The System Apocalypse

Short Story Anthology

Volume 1

With Stories By

Craig Hamilton
Alexis Keane
Ix Phoen
RK Billiau
L.A. Batt

and

Tao Wong

License Notes

The System Apocalypse Short Story Anthology Volume 1

Copyright © 2019 Tao Wong. All rights reserved.

Copyright © 2019 Sarah Anderson Cover Designer

A Tao Wong Book

Published by Tao Wong

69 Teslin Rd

Whitehorse, YT

Y1A 3M5

Canada

www.mylifemytao.com

ISBN: 9781989458198

Contents

Intermission One

"Why are we doing this?" Amelia Olmstead, the hefty ex-RCMP officer; now turned settlement investigator grumped as she stared at the virtual pile of data. To simplify the sorting of information, the pair had created this virtual workspace, allowing them to move within the room and find the pieces of information that they needed. In reality, the pair were back in Whitehorse, seated in comfortable lounging chairs while they processed the information. Information that they had acquired after the acquisition of the Svartfalar base in eastern BC, hidden in the Rockies.

"Information gathering. The Svartfalar collected this information for a reason. The question is, why?" Vir picked up one data slat, waving it at the human. The thin, impeccably dressed Truinnar guard – and spymaster – half-smiled at his friend and partner as he educated her on Galactic politics. Not that she needed it, not after so many years. "My assumption is that they are looking for the exceptional. An AI generated algorithm will have mistakes, thus producing. Well, this."

"Because AIs don't have true sentience," Amelia said and sighed. "So now, we read through everything, hoping to figure out what the Svartfalar were doing with this information?"

"Yes. If we can head them off, or at least, understand what their interest is, we might be able to stop them. Even if this information is a little old, there is still information to be gleaned," Vir said. His brows drew down, as he stared at the completed System recording and sighed. "Like this."

A flick of his fingers sent the recording over to hover in front of Amelia. She stared at the recording dubiously, knowing that records of the first year had a tendency to be both violent and depressing. But, they were here because some information was too sensitive to let the other guards know.

Among things – the fact that they had taken action against the Svartfalar at all.

Hunting Monsters

by Craig Hamilton

Only a monster could have left such carnage.

I stood in the doorway of a tiny apartment, the stench of decomposition wafting out to fill the dimly lit hallway. The deputy who had opened the door had already fled down the corridor before retching and emptying his stomach. I ignored the officer. Just as I ignored his partner, who glared at me as I took in the scene inside the room. His skepticism affected me as much as the smell—not at all.

The cops may not have known me, but death was no stranger. Nearly two-thirds of humanity had died ten months ago, the day the System came online and ended the world as we knew it. Monsters spawned everywhere and massacred mankind as our lives became governed by the System's video-game-like rules. Rules that allowed no replays or extra lives. Those of us remaining had seen plenty of death, but I may have seen more than most.

That fateful day began as I pursued a man who had skipped out on his bail. When the armed man unexpectedly opened fire and fled, I had refused to let the criminal get away, even as our world changed. The pursuit, and ensuing gunfight, led to my first experience gained under the System. Before I even had a chance to select a class, I had earned a level from killing another human. The System rewarded that achievement with an Advanced Class that matched my actions, and I had been hunting monsters ever since.

I stepped cautiously into the hotel room turned apartment. There was no avoiding the dried blood that stained the floor a rusty red, but I kept my feet away from the larger lumps. Crouched beside a pile of organic material, I let myself study the viscera that remained of a human torso. The edges of the gaping wounds were sharply cut. My eyes traced over the slashed flesh to the arcing spatters of dried blood, following the pattern backward and rebuilding the scene in my mind. I moved from one chunk of gore to another, careful to touch nothing. Slowly and deliberately, I lost all track of time as I pieced together the horrific puzzle.

Eventually, I stood and brushed aside a System notification for a skill increase in Forensics. As I turned toward the door, a glimmer of reflected light caught my eye. A framed holograph, splashed with blood, was centered on a bookshelf filled with knickknacks. I picked it up and wiped the glass covering. Crusted flakes fell free and revealed an image that made my breath catch in my throat. The six smiling faces in the image were a jarringly bright reflection of the agonizing jigsaw assembled in my mind. A family—as much as anyone had these days after the System Apocalypse—with parents caring for children not their own and children clinging lovingly to adults with no blood relation .

After replacing the holograph on the shelf, I absently pulled a flask from my inventory and took a long pull. I should have felt more for the family. Anger that their lives had been stolen. Rage at the potential snuffed out. A passion to bring their killer to justice. Instead, I felt nothing. Not even the burn of the whiskey pouring down my throat. My System-enhanced constitution easily resisted weaker poisons and dulled any sensation the alcohol may have once given me. Though I had no proof, I suspected the System similarly affected mental resilience, blunting the horrific impact of how many humans had died in the previous ten months. Despite the tragedy, people had simply moved on with their lives. Most even calmly accepted the arrival of the Galactics—aliens from throughout the wider System universe—

as they settled in on Earth. In most places, these new arrivals promptly took over.

I was currently in one such location—a Truinnar-owned village in what used to be Western Pennsylvania. When I'd crossed into the town limits, I had picked up a System-generated quest to track down a killer menacing the human population. The few local law enforcement officers left alive had apparently been unable to catch this killer. While the identity of any criminal could be purchased from the System, that criminal could also have Class Skills or spells that would assist in hiding them. The cost to purchase the identity from the Shop would increase with each obfuscating ability added, quickly making the price prohibitively high. It often worked out cheaper to hire or post a quest for someone to hunt down the criminals who took these precautions. Which led to Adventurers picking up side gigs as bounty hunters.

Turning my focus back to the room, I closed my eyes and cast a newly acquired Class Skill. The nauseating aroma of the room assaulted my nose as Blood Scent settled into place. Six distinct tangy bouquets hung heavily tangled in the air, and I spent several minutes locking each one into my memory. I wasted no time looking for the scent of the killer since no evidence had been found at any of the earlier crime scenes and I expected the same again here.

I cracked my eyes open and left the room but stopped where the two police officers waited. The younger man, sweating and pallid, stood behind his partner and looked anywhere but through the apartment door. Both noticed the flask still in my hand, neither able to hide their disdain.

Officer Robert Richardson (Level 36 Guardian)
HP: 960/960

Officer Thomas Cook (Level 11 Guardian)
_HP: 280/280_

"Six dead," I said, addressing the more experienced officer. "Three adults, two teenagers, and one toddler. Two days ago."

"That matches the apartment registration," Officer Richardson replied stoically. "And the last time anyone talked to the occupants."

"No one heard anything?" I asked.

"No," Richardson said, his eyes distant. "No one heard a thing."

"The killer disabled them all quickly," I said. "Then he took his time cutting them apart bit by bit. The others were forced to watch."

The rookie cop looked as if he was about to be sick again.

"The killer?" Richardson peered at me sharply. "Not a monster?"

"Oh, it was a monster," I replied. "Just not a System-spawned one. Your killer is human."

Leaving the two astounded cops, I headed down the hall toward the stairs. Maybe it was a leap to claim the culprit was human, but my gut was convinced. This building was a Safe Zone, so no System monster could have spawned inside the room. The Galactics who ruled this town had no issues striking down a human in cold blood, but none of them had any reason to hide it behind closed doors. Just the opposite, in fact. Any killings were usually public examples being made of criminals, troublemakers, or those who violently resisted Galactic rule. Most humans were second-class citizens, if they mattered at all, so no Galactic would go through the trouble to cover up a series of murders. On top of that, most Galactics now on Earth were so highly leveled that they would gain little, if any, experience from killing low-level humans.

Only a human would have felt the need to hide these massacres from their own kind. Especially murders performed in a place like this—an apartment building converted from a pre-System hotel—in the middle of a Safe Zone. A home where the most vulnerable, those without combat classes, were meant to be protected. Instead, the people here were terrified, knowing a killer lurked in the night and anyone could be next. I was certain the culprit fed on the desperate atmosphere, relishing the terror his work left behind.

More than the deaths of the family, this annoyed me. That a predator could feel superior in stalking the weak and the helpless left me feeling raw. Despite my antisocial tendencies, I still regarded humanity as my own. I felt a primal need to deal with that which threatened my people. The Galactics were outside of my capabilities for now, though that was an itch I looked forward to scratching.

Once outside on the sidewalk, I took a deep breath of the fresh evening air. Blood Scent remained active, slowly draining my mana and allowing me to follow the faint coppery tang. The sun had dropped below the horizon, but enough light remained for me to get my bearings in this unfamiliar small town.

Other than pursuing System-generated quests or bounties for broken Galactic Contracts, I spent the majority of my time alone, grinding out levels in the wilderness and occasionally partying up with other Adventurers to clear the odd dungeon or two. I had passed through here before, but the few surviving rural burgs throughout this part of the country sort of blended together at this point.

"So, you're the latest to pick up the quest for our town's little murder mystery," said a voice from behind me.

I looked back at the man who leaned casually against the building, beside the door I had just exited. I raised an eyebrow in response, looking him over as he examined me. The man wore civilian clothes—a beige trench coat over a light-blue collared shirt and khaki pants. He was shorter than average and slightly balding, which told me the man was either too proud or too broke to purchase Genome Treatment from the Shop. An examination of his System status revealed his class and indicated the latter .

Scott Davis (Level 7 Journalist)
_HP: 140/140_

"Latest?" I asked.

"Adventurers passing through, like you," Scott replied. "They all disappeared shortly after beginning their investigations though."

"Is that a threat?" I growled. My eyes narrowed as I turned to face the man completely.

"Not at all," the journalist replied hurriedly. "I just wanted to warn you that whatever is doing the killing doesn't seem to want anyone investigating too deeply."

"And a journalist doesn't investigate?" I asked.

"I report the facts," Scott said defensively. "It's common knowledge, once the police publish their reports. At least for the bodies found in town."

"So, there are also bodies found outside of town?"

The journalist looked around nervously then nodded. "Back when the System first came online, the town hunters would find convoys that had been slaughtered outside the town limits. People headed here for safety but never made it. Or roadways covered in blood with the area all torn up but no bodies. Everyone thought monsters did it, but then the killings started in town."

"This almost sounds like the work of a System-enhanced serial killer," I speculated. "What's the body count from in town?"

"Nobody is really sure," Scott replied with a shrug. "The numbers really climbed after families started showing up as victims, so at least fifty have been confirmed. But with the number of transients and Adventurers passing through, on top of the killings outside of town, it could easily be hundreds."

The ominous bits of news were troubling since the System quest had made no mention of anything outside the town or that the body count was so high. If the killer had been active since the System came online, the experience they'd accrued would be sizeable and would have led to the killer obtaining higher levels than normal.

"Why has no one bought the killer's identity from the Shop if things are this bad?" I asked.

"It's too expensive," Scott replied. "No one can afford it on their own, and every time people try to pool their resources to buy it, the price jumps."

That was really bad news. It meant the killer was inside the community and able to take precautions.

"That's really all the info I've got for you. I hope it helps." The journalist turned and walked away. After a few steps, he turned back toward me. "Good luck," he said with a solemn nod.

The journalist had given me plenty to think about. That the man had been waiting for me outside the latest crime scene meant that word was spreading that a new Adventurer was looking into the killings. As plugged-in to the community as the killer seemed, they would soon be aware that I was hunting.

I headed south, tracking the faint aroma of blood that the killer had left behind. With dusk setting in, most of the local businesses along Main Street were closing up as I passed. The shops sold locally made goods using resources looted from System-spawned monsters. The human craftsmen making those items were still fairly low-leveled, so the System Shops generally had higher-quality, and thus more expensive, goods. The likelihood of finding upgrades for my gear was slim though, so I passed the stores without a glance. Most of my attention remained focused on following the scent, but I was well aware of a few townsfolk eyeing me nervously and giving me a wide berth.

As I reached the southern edge of the business district, the storefronts of the downtown area gave way to residential homes. I also felt the onset of a headache caused by low mana and quickly cut off Blood Scent before mana fatigue could fully set in. The conversation with the journalist had taken longer than I would have liked, and leaving the Class Skill active during that chat had drained my mana. I would have to let my mana regenerate before I could continue my hunt. A downside of the physical benefits of my class was that I tended to be far weaker on the spell-casting side of things.

No longer focused on my Class Skill and intently following my nose, I became aware of the music that emanated from a solid brick building ahead of me. Live music tended to be somewhat rare since musicians had generally fared poorly in surviving the apocalypse. The full sound of a stringed instrument pulled, at me and I found myself walking several steps toward the building. I forced myself to stop, disconcerted that the unexpected music had attracted me so strongly.

Mental Influence Resisted

The conscious mental effort and notification explained the powerful draw and aroused my curiosity. I had fairly significant mental resistances, so a musician who could challenge them with a compulsion certainly seemed worth checking out. Now that I was somewhat closer, I gave the building a more thorough examination. It looked like a pre-System dive bar, only somewhat cleaned up by new management. Galactic runes above the door proudly proclaimed Gimsar ownership and that Adventurers of all types were welcome.

Gimsar were like dwarves from fantasy legends, except that their craftsmen were no more talented than anyone else in the System universe. Hard drinking and hard fighting, they were often seen as honorable mercenaries. So long as one avoided insult to a Gimsar's clan, beard, or axe, they tended to be fairly good-natured .

I stepped into the building and found every eye in the place glancing in my direction as I eased the door closed. I was pretty confident of what they were seeing. Some used high Charisma to enhance their looks. I used my Charisma to ensure others saw exactly what I wanted them to see. A tall, brown-haired human man with a muscular build wearing a dark-gray combat jumpsuit. A sword sheathed across my back and holstered pistols on both hips. Standard Adventurer chic, nothing out of the ordinary.

Hal Mason (Level 29 Hunter)
HP: 220/220

A granite-topped bar counter ran along one side of the room. Surprisingly, the bar top looked to be at a normal height for a bar despite the older, gray-bearded Gimsar tending bar from behind it. The bartender conversed with a group of Gimsar taking up about half the high stools at the closer end of the bar. Behind the bartender, above the racks of liquor, hung a massive double-headed battle -axe. From the notches and scrapes on the weapon, I could tell the axe had been well used.

Several tables of Hakarta mercenaries promptly ignored me, going back to a complicated series of card games. The green-skinned aliens were similar in appearance to fantasy orcs, but I preferred to think of them as high-tech supersoldiers . The Hakarta typically operated in well-disciplined squads, so if you saw one out in the wild, there were probably several others nearby keeping you in their sights.

A group of Yerrick took up a large table in the far back of the bar, out of the way. The nine-foot-tall minotaurs were thick with muscle and commonly employed as Adventurers. I recognized none from this particular group, but I had worked with Yerrick in the past and found them more than capable.

The rest of the clientele scattered throughout the bar was a mix of human and Truinnar. Nothing about the humans stood out—exactly the shady types of people I would expect to find in a seedy dive bar. The Truinnar, on the other hand, were eye-catching. Dark elves with lithe figures, midnight-black skin, and exotic hair colors, they moved with ethereal grace. Truinnar politics followed a labyrinthine feudal system I barely grasped enough of to know that Earth fell just inside their Galactic territory. Like this town, large portions of North America were now also under direct Truinnar control.

Across the room from the bar, an elevated platform served as the stage for a Truinnar woman vigorously playing a stringed instrument similar to violin. As captivating as the music had sounded outside, I found the instrumentalist dancing across the stage even more mesmerizing. A silver corseted dress hugged the woman's slender, athletic frame and sharply offset the onyx skin of her bare shoulders. Her shapely legs flashed through slits in the dress as she spun, kicked, and twisted around the platform. Platinum hair dyed in waves of cerulean and crimson streamed behind her as she danced with her eyes closed, lost in the enchantment of her own musical creation .

Pulling away from the enthralling vision on the stage, I headed to the empty end of the bar and perched on one of the high stools.

Walking along a ledge on the backside of the bar, which kept him at a normal height, the Gimsar headed toward me. "What'll it be, lad?"

"Whiskey," I replied. "Neat."

The dwarf grabbed an empty tumbler from a rack behind the bar and poured in a generous quantity of amber liquid from a recognizable green-tinted bottle. Sliding the glass toward me across the bar, he held up several fingers, and I transferred over the requested number of Credits as well as a small tip. The dwarf nodded in acknowledgement and headed back to the other end of the bar.

Glancing at my status, I saw that my nearly empty mana pool had barely begun regenerating. Making a mental note to put more points into Willpower, I resigned myself to waiting until my mana refilled.

"Well, well, you're certainly an interesting human, Harold Mason."

The sultry voice from behind tingled down my spine, and the use of my full name sent adrenaline rushing through my system. Twisting around on the barstool, I instinctively dropped my right hand to the pistol on my hip as I found myself facing the musician from the stage.

Dayena Baluisa (??? Level ???, Sultana of the Whispering Strings, Mistress of Shadows, ???)

HP: ???

Up close, I found her even more stunning, and her loveliness momentarily arrested my panic at the realization that she had likely read my full System status. I'd barely glanced at her before luminous amethyst eyes captured my attention completely. Caught by surprise, I vaguely felt a sense of being analyzed and mentally stripped bare. I forced myself to blink rapidly and shifted my gaze away from her sharply angular face, breaking the spell.

Mental Influence Resisted

"That was rude," I growled, now on guard as I looked back at her.

"Oh, I'm sorry," Dayena replied, her skin flushed as she blinked innocently. "I forget how easily my influence overwhelms most humans."

Despite my initial reaction, her response struck me. Maybe her influence still affected me, but my intuition told me that her words sounded genuine. She appeared as ageless as most Truinnar, yet I got the sense that this woman was younger than I would have expected.

"May I join you?" she asked politely.

"Sure," I said as I released my right hand from the holstered pistol and waved at the barstool beside me.

Dayena gestured to the bartender, who brought over a recognizable cocktail as she gracefully slid onto the stool.

"You drink Manhattans?" I asked incredulously as I turned back to my drink.

"It's a recently acquired taste," she said defensively. "Pity about the city."

I snorted. "Pity about most of our cities."

She looked at me with her eyes narrowed. "You don't actually care, do you?"

No accusation tainted her tone. No judgment. Just observation. I sipped my drink while I considered my response.

"No. Not really. Nothing can change what happened, so there's no point in feeling upset. And yet I feel the need to do something about it. To protect what little is left." I knew she was getting me to open up more than I should, but I was always a sucker for a pretty face. "So, what's a high-class dame like you doing in a dive like this?"

Dayena's lips quirked into a slight smirk, acknowledgment that she was well aware of my attempt to change the subject away from myself. "Checking out all of the opportunities a new Dungeon World offers. There are plenty of possibilities in a place like this for those seeking fame and fortune."

"Sure, but you don't strike me as someone lacking in either," I said.

Dayena flinched and turned her head to look at me sharply. I had struck a nerve. "No, but sometimes accomplishments gained by others leave one wondering what can be achieved on their own without depending on others for protection."

I nodded in sympathy for the young Truinnar. Alone in the wilderness, reliant on only my own abilities to survive and eliminate System-spawned monsters, I felt invigorated. The chaos of combat banished the numbness and emotionlessness that had ruled me ever since the System initialized. Out in the untamed wilds, I fought to become stronger. If she desired to get out from under someone's thumb, building her strength on a Dungeon World was certainly one way to do it.

"Sometimes the most freedom comes when there are no strings to catch you if you fall," I replied.

"Exactly!" Dayena exclaimed, then sobered. "But my family doesn't see things that way."

The young woman stayed silent for a minute. I waited. She would either choose to continue and open up more or not.

"I'm just a pawn to marry off," Dayena said as she stirred her drink. "I won't be free to be my own person. Bundled off into an arranged marriage with another house, I'll be safely tied up in responsibilities and obligations."

"Maybe your family is right," I warned with a shrug. "On your own is a dangerous way to live."

"That's the only way to thrive under the System," she countered emphatically. "And so I ran away."

"It doesn't tend to work out for everyone though. What's stopping your family from tracking you down?"

"Nothing." Dayena sighed. "I'm sure they already know where I am. They just have to send someone to get me, and I'm not strong enough to stop them. Galactic society respects the strong." She turned half toward me, her look analytical. "The strong and the resourceful."

"I've been lucky." I shrugged. At this point, we both knew she could easily read my System status despite my pretended nonchalance.

"What if I said I'm interested in hiring you?"

"I'd be skeptical of what someone your level would need of someone as low-leveled as me," I replied. "Besides, I'm currently on a job."

Dayena looked away as she fidgeted with her drink. The sense of youth was back, along with a hint of vulnerability and a whiff of desperation. "That quest hasn't gone so well for anyone else."

"So I've heard. Fortunately, I'm not just anyone. But why do you care?"

"I'll tell you if you take the job," she shot back. "I guarantee that I can pay more than you'd make collecting on contract breakers or crime solving anywhere on this planet."

Clearly Dayena knew that bounty collection on individuals who broke their System-enforced Contracts was a lucrative business and my primary source of Credits. My current income was higher than average and one reason I still lived when so many others lay fallen. If she had access to the kind of resources necessary to research me with little more than a glance, her job offer would be interesting and likely worth my while. More Credits meant I could afford more, and better, skills and equipment from the Shop.

"Tell you what," I said. "Look me up after I finish up this quest. If you're really offering that many Credits , I'm interested."

"Good," Dayena said. "I'll be in touch."

With that, Dayena threw back the rest of her drink and returned her cocktail glass to the counter as she slipped off the barstool. She glided back to the stage and quickly returned to her melodic performance.

The position Dayena offered would likely involve me heavily in Truinnar politics. Once finished with this job, I needed to research Truinnar society. My lack of knowledge would be a significant handicap if I ended up working directly for a Truinnar noble. Especially with the cutthroat politics her family history implied. I had little doubt she was far more than a minstrel.

I shelved that train of thought and lost myself to the music flowing from the stage, helped along by a few more of the bartender's generously poured rounds. Eventually, I checked my status to find my mana pool nearly full . I finished my last drink and nodded respectfully to the Gimsar bartender as I stood to leave. It was time to get back to work.

Back outside the dive bar, I reactivated Blood Scent and once again followed the faint trail south. Night had fallen completely, the darkness broken only by sparse streetlights and the occasional storefront sign. The streets were deserted, not a person to be seen. I followed the scent traces, the footsteps of my armored boots the only sound in the stillness.

The scent soon cut across the main thoroughfare, then turned back north, still following the sidewalk along Main Street. Before long, I passed back through the downtown area and found myself across the street from the hotel where I'd begun tracking the killer.

The trail continued north, and my gut told me the end of the trail was nearby. I followed the scent for another half block before the trail cut back across Main Street and west down an alley, between an old theater and a store built of weathered brick. At the end of the alley, I found a small parking lot bordering the backside of several buildings. The trail crossed the parking lot and led to the back door of a narrow two-story house.

I stood in the middle of the dark parking lot and stared at that door for several minutes. I then turned toward the back of another building that bordered this small parking lot. The beige brick building that had been my first stop in town after I'd accepted the quest to hunt down the killer. It was the old pre-System municipal building, which currently served as the police headquarters.

I was unsurprised when a shadow detached from the building and glided toward me. The figure stopped a dozen paces away. I knew who it was long before the figure came to a halt. Human, levels above average, and able to wander leisurely around town after making any kill.

"Officer Richardson," I said.

The police officer, still in his uniform, cocked his head and examined me. "How did you follow the trail? No one else has ever come anywhere close to figuring it out."

"Easy," I replied. "I just followed my nose."

"Impossible," Richardson said, his brow furrowed in confusion. "I cast the Cleanse spell. There was nothing of me to scent."

"Sure," I said with a triumphant smirk. "But you cast it while you were still in a small room reeking with the blood of your victims. I followed their scent, which clung to you as you left."

"Well," said Richardson, his eyes wide, "I'll have to remember that the next time."

"There won't be a next time," I growled.

"Sure," he replied as he gestured to cast a spell at the surrounding area.

Despite the spell not being cast directly at me, I identified it as some kind of area silencing ability. The spell prevented any noise from escaping the area—clearly how the killer had kept anyone from interrupting his killing sprees.

Long knives shimmered into existence in Richardson's hands. As the weapons appeared, I pulled a pistol from each of my thigh holsters. The comfortable weight of System-upgraded Colt M1911, magazine loaded with hand-crafted ammunition in .45 caliber, filled my right hand. My left carried a sleek, lightweight beam pistol constructed of Galactic composite materials, the popular Silversmith Mark II.

Richardson charged toward me with a speed that defied belief. Just as quickly, I opened fire. The beam from my Silversmith hit a shield before reaching the advancing officer, and the rounds from my M1911 sparked off the same shield as they were deflected. The shield flickered as I fired my fourth round from the Colt, and it dropped completely on the fifth, but Richardson was now within arm's length.

I tried to step backward as he swung, but momentum was on his side, and I was forced to deflect his blades with the barrels of my pistols before I could get out of range. The upgraded metals in the Colt held up to the blow, but the other knife sheared completely through the Silversmith. I hurled the sparking mass of severed electronics at Richardson, but he ducked under the throw. The officer's dodge gave me time to fire several more shots from the Colt. Each round took small chunks from his health.

Then the slide locked back on the handgun, the magazine empty.

A downside of the physical ammunition fired by the high-powered weapon was the magazine only carried seven rounds with an additional one in the chamber. The advantage of handcrafted ammunition was that each round could be given bonuses by the crafter, which provided significantly higher damage than any mass-produced ammunition. In this case, my first magazine had been filled with rounds designed to break energy shields.

I summoned a full magazine from my inventory as I reversed direction and twisted in an attempt to get past the rushing cop. A line of fire ripped through the back of my left thigh as Richardson caught my leg with one of his knives.

Hamstrung!

You have received a debilitating blow to your left leg. You will not be able to run on your left leg until you are healed.

I managed to finish the reload on the Colt despite the crippling pain in my leg. With my mobility severely limited, Richardson was all over me within a moment, and his knives tore through my defenses. My status became a mess of debuffs and damage notifications.

Stunned!

You will not be able to move, use mana, or react in any way while stunned . You are stunned for 4.3 seconds.

Disarmed!

Your weapon has been removed from your grip. You will need to pick it up or equip a new weapon.

Bleeding!

You have received a bleeding debuff. You will lose health so long as the wounds are not treated.

-2 Health per second

Richardson swept a leg through mine, which collapsed me onto the pavement on my back. I lay unable to move as the stunned debuff ticked down ever so slowly. I looked at the killer above me as Richardson stared into empty space just above my head. I realized he watched my health bar as my nearly empty health pool drained from the bleed ing effect.

"Why?" I asked. "Why did you kill all those people?"

"Because I could," Richardson sneered. "They were weak, and this is a world where only the strong survive."

"I don't believe that," I replied quietly. "You're a monster."

"You're a monster too," Richardson said gloatingly. "You care for nothing but the thrill of the hunt, and you're too weak to survive, just like everyone I've killed. That's why you're about to die."

Maybe he was right to call me a monste r, but I felt almost disappointed by the trite explanation. I'd thought a killer with such a body count would have a better excuse, even if only a deluded one.

As the last of the health points disappeared from my visible health pool, I remained absolutely still and held my breath. This was my favorite part of the hunt. When the monster sensed victory and I got to snatch it from their grasp.

Richardson still stared above me, fixated on my empty health pool as he waited for his experience notifications.

Nothing appeared for him.

Richardson's gaze flicked to me, then back up at the empty health pool. Confusion crossed his face when he looked back down at me again. This time, I blinked.

"What?" The killer recoiled in surprise.

I pushed myself to my feet with no sign of my earlier injuries. I activated The Right Tool for the Job as I stood. The Class Skill instantly pulled weapons from a dedicated inventory space and filled both of my thigh holsters with new pistols, equipped a shoulder harness rig with a pistol under each armpit, and materialized a pair of MP5K machine pistols, one in each hand.

Confusion warred with surprise across Richardson's face as I kept my eyes locked on his. I relished his expression as I deactivated most components of my penultimate Class Skill, On the Hunt. With my true class and attributes no longer disguised by the System, my health bar snapped from empty to over three quarters full.

Harold 'Hal' Mason (Level 29 Relentless Huntsman)
HP: 710/930

Wide-eyed, Richardson stared at me as he gaped. He closed and opened his mouth several times as he attempted to say something. "How?"

"Maybe I am one"—I grinned savagely—"but I hunt monsters."

I raised the MP5Ks and squeezed the triggers of both automatics. Flame and thunder poured from each weapon. Normal recoil from fully automatic weapons would have been difficult to keep steady, but my System-enhanced strength was easily up to the challenge. Richardson attempted to dodge by diving to the side and rolling to escape the line of fire.

Despite his attempt, my rounds stayed on target. The fire from my guns robbed Richardson of his momentum and knocked him prone. He stopped moving as my weapons ran dry. After only seconds of automatic fire, the thirty-round magazines were empty. I stashed the weapons in my personal System armory provided by The Right Tool for the Job and strode over to the broken body of the killer I had tracked through town.

Richardson wore armor under his uniform, but the close-range fire of armor-piercing ammunition had left his torso a shredded, bloody mess, and air wheezed from a punctured lung. Even with those injuries, he would recover if given enough time. Time I would not allow him.

I summoned a Smith & Wesson Model 29, once claimed as the most powerful handgun in the world, from my inventory and pointed the massive revolver at Richardson's head. The hammer clicked back as I pulled the double-action trigger and continued to squeeze. The .44 Magnum round almost blew off the killer's head. I fired a second time, finishing the job.

Notifications flooded my vision. I quickly flipped through them to confirm the quest completion for tracking down the town killer.

I touched the corpse and pulled it into another System inventory space with the Meat Locker Class Skill. Never knowing when the next conflict might come, I took the time to pull the spent weapons from my inventory, checked them for damage, and reloaded them. I then picked up the pieces of my Silversmith beam pistol, found my dropped Colt, and looted Richardson's daggers. With those items picked up, only the pooling blood splattered across the pavement remained as evidence of the fight that had taken place. I glanced around to ensure I'd left nothing behind, but I quickly noticed that I was no longer alone.

Surrounding the parking lot, Truinnar in the uniform of the town guard formed a perimeter that cut off any route out of the area. At the mouth of the alley waited a Truinnar more finely dressed than the uniformed guards who stood behind him.

The guards eyed me warily as I approached the finely dressed figure, which gave me time to examine the man. He had the typical tall, slender build of the Truinnar, though he somehow seemed softer than the guards and most other dark elves I had encountered. The elf also seemed younger even than Dayena. He carried no weapons, clearly trusting the escort behind him for protection.

Lord Aradin Daxily (??? Level ???, Baron of the Argent Sea)
HP: 790/790

The noble's level and class were hidden, likely by a Class Skill, but the meager health points hinted at his level being quite low. Especially low if he was the man who, I suspected, ruled this town.

The System Apocalypse Short Story Anthology Volume 1

"Adventurer Mason," greeted the young dark elf in a high, nasally voice.

"Lord Daxily," I replied politely.

"Thank you for ridding my village of that menace," said Daxily, which confirmed that he indeed owned the town. "He was a drain on resources and lowered my village's value."

"You knew he was the killer."

Daxily sniffed. "Of course. I know what goes on in my village."

"And you did nothing?" I asked, annoyed by his inaction in the face of lost human lives.

"It was a human problem." The dark elf waved dismissively. "I leave human problems to humans. But now you've become a problem for me by breaking the peace in my village."

I was seriously aggravated by his knowledge of the killer and his lack of action. That he now declared my action of taking out the killer as problematic made me debate whether to show this spoiled punk a real human problem. I kept my face blank, but something of my intent must have leaked out because two of the guards stepped up beside the noble, their weapons half-drawn.

I examined the guards critically. I figured I could take the ones in front of me, along with the noble, but at least another half dozen guards were somewhere behind me. They would call for assistance, and I would certainly not survive if the entire town guard were called in.

Before the situation could escalate further, a figure materialized out of the alley shadows. Hips swayed as the figured sauntered toward us, and I recognized the seductive silhouette of the musician from the bar. The sensuous dress from earlier had been exchanged for an armored jumpsuit, one of significantly higher quality than my own, but it still managed to give her slender figure mouth-watering appeal.

Mental Influence Resisted

"Take it easy, boys," said Dayena.

The sultry voice grabbed the attention of everyone in the alley.

As if hit between the eyes by a hammer, the wide-eyed Truinnar noble seemed stunned. "C-countess? I knew you were in town, but what are you doing here?"

Fantastic. The spoiled noble had revealed my potential employer as a ranked member of the Truinnar peerage. Her comments in the bar made more sense now. I needed to be wary, or else I'd quickly become buried in Truinnar politics. Unfortunately, my gut had the sneaking suspicion my caution was entirely too late.

Dayena gestured toward me and looked pointedly into my eyes as a prompt appeared before me.

Contract Initiated between Dayena Baluisa and Harold Mason.
Do you accept? (Y/N)

"The huntsman works for me," Dayena stated confidently while she stared at me intently and ignored the other noble.

I got the hint. She'd just made me an offer I couldn't refuse. I accepted the prompt and resigned myself to working for the gorgeous elf in a deal that would clearly be in her favor.

Contract Agreed Upon by Dayena Baluisa and Harold Mason.
Further Details? (Y/N)

I ignored the prompt and hoped for a chance later to read through the fine print.

"What? Is this true?" the young noble demanded, finally recovering from being hit with the full force of Dayena's charms.

"Yes," I replied, though I found it safer to say as little as possible.

"Fine," Daxily huffed. "I want you both out of my village. I rescind my hospitality, Countess."

"We'll be gone before daylight." Dayena turned to leave the alley. "Come on, Adventurer Mason."

I followed the woman and nodded to the town guards as I passed. I ignored the spoiled noble. The guards tracked me warily, likely aware that any violence would end poorly for all involved.

Once we reached the main street at the end of the alley, Dayena turned back toward me. "Is there anything you need in town before we leave?"

"No. I only needed to finish the quest here, and that's done."

"That was an impressive fight," she said. "I enjoyed how you toyed with him. It almost reminded me of court politics back home."

"Speaking of politics," I said with an arched eyebrow. "Countess?"

Dayena shrugged dismissively. "It's just an honorific. My family is complicated, so I have no lands or responsibilities. I want to forge my own path and not have it dictated to me. And now I have you to help."

A moment later, the woman climbed onto a sleekly armored motorcycle that materialized on the empty street in front of us. I summoned my bike from my inventory and mounted it beside her.

"Help with what?" I asked.

Tao Wong

"Hunting monsters, of course," Dayena replied with a wink. A helmet snapped up out of her collar and over her head. Tires squealed, her bike shot forward, and she quickly left me behind.

Resigned, I kicked my bike into gear and followed the Truinnar countess off into the night. Hunting monsters, indeed.

###

Some Class Details

Advanced Class: Relentless Huntsman

Relentless Huntsmen are elite combatants skilled at tenaciously pursuing bounty targets for capture or elimination.

Class Abilities: +1 Per Level in Strength. +3 Per Level in Agility and Constitution. +2 Per Level in Intelligence and Charisma. +1 Per Level in Perception and Willpower. Additional 2 Free Attributes per Level. +60% Mental Resistance. +20% Elemental Resistance.

Class Skills:

Blood Scent - The Relentless Huntsman may select a scent present in the current environment and follow any object or individual to which that scent clings.

Cost: 30 Mana per minute

Meat Locker - The Relentless Huntsman now has access to an extradimensional storage location of 20 cubic feet. Only deceased bounty targets or creatures may be added to this location and must be touched to be willed inside. Mana regeneration reduced by 5 Mana per minute permanently.

The Right Tool for the Job - The Relentless Huntsman now has access to an extradimensional storage location of 5 cubic feet. Items stored must be touched to be willed in and may only include weapons, armor, equipment, or supplies owned by the Relentless Huntsman. Any qualifying System-recognized item can be placed or removed from this inventory location if space allows. Cost: 5 Mana per item.

Implacable Endurance - Reduces Stamina cost for physical exertion and activated physical abilities by 50%. Does not stack with other Stamina-reduction skills. Mana regeneration reduced by 25 Mana per minute permanently.

On the Hunt - The Relentless Huntsman has a reduced System presence and increased ability to disguise their visible titles, class, level, ability scores, and any status effects. Effectiveness is based on the user's skill level and Charisma. Mana regeneration reduced by 15 Mana per minute permanently.

Intermission Two

"There's a runaway Truinnar Countess and a human slash monster bounty hunter wandering the continental United States," Amelia said as she finished the recording, fingers tapping against the armchair. Once again, Amelia shifted position, trying to find a comfortable place to sit. The Svartfalar were taller and thinner than humans, but that was not the reason their chairs were so uncomfortable. It was because the chairs themselves conformed to the unusual rib structure in the Svartfalar backs, giving them additional support in the middle of the sentients backs. Which, for a shorter human, meant that it poked directly into their backs.

"Yes. I'll have to inform Lord Roxley about this. He will be quite interested," Vir said, tapping on the armchair.

"Going to track them down?" Amelia said.

"Unlikely. Involving oneself in familial matters can be tricky. We will need to be on watch for them, but it is a matter for others." Amelia nodded, content to leave it at that. She had more than enough work as it stood, being the go-between the human policing faction and their Truinnar Overlords.

In silence the pair worked before Amelia choked down a laugh.

"Something the matter?"

"Nothing official," Amelia said. "Though Lana might be interested in it."

Vir cocked an eyebrow and chuckled again, flicking a finger to pass on the video.

"Just someone being a good boy."

Tooth and Claw

by Alexis Keane

Chapter 1

Two rooms across, I hear movement. The big humans, my pack, are up.

Almost regretfully, I stretch out all four of my limbs, my muzzle opening in a wide, lethargic yawn. As I move, my back presses against something soft, something small, smelling of soap, cornflowers, and oranges.

Katie. My human.

My tail twitches, tapping against the blanket, and I turn around quickly. I plant one of the big, slobbery kisses that Katie loves all over her face—from her tiny chin, to her button nose, to the wide, blue eyes between angelic blond curls.

"Morning, Buck," she murmurs, still asleep but reaching for me.

My tail taps the covers a little faster, a little more loudly. But I don't want to wake Katie up... not yet.

The big humans in the other room are awake. And that means one thing.

Food. Tribute!

I bound off the bed and out the door as the big humans chuckle in the other room, able to hear me even with their poor senses. I leap down the stairs, taking them two at a time.

My ears—covered in downy, well-kept fur—flop against my face as I charge toward the Tribute bowl, the metal tags on my leather collar jangling wildly. I sit by the bowl. A horde of cats couldn't move me from this spot.

Movement at the edge of my vision catches my attention.

There! Through the see-through doors that always hurt my nose when I run into them. Temptation! Several of them. They stare at me mockingly with their thin, ratlike faces and their long, fluffy, bushy yellowish tails streaked with white and gray.

SQUIRRELS!

I want to chase them, but I keep my backside planted next to the Tribute bowl. Nothing will move me. Not even the Temptation.

Then one of the squirrels runs up to the glass door, its little rodent nose twitching. I don't like where this is going...

Oh dear.

***

"Geez, Buck, cut it out!" the human with the deep voice shouts from the top of the stairs.

I come to my senses standing on my hind paws. My forepaws are pressed flat against the cold glass, claws scratching futilely against the cruel surface that keeps me from the Temptation. The squirrel is long gone now, so I drop back down to all four paws and turn around, seeing the human—the tall one with the square face, dark hair, and blue eyes—peering at me from above the banister.

He caught me in the act!

A small whine escapes my throat. Well... this is embarrassing.

Wait a minute. Wait. I have a brilliant plan. Maybe if I forget about it, he'll forget about it too.

I purge the embarrassing situation from my mind and sit back by the Tribute bowl. Success! The big human—the humans call him Jeff—nods, then goes back upstairs. When he returns, he lugs two large bags downstairs, one under each arm, and places them by the door.

Then he approaches me and pours a glorious stream of kibble into the bowl.

My tail wags a little faster. But I do not move. I wait and wait and wait. It's torture at its best. Or worst? I'm not sure.

The big human looks at me, then nods. "Go on, Buck. Good boy."

I recognize those words even if I don't understand them. It means that it's time to eat.

Dignity to the wind, I descend upon the bowl, gobbling down my food before it runs away. It's nowhere near as good as table scraps, but I'm not complaining. Much...

I hear a tut from above, but I don't look up.

"Greedy pig," Jeff mutters.

Ah, this is the life!

Once I'm done, I'm let outside to do my business.

The Temptation and I have plenty of it, and it's all unfinished.

One spots me as soon as I spot it, and it breaks into a run toward the nearest tree. I, of course, being a proud and self-respecting canine, chase it, barking at the top of my lungs.

That's right. You better run. Not so tough now, are you, little guy? The Glass Door of Doom can't protect you now.

I almost have it in my jaws when, with a graceful leap, it sails the last of the distance toward the tree and latches onto the bark with stubby claws. It skitters up the side before turning and chattering down at me. Mocking me.

And just like that, I lose control again.

***

This time, the big humans don't shout at me. After several minutes of cathartic barking up the right tree, I forget all about the squirrel—which has long since fled—and do my actual business outside.

Keeping the Temptation away is hungry work—squirrels are a menace—but I do it anyway. For the pack. I'll keep them safe. No matter what, I'll keep Katie safe.

The thought reminds me...

I miss Katie. I need to go see her.

I sprint upstairs, tongue dangling out of the side of my mouth as I run. I dash toward her room and leap onto the bed, surrounded by the smell of cornflowers and oranges, before soaking her face in kisses.

She wakes up with a happy squeal, blue eyes opening. "Ewww, Buck, gross! Stop it!"

She says this every morning. Unlike most of the other noises humans make, I know exactly what these words mean.

Katie wants more kisses.

I'm happy to oblige.

Chapter 2

Time passes slowly as the humans do human things around the house before coming down to the kitchen to eat. Katie bounces down the stairs with her favorite plushie—a rabbit called Mr. Flopsy—in her arms.

I gaze at her expectantly, psychically projecting my hunger toward her. As usual, she slips me a few scraps of bacon beneath the table. I lick my chops and gobble the scraps out of her hands, licking her greasy fingers under the table as the glorious taste melts over my tongue.

She giggles, and I lie down, content, and slowly doze off with my head on my paws.

***

All of a sudden, the humans are moving.

"Are you excited to stay at your grandparents', Katie?" the big humans ask as they walk toward the door.

Katie nods as she puts on her shoes, and my tail helicopters in excitement. I know what putting on shoes means! It means we're going for a walk.

The pack laughs at my antics as I romp around their legs.

"Maybe later, Buck, maybe later. Good boy. Good boy!" the smaller of the big humans—Sarah—praises me, long, blond hair framing blue eyes that are crinkled at the corners, and her radiant smile tells me I've done well.

I sit by the door, tail wagging, basking in their praise.

The humans slip on their shoes and pick up the two bags.

"Are you ready, Katie? Okay. Let's go," Sarah says.

The door opens, a magical portal to the outside world full of incredible sounds and scents waiting to be smelled. Maybe I'll even mark the tree that bitch Karryn marked two days ago.

However, no sooner do I attempt to step outside than a leg blocks my progress and the three humans, my pack, brush past me, hurrying toward the car without me.

Tao Wong

They're going without me. I give a small whine.

The shorter of the big humans turns back to me. "Stay, stay, Buck, good boy. We'll be back soon."

The praise gives me confidence. Maybe they're not leaving after all.

My tail wags with feverish hope as the shorter of the big humans places the bag she was carrying by the car and walks toward me. I jump to my feet, my tail moving so fast it might catch on fire. The human has come to take me with her.

"Good boy," Sarah says and closes the door in my face.

I lie down by the door, whimpering as I listen, with rapidly fading hope, to the voices outside. Then, through the crack in the door that always lets in a cool draft when it's hot, I hear Katie say my name.

My hero. My human's coming back for me. I hear footsteps.

The door opens, and Katie gives me a big, warm hug, blond curls bouncing. My savior. She's convinced the pack to not abandon me. I demonstrate my gratitude by planting several sloppy kisses all over her face, eliciting her usual response.

Then she's gone, the door closing once again in my face.

I hear the familiar sound of the car starting—with me not inside it. It rolls onto the road with a slight bump, and the engine revs. And slowly, tormentingly, the sound of the pack's car fades into the distance.

It's too much to take.

I howl at the closed door, begging them not to leave me behind. But I don't think they can hear me; they're too far gone.

The pack's abandoned me.

I feel a slight prickling behind my ears. But I ignore it. This situation is too serious for idle scratching with my hind paws.

With nothing else to do but wait, I press my nose to the crack beneath the door, trying to make out the freshest patch of their scent trail, taking comfort in the faint whiff of cornflower and orange.

But as I sniff it, my nose pressed close against the wood, the smell only gets fainter and fainter.

For who knows how long, I wait.

***

All of a sudden, I'm hauled out of my personal pit of loneliness and despair as the prickling returns in force.

It's a foreign feeling. But I instantly recognize it for what it is—danger.

Not just for me, but for Katie, my human.

I stand and scratch at the door, whining. Katie's in danger. I dash around the house, looking for a way outside, but the house is sealed up and the prickling is intensifying. Now it's an invasive ache that makes my hackles rise and my tail drop, my teeth baring in an involuntary growl. Danger. Enemy.

Katie's in danger, my pack's in danger, and my pack is far away.

I growl again and snap at the air, trying to tear the horrible sensation from the world with teeth, but I find nothing. The feeling continues. Suddenly, it's as if I'm choking. I can't breathe.

I roll on the floor, trying to scratch away the feeling on the doormat. Body racked with unbearable pain, the doormat seems smaller than I remember, barely enough to scrape away the unbearable itch. The choking feeling around my neck tightens before, with a sudden snap, the feeling stops.

A screen flashes in front of my eyes, conveying to me, with sight and scent and sound, a simple message.

Would you like to form a bond with Katie? **Y/N**

For the first time in my life, I truly understand something that's not another dog—or Katie asking for kisses. In an instant, I make my choice.

Yes.

And just like that, another series of screens flashes before my eyes.

Through Katie's actions, you have gained a class.

Basic Class: Beast Bonded

A Beast Tamer forms a lifelong bond with their animals. For a Beast Bonded, that bond lasts through death. Rather than allowing for the taming of multiple animals, a Beast Bonded may only bond with a single animal.

Class Abilities: +1 per Level in Strength and Constitution. +2 per Level in Perception. Additional 2 Free Attributes per Level.

Class Skills unlocked.

1 Class Skill available to be distributed. Would you like to do so?

I understand the meaning of the screens' contents. But Katie is still in danger.

I try to walk, but the screens remain in front of my eyes and I slam headfirst into a wall. Annoyed and confused, I brush away the screens with a paw, and surprisingly, they disappear.

I see the broken drywall in front of me. Oh dear. I think I did a bad thing.

The part of the wall that I impacted is cracked in places. The smell of dust and powdered plaster puffs out around me. But what surprises me is the height at which the fractures in the wall are placed. Everything seems smaller now. And it takes me a moment to realize that I am what has grown.

I turn around and see a thin strip of leather lying by the doormat. My collar! Except it's not on my neck anymore. One side of it has snapped.

Absently, I scratch my neck, remembering the choking sensation that had overcome me. If the collar hadn't broken, I might have choked as my neck grew too big for it.

I'm tired, and my neck is still in pain, but Katie is in danger.

So, without much thought as to how not a good boy I am being, I seize the broken collar in my enlarged jaws and jump through the nearest window.

The breaking glass reminds me of lots of shouting—like the first time I broke the Glass Door of Doom. Glinting shards cut into my belly and the pads of my paws, but the pain fades quickly and my wounds with it.

Anyway, there's no time to dwell on pain. I have to find my pack. They are in danger. I know it. I can smell it in the air.

I sniff where the car was, committing the scent of the tires and everything they touched to memory. Particularly the roadkill from two days ago. A decaying frog, I think—strong, earthy, and bursting with the sickly sweet twist of rot.

Somewhere in the back of my mind, I hear the frantic shouts and screams of people inside their houses or on adjacent streets, as well as the distinct lack of running engines. But the noises don't matter to me. Only one thing holds any importance at the moment, and that is finding my pack.

I set off down the road, pursuing the trail of the frog on the car's wheels. With my nose close to the ground, I run as if my life, and my pack's lives, depends on it.

Small critters, now massively enlarged, roam around the town as the first threads of smoke weave through the sky.

The smoking shells of cars, the remnants of sudden and violent accidents, snarl up the road, leaving behind the acrid smell of burnt rubber, hot metal, and leaking petrol. The surrounding screams get louder and more frequent as monsters rampage through doors and windows. Shatters are followed by dull thuds and thumps—and all too often, no more screaming.

Hearing so many humans in distress makes me stop, but then I remember my goal.

I need to find my pack, and *these humans* are not my pack.

So, I keep on running, sprinting faster when several monsters turn their heads toward me and attempt to run me down. But I am too fast for them. I leave them all in my dust.

As I leave town, the density of screams and smoke and accidents lessens. I follow the road up a gentle incline into a quiet pine forest, the air thick with the scent of fallen needles and sweet, sticky resin. Several trees rustle as I pass, but I pay them no heed except to give them a wider berth as I continue chasing my pack.

I dash past a group of humans huddled together, shaking as they see me. I can smell their fear. I suspect it might be due to my increased size.

One of them raises a long metal tube toward me. A thunderclap rings out, and I feel as if I have been punched in the hindquarters. I stumble, not quite realizing what's happened, even as the first hints of pain spread like sharp spiderwebs.

However, a singular purpose consumes me. I power forward, and the man with the loud metal tube lowers it as he realizes that I'm not a monster intent on ripping him to shreds. Several of the women in the group shout at him, but I don't understand what they're saying. I don't care either.

I just want to find my humans.

The pain in my hindquarters has progressed into a frothing agony. I can't run as fast, but the strength of the scent I am following spurs me on. I follow the trail, climbing ever upward toward the mountains in the distance, the air becoming increasingly unpolluted as I pull away from the town.

The pain fades quickly, and my speed returns to normal; a slug of metal—smelling of brass, blood, and smoke—drops from my side. I continue for interminable hours until fatigue overwhelms me.

My humans are close now. The smell of rot from the roadkill that coats the tires is stronger. But my muscles ache, and I don't think I can run any farther.

I'm tired and hungry and alone. And my pack isn't here to make any of the aches go away.

Whimpering, I curl up beneath a bush and lick my wounds.

Chapter 3

When I wake, the world is crisp and clean and the air is clear. It must have rained during the night.

The pain of overexertion has passed, but I give my hindquarters an examinatory lick to make sure I'm okay. My skin is unmarked, but a slight patch of hair on my flank is shorter than before.

I give a noisy yawn, then pause as a familiar scent wafts toward my nostrils. A new one, given the cleansing effect of the rain that washed away scents and tracks. Even in my dozy state, the scent sends a shiver of excitement down my spine, vibrating through my tail.

I poke my head out of the bushes. Nothing.

Droplets of water and dew cover leaf and grass alike, making the forest and road smell muted and muffled, emphasizing the familiar scent of the Temptation.

Slowly, making as little sound as possible, I slink out of the bush, following my nose toward the scent.

I hear a large rustle in the bushes before me. A squeak. Taunting me, daring me to come chase it as it flees into a tree, as it has so many times.

But not this day. Today, victory will be mine. A screen flashes in front of me. Something about stealth. I bat it away. Now's not the time.

Throwing caution to the wind, I charge through the bushes, eager to finally seize my prey. Foliage explodes around me as I accelerate, leaping toward my quarry.

And then I see it. Hulking and huge.

I try to halt my charge, try to skid to a stop, but I'm too late. The ground beneath me is slick with dew, and I slide straight into the side of Temptationzilla.

I bounce off its side and fall to the ground. Horror of horrors, the giant squirrel's nose twitches. Its head turns toward me, bushy gray tail twitching like a spaniel struck by lightning.

Not prey! Not prey!

With one paw, it swipes at me, but at the last moment, I roll to the side, evading its questing claws. Yelping in surprise, I scramble away, but the monster leaps over me, heading off my escape.

No, definitely not prey.

It takes another swipe at me, and I dodge again, backing away slowly. Even with my growth, the squirrel is larger than me, but I can't run. I growl at it menacingly, trying to exude a confidence I don't feel. I eye the monster, trying to get a sense of what it'll do next.

Then another ground squirrel, one of the smaller kinds, skitters up a nearby trunk. Out of habit, I stare at it.

As I'm distracted by the big squirrel's buddy, the squirrel's swipe strikes me on the side and sends me careening into a tree, whimpering and yelping in pain.

I heave myself to my feet. *Fine. If this is how you want to do it, have it your way.* I charge the oversized squirrel, ducking beneath its hasty counterattack.

Latching onto its back foot, I bite down hard. I maul its leg, feeling my teeth scrape against bone as I shake my head from side to side, trying to rip and tear tendons and flesh as quickly and as savagely as possible. The squirrel whirls, slamming a lumbering paw into my torso, trying to dislodge me.

All four of my feet leave the ground, but my jaws are firmly attached to the squirrel. As it takes me for a ride, I hold on for dear life, and its life trickles away between my teeth.

The squirrel spins me straight into a tree.

I'm winded by the impact, and my grip loosens. I collapse in an aching heap. The squirrel looms over me as my ribs shift, sending shooting pain through me with each breath.

Vengefully, its flat teeth clamp down around my forepaw, and it shakes me with vicious jerks of its head. Between the haze of agony as my life bleeds away and my ribs rattle within me, I manage to grasp its neck between my jaws.

The dumb monster continues to shake me, both of us ignoring the pain as we maintain our death grips on each other.

My grip is deadlier.

It gives my leg a sadistic jerk, almost tearing it off, but my jaws are still clamped around its throat, and the squirrel pulls hard. It aids in ripping out a bloody chunk of its own neck, its heart pumping a rhythmic pulse of arterial spray onto the ground.

Several notifications pop up in front of me, but I brush them aside. Embracing my instincts, I wolf down the gobbet of warm, fur-covered flesh, then clamp my teeth onto the wound once more. Hot blood gushes around my teeth, some pouring into the back of my throat.

The monster weakens, no longer tossing around my abused body, and we both impact the earth hard.

I lie there for what seems like hours, unable to move, unable to pry its jaws from my paw in my current pitiful state. Slowly, however, the aches in my ribs and legs abate, and I notice the screen that pops up in front of me.

Level Up! *2

You have reached Level 3 as a Beast Bonded. Stat Points automatically distributed.
You have 4 Free Attributes to distribute.
1 Class Skill available to be distributed. Would you like to do so?

From the sense the message gave me, this is a good thing. I just don't know how to actually allocate my free attribute points.

As if responding to my thought, a new screen appears in front of me. Intelligible in a somewhat surreal way, since I had no real grasp of numbers prior to this, it all makes sense. Maybe it's the bond with Katie, or something else, but I find myself slowly coming to grips with counting and numeracy, abstract concepts though they are.

Status Screen			
Name	Buck	Class	Beast Bonded
Race	Canine (Scotch Collie – Male)	Level	3
Titles			
None			
Health	100	Stamina	100
Mana	50		
Status			
Normal			
Attributes			
Strength	13	Agility	16
Constitution	10	Perception	26

Intelligence	5	Willpower	5
Charisma	17	Luck	11
Skills			
Tracking	4	Athletics	2
Natural Weapons	2	Sense Danger	1
Stealth	1		
Class Skills			
None			
Spells			
None			
Perks			
None			

It seems that I gained several Levels in tracking—probably a result of chasing the pack—as well as four other Skills from my fight.

With four points to spend, I put two in Willpower and two in Intelligence. I have noticed a surge in my strength, vitality, and senses from my automatically assigned attributes, but somewhere deep down, I know I need more Intelligence so I can be more like the humans.

Am I doing this counting thing correctly?

Given that, on subsequent tries, I am unable to allocate further points, I guess I am.

And what were the other things? Class Skills? I have two of those, right? Upon the mental prompt, a new window opens.

Beast Bonded Class Skills

Wicked Claws		Swiftfoot	Adapted Observation	← Improved Senses
↓		↓		↓
Rending Strike ➡	Blackpaw	Sure Stride		Toughened Hide
↓	↓	↓		↓
Bulwark	Rift Strike	← Shadow Dash		Zone of Eyes
↓		↓		↓

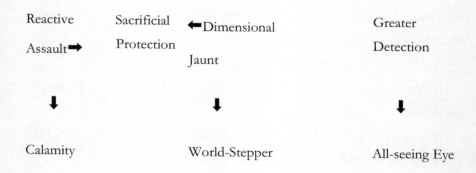

My Class Skills are divided into three categories: combat, mobility, and utility. Only the first row is actually available to me though. The second through fifth are only available at increasing increments of ten Levels each.

As much as I want to take a combat ability, I'm in a corner at the moment.

I have to find Katie and the pack before something terrible happens. Swiftfoot would let me reach them quicker, but without improving my senses, I can only follow the road. Perhaps I won't even be able to follow that since the rain during the night has probably scoured it of the easier-to-track scents.

Coming to a decision, I spend my first and second Class Skills.

Class Skill Acquired

Improved Senses (Level 1)

> *Effect: User's sensory range is expanded, allowing you to hear sounds of higher and lower frequencies, view an expanded range of wavelengths of light, and more. Additionally, Mana may be sacrificed to temporarily increase your Perception attribute by an equivalent amount when this Skill is activated. Observe Skills, Class Skills, and your Perception attribute will influence the effectiveness of this Skill. This Skill can be boosted with additional Mana.*

Mana regeneration is permanently reduced by 5 Mana per minute.

Active Cost: 1 Mana per minute per point of Perception gained.

Class Skill Acquired

Adapted Observation (Level 1)

Effect: Draws from the System to provide additional information on monsters and individuals encountered. Data is converted to be compatible with your Olfactory System instead of Visual System. Observe Skills, Class Skills, and your Perception attribute will influence the effectiveness of this Skill.

Cost: 1 Mana per use.

Immediately, I feel my vision growing clearer, sharper, as the effects of the Class Skills come into force. And I see something new. Red and green.

Previously, green had appeared white, but now it has an actual color that is... *green*. Even I recognize that as a lame explanation, but there's no other way to explain it. I see *more*, and that's all there is to it. Something in my skull has changed, and green is suddenly *a thing*.

I gaze at the corpse of the squirrel and find another surprise. Red blood on a brown coat.

Red used to be a boring gray, but now it's *red*. I really need to find a better way to think of this. And brown, which used to be a dark grayish-yellow, is a rich *brown*.

I shake my head, ridding myself of the odd thoughts that bombard me as a result of my newfound intelligence. Thinking is uncomfortable. It's like having humans in my head.

My stomach growls, and I squirm out of the ground squirrel's mouth, taking a bite out of its neck. As I do so, a gray box pops up with several hunks of meat inside, tender and juicy, and a brownish-gray pelt.

After releasing the monster's neck, I prod at the contents of the box with my muzzle, surprised when I *touch* the meat inside. The gray box has given me Tribute!

Excited, I pull the food from the box, making the screen close.

The body remains behind, but I've already gained too much meat from the gray box. I can't eat it all, plus the body, in one sitting.

Leaving so much food behind hurts me, but I scarf down as much of the Tribute as I can, then I go to find my collar. I left it somewhere, and I need to find it. The pack gave it to me when I was only a puppy.

I backtrack to the bush where I slept and find the strip of red leather where I left it in my rush to defeat the Temptation. Giving a growl of approval, I pick it up then meander to the road, keeping an eye out for more monsters.

However, no matter how fervently I search, I can't find the pack's scent. It's there in faint hints and directionless splashes, but there's no trail to follow. The clear unbroken line of odor was obliterated by the rain.

I whimper. The pack's gone. I'm lost. I'll never see them again.

Then I remember.

I have seventy Mana in the tank right now, and I just got Improved Senses. Doesn't it have an active ability? It allows me to spend Mana to increase my Perception.

I immediately do so, spending four Mana per minute, and bump my Perception up to thirty.

With that done, I take a good long sniff at the road. The world dilates around me. I can detect the gravelly, bituminous surface of the road, the smell of wet tarmac, and the overpowering fragrance of pines and damp needles. And beneath it all, so faint...

There.

I have it! A scent. The one I'm looking for.

It's faint, even at thirty Perception, but it's there.

However, I won't be able to run while tracking. Which means…

I boost my total up to thirty-five. But it's not enough. At thirty-seven, the trail is far stronger, but it's still not sufficient to track while running. I'm guessing forty won't be either.

Throwing good sense to the wind, I bring it all the way up to forty-five. The world expands around me. Even the water has a scent; it's dusty and ever so slightly cool, but beneath that scent is another. Suspended within every droplet is the remnant of the path my pack took.

I'm hemorrhaging Mana, losing almost one Mana every three seconds, and my regeneration can't keep up with it, especially with the permanent reduction from Improved Senses. In the time it's taken to look this far, I'm down to fifty-one out of seventy Mana. The boost to my Perception will last for three and a half minutes, then there'll be nothing left.

But the trail is there. Before me, my pack's trail spreads out like a golden path. I take a moment to remember the exact direction. Then I deactivate Improved Senses, letting the boost to my Perception expire after sixty seconds have elapsed.

But I remember the path the pack took. I race down the road, only turning on Improved Senses every now and then to confirm I'm going the right way.

My Tracking skill is increasing at an incredible pace thanks to boosting my senses. It seems there are benefits to abusing a Perception score of forty-five at Level 3. As I run, I do the math. If I put all my future attribute points into Perception, it would take me five more levels to passively reach what I am already managing.

And that's insane.

Able to smell and see everything, my Tracking skill improves commensurately. I hit Level 7 in the skill with little to no difficulty, and my progress shows no signs of stopping anytime soon.

My Stamina runs out faster than my Mana, given that I'm not using Improved Senses all that often. Not that it's too much of a burden. I can still run for longer than I used to be able to by virtue of my improved Constitution.

I run, stopping for breathers every twenty minutes or so. My improved Tracking skill is paying off. The trail is strong now and…

In the distance, I see something.

My humans' car. Was it always red?

I give a big, wolfish grin and tear down the road toward it. A notification about a high-level zone appears, but I swat it away. I'm close now.

The car is abandoned, not wrecked like some of those in town. The tank smells as if it's still half full of gas, which means the engine probably isn't working. I know how fast these things go.

If they're not here, they went on by foot. And humans are *soooo* slow.

I wait to recover my breath, then I set off along their trail, recognizing the smell of soap, cornflowers, and oranges that belongs to Katie. As I chase them down, a story in scent form plays out before me.

They walked around the car for a while, likely scratching their heads as the first of many notifications they would see appeared. Then they set off down the road in the direction they were going.

If I remember correctly, two of the elderly sometimes-pack, sometimes-not-pack live close by. Not that I could say so with any confidence. My memories from before I was able to increase my Intelligence are fuzzy.

What was the word?

Grandparents. That was it.

But suddenly, they veer off into the trees, leaving bags and possessions scattered behind them. A new scent trail, one that reeks of rancid sweat and danger, joins up with them.

Their scent strengthens slightly as they run, dead skin shaken loose.

The sweaty one follows, and it's big. Where the pack, my humans, dart through bushes, leaving behind a trail of broken branches and scattered leaves, the sweaty one muscles through trees, leaving a trail a blind cat could follow.

It pursues them slowly, spending time picking up their trail.

And it loses them.

I breathe a sigh of relief and continue tracking my humans, now up to a Tracking skill of Level 9.

The wind shifts, and I smell something different. Damp fur and the smell of rotten meat billowing from hungry jaws. There are other monsters nearby, and they aren't following my humans. They're following me.

As if waiting for that thought, the dappled shadows beneath the trees nearby shift and realign. Four beasts with mottled black-and-green fur emerge, seemingly from the forest itself, tongues lolling out of open mouths and long strings of saliva dripping from between their teeth. Their bodies are oddly canine, yet more muscular, but their heads are crested with antlers that resemble the branching boughs of trees.

Their eyes are beady and well adapted to seeing in shadow and sunlight. Their paws glide silently over wet leaves as they stalk toward me, gazes fixed on me. They're predators through and through, obviously specialized in stealth.

My Class Skill, Adapted Observation, activates as I see them. Information fills my mind, conveyed by sentences of phantom scent that twist within my nostrils.

Keranid (Level 5)

Three of them are Level 5, but one of them, slightly larger than the others, sits at Level 6. I step back from them. I doubt I can easily defeat these things.

They growl at me, baring fangs with wolflike menace, antler-topped heads tossing in irritation. For a moment, I feel a twinge of offense at their canine likeness, but that's replaced by fear.

I turn and flee as the Keranids announce their pursuit with yips and baying howls. I risk a backward glance.

They're closing in, silently gliding over the forest floor on flashing feet.

I push my body further and accelerate.

It's not enough to matter. These Keranids are built for speed, stealth, and pursuit. They eat up the space between us with every stride, veering gracefully around bushes and trees.

They're gaining on me. I can almost feel their hot breath on my heels now.

Out of the corner of my eye, I see an antler sweep toward my leg, aiming to trip me and send me to the ground—and to their jaws moments later.

I leap just in time. The head swipe makes the lead Keranid fall back as it regains its balance from its failed attack, but it's a temporary pause and it soon rejoins its pursuit.

I might not spot them next time, or they might flank me, box me in. I can't let that happen. I struggle to think up a solution, kicking my brain into gear.

I glance back again.

The Keranids weave around trees, antlers grazing leaves and twigs as they leap soundlessly over low-lying obstacles—but never getting close to trees or thicker vegetation.

Realization slams into me like a two-hundred-pound squirrel.

Their antlers. They're affixed to their heads, so if they run too close to a tree, they'll end up impacting a solid object, like charging into a glass door. And unlike the Glass Door of Doom, their necks will give out long before a tree trunk does.

I spot a funnel of trees nearby, the verdant corridor's gaps connected by banks of shrub and bush. I angle toward it, pushing myself faster as my Stamina drains.

The Keranids are close now, but I break into the avenue of trees before them. I can feel their spittle flecking my hindquarters, and as the last of them enters, I veer through one of the smaller gaps, my body slamming painfully into a tree.

But unencumbered by antlers, I make it.

The Keranids screech to a halt, piling into each other as they struggle to stop.

I remember my embarrassing days of struggling to fit through gaps too small to fit my frame, neglecting to go around the obstacle instead. I'm past that now. The Keranids aren't.

They thrash their antlers against the nearest gap of trees, not even trying to fit through the bushes for fear of becoming hopelessly entangled.

But I'm not done.

I turn on my heels and charge back at the one working itself through the gap. Restricted as it is, it's unable to meet me properly, neither can it pull away in time.

I stop short, and with a cheeky grin, I drop the collar from my mouth and seize its antlers in my jaws in a game of tug-of-war.

Not expecting the change in tactics, the lead Keranid's feet give out as I yank its head, then tangle its antlers between branch and bush and tree. It thrashes as it realizes, too late, what I've done. I crouch under and around it, then tear at its throat and exposed belly.

It dies in moments. As fast and as strong and as stealthy as they are, the Keranids lack resiliency. A Level-up notification appears, but I dismiss it. The other three Keranids are still milling around behind their leader, trying to disentangle themselves and back away from each other. I don't intend on giving them time to do so.

Time for phase two.

I bite into the defeated Level 6 Keranid, letting a gray box pop up. Once again, Tribute appears inside the box. My hopes have been realized. Like with the squirrel, the Keranid's Tribute box contains meat, but more importantly, a rack of antlers, complete with a clean white skull.

I pull the antlers out of the box and dart into the middle of the corridor. Balancing on the downed Keranid's corpse, I wedge the upper end of the antlers into a crooked bough above the dead monster, and dig the tines of the lower end into the flank of the dead Keranid, providing another obstruction if the other three Keranids try to step over it. Then I dart back before they have time to snap at me. A notification about Tactics fills my vision, but I ignore it, rushing around to the beginning of the avenue of trees.

The back Keranid's flank faces me, and it struggles forward when it realizes I'm now behind it. Its frantic actions cause more chaos, and the Keranids press up against the wedged antlers and skull of their former leader.

I hamstring the Keranid and savage its spine until it falls still. I crawl over its cooling corpse and move on to the next.

There's a savage song in my blood, wild and primal, as I rip and tear through the monsters that make a mockery of the canine form. I work methodically, going for vulnerabilities and slicing the Keranids open with maximal efficiency.

Yelps and whines fill the forest as I clean up, but by the end of it, all the Keranids have been disposed of and I have earned yet another Level and several new skills.

Level Up! *2

You have reached Level 5 as a Beast Bonded. Stat Points automatically distributed.
You have 4 Free Attributes to distribute.

1 Class Skill available to be distributed. Would you like to do so?

I place two points in Agility and two in Intelligence. Both attributes were the only reasons I survived that encounter. Agility because I was fast and maneuverable, and Intelligence because of… well… that's obvious.

With that done, I pick up my collar and allocate my latest Class Skill. Wicked Claws.

Class Skill Acquired

Wicked Claws (Level 1)

   Effect: Natural weapons may now be imbued with mana to deal more damage on each hit. +5 Base Damage (Mana). Partially ignores armor and resistances.

Cost: 10 Stamina + 10 Mana per minute

Then I check my Status once again, noting the changes before setting off back toward where I came from.

Status Screen			
Name	Buck	Class	Beast Bonded
Race	Canine (Scotch Collie – Male)	Level	5
Titles			

None			
Health	120	Stamina	120
Mana	90		
Status			
Normal			
Attributes			
Strength	15	Agility	18
Constitution	12	Perception	30
Intelligence	9	Willpower	7
Charisma	17	Luck	11
Skills			
Tracking	9	Athletics	4
Natural Weapons	5	Sense Danger	2
Stealth	1	Observe	1

Tactics	2	Detect Vulnerability	2
Class Skills			
Improved Senses	1	Adapted Observation	1
Wicked Claws	1		
Spells			
None			
Perks			
None			

I make my way back to the humans' trail without much difficulty. With my skill in tracking and the messy trail I left in my mad dash through the forest, it doesn't take long. Thankfully, my return journey is uneventful.

I occasionally boost my Perception with Improved Senses once again, reading the story in scent my humans left behind.

Chapter 4

The humans' scents are gathered in three patches of squashed grass and leaves, two big and one small, beneath the low-hanging boughs of a pine tree. The strong smell of resin masks their scent further, but it's no match for my superpowered sniffing.

They obviously bedded down for the night, then continued after dawn.

The humans continued on, lost in the woods. There's the sound of a waterfall nearby, and their trail begins veering toward it. A path slowly emerges, one trodden by hundreds of humans. There are two fresh sets of footsteps in the damp earth, one—the father—carrying Katie by the way his footsteps vary in depth, as if his burden wiggled in his arms.

And a plush rabbit, Katie's favorite, lies to one side—left behind as their pace quickened.

I carefully open my mouth, maintaining a grip on the collar as I catch ahold of the plush rabbit's torso.

A new set of massive footprints joins the trail, chasing them, the same stink of sweat and dead skin as I detected by the car. They're all running now, the monster in pursuit.

A roar breaks the stillness of the forest—right ahead of me! I snap out of my tracking trance.

I can see them with my own two eyes. My pack. And something else. They're on a wooden bridge that passes over a raging river, a waterfall slightly upstream.

A hulking creature of warty gray flesh, ridged with multiple calluses, hefts a tree-branch club over its head as it bellows at them.

I pick up speed. I can't let the ugly beast catch them. I focus on its form, taking in its sweaty scent. Adapted Observation delivers a scent-based analysis of the creature.

Rock Troll Youth (Level 14)

Given that there were no signs of a struggle on the way here, I assume that my pack are still only Level 1.

Which means the Rock Troll will squash them like frogs beneath a car tire.

Muscles burning, I lope toward my pack, interposing myself between them and the enemy. My pack flinches as I approach—I'm different now, bigger— and the warm flame of reunion almost dies in my chest. Then Katie speaks from her father's arms. A single word.

"Buck?"

Gently, I drop my cargo at my human's feet and kiss her ankle where her dress hitches up.

Then I turn to the Troll, menacing it with a vicious growl. The Troll steps forward, swinging its club in wide arcs, the wind whistling around the bough of knotted wood. It expects me to flee, but I'd rather paint the bridge red with both our blood than let it get past me and reach my pack. No way in hell.

I charge, sliding beneath the wooden bough that comes screaming toward me, feeling the rush of air tickle my fur and smelling the thick, sticky sap that still sticks to its surface. I end up behind and to the side of the Troll. I see my pack staring, frozen in shock and terror.

I yip at them. *Run.*

But they just stand there.

The Troll kicks me, the impact of its warty foot sending me slamming into the wooden siding of the bridge. I limp to my feet. Chunks of broken baluster fall into the river below, their splashes masked by the turbulent roar of water.

"Buck!" Katie cries.

I bark at them again, but it's mixed with a yelp as broken ribs grate. *Run!*

The Troll, now ignoring me, takes another step toward my pack. The movement breaks them from their stupor, and they back away, picking up the collar and toy as they move.

The Troll follows them. I leap toward it, pain forgotten. But at the last moment, I remember something.

My claws scrape against wood as they lengthen and sharpen, reforged into cruel points. My new Class Skill.

And one more thing.

Golden explosions of scent detonate around me, and I see so much more. I slam my Perception up to sixty, my Mana falling by thirty every minute. Forty, if you include Wicked Claws.

The Troll is too high-leveled though. I doubt I'll have another minute of Mana to use.

Time seems slower, the waterfall louder, and every pulse of the Troll's blood is all the more distinct. The Troll had once been a beacon of sweat and rancid odor; it's so much worse now. Foul scent puffs out from between folds of fat, flesh, and callus every time the monster moves.

It's all too much. Everything is exacerbated. The sunlight is nearly blinding, the grain of the wood beneath my paws too distinct and unique, the noise of the churning water verging on deafening. Time trickles past me, like tree sap between my claws, and I stumble, my head bursting from the sensory overload. I feel a faint prickle in my ears and nose as blood begins to pool and run—a repercussion of too high a Perception and too-low Intelligence, perhaps.

But it's worth it.

I know every inch of the Troll's hide, every crack and crevice between dry and crusted callus. The beat of its heart is so loud I can *feel* it on my skin, and the murmur and gurgle of backwashing blood through sclerotic veins—brushing up against stiffened valves—rivals the waterfall for sheer volume.

I push further, adding another fifteen Mana per minute to boosting my Perception. Seventy-five now. I leap forward, intent on tearing the Troll's veins from its malodorous bulk.

The Troll spots me and roars. Loud. Too loud. I feel my eardrums burst.

And like that, I hear nothing at all. My world becomes noise and through noise becomes silence.

My claws strike the Troll's leg, raking it from ankle to knee. Empowered claws score clean lines through its tough, callused skin. Not too deep. Not deep enough to reach the vessels pumping vital blood beneath, but certainly revealing them.

Blood flows freely, twice as foul-smelling as I expected.

The Troll stumbles, leaving a red-smeared footprint on the planks of the bridge. The smooth-planed timber creaks beneath the sudden shift in weight.

I tear at the exposed tissues with my teeth. My canines—I take a moment to reflect on the hilarity of the unintentional pun—puncture farther, perforating an artery. The Troll's roar vibrates my chest with a bass rumble. Unheard but still felt.

And then, the worst happens.

The wounds I inflicted heal. Even with Improved Senses and Detect Vulnerability working together, seeing every place I can harm an enemy doesn't matter if the harm doesn't last.

I jump back as the Troll stomps its foot, sending its heavy limb straight through the bridge, down into nothingness, and it collapses to one knee. I pause, hoping its momentum will carry it through. But it's not to be. Slowly, the Troll raises itself on one hulking foot.

I look at my pack, at Katie, at the far end of the bridge, and I know what I have to do.

Before the monster can free itself, I dance in front of it, tearing at its fat fingers as I pass. Enraged, it swings at me, no longer trying to stand. It ploughs through the wooden planks, sending a tidal wave of splinters flying.

I dart toward it again, this time standing near the siding.

The bridge groans and tilts as the dumb monster continues to destroy the only thing keeping it from the river. I dash to the other side, and the club smashes after me, tearing the structure we stand on to splinters.

I bark once at my pack. Five years of love and memory contained in the single sound.

And the bridge falls.

Suddenly, there's a chance. The other side of the bridge remains stable, buttressed by a fortuitous support column. With the last of my energy, I leap.

And the Rock Troll's club clips me from behind, the glancing blow nearly tearing my back paw clean off. My leg hangs on by the faintest string of sinew. The force sends me flying over the siding, hurtling toward the river.

There's nothing left to lose. I turn up Improved Senses as far as it will go. With the last of my Mana, I hit a hundred and ten Perception.

Perfect.

The smell of orange, soap, and cornflower fills my nose from across the river. Time slows to a near halt, and for two blissful seconds that stretch out forever with my impossible Perception, I remember.

I remember being tiny, a puppy, not a single summer old, staring at a swaddled bundle of warmth and comfort and realizing that I had found my world as I laid the first of many kisses upon her button nose. Her breathing was bad, and they had to take her away.

That month was a year in itself, waiting to see whether the candle in my heart would flicker out so soon.

It didn't, and I've stayed beside her since.

When she was four, she broke her arm on the garden swing. The swing was cut down, but I stayed with her in the ambulance, growling at the paramedics when they tried to separate me from her.

Katie. She gave me purpose, meaning. And when the monsters came, when the cars stopped dead in the streets, she *chose me*. She saved me from becoming a monster. She saved me.

I stare at her, drinking in every inch of her face as I fly toward the water. I see her lips form my name as she strains forward, eyes wide, desperate, already brimming with tears.

I wish I could stretch out and kiss those tears away, but I'm too far. And I always will be.

"Buck!" she screams.

But of course, I don't hear. I can see her mouth move.

My head is burning from having my Perception so high.

But it's worth every moment.

Just a moment more.

My human.

Katie.

And all too soon, it's gone.

Air rushes past me, ruffling my brown-white-and-black fur. The water approaches so fast, even with a hundred and ten Perception.

For the pack? My love, my life.

For Katie? My everything.

I close my eyes as the Troll falls beside me like a meteor.

I don't hear the impact as we hit the water.

I don't hear anything at all.

Chapter 5

The waves lap silently against my back paws. The cold water splashes over pebbles, sending cool spray flicking into my fur.

Beside me, driftwood litters the pebbled shore, the detritus of the slow part of the river. I should get up. I don't want to.

Screens cover my vision, and slowly I read through them.

Hidden Quest Completed!

You have sacrificed yourself to protect your loved ones regardless of any repercussions that might befall you. Your love and sacrifices echo throughout the scope of the System.

Reward: 5,000 XP, Title Gained: Unto Death. All damage taken in defense of others reduced by 15%.

Congratulations!

For achieving your first title, you receive a bonus +5,000 XP.

Level Up! * 2

You have reached Level 7 as a Beast Bonded. Stat Points automatically distributed.

You have 4 Free Attributes to distribute.

1 Class Skill available to be distributed. Would you like to do so?

The words float before me, understood but without context. The remnants of another life.

Aching, I ease myself to my feet. My movements are lethargic and apathetic, my thoughts clouded. Where am I? Who am I?

At the thought, another screen appears.

Status Screen			
Name	Buck	Class	Beast Bonded
Race	Canine (Scotch Collie – Male)	Level	7
Titles			
Unto Death			
Health	140	Stamina	140
Mana	40		
Status			
Deaf (-15 Perception, cannot hear) Crippled (-10 Agility, -30% Movement Speed) Brain Damage (-5 Intelligence, Amnesia) (19:42:16)			
Attributes			
Strength	17	Agility	8
Constitution	14	Perception	19
Intelligence	4	Willpower	7

Charisma	17	Luck	11
Skills			
Tracking	9	Athletics	5
Natural Weapons	6	Sense Danger	3
Stealth	1	Observe	2
Tactics	3	Detect Vulnerability	4
Class Skills			
Improved Senses	1	Toughened Hide	1
Wicked Claws	1		
Spells			
None			
Perks			
None			

A name that is not my own hovers at the edge of my mind, too far to touch upon yet obviously there.

Irritated by the screens, I swipe at them, clearing them from my vision and unbalancing myself in the process.

I look back at my hindquarters. Ah, only three working legs. My fourth is slowly reforming, flesh knitting back together.

I'm not sure to do. I can walk, but who knows where? Or I can just lie here. Both options seem equally appealing.

Once again, the name intrudes upon the boundaries of my thoughts.

I don't know why, but it's impossible to lie still. I stand, and all the colors I see hurt my eyes. But I walk.

Something large attacks me, and I swipe it down, feasting on it, not understanding the gray box that appears before me.

It doesn't take long for my paw to heal properly and for my hearing to return. Soon I'm able to run and hear without issue or impairment. Those status effects are gone, although the Brain Damage and its Amnesia remain. Numbers slowly tick down, one second at a time. My Attributes have mostly returned to normal. But I'm still missing something.

Whatever memories I had, my understanding of the world, were excised from my brain by whatever injury I sustained. My body might have healed, but my mind is still a long way off. Not only that, I recognize my mind. I recognize it as *more* than other creatures'. But something within it is out of reach. Things I should know are there but slippery, within the scope of my mind but as intangible as smoke. My consciousness seems like an empty field. It has scope and scale and dimension; it is mine. But part of it now is... not for me. I know it's there. I know that it once *was* mine. It's not anymore. Not until the last status effect fades.

It is… frustrating.

And I worry. That maybe what I had will not return. That the voices and names, the fragments of memory that feel so familiar yet unreachable, will stay that way forever.

The mystery of the name I do not know haunts me. And my Status screen tells a story. My Class, my title. My high Tracking skill. All of it.

I was looking for someone, connected to someone. And they are not here.

Rather than wander in circles, roving aimlessly, I return to the pebbled bank of the river. With nothing but a purpose I do not remember and can only infer, I follow it upstream—climbing as the terrain curves up into a canyon with the river at its center.

A bridge, splintered and broken, spans the water. I approach it. Blood stains many of the ruined planks. I sniff at it, and I instantly recognize the smells. My own blood and that of something foul.

I was here.

Beneath the sweet, coppery cloy of blood, I find something. A scent. Three of them.

There's a rustle from across the river, and my ears perk up, swiveling to detect the noise as my gaze snaps up toward its source. A human stands there, pale skin covered by hair and fabric. The wind blows toward me, and I sniff, but his scent is not one I recognize. Then the human spots me and stills. Ever so slowly, he lifts a long metal tube.

I stare at him, head tilted inquisitively. The metal tube flashes, spitting fire and a whining round of metal that stings my side. The human curses, and I turn to flee. I might not remember what happened here, but I know when I'm unwelcome.

As I run, I pick up my own trail—and that of the three other scents on the bridge.

The scents weaken the farther I go, and it becomes clear I was following the three humans, for whatever reason. I feel unsure. Maybe I'm going the wrong way? But I forge ahead, following the path I took back to its source.

The scent of the humans is weaker when I reach the car, but my own trail is still pretty clear. I must have been running hard to catch up with them. Though I still wonder for what purpose.

Their scent stops inside the car, and I've hit a dead end on that front. One of the wheels holds a residual stink of some small animal caught beneath its tracks, but the scent it laid along road is too faded to track.

Not that I have to. I can follow my pursuit of the car just fine. Not that I need to. The road continues on straight for quite a ways, no tributary streets leading into or away from it.

So, I follow the road until I reach an intersection, sniff around to verify which way I had first come from, then continue to follow the road.

***

The first things I hear are gunshots.

They come from within the town, where a sleek metal building towers over the rest of the houses. But the expected pain searing across my side does not come. They're not firing at me.

Reassured, I crouch lower, creeping into the town, forgoing speed for stealth. I'm still wary though. The shining metal construction is out of place compared to the plaster and brick that sprawls past it. What's more, the gunfire issues from that direction, along with shouts and growls carried on stray gusts of wind.

I creep between buildings, following my trail to its source, only to be unpleasantly surprised by a threatening hiss from above my head.

Too quick to dodge, a lizard-like creature leaps from the wall it had been clambering on. It descends on me, the gripping pads of its dewdrop feet extended toward me, unbroken by claws but tinged a sickly yellow.

Acting on instinct, unable to evade in time, I get a look at the creature, surprised by the sentence of smell that fills my nose.

Yellow-Toed Lacerta (Level 9)

Its toes plop against me with force, bowling me over. Its attack completely bypasses my skin and fur. An insidious, creeping numbness spreads across the place I was struck. I give the affected area an experimental lick but feel nothing except a tingle across my tongue. The paralytic agent imparted by its toes does its job.

My hackles rise, and I snarl at the Lacerta, activating Wicked Claws. Murderous energy surges down my legs, lengthening and empowering my natural weapons.

The Lacerta leaps again, but I roll to the side, now wary of its paralytic touch. I give it an experimental swat with my left paw as it passes, and my empowered claws skitter off strong scales for a second before tearing through the flesh beneath like dried leaves.

I could get used to this.

The Lacerta gives a pained hiss. Viscous yellow blood oozes from its wounds like tree sap. I make a note to myself to not come in contact with the blood. Its color is too similar to its toes to be a coincidence.

We circle each other warily, then the Lacerta's tongue flicks back to touch the blood at its side. I take the opportunity to lunge, but quick as a startled snake, the lizard monster's tongue retracts, gooey blood coating its length. With a foamy whistle, a jet of part-saliva, part-paralytic-blood shoots out of its mouth, and I dodge just in time.

The thing is fast.

Realizing I have four points to spend on my Attributes, I dump half into Agility and the rest into Constitution—the latter in the hope that it will help ward off the paralytic effect.

Sure enough, the margins of the numbness recede slightly, only to be replaced by pain. It's then that I realize something is off. The sulfurous smell of burning hair fills my nostrils, and I glance at my side. It's an angry red mass of sizzling skin, melted hair, and dangerous-looking blisters. The paralytic agent is apparently only one part of a two-pronged attack, the other being a potent acid to damage the Lacerta's prey.

As if to confirm my thoughts, the Lacerta's mouth gapes open again as it hisses at me once more, revealing flat, stubby teeth that have no hope of biting through prey that hasn't been significantly softened.

Aiming to head off another attack that might paralyze something more important—my legs or my skull, for example—I strike, leaping forward to rake my claws against one leg. The Lacerta raises its foot to ward me away, but not fast enough. I feel my claws scrape against bone, savoring the elastic snap of severed tendon.

It crumples, but the monster has another surprise in store for me. Its tail whips around, slamming me into its side. As if waiting for this moment, the Lacerta drops onto its flank, three feet reaching out to encompass me in a paralytic embrace.

I wriggle away, but not in time to avoid getting tagged on the forepaw. Before the quick-acting paralytic sets in, I retaliate, sending several sticky yellow toes pattering to the ground. Blood oozes from the severed stumps on the Lacerta's foot.

The Lacerta struggles toward me, but the lack of one working foot and having no toes on another significantly impedes its motion—the sinuous alternating step of the lizard becoming a clumsy stumble. My own front foot is in a bad way too, now numb and slowly dissolving. But in this, I have an advantage.

Having already experienced walking with three feet, I have a passing familiarity with it. The lizard has none and is in far worse shape.

I half-hop, half-wobble backward, letting the wounded Lacerta try to angrily close the distance. And I wait for my opportunity.

Growing impatient, it lunges forward, overbalancing as I dash past it.

This time, I'm wary of the tail and just about manage to dodge it, even with my Agility crippled by having only three working feet. Then I turn.

As expected, the Lacerta lashes its tail back, trying to get me in the returning motion. Instead, I arrest its motion with my teeth, tearing chunks out of its tail and spitting it away before too much of its blood comes in contact with me.

The Lacerta hisses at me again. The combination of its ill-advised rush and its double sweep with its tail sends it collapsing to the ground before it has the chance to steady itself.

Even with the precautions I took, my jaw is turning numb. But I don't need it anymore. I climb onto the back of the downed Lacerta, letting my claws puncture its scales and spine with an atavistic relish. My weight pins it.

With one leg incapacitated, I can't swipe at it as I would like to, and with my jaw partially paralyzed, I can't gather enough grip strength.

But walking? I can do that. And I walk with extreme malice, especially since the pain-blocking and immobilizing effect of the paralytic is wearing off. My skin feels as if it's on fire, but it's only pain. If I let the Lacerta get the upper hand, I'm done for.

After a second or two, I get lucky or accurate—I'm not sure. A claw stabs into the lizard's spine, and the Lacerta gives a screeching hiss, finally mustering the strength to throw me off.

It doesn't go well. For the Lacerta, that is.

Still buried halfway into its spinal column, the claws of my hind feet catch, then glide gratingly through bone and the spongey cord at its center. I'm thrown away, injured by the landing, but the back half of the Lacerta is completely limp.

I lie there, paws tingling from contact with its blood, but I'm not too worried. No matter how quickly the Lacerta might regrow its spine, I have little doubt the paralytic effect will wear off faster.

It does. I limp toward it on unsteady legs, the pads of my feet dissolving from walking on small droplets of its oozing yellow blood. Then I take a swipe at its head.

It's slightly smarter than I gave it credit for. Waiting for me, it releases a jet of spit and blood that sends a stream of numbness down my neck and shoulder. But it's too late for the creature. All it takes is one swipe, then two, and its brain lies exposed for my teeth to sink into.

I'm still unable to get a good grip strength, but I don't need to. I'm too numb to shake my neck, rip my teeth through the brain as my instincts scream at me to do. I don't need to. Brains react badly to being squeezed by teeth. Who knew?

The paralytic blood only helps me, locking my jaw into place as the lizard thrashes its head. A spasm beyond its control racks the upper half of its body. I'm sent flying once more, this time with a lump of spongey brain matter trapped between my teeth—unable to be released—and a new notification before my eyes.

I take a moment to heal and collect myself. My teeth ache as they dissolve, but once they're gone, the torn chunk of Lacerta brain falls to the ground. I shake my head, waiting for the pain in my jaw to subside.

Once I feel fit to continue and the pain is an unpleasant memory, I continue following the trail of scent. It's been partially erased by the scuffle, but it continues farther down the road.

I leave the body of the monstrous lizard—not wanting to eat or touch the meat—and plod forward, keeping an eye on the surrounding walls. The encounter with the Lacerta was surprisingly harrowing. Despite being only two Levels higher than me, it was well-adapted to close combat with its ability to paralyze with a touch and spit its own blood.

If it had gotten a proper grip on me…

I don't give the subject any further thought. In front of me lies a house, untouched by the apocalypse except for a broken window. And unlike the road, where I can only find my trail, here I find the other three scents from the bridge.

After cocking my head to listen for any abnormal sounds inside and detecting nothing, I clear the sill and the protruding shards of glass, landing easily on wooden floor. This place was obviously the home of the three humans and myself. Their smell permeates the walls and floor and every scrap of fabric nearby. But I have more senses than smell, and I have the brain power to interpret them—even if my memory is shot to hell.

Pictures hang on the walls. Three humans—two big, one small. I stare at them, committing the faces to memory, feeling a twinge of familiarity from all three despite my inability to remember them.

And something that looks like a smaller version of me is there too. Sometimes with just one of them, sometimes with all three.

Deep down, on a visceral level, I know they're my pack. But they're not here.

So, I set off running.

Chapter 6

I make good headway back to the bridge, narrowly dodging the ambush of another Yellow-Toed Lacerta as I'm about to leave town. I give it a wide margin instead of fighting it. There's no point in risking my life for little gain.

As the sky darkens, I want to continue running, but I don't want to push my luck either. So, I curl up beneath a bush and wait for morning.

***

Morning comes without fanfare, unless you're in the habit of calling birds a brass band.

I rise without ceremony despite a vague tiredness that begs me to rest a few hours more. And like that, I'm running once again.

There's no need for sniffing around, trying to make sure I'm going the right way. I've been here before, I know I'm going the right direction, and I make excellent headway. My speed increases when I place my latest Class Skill point in Swiftfoot.

Running at an unprecedented pace, it's only a few hours before I reach the bridge. The gun-toting human is gone, but the bridge is just as broken as it used to be.

Still…

It might be possible.

I take a moment to check the distance between the broken pieces, careful not to look down. It's a long way across, but I'm strong and faster than I've ever been. If I time the leap right, I'll probably make it… just.

I walk backward for a running start. Then I sprint as fast as I can go.

I time the jump perfectly. And I immediately know it isn't enough. I'm several feet shy of the other side as I drop with a yelp, and all the air is pushed out of my lungs as I crash against a wooden brace. By sheer fortune, I teeter on a small length of wood between two support columns—with nowhere else to go.

Slowly, carefully, I push myself to my feet, careful not to overbalance lest I end up tumbling headfirst into the river. That sounds like a bad idea.

I've reached the other side, but where I wanted to land is fifteen feet above me and there's no convenient way to get anywhere.

Well, damn.

I pace up and down the beam, gut turning circles with the feeling of failure. The water roils below me. I could jump. I should jump.

Maybe I'll end up on the pebbled riverbank like last time. But it's impossible to tell whether I could safely reach the riverbank a second time. I don't even remember if I know how to swim.

And I'll lose nothing but time if I try something crazy first. I do have brain damage after all.

I activate Wicked Claws and dig my left forefoot into the side of the wooden support column that holds up the bridge. I give an experimental tug, and it holds. Just. There's a little bit of slipping, as expected. That means I'll have to move fast.

I follow with my right, using my strength to pull me up until the claws of all four limbs are embedded in the thick wood. Then I climb, one foot at a time, slowly working upward until I reach the top and a ceiling of planks and woodwork blocks my progress.

Now for the tricky part.

I grasp a supporting strut with my teeth, jaw aching with the strain as I carve out chunks of wood above me with a freed-up paw, letting the broken timbers fall into the river below with a splash. Finally, muscles aching, I cut a small hole to wiggle through. And I'm on the other side. I'm cut up badly from the tight squeeze through, but I've made it.

Tail wagging with excitement, I locate my pack's trail and chase it, the inconvenience at the bridge forgotten.

Several critters try to block my path, but they're low level and are easily cleared with a few casual swipes. I'm too pumped up to care about such minor things now. The urge to be with my group is strong even though I don't remember who they are. It spurs me on, so I hurtle through trees toward my destination.

The bond from my class sings in my blood, telling me I'm close to someone whose name I don't remember, someone who means the world to me. Telling me I'm home.

I keep on running, chasing the feeling. Their scents stretch out before me, strong, fresh, and one in particular—oranges, cornflowers, and a good deal less soap. My tail is wagging so fast I'm having difficulty running.

I barrel through the woods on the other side of the river, breaking into a small clearing with a campsite at its center, and hear a voice that makes my world stand still.

Soft. Tremulous. Questioning. "Buck?"

Not recognizing anything else, I recognize that.

Katie.

Intermission Three

"I can see why you'd think Settlement Owner Pearson would be interested," Vir said. His eyes darkened as he considered the potential implications of providing this information. Improving political ties with humanity was always good, and the Beast Lord was their closest and most dependable ally. Best of all, she was much more stable and had no romantic ties to his liege, making interactions with her easier to anticipate. On both sides. Still, was there a way the could use this information in the next negotiation? Maybe throw her off guard. The Beast Lord did have an inordinate fondness for animals, not just her own pets…

"You have your plotting face on," Amelia said, waving a finger at Vir.

"I do not have a plotting face. If I did, I would never have passed my third-year examination," Vir said. "That is all you, Guard Captain."

"Sense truth and sense motive do make a great Skill combination," Amelia said. "But, all these changes, all these reports. What makes all of you Galactics so damn interested in our little blue ball?"

Vir tilted his head to the side, considering his partner. As he did so, a memory rose. A conversation, one held a long time ago. "Well, I don't think we all planned for Earth.

"Not as it is now."

Debts and Dances

By Tao Wong

1.2 Earth days before the System Initiation

Dark blue light from System windows illuminated the displayed information and nothing else, leaving the information they displayed only available to the viewer. Seated in the mounting darkness of his office, the obsidian-skinned, smartly dressed man read over the reports, sensuous lips pursed. With thin, long fingers, the man pushed back some of the long hair that had escaped from behind his pointed ears. Lord Graxin Roxley, Baron of the Seven Seas, Hunter of Drakyl, Master of the Sword and the Black Flame, Corinthian of the Second Order, and acclaimed Dancing Master of the 196th Ball sighed as he finished reading the latest reports, shutting down the notification windows with a contemptuous wave of his hand.

"My lord?" Vir said, attracting the attention of his liege. Standing at parade rest, Roxley's personal aide, head of security, and spymaster was a model Truinnar, short-cut white hair setting off his black and silver uniform. As a personal servant to Lord Roxley, the lieutenant was not allowed, by custom or law, to keep his hair longer.

"What next disaster do you bring?" Roxley said snippily. In the privacy of his quarters, Roxley could afford to show his closest and longest companion the worries that weighed down his broad shoulders.

"None new. Pauka" —second son of Baron Kumi, a long-time rival of the Barony of the Seven Seas— "came by, seeking a game of cards again. I indicated you still were not available. The Lady Bauber wished to know if you were attending the next Sembla Ball." At Roxley's frown, Vir continued. "But I came for another reason. The vote results are in."

The sentence made Roxley straighten abruptly, eyes narrowing. A mental command had the lights in the room flick on. "Out with it! Don't you dare tease me. Not today."

"It passed."

Roxley relaxed, tension draining from his body. His eyes flicked to the side, his AI generating the notification screen that he had been perusing before. It was a complex spreadsheet of numbers and graphs, but the final tally offered a simple answer—the barony would go bankrupt in nine months. The obligations incurred by his father and those of the previous generation stacked against the meager revenues of his ruined lands ensured the Barony was set on an unrelenting path of ruin. If the Titan that still lived on the lands had left, they would have stood a chance to right the ship. Unfortunately, the monster refused to leave, and they had no funds or ability to make it leave. The Titan's presence and occasional rampages ensured that any reconstruction efforts were short-lived.

"Where? When?" Roxley said, a burning light erupting from his eyes as he focused on Vir.

"Sector 182.3. A small blue planet, third from its sun…" Vir listed the little that he knew of the newly initiated System planet. A small, unimportant world.

0.98 Earth days before System Initiation

Acquiring the information on the planet "Earth" was simple enough. The System could provide significant data as it had gathered everything from the planet's numerous and rather extensive entertainment channels. The entertainment methods of the majority sentient species were an archaic form, with a wide variety from solo musical components to flat-imaged projections. Through these entertainment channels, Roxley had access to the entire written history of the planet. Or at least, the important parts. Unfortunately, sifting the data for truth, especially those sourced from this "Internet," had been interesting. Numerous sources were available, often contradictory in all but the most basic facts. Finding and understanding a "true" source would have been impossible in the hour or so that they had without the aid of their AIs. Luckily, competing historic sources were not a new thing in the Galaxy.

To speed up their assessment of the information, Roxley and Vir had split the task. Roxley tackled the information glut to understand politics, society, and the psychology of the dominant species on this "Earth" while Vir tackled the security aspects and the Galactic competition they were likely to face.

"It has been two hours," said X-124, Roxley's AI.

Roxley eyes narrowed, dismissing this rather interesting treatise by this human—Nicollo Machiavelli—as their self-imposed deadline passed. The Truinnar found much of Machiavelli's recommendations simplistic at the very best, and rather naïve at the worst. Still, the politician might have survived all of three months in a Truinnar court. Long enough to be set aright by the more experienced players.

"My lord?" Vir said, cocking his head as he indicated for his liege to begin.

"These humans seem to be the dominant species on the planet, by virtue of their population and ground covered. In fact, they have stamped their dominance on the planet in a very Movana fashion—the number of competing species they have destroyed in the last millennia is staggering. Obviously, the wholesale destruction exhibited is less than optimal for the continued variance in the bioculture of the planet if the System was not arriving. In light of System initiation, their actions might actually have provided them some small grace," Roxley said. "There are other species of notable intelligence, but it is unknown if they are sufficiently sapient for the System to register them. Certain giant cephalopods come to mind as potential System-registered species, but for our purposes, they are superfluous to our plans.

"In light of that, I have concentrated research on these humans. They are a relatively young society, low on the initial technology scale, with a lack of fusion engines or space exploration. Sociologically, they have only recently begun their integration as a species. On the Ofpaudr scale, maybe a four, bordering five?"

The Ofpaudr scale was a well-used scale that denoted the technological development of a society before their initiation into the System. Created by Technologists to classify various races during their regular and insane jaunts outside of the System, the scale helped colonizing System races to grasp the intricacies of such societies. How a System-integrated race dealt with a pre-powered society was very different than how they dealt with a powered society that had begun informational integration.

"After ascertaining their current level on the Ofpaudr scale, I delved into their psychology. Thankfully, it seems that much of their cultural biases are similar to many of our Galactic brethren—another point in the Technologists' favor," Roxley said.

Vir waved, gesturing for Roxley to continue. There was little point in the discussion, especially with the time crunch they were under.

"Humans—on a societal level—are easily led. They can be manipulated with a series of benefits and punishments, with only a few specific sticking points. I briefly considered manipulating these 'religions' of theirs but discarded it as too short-term a gain for the expenditure of time and Credits required. On a societal level at least, it seems that being the least bad alternative—within an acceptable band, of course—would allow us to gain control in a quick manner."

"Good," Vir said. "That aligns with much of what I have gathered. Your take on an individual level?"

"The individual..." Roxley shook his head.

That was the crux of the matter, was it not? In the System, with its rewards for experience, Leveling, occasional Titles, and—on introduction to the System—individualized Perks and new Classes, individuals mattered. Not immediately, of course, especially not for a newly integrated System world. But in the future? In the future, a gifted individual could cause significant problems.

It was part of the reason why many newly-System integrated worlds were repressed immediately. The level of repression varied of course, and in times past, wholesale slaughter had occurred. The destruction of sentients in newly created worlds had brought about rare direct action by the Galactic Council, with the offending groups and their kin enslaved. Conducting genocidal actions on another group was one of the few System-wide taboos now. While not expressly forbidden, the examples made of many groups who lacked the political backing and power to conduct such actions were a significant deterrent.

"The individual is more difficult to handle. Humans are varied. I would mark them as an eight on the Dairgax scale," Roxley said. "Too varied for a general discussion in fact. Local histories have shown that they can be extremely stubborn, worse than the Grimsar. Idiotically suicidal, honor bound, and driven to irrational positions as often as they can be rational, pragmatic, and violent."

"You sound like you admire them," Vir said.

Roxley smiled slightly, offering a half-shrug. "And your research?"

"The Duchess Kangana, the Duke Zuka, Viscount Nivoosi, and the Marquise of Pourbet are all looking to expand. Their various liegemen will be in charge of course, notably the Barons Pehan, Erallia, and Kodrix," Vir said. "Those are the notable opposition we can expect. Various other merchant firms and the like, but with System integration in our sphere, a non-issue."

"And not our own liege?" Roxley said sarcastically.

Vir snorted, just as amused as Roxley by the concept that their liege, the Duke of Ravius, would do anything but sit on his redolent ass and be fellated. "No, my lord."

"And the other Barons?"

"Content."

"Then we will be alone in this endeavor."

Vir nodded.

Roxley said, "Not as if that is anything new. Not anymore."

"Yes, my lord."

Roxley rubbed his chin, considering, then gestured for Vir to continue.

The guard hesitated before he spoke. "I spent the remainder of the time researching potential threats in the city itself. Considering the likely zone levels that we will face and the geography of the locations, I have narrowed options down to three locations—the United State known as Montana, the island nation of New Zealand, and the nation of Liberia."

"Why these three?"

"Geography, population density, and wildlife. While mutations and spawnings are expected to be controlled for the first few months, we want to edge around existing dangerous creatures," Vir said. "In that case, we'll want countries with a low number of dangerous animals. A counter-example of locations we want to avoid would be Australia and the Amazon."

"I see," Roxley said. "And population density?"

"As discussed. Not too high—or we'd face too great a competition from the Dukes and their men—and not too low, to allow us to coerce help." A flick of his hand sent Vir's detailed results and conclusions to Roxley, who perused the information with X-127.

It took him a few moments before Roxley nodded to Vir to go on.

"Geography, of course, shapes both potential mining and farming returns, as well as zone expectations. Again, we're looking for a balance."

"As is everyone else," Roxley said bitterly. "Can we win a bidding war, with our current resources?"

"No. Which is why I recommend you agree to the Lady Bauber's request."

"You know what she wants…"

"Yes," Vir said, his gaze firm. "And it is not that great a sacrifice, is it? For your people."

"For my people…" Roxley sighed. "Very well. Arrange a meeting. And send for Vaiko."

Tao Wong

0.82 Earth days to System Initiation

"You have done well to keep fit, my lord," Vaiko said. The hermaphrodite Truinnar tailor moved around Roxley as he carefully adjusted the fit of his latest creation. Of course, the black and silver of Roxley's house was required, but in this case, it was used as trim for the bright yellow-and-green creation appearing under Vaiko's flowing hands. The combined Makun hemp and aracahni silk meant that the vest, tails, and pants were both highly protective and comfortable.

"Thank you, Vaiko. And thank you for coming at such short notice," Roxley said as he looked at the finished creation before summoning a hologram to review his new image.

"You know thanks is not needed, my lord," Vaiko said. "It was my pleasure to craft this for you. Your return has been much anticipated."

Roxley smiled thinly, looking at his clothing. He tracked the green and yellow of his suit, a sure sign that he danced for the Lady Bauber and not himself. A dangerous thing, just like the Ball itself. Returning to the floor after so long, he had no knowledge of the newcomers, their Skills and abilities, their partners and their interests. Doing this with so little prep…

"This venture of yours is less than wise, dear one," Lady Bauber had said.

The Lady was no longer the matriarch of her clan, having been displaced by the marriage of her only son. Yet not once in the last four hundred years had anyone dared to say that the Lady was not a force to be reckoned with. She was, and would be, a power in Truinnar society for many years to come— both due to the immense wealth she had collected and the details of the bodies she had gleaned. If her Class of Society Gossip had not provided significant shelter against assassination attempts, she would have been targeted for her knowledge long ago. Even now, the Gambling Boards kept a running bet on her eventual death or kidnapping.

"Perhaps. But it is the only one left for me," Roxley had said. *"Will you agree to my request?"*

"My support for you wearing my colors?" Lady Bauber nodded. *"But I expect a good showing, you understand that, no?"*

"Have I ever provided one that was not?" Roxley said. Left unsaid was the fact that he needed to place because even with the Lady's support, Roxley needed to acquire more funds. While Vir would speak with the usual array of bankers, industrialists, and merchants to acquire Credits, it was unlikely he could get enough. The remainder was something Roxley would have to find. Doing the only thing he really was good at.

"Good. Then we have a deal. Dance for me, dear one. Dance and beat that hag Lia."

In his mind's eye, Roxley saw himself bowing to the holographic projection. Saw the vindictive flash of a smile on Bauber's face as she'd killed the connection. And the chill that ran through him when he considered if he was the one who had fallen for her trick, or was it Lia?

Who was he kidding? Roxley's smile turned bitter. With the real players of the Great Dance, like the Lady Bauber, those two objectives were not mutually exclusive. And were likely just the start of her plans. All someone as inexperienced as Roxley could do was grit his teeth and accept that he was a backup partner in the Dance.

It was up to him to make sure he was not a disposable partner.

0.69 Earth days to System Initiation

The site of the Ball was one short, sponsored Shop teleportation away. As Roxley stepped away from the teleportation pad, he winced at the brutal heat of the dance floor. The regulations were very specific on the kinds of clothing and armaments that could be used, leaving only the Skills of the dancer and his partner for the most part. As such, while his clothing had increased durability enchantments, it had no enhanced attributes, Skills, or other advantages.

To ensure the sanctity of the rules, the glowering Grimlak referee stomped over, his four-foot frame holding up a portable scanner. The Baron took the intrusion to his personal space with equanimity, having gone through the routine multiple times. He even vaguely recognized the bearded Grimlak, though his memory offered no name. It was possible that Roxley had never received it—the last time he had been on the floor, he had not cared to learn such trivialities. On that note...

"Thank you," Roxley said, inclining his head as the Grimlak indicated he had completed his job.

When the Grimlak looked surprised, Roxley tried to suppress a twinge of irritation, knowing that such a reaction was understandable. Most of the dancers had little care or consideration for the referees who oversaw the contest. Unlike the judges, the referees could do little to help a competitor win but much to ensure they lost—mostly in catching the competitors breaking the rules. Better to be cold and cordial, professional instead of friendly. Less likely to see accusations of favoritism.

As Roxley stepped away from the teleportation pad, he took in his surroundings with practiced eyes. Black stone and off-white metal beneath his feet and the fluttering banners of contestants and their sponsors all reminded Roxley of dozens of other dance floors. The Ball—which was just another name for the contest—was being held on a platform that floated on a sea of lava. While the volcano was unlikely to erupt, the potential that it could added spice to the viewing numbers. Only high durability, stacked Resistances, and the careful regulation of force shields kept the platform from completely melting under the intense heat. Even inside the force shields, the air rippled from the heat that bled through. Outside, the inferno would consume all but the most powerful Master Classers.

"You're here," a wintry voice greeted Roxley.

The Truinnar turned to spot his partner. The tall, elegant man was clad in yellow and green, but the trimming of his clothing indicated his rank—the pure white of a commoner.

"Bress." Roxley tried—he really did—to keep his voice serene and calm. But the slight hitch in his voice, the increase in his pulse gave away his real feelings. Bress Kogen, his ex-partner and now partner again, was as handsome as he had always been. The minor scar on his forehead that drifted into his hairline caught Roxley's eye. The cursed attack refused to heal, even now.

"What do you think you are doing here?" Bress said, cold fury in his voice.

"Dancing for our lady, no?"

"Without practice. Without research," Bress growled. "Tell me that you at least brought Purity."

"Of course. Tell me about our competition."

"Funnily enough, you know most of them. It seems many of the younger competitors pulled out when they heard the Corinthian was joining. Only the truly angry or ambitious have stayed." Bress's hand shifted, pointing at a pair of Truinnar. After a couple of disastrous Balls, these days only Truinnar were allowed to compete. "You know Iod. Her new partner, Amelu, is one of the latter group. He feels your title is a sham. Fast, known for his use of the Six

Helix and a heat shield that is doubly effective here. The former leading pair on the boards."

Roxley inclined his head, flexing his will for a second as he attempted to Observe the other two. To his utter lack of surprise, the Skill did nothing. Only a total fool left his Status open for viewing, especially in such a competitive environment.

"Next up. The pairing of Carz and Sopin."

Roxley sniffed, giving vent to his views on the infamous pair. Even in his time, the pair were well-known rogue competitors, inclined to break the rules to win and hope not to get caught. Since the referees were mortal and playbacks weren't allowed by tradition, rule-breaking was viable.

"They've added a new trick to their repertoire, a semi-sentient ice whip that gives them area control of the floor. A bad choice for this location."

While magic and System-registered artifacts were protected from "normal" environmental factors, they were in no way in a normal location.

Bress inclined his head further to the right. "Tomaidh and Xoxe. Up-and-coming pair. Ranked third. She's a summoner, he's an acrobat."

"Is he now?" Roxley's eyes raked over the pair. Tomaidh was tall, nearly seven feet, and angular, but the tight, almost leotard clothing showed off the sculpted muscles that covered his body. As for Xoxe, she was clad in a flowing red gown with orange and yellow highlights, showcasing their sponsor, the Viscount of Renyeh's colors and her own house colors. That made Roxley hiss. "What is a Herdan doing here?"

"Black sheep."

Roxley's lips turned up as he eyed the shoulder length of her hair. Second cousin at most, not one of the main branches. "Very well. Next?"

Before Bress could continue to detail their opponents, the referee walked to the center of the stage. A staff appeared in his hand before the short, portly referee pounded the end of the metal-tipped staff on the floor. A rolling rumble echoed through the volcano, calling the participants to attention.

"The time has come.

The hour is here.

Let all those who seek honor stand.

Let all those who seek glory step aside.

The dance is now.

Let the blood flow."

The traditional opening chant rolled over the silent participants. Some tensed, others relaxed as the words wrapped them with the bonds of tradition before unleashing the waiting participants on each other. Unseen, hidden beneath protective force shields, the orchestra struck their first notes, the swell of music rising as the beginning beats of the dance began.

"Shall we?" Roxley said, stepping away from Bress. He offered the other man a deep bow, one that was mirrored by his partner.

Even as he straightened, Roxley began layering his buffs and Spells on himself. Fleet Foot, Lord's Grace, Shield of Nobility, Dance of the Night. Out of the corner of his eyes, Roxley saw Bress cast his own series of buffs. As the follower in the dance, Bress also layered party buffs on Roxley and himself, from the basic Mana Drip and health regeneration Skills to more complicated ones geared for use on the floor, like Falling Partners. As they straightened, above the dance floor, previously hidden beam cannons appeared, tracking each of the participants with no less than two turrets.

"Overkill, no?" Roxley said. The beam cannons were just the start of the potential attacks that would be levied against them.

"The dance has grown more vicious since you left."

Roxley flashed Bress a reassuring smile. "It's fine. We don't need to win, just last to the top three."

"You say that now."

"Have I ever lied?"

Bress's roll of his eyes was telling. But there was no more time, as the first note of the dance proper resounded. The pair spun in synchronicity, never touching. Each step was practiced and ordained, each dip and shuffle dictated by the centuries-old tradition of the song being played.

As Roxley's body moved without thought, matching Bress's toned body, Roxley felt himself falling into the familiar routine without missing a step. The first few songs were traditional, a known factor meant to weed out participants who did not meet the fundamental requirements of the Ball. For the high-level participants taking part, not a single step was missed. Roxley took the time to listen to the commentators and locate the dancers they considered a threat.

The music changed, abruptly and without warning to untrained ears. Of course, for the participants who knew each song by heart, each step drilled into their bodies through unending hours of practice, the surprise was no surprise at all. After all, this was a Ball, and the harmony of the music and the dance was paramount. As such, there were only a few points where a shift in the music could occur—and only a few songs that could fit at each point.

Once more, the dancers shifted, twirling, dipping, and jumping in time. Roxley could not help but shoot an admiring glance at his ex-partner. Bress had improved, growing smoother, more aware of his surroundings and the dancers. Deftly, the pair guided one another around the dance floor, avoiding other pairs moving toward them in an attempt to disrupt and injure. Most of those attempts were half-hearted at best and easily avoided. None cared to anger the top-ranking pairs, not yet.

The first major clash happened during the fourth change of song. There was little warning beyond the fluctuation in Mana as oil bubbled up from the metal floor. Two dancers in two different pairs were caught in the initial attack, their footsteps missing a beat. That was all that was required.

The beam cannons opened fire, slamming into the defenses of the two dancers and their partners. Under fire, the quartet attempted to regain their footing and keep dancing, but the high energy beam attacks set the oil on fire, adding to the woes of the participants. A hastily cast Skill cooled the floor, layering a thin mixture of ice on the flames and killing the fire while providing marginally better footing. It was too late for one pair though, as they fell to the focused fire of the beam turrets before they could rejoin the beat. The other pair managed to escape the murderous attacks of the automated weaponry— only to be felled by a casually swung ice whip that sent the pair back into the ice field where the beam turrets refocused their attacks.

"And so it begins," Roxley said, watching the quartet get teleported out.

0.51 Earth days before System Initiation

Roxley flipped through the air, his body arcing horizontally between a pair of attacks and the beam attack from a nearby turret. He landed lightly, his feet tapping out a beat as he spun around his attackers, the tips of his fingers flashing across a pair of double-pupiled eyes. An involuntary flinch sent the dancer out of time, adding another quintuplet of cannon fire to their surroundings.

"And that, Lords and Ladies, is why Lord Roxley is known as the Corinthian. Athletic and versatile, the perfect athlete, dancer, and socialite," the announcer's voice buzzed in Roxley's head, piped in via X-127.

While Roxley might hate the inane commentary, he had, on occasion, learnt something useful. And so, he listened.

As beam fire bathed his former position, the pair of dancers struggled to stay on time, to re-establish their rhythm. As the hours ticked on, the cannons' reset period increased, forcing the dancers to dodge for longer and longer while staying on time with the beat. Toward the end of the Ball, the beam cannon fire could last for tens of minutes for a single mistake. As the pair attempted to spin away, a prismatic wall of dust and nanites floated into the middle of their escape route, draining the pair of Mana and assaulting their bodies. In seconds, riddled with tens of thousands of minor cuts, the pair went off-time again and were riddled by more beam fire.

"That leaves a total of eighteen participants," the announcer burbled as the pair flashed and disappeared.

A slight grinding sound came as the stage shrank for the next stage of the dance. Dancers who were near the edge were forced to move inward or lose their footing entirely, which none of them would survive—never mind their automatic dismissal from the competition.

As Roxley met up with his partner once again, Bress flashed a thin smile. The second stage was where the fighting truly begun. Until now, the majority of the seeded pairings had been left alone, allowed to dance and pick off the lower-ranked opponents. Now, with only nine pairs remaining, it was time to get serious. Worse, the upcoming changes in the stage would increase in speed as additional environmental hindrances were put in play.

"Incoming," Roxley said.

The first to come at them was Carz and Sopin. A shift in color and the previously sluggish ice whip changed, turning into fire that lashed out at the pair. Roxley twisted his body, almost going parallel to the floor as his feet never stopped moving. Bress, on the other hand, brought his hand up in a flourish, deflecting the whip into the sky. That movement sent the attack skyward before it retreated, a motion that Bress followed as he hot-footed toward their attackers. Carz moved to block Bress, only to find Roxley in his way. A shift in music had the pairs pause, their motions forced to change.

"Already, C?" Roxley said.

"It's Lord Ishoia," Carz said. "And it's not personal, Graxin."

And then there was no more time to talk. Rather than draw his weapon, Roxley stepped closer to Carz, invading his personal space as his hands struck in short, staccato attacks. Carz refused to back off, the pair blocking and twisting, their feet never stopping while their postures stayed upright and proper as required.

"Oh! Both the Corinthian and his partner and the Abiding Duo have begun fighting! New audience members, watch carefully, for this is a sight you might not see again. Unless Lord Roxley has permanently come out of his retirement. As long-time fans know, Lord Roxley's abrupt retirement due to his ascension to the seat of his house was much criticized, many pointing out that the new Lord had shown no interest in running a holding—and certainly not one as troubled as the Seven Seas," the announcer's voice droned on. "And of course, the persistent rumors of the Abiding Duo's imminent retirement have swelled in the last few months."

"As if that'd happen?" Roxley said as he jumped, dodging backward.

His actions were mirrored by Carz and not a moment too soon. An explosion erupted between the pair. Almost as if they had rehearsed their reprisal, the pair spun and sent Skill and spell shooting toward the impertinent youngster who had chosen to interrupt their fight.

As Carz closed with Roxley after sending the youngster scurrying away, his smile quirked sideways. "Actually, this might be our last dance. We do need the Credits but…"

"Oh?" Roxley hesitated, his left hand dropping.

As if Carz had been waiting for that, his hand flashed toward the suddenly exposed chin. But instead of blocking, Roxley dropped his left foot backward, shifting himself backward. Carz's attack never finished, his own attack a feint meant to cover the true attack of a kick to Roxley's right. That attack was intercepted by Roxley's right elbow, eliciting a grunt of surprise from Carz as he finished with a twirl and stamp. In seconds, the pair was bathed by beam fire as the mistimed motion on Carz's part forced the pair apart.

"You feinted, you sly dog!" Carz protested.

"So did you."

That answer elicited a laugh from Carz. Using the beam weaponry to disengage was a perfect example of an exchange between masters of the dance. Yet Carz sobered up as he realized that his partner was being hard-pressed by Bress. The former ice whip had turned to flame, the shift in elemental nature doing nothing to stop Bress's indirect attacks. Swirling balls of electricity and plasma flowed from Bress's hands. They shot off into the distance at times, and at others, they curved to swirl around Bress in a protective shell. As more and more chasers of plasma and electricity formed around Bress, the more difficult it grew for Sopin to dodge his attacks.

As Carz struggled to close in on his partner, Sopin narrowly dodged a plasma blast. The attack singed her green-gold hair, fraying the ends and infuriating the woman. Her anger manifested in a too-hard stamp of her foot and a slew of ice spikes that caught Bress in his hip and sent him stumbling. The ice spikes shattered under the brutal assault of additional beam fire, some of which struck Bress.

"Bress!" Roxley snarled.

A tap of his foot had Roxley disappear, the Flash Step Skill getting him across the space to catch his partner and spin him away, weaving the pair through the redoubled beam attacks.

"Oooh! The Phoenix Dance!" the announcer cried out as Roxley continued to hold Bress close, ducking, twirling, and weaving around the ever-growing beam turret fire, shifting position to bring them closer to their opponents. "The Corinthian gambles once again."

A dry, mechanical voice interrupted the main announcer. "There is a 48.9% chance of a shift to a partnered dance at this time. This is not as much a gamble as the Honored Pierson might lead you to believe."

"Rubbish," Pierson said. "That percentage calculation of yours is an outdated model. You know the distribution of music saw an algorithm change four Balls ago. Due to the purchase, I would point out, of someone's mathematical model."

"Which shows that the model and the underlying assumptions are not wrong. And we have updated the model to take into account new changes," the robotic voice said.

Ignoring the bickering announcers, Roxley continued to weave around the dance floor. By this time, nearly three quarters of the beam cannons were firing at them, lighting up the entire dance floor in splashes of white and blue. No one, not even a Titled Master Class dancer, could avoid all the attacks. Even the bystanding dancers were struck as Roxley guided attacks into their floor space, sending them off-beat as they were struck.

"Suicidal fool," Bress said when the pair spun back to face one another. In the glow of the beam weapons and the thudding impact of bodies and the orchestra, anything they said would be missed.

"But isn't this more fun?" Roxley said, lips pulled back into a wide, devilish grin.

"Fool!" But Bress could not hide the smile in his eyes or on his lips. Then Bress fell silent, for his job of keeping the pair alive and their health topped up grew more and more difficult.

For long minutes, the music played and the destructive energy rained upon the stage. As time dragged on, additional attacks joined the stage. Nanites drained Mana. Webs of heat-resistant arachni silk clotted the floor. Buzzsaw blades fired from the edges of the stage flew in. Pillars of lava exploded through sudden gaps in the flooring. Participant after participant fell aside, their defences insufficient against the abuse being layered upon them as Roxley Flash Stepped, ducked, and pirouetted through their midst. Even the announcers had fallen silent, robbed of their words as viewer numbers racked up.

Then the music shifted. In the small break, Roxley broke from Bress, leaving his partner as the music changed to a song that would not allow them to dance touching. By now, even their impressive resistances and Skills were insufficient for the incoming damage. The pair soaked up the blasts, sucking in the pain as clothing burnt, skin chapped, and hair crisped. In the end, when the fire finally ended, only six participants were left on stage. A glance to the side brought up Roxley's Status.

Health: 1376/ 2830
MP: 1023/ 1830

Six left. Roxley took a moment to inspect the remaining opponents. Iod and Amelu, the ranking pair in the group, and the newcomers, Tomaidh and Xoxe. Sopin had fallen under the barrage, forcing Carz from the floor by default. Iod had created a protective dome, keeping attacks away from them by using a Mana-intensive Skill. Since they were not directly targeted by the beam cannons, the duo had been fine—the amount of space within Iod's dome just enough for them to continue dancing without issue.

Bress dipped close, clapping his hands at the apogee of his movement. "Iod's at half Mana now."

"How'd the newbies make their way through?" Roxley said.

"Just like us," Bress said. "Speed, coordination, and a little bit of stubbornness."

"Good regen rates then." Roxley eyed the health and Mana bars of the two newcomers. At least those he could get, their Obfuscation Skill not sufficient to hide that most basic of System information.

As if the participants had decided at the same time, everyone stopped their elegant posturing, purposely moving toward each other. Roxley kept an eye on the newcomers while Bress focused on the other pair. Iod and Amelu hung back a little, just a fraction of a moment, their steps a little smaller.

Amelu was the first one to break the silence as she called to Tomaidh and Xoxe, "Let's get rid of the antiques."

Iod shot a glance at Amelu but kept silent as Tomaidh answered, his voice hoarse. "What makes you think we need your help? They've already played their hands."

Roxley shook his head as Bress bristled, buffing himself. Xoxe, watching the quartet, had a half-smile and disdainful amusement in her eyes as she stared at the group. Feeling his hair stand on end, Roxley looked around for unseen danger, only for his eyes to widen as he stared past the force curtain holding back the lava.

"Scramble!"

Bress's feet beat a double-time of steps to bring his body to the other side of the Flash Stepping Baron. As he retreated, Bress turned to spot the reason for Roxley's command.

Rearing out from the lava, a monstrous Elemental lava worm came crashing down on the force shields. Unable to handle the attack, the shields gave way, shattering and bringing in a wave of lava. The once-stable dance floor tipped under the weight of the Elemental as it landed, forcing the dancers to trigger additional Skills to maximize their footing. Liquid rock lapped at the floor, threatening the feet of the participants as the Elemental squirmed forward.

As the Elemental closed in on the slow-moving pair, Iod triggered his protective Skill and staggered as the sudden loss of all his Mana broke his careful dance. Immediately, multiple beams focused on the dancers. Under the intense barrage of beam turrets and the explosive lava bursts, Iod's protective dome cracked.

"That was a mistake," Xoxe remarked contemptuously. The woman was gliding along, clapping and spinning in time with ease. There was a hungry look in her eyes as she stared at the dome.

"Autoteleports are down. As are some of the cannons," Bress remarked to Roxley as data scrolled by his eyes. The dancer had chosen to adjust his footing by triggering a series of metal chains that erupted from his body and sank into the floor around them, the Skill offering the dancer greater stability on the tilted floor.

"Not good," Roxley said. Unlike many others, the Baron chose a more direct route to establishing his footing, each graceful step denting the metal beneath his feet.

Panicking, Amelu cried out as she reached for a pin on her dress. "I won't die here!"

Her contingency enchantment triggered, throwing her out of the dance floor even as the dome shattered, bringing with it a flood of lava and high-energy beams. Unable to react, Iod curled up reflexively, his health dropping so quickly that he was unable to trigger his own backup enchantment. Before help could arrive, the Elemental fell, covering Iod within its lava-formed body. Choked-off screams ended abruptly, and the System scoreboard flashed once with Iod's demise, removing his name from consideration.

"As I said," Tomaidh said with a smirk. "We don't need your help. Now, let's end this."

"Roxley…" Bress sounded concerned as he felt the wintry silence coming from his partner. Long years of partnership informed his suspicion.

Roxley faced Tomaidh, his feet continually pounding the floor as he asked Bress, "Can you hold her off for a few moments?"

"Her and the elemental, you mean?" Bress tried for a light tone, but his voice trembled. "Thirty seconds."

"That's enough." Roxley darted forward as the music swelled and changed, a familiar tune appearing. Cowan No. 3 in E Major. Fast, percussive, allowing for myriad changes in forms and steps.

Tomaidh smirked, hands opening as if to welcome Roxley. His smirk did not fade even when Purity appeared in Roxley's hand, the soulbound weapon bypassing rules about equipment and clothing by being the prized weapon he had earned in a previous Ball. The sharp blade was thrust forward toward

Tomaidh's form, only for the dancer to open a gap in its body where the blade would land.

His attack thwarted, Roxley had to break his momentum with a fast staccato of taps. The motions were flourishes on the original dance and allowed—marginally—though Roxley absently noted that his style points dropped once again. In quick succession, the pair exchanged a series of attacks, Roxley continually missing as Tomaidh shifted and morphed his long body. Roxley dodged and received the attacks with determination, searching for Tomaidh's flaw.

"Ten seconds!" Bress called.

As Roxley twirled away from a strike, following the beat of the music, he spotted his friend's straining face as metal chains formed from the platform gripped the Elemental. Chain after chain melted under the onslaught of the Elemental's molten body, only to be replaced by others. Occasionally Bress released a blast of cold air, solidifying some of the melted metal around the Elemental's body and pushing Xoxe off course. The attack should not have worked on a participant at this level, but between the sloped platform and the now constantly altering beat of music, the additional disruption seemed to be causing Xoxe great discomfort.

Eyes glittering with understanding, Roxley laughed and stamped his foot. He spun aside, turning his Aura and other enhancements to full blast as he focused on Tomaidh. An overhand cut targeted at Tomaidh's neck sliced at the edges of the man's skin, the sudden change in environment throwing off the dancer. Another step, another cut, another Skill—Commanding Presence.

"Stop!" Roxley snarled.

Tomaidh froze as the words struck him, and Roxley buried his sword in the man's skull. A twist sent arcs of Mana directly into the man's cortex, driving his opponent to the floor. Roxley turned and kicked, sending the man's body flying toward the corner of the tilted platform where the lava waited. Seconds later, beam cannons opened up.

"You fool!" Xoxe screamed as she dodged the fire, but it was too late.

Her focus disrupted, the Elemental dismissed itself, leaving her to the tender mercies of the beam cannons and Bress. Roxley smiled grimly, waiting for the ending teleportation. Time to go home.

0.43 Earth days before System Initiation

High above, the surviving participants stood on a floating platform. Below them, the remains of the dance floor were being slowly broken up and taken away to be fixed and reused. Floating repair ships scooped up broken portions of failed technological pieces, attempting to recover as much possible. On the platform above, none of the broken detritus was paid any attention as the winners were showered with accolades and gifts.

In a lull between guests, Bress turned to Roxley. "I thought we weren't supposed to be winning?"

"Things happen." Roxley glared at Xoxe, the woman looking away from him. From the corner of his eyes, Roxley noticed the attention of an older Truinnar focused on him, clad in the house colors of House Hedran. That could be a problem... "Did her partner survive?"

"Barely," Bress answered. "I noticed you dodged the question of whether you're coming back."

That had been the most common thread among the well-wishers.

"That..." Roxley paused as Vir appeared, tense and intense.

Vir bowed slightly. "My lord."

"We should be done in another fifteen minutes."

"I do not believe we have the time, my lord. There has been a development."

Roxley frowned as he realized that Vir was not the only individual to have appeared. All around, servants were entering the reception hall and speaking with their lieges and mistresses. A particularly short noble lady frowned as her servant whispered into her ear. Stretching his senses briefly, Roxley caught the tail-end of the conversation.

"… change to a Dungeon World."

Eyes widening, Roxley cast a glance at the imperturbable Vir. The guard nodded, as if confirming the news Roxley had heard, or perhaps just to hurry Roxley onward. Noblemen and some of the businessmen were streaming out of the viewing platform, some going so far as to teleport away.

"It seems the reception is over," Bress said. Unlike many others, the dancer looked nonplussed by the change in atmosphere. Then Bress's expression drooped, sadness crossing his face as he stared at his old friend. "You have fingers in that pie too, don't you?" At Roxley's nod, Bress smiled and stepped back, offering his old friend a bow. "Then, my Lord, I will not keep you."

Roxley opened his mouth then shut it, looking at his ex-partner with a trace of sadness before he nodded. "Thank you, old friend."

Together, Roxley and Vir pushed through the crowd, leaving Bress with the trophy and the accolades and the few Truinnar who cared little for the new world. The new Dungeon World. The Great Dance went on, and if you did not keep to the beat, you would only be left behind.

0.39 Earth days before System Initiation

"Why would the humans do that?" Roxley's lips pressed tightly as he stared at the ghastly image. To do that. To an Ambassador. How insane were they? Certainly the humans had shown some degree of insanity, but to this level? Vir could not answer and Roxley shook his head vigorously, dismissing the thought. Better for him to focus on what was important. "How does this change things?"

"Many of our competitors to enter the cities have dropped from the world at this time. Others are scrambling to adjust their exploration teams," Vir answered.

"No surprise there. Merchants are not who you send to a Dungeon World. Zone levels?"

"Up to one hundred fifty."

"For a recently implemented Dungeon World?" Roxley's eyes popped wide. "That is insane. Why?"

"It seems that the Council desires to make a statement."

"I smell politics," Roxley said, fingers flicking as he scanned down information screens, his eyes narrowing in thought. "There. The vote distribution. It was the Movana." Lips peeled into a snarling smile. "They were the ones who pushed this."

"Why? It makes no sense." Vir shook his head. "It gives us a localized Dungeon World, one that will increase our strength."

"Ah, but you forget. No one controls a Dungeon World." Roxley snapped his fingers. "They're going to try to take over the cities. Buy them out from us."

"But won't the Great Houses stop them?"

"You would think so... we're missing something."

"I shall check in with my contacts."

"And I'll do some research," Roxley said, his fingers dancing. "X-127, run me a search on Dungeon Worlds and their entry into the System. I also want the latest histories of Dungeon Worlds, their most common monster distribution, and the spawning effects on local populations."

As Roxley focused, Vir smiled and bowed once more as he retreated to check in with his contacts. Even if many of the other houses were unwilling to take part in the mad scramble for land in a Dungeon World, there were those who would not shy away from the competition. It would be up to Vir to find out who, and what, if anything, he and the guards could do to forestall future problems.

0.21 Earth days before System Initiation

"What, my lord, is that doing here?" Vir said as he stalked back into the room. Hanging in Roxley's spartan, futuristic study was a massive notification screen showcasing an unfamiliar continental map.

"That, Vir, is North America."

"Yes, my Lord," Vir intoned flatly. "I am inquiring to its purpose."

"There."

A beacon flashed far up on the map. The topographic map showed that the location—a city—was set amidst a series of high Level zones. Around the city, unlike many other high Level zones, was nothing but more wilderness. In fact, the total population of that village was less than a block in the capital.

"There, my lord?" Vir said. "I see but a minor settlement. One with a high possibility of a Shop, but a minor settlement nonetheless. Surrounded by monsters."

"Exactly!" Roxley almost bounced on his feet, his eyes glowing with excitement. "Too small for the big Houses. They'll be busy fighting over the other locations."

"Other locations?"

"Yes. A Dungeon World is a free-for-all ten minutes before the System Initiation begins," Roxley explained. "In that time, anyone may purchase a location. There's a percentage that must be left alone and another that is designated for the native sentient population, but historically, it's been impossible for that number to be reached."

"Ten minutes, my lord?" Vir said.

"Exactly. In that time, all the Great Houses and other interested parties will be looking at the bigger and more financially viable locations. They'll hedge their bets, buy multiple locations in bigger cities. They'll establish their territories and try to gain a real Settlement while keeping their exposure low." Roxley flashed a shark-like grin. "The more cautious players won't even get involved. It'll be the usual rag-tag bunch of explorers and desperate to start." Vir cocked his head, and Roxley shrugged. "Yes. Like us. But while the rest are going for the safe bets, we'll steal this territory from right under them."

"High risk, high reward. A marked change from our initial plans."

"Our initial plans would float us for a few years. This, if it succeeds, might actually bring us back to where we belong."

"We won't be the only one considering those tactics."

"Which is why we'll have to bid aggressively. I've already put up the mansion, fortifications, and Settlement Mana Engine." Roxley patted the air placatingly as Vir narrowed his eyes. "I know what you're going to say. But we're about to lose it all. Better to gamble."

"Lose the Barony, my lord. But not our holdings," Vir said disapprovingly. "If you do this, you will have nothing left. Your personal loans—"

"I know."

A heavy silence fell over the pair. Without personal funds, Roxley would not be able to pay for the guards and security personnel. Many were liege-sworn, but it was a hard thing to ask a man to work for free, no matter personal honor or obligations. Harder still when it was clear that doing so would lead to their death. A bad liege might feel that it was their right, by blood or status, to request such matters. A good lord, and Roxley strove to be a good lord, never let such a situation develop. In his heart, Roxley knew he would dismiss those he could not pay when the time came. If the time came.

"Well, if you've taken the loan, then we best make sure this works," Vir said. "What else do we know of this location?"

"Not much. I expect these 'First Nations' to be of use. There are a higher percentage of hunters in this subgroup, though the numbers in total in the state are relatively high," Roxley said. "Creating a number of safe havens will be important to reduce deaths. If we can provide them with weaponry, that would be best. But safety will be the main concern."

"I'll make arrangements with the personal guards then, to journey over."

"Volunteers only."

"Of course." Vir bowed and backed out.

Roxley continued to research, searching for details about the location, attempting to not only narrow down his potential opponents in the bidding process but also the monsters that would arrive. That, he knew, was key. If a dragon appeared nearby, it would scupper the plan. Even the safety zone that a Shop created by drawing a large amount of ambient Mana into it was not perfect.

0.0503 Earth Days before System Initiation

"That would be the third." Vir turned away from the wall where the reverberations of an earlier battle died off.

Roxley dragged his attention away from the glacially slow moving clock. "Anything to be concerned about?"

"Local miscreants. I doubt we'll see anything until just before System initiation." Vir sniffed. "Our men are more than enough to handle them."

"Good."

Silence fell, the pair staring at the countdown. Their agonizing wait was only punctuated by the occasional thrum of laser fire, the crack of a spell or attack breaking the sound barrier, and the crackle of ice and fire as additional assaults occurred around the mansion.

Vir would flick his gaze sideways to his notifications about the continued battle, but he refused to disrupt his liege any further. Yet as the timer dropped to the last few seconds, he grew ever more tense as he waited for the last shoe to drop.

Roxley broke the silence thirty seconds before the end. "Any idea who?"

"The Duchess Kangana. Yuriel. Perhaps a few others," Vir said. "Our information-gatherers are working on it, but—"

"Multiple cut-outs."

"Always."

Silence, then Roxley's lips pursed. "Ten seconds."

The attack came without warning. An innocuous chair exploded, the shell showering the pair with poison-coated splinters. Only personal shield barriers stopped the initial barrage, though a few slivers struck exposed skin and armored clothing. Even as Vir shifted to block the rain of wood, a form emerged from the curling smoke.

"Chameleon," Vir snarled. He caught the Chameleon's arm, attempting to throw his opponent aside, only to find the Chameleon had left him with a fake arm as he swung around and beneath Vir's feet to attack Roxley.

Roxley danced backward, his hands up to protect his face and reach the notification screens faster. He only needed a few seconds, just long enough to search, purchase, bid, and win the location. Just a few seconds...

Vir snarled, stamping his feet. A flash of light filled the room, drawing even Roxley's attention. Yet the assassin ignored the distraction, focused as he was on the Baron. Another pair of strikes laid poison on Roxley's shield, eating away at its integrity.

"Damn it. Taunt resistance. Let's see how good it is." Vir clapped his hands again.

Roxley disappeared, replaced by Vir, who opened his hands. Cupped in his palms was a glowing ball of flame, one that wrapped around the Chameleon's body as he struck the undefended Vir. As Vir fell back, blood pooled from the wound in his abdomen—blood that turned black and hissed as his healing factor attempted to remove the poison. The Chameleon was having his own trouble with the chains of fire that bound him. Every time he attempted to turn away to attack Roxley, the chains tightened. Only when he faced Vir did they lighten.

"What kind of taunt Skill is this?" the Chameleon snarled as it gave up, focusing on Vir.

In answer, Vir popped up a notification screen in front of the Chameleon, one that was fully opaque.

Chains of Forced Attention

The Gokrus Priests of Mizag are known and loathed the Galaxy over. Their preeminent Skill, the Chains of Forced Attention, is a taunt Skill that binds opponents to listen to them drone on about the multiple levels of saintliness. This Skill cannot be blocked by common anti-taunt spells as it applies mental, physical, and magical bindings on a target's attention.

"You'd use that?" the Chameleon said, eyes widening as it forced the dismissal of the notification.

"I would use anything for my lord."

Behind the pair, Roxley focused on the new screens that flashed before his eyes. The marketplace for the world known as Earth had opened and he had to navigate the maze of System notifications, System data, and warnings to locate the information he needed. Even with X-127's help, the notifications kept changing as parties purchased and took pieces of the new Dungeon World off the market. It did not help that the System would close new notification windows when a certain number was reached as it recalculated the necessary holding percentage for the sentient species.

Again and again, Roxley closed in on his desired location and it disappeared. In the corner of his eyes, he saw how locations with the most repetitive of names, like New York, Yorkshire, London, New London, London again appeared and disappeared. In some cases, the System locked out purchased lands, ensuring that the purchasers could not gain access to them for weeks, even months.

"There!" Roxley crowed and tapped the buy button.

His view changed as his purchase intent was confirmed, shifting to a new screen. Minimum requirements, rules, and laws that would bind him—or not—were offered. Each of those were then expanded upon and detailed in System legalese, which could be as clear and direct or obtuse and hidden as its original scripter. No single settlement sale was the same, as the System constantly altered the rules and requirements.

Roxley's fingers flicked and twisted, throwing aside the majority of the rules, searching for a series of regulations he could live with while discarding the majority that he had no desire to be bound to. Even with the binding options being created, Roxley knew other parties would be willing to take the unfavorable trade, so he hurried. In the corner of his notification screen, the Credit cost for all this kept changing, shifting as he discarded options or took on other obligations.

"My Lord!"

A call from outside his viewpoint alerted the Baron and he tugged his hands close as he discarded one last binding, leaving him with a trade-off that he could accept. A mental confirmation was all that was required and the Credits streamed out, even as he received a notification of his successful purchase.

As Roxley came back to his senses, it was to the sight of a sharpened wooden stake stopped inches from his eyes.

"Well, that sucked." The Chameleon straightened, morphing the stake back into its original form as his hand. "I hate failing."

"But fail you did." Roxley shook his head at Vir, who had walked up to the Chameleon, still bleeding black and boiling blood from numerous wounds.

"I'll just take my leave then."

"I do not think so," Roxley said. "You did attack me."

The Chameleon's eyes narrowed and its snout-like nose wrinkled before a notification flashed before Roxley's face. The Baron barely glanced at it, the membership of the Yellow Sashes spotted and dismissed.

"It's a pity you died in your attacks," Vir said, his voice dripping with sarcasm.

"Do you think that lie will hold?"

"Long enough for us to arrive on the new Dungeon World."

The Chameleon fell silent, weighing his choices and the seriousness of his opposition. Eventually, he relented under the pair's silent focus. "Fine. What do you want?"

"A token," Roxley said, holding up a hand. "Three uses."

"One. No more than Master Class."

"Done."

The Chameleon's nose wrinkled again, a new notification and Contract showing up on both their sides. After a quick acceptance, Roxley dismissed the assassin, watching it stroll out.

Vir snorted as Roxley turned to him. "We're looking. But at a guess, it'd be the Duchess."

"Her Envoy does favor Chameleons," Roxley agreed. "Please do ensure the mansion is properly set-up. We have much to do."

0 Earth Days before System Initiation

In his study, Roxley watched as the sentients on Earth reacted to the new notifications. Hands clasped behind his back, he looked at hundreds of open windows, letting the details flow into his subconscious mind as he searched for a common thread, for understanding. Soon enough, he would be their liege lord, and understanding his new people was paramount.

In one corner, a woman stopped speaking, her voice stuttering as her presentation was interrupted. Dressed in a brightly colored sari, she gaped, swinging her gaze from side to side as her board members all stared dumbly into space. One after the other, the board members roused from their stupor and conversation broke out.

A chimp wielding a stick and smashing it against a nut held in place on a split rock paused before it continued swinging, the notification dismissed, never to be seen again.

Screaming, a construction worker in a fog-filled city fell from scaffolding, his footing lost as a blue screen appeared before his eyes. Frantically, the worker waved his hands, desperate to catch something, anything as he fell, never to see the new world.

A killer wielding a knife was surprised when the knife sank into his victim's shoulder, only for himself to be blinded. As he stood still in surprise, his hand was pried off the blade and the weapon taken for use by his victim. Blood flowed anew, in a surprising twist.

In a prison, hushed silence fell over a previously noisy block. Shouts erupted before klaxons sounded, driving inmates who were hanging out back into their cells. The hubbub of conversation did not end as the outnumbered guards dismissed the notifications and attempted to quell the rising riot.

A million stories, a billion of them. Some were peaceful, the new System members asleep and unaware of their introduction. They would receive a grace period when they woke. If they woke. In other locations, thousands, millions chose blindly and in haste, confirming the most important decision of their life as they dismissed it as a mass hallucination. Others grew quiet, concerned, a subconscious understanding giving them the time, the place to choose properly.

In a small village, a "city" supposedly, its inhabitants were beginning to wake. Many dismissed the notifications as nothing more than a brief hallucination. Others chose more wisely, seeing the potential in this new world and hoping desperately that it was true. They wanted an escape from their mundane lives.

And on one lonely mountain, a young man drew a deep breath, calmed himself, and achieved a world first.

"How goes it, my lord?" Vir asked.

"It goes well." Roxley's eyes drifted to the young man who stood in the middle of the wilderness, who would not survive the new few hours. Roxley dismissed the windows, turning to Vir. "Make arrangements. I had to spend more funds than I planned. We'll have to travel via mundane teleportation."

"Not ideal."

"No. But it will do."

"Yes, my lord. We are ready to leave," Vir said, bowing to his liege.

Roxley drew a deep breath, casting his gaze once more to where the windows showing Earth had hung, then let it out. "Then let us go. To Whitehorse."

***

Intermission Four

"Glad to hear you continue to mess up your Galactic expectations," Amelia said with a smile. "But, any ideas of what they're looking for. Other than the exceptional?"

"Individuals – humans – of concern. Galactics as well, especially those who have been hampered in their progression before their arrival. I have already found the notices about myself and my lord," Vir said. "But as well, any major Galactic incursions or takeovers."

"And what would you do with this information?"

"It depends on the importance of that information, no?" When Amelia continued to stare at him, Vir sighed. "At the base level, we track and watch for such individuals. The Bounty Hunter might be of use in our own operations. His… companion… might be of interest if she continues to be around. At least, on a political level.

"Others, like that creature are of no more than a passing interest. On a Galactic basis, it is not worth speaking of."

"Interesting. And if you'd found a human settlement who'd found a place with a Galactic? Who'd changed species?" Amelia said.

"Like Tim and Carcross?" Vir said. "It would depend."

"Then tell me about this one," Amelia flicked a new video over.

Rebel Within

by IX PHOEN

Milliscorpion

I jumped behind a mass of cacti and activated Subversive Stealth as my companion, Sumay, hovered above my head. Her wings were spread to keep her aloft, even though she could just as easily float while curled into a ball.

"It's tracing your scent trail, Adrian. You've got about ten seconds before it comes over the ridge," Sumay sent. Our telepathic connection and her invisibility made it easy for her to spy while I stayed in hiding.

My short brown hair and tanned skin would once have been my only reasons to believe I might remain invisible. When the System arrived, I had given up my humanity to become a Polymorph, able to change form and hide in plain sight. Now, my carefully reconstructed human appearance allowed me to fit in, and I was grateful for it.

My best friend, Tae Song, caught my eye and offered an encouraging thumbs up as he crouched behind a drop-off. He held his Soulbound swords, ready to attack. As a Level 21 Twin Blade Defender, his job was to block the Level 60 Milliscorpion on my tail, preventing it from hitting me as I lured it into our trap. The creature had been prowling the mountain above our remote boarding school's property for the last few days. We had decided to trap it on our own terms instead of waiting for it to surprise us.

My Mana ticked upward as I waited for the signal to run.

"It's here. Go!" Sumay swooped toward the path I'd already mapped during our practice run.

I activated Environmental Barrier, and the concealing cacti collapsed around me, flattened by a surge of Mana. My body absorbed the plants' fluids in a revitalizing rush as the residue bonded to my skin for an extra few points of protection. Using Speed Boost, I leaped across the deeply carved stream bed at the cliff base and clambered upward.

"Left! Stinger incoming!" Sumay sent.

I dodged along a narrow, crumbling ledge, and a burst of stones rattled against my armor as the tail struck beside me. Already running low, my Mana drained rapidly, forcing me to release Environmental Barrier before the fibers could revert to shredding my skin. A cascade of thorns rattled toward the dry stream bed below.

When I glanced down to check my progress, I realized the Milliscorpion had made it partway up the cliff behind me. Tae Song balanced on its back, his swords slicing at the joints of its tail. Hoping to distract the creature, I leaned to spit my own venom into its face. It jolted back, lost its grip, and skidded onto its side in the crevice below. I jumped to safety as Tae Song sprang away, leaving the stinger dangling by a thread. He flung himself behind a massive boulder as Cher launched Smite.

A wave of light erupted from the earth beside me. On its own, the area-effect Spell wouldn't have caused much damage to the Milliscorpion, but the cliff was another matter. A pulse shuddered through the ledge beneath me as the surface almost seemed to liquify and the truck-sized rock at the top tilted precariously. Dust billowed over the scene as a series of loud snaps, followed by a deep rumble, filled the air. I scrambled to find an unaffected location as my perch cracked and shuddered.

When the air cleared enough to see again, I gave a sigh of relief. The landslide had pinned the Milliscorpion in the crevice, so even the lower-Level kids could safely participate in the kill. Its tail segments still swung violently free of the rubble, but Tae Song was already in motion to continue his initial task as the others ran to back him up.

Cher lit up. As a Level 19 Holy Warrior, her Armor of God Skill coated her in literally shining Mana armor, and she drew her Radiant Sword Perk from storage. Her golden ponytail bounced as she jumped down the hillside to join the rest in bashing the writhing creature to death.

I relaxed into my new role, keeping an eye out for anything that might be lured in by the battle while everyone was distracted. Sumay curled her lizard-like tail around my neck, offering a running telepathic commentary on the fight below. I tuned her out for the most part, assuming our plan would continue to work. We had enough experience by now that I knew everyone fought well as a team, and it was rare to have a moment of privacy to consider my situation.

I was beginning to feel more and more useless as everyone Leveled. My morphed claws weren't strong enough to pierce the Level 50 or higher monsters dominating the area. Frontline fighting wasn't my strong point anyway. I needed some kind of ranged weapon that would mesh well with my Skills, and all the guns were taken. At least my Class would never paint a glowing target on my back, but hiding wasn't of much help in a fight.

Several of our party members cheered over gaining a Level when the Milliscorpion finally died. Distracted from my thoughts, I looked to see if anyone had poison debuffs for me to Purge, but everyone was already regenerating, some with the help of Marcus's Minor Healing. Cher's armor faded, and she wiped goo from her hands onto her ragged jeans as she found a perch where she could rest and keep watch with the others. Somehow, she still managed to look like a model, even while covered in muck.

"Anything useful?" I swung my legs over the edge of the cliff as Mr. Sanders activated his Use What You've Got Skill to check for additional resources. He was our token teacher, sent along so the rest could imagine they were trying to keep us safe. Thankfully, he'd done a lot of hunting and hiking over the years and happened to be one of the few adults who treated us like equals.

His rich, dark skin was dripping with sweat, drawing muddy lines through the pale dust coating his shaved head and muscular torso. He'd have made a terrifying Warrior, but everyone loved how his Logista Class Skills gave him the ability to break a carcass down to the parts that would be most useful to our crafters.

He gestured for me to climb down. "Nothing we'd risk consuming, since you poisoned it. Thanks for that, by the way. The damage over time was a big help."

I shuddered. "The thought of eating bugs is just nasty!"

"You've never tasted crab, have you?" He laughed and flicked through a screen, linking me in so Sumay could review the options.

"We'll use some of the meat for our cockroach herd. There are also several useful crafting components and a new toxin for you. Sumay might know if any of the rest could be worth more than our current stash. We won't unearth the whole corpse this time."

I jumped from rock to rock back down the cliff, carefully avoiding the unstable area, then absorbed the venom sack with a touch. My Dimensional Lab would break it down and record its components later. Having a racial resistance and the ability to reproduce toxins meshed well with my Toxic Apothecary Class, even though I could only secrete one toxin at a time.

Sumay became visible and, as usual, took a moment to preen, enjoying everyone's admiring glances. Sunlight skimmed her black scales and wings with a shimmering rainbow. She had plucked the daydream of having a wyvern companion from my mind when I'd chosen her as my first Perk, and she decided the form suited her.

"Keep the pincers," she told Mr. Sanders. "They're the most likely to be valuable. I'll need upgrades from a Shop to be more accurate." She disappeared again, unable to maintain visibility for long.

Mr. Sanders nodded respectfully toward where he'd last seen her, then turned to direct the others. "Let's finish up and head back before the light fades."

After wincing at the sight of Tae Song and a few of the others chopping into the creature, I hurried away. Ever since they'd learned I could secrete poison, I wasn't allowed to help with harvesting. I couldn't decide whether I felt grateful to avoid the disgusting task or excluded.

"Sumay? I could just head along the highway to search for a Shop on my own. I'm not much use here." Maybe I could create a better role for myself.

"You need to bring a group." Sumay landed on my shoulder as I groaned in irritation. *"You'll need help to carry enough loot to purchase some of the school buildings and turn the property into a Safe Zone. If you bring along an administration Class like Mr. Sanders, there's an additional discount too. I could list even more reasons if you'd like."*

I shook my head, feeling even more inadequate. Leaning back against the cliff, I practiced Chameleon Skin, taking on the color and textures of the stone behind me. Merging into the landscape this way took a lot less Mana than Morphic Disguise, but I sometimes wondered if I'd forget how to recreate my own face one of these days.

Giving up my humanity had saved me in more ways than by simply making it easy to hide and run. Ironically, it was the end of the world that had given me hope.

After my own parents called me a liar for asking for help after Coach Watson assaulted me, I had taken off for the national park behind the mountains. I'd spent multiple summers learning jungle survival skills from my Ayoreo friends. Based on those experiences, I'd planned to live off the land until the mission stopped looking.

Then the System arrived and gifted me with both the supportive companion I'd always dreamed of and the power to protect myself. After surviving a hellish first day, I'd decided to fight my demons by returning to help protect my friends. I'd made it back to the school a few weeks after the System arrived.

Ever since, I had been waiting for the chance to expose Watson, but the creep always found ways to make himself look good. He'd somehow ended up with the Missionary Class, which had tipped quite a few of the teachers toward believing that the System must somehow be a gift from God. Knowing the man's true nature, I couldn't help but worry about the abilities he must be using.

"Adrian?" Tae Song was staring in my general direction, obviously unable to see me in spite of his Perception Skill.

"Here!" I dropped Chameleon Skin and grinned as his eyes focused on me. It didn't take long to refresh my human appearance these days, since I practiced so often. I assumed everyone had guessed that my suspiciously spotless black pants, boots, and shirt weren't real, but I hoped they assumed it was a System clothing Perk. Better that than the truth of a crafted adaptation of fur and thickened skin that had taken two weeks to design and remember.

"We're heading back. You're covering the right."

I nodded and moved to prowl alongside the party, keeping an eye out for danger as we hiked home, following the rambling animal trails between the thorn bushes and cacti covering the hillsides. Even before the System, many of the plants had been dangerous, seeming to jump forward to dig into our clothes and skin. Now that some had developed a truly conscious aggression, we had to keep an even closer eye on our surroundings.

This time we only encountered a giant chicken the size of a small car, which Mr. Sanders forbade me from touching for the sake of our food supply. At least standing watch resulted in repeatable Quests, giving me XP for staying alert and warning of potential threats. Otherwise, I'd have started to worry about my Leveling strategy. I needed to keep ahead of Watson.

Fort Tin

We eventually crossed the highway as the sun was setting. After making our way through a maze of traps, we reached what we now called Fort Tin.

Located halfway between the cities of Cochabamba and Santa Cruz, our boarding school had offered safety, spiritual community, and education. Only the children of missionaries and a few others who had paid extra for the privilege of an English education were accepted. The only reason so many of us had survived was that a random System Fort had selected the walled-in hilltop that had once been our basketball courts as a Safe Zone. As the first sentients to find the location, we claimed it. This included a storage building and game room where we used to hold class parties. With no way to get System Credits, we couldn't expand our Safe Zone or purchase upgrades to Fort defenses and facilities, though our crafters did their best with the resources at hand.

Even the newly salvaged rows of bunk beds under ramshackle tin shelters didn't offer enough space for everyone. We were grouped into shifts for everything from meals and shower runs to rest times, making privacy a rare treasure. From the middle grades on up, we all took turns at watch, though the hunting and defensive parties tended to fill in the gaps whenever we were inside the walls so the watchers could catch a break.

I waved at the group of little kids near the food shelter as our party dispersed. They had a card game scattered across one of the tables, and I sighed in relief to count all seven still alive. Far too few of the kids had survived the first days before moving into the Fort's brick-walled storage room, and the predators in our vicinity were only getting stronger.

The ancient army truck that had been maintained by the school for decades rumbled up the narrow track toward the kitchen area. Its wooden bed bulged with yet another load of salvaged propane tanks, boxes of supplies, and a massive iron stove from the old dining hall. Everyone believed Chef Richards must be a true genius to have managed cooking for sixty-three people over an adobe fire pit, with only the puny, game-room snack stove for backup.

I headed along the track between the shelters, knowing Rachel would be checking in with her brother at our watch post. A Level 18 Air Mage, she'd been assigned to the party guarding the foraging team for the day. Tae Song had promised to join us once he finished emptying his inventory into storage.

"Any news?" Rachel was already in the tower gazing out over the shadowed soccer field, now a torn-up graveyard. Nobody else wanted the post for that reason, so our little group had claimed the responsibility. This section of the wall came with more privacy than the rest.

Rachel's younger brother had already loaned her his Mana Rifle, a much-appreciated Perk he'd chosen to go with his Sharp Shooter Class. I glanced down at the hammocks we'd hung between the support posts and saw John already asleep, his face pale with exhaustion. He'd been keeping watch on his own since dawn in spite of missing half his sleep schedule the night before.

I found it ironic that the System counted him as an adult already. The teachers still refused to treat me as one, even though I'd turned nineteen a week ago. According to Sumay, the System used the local age of adulthood to calculate, and the Quechua considered their children grown at fifteen.

"They're planning a joint river run tomorrow," I told Rachel as I clambered up the ladder and slumped in the corner. "Both of the fighting parties desperately want to bathe, and the rain barrels by the kitchen are nearly empty again."

"But no plans to search for more survivors or find a Shop?" Rachel shook her head.

I scrubbed my face, irritated by the gritty feel of the ever-present dust. "Mr. Sanders hopes the adults will come to an agreement tonight. I know he wants to believe they'll send us out because we won't survive much longer without System resources. Still, even his perpetual optimism can't help but acknowledge that at least half of them still imagine God will Rapture us all into Heaven at any moment."

Tae Song scrambled up the ladder and yanked himself onto the platform with one arm, clutching a fabric bundle in his other hand. "Chef sent along some snacks since we missed lunch and dinner. Cold meat as usual, but Doña Maria's new mud oven has dried enough to bake the first batch of *marraquetas*, and we're her guinea pigs."

"Bread!" We tore open the bundle and shared the still-warm rolls, even waking John long enough to stuff his face with the treat.

I breathed in the steam as I tore off a bite. For just a moment, I remembered how it felt to be safe and happy. "Now all I need is a Guaraná."

Rachel sighed. "Too bad we finished the last of the soda weeks ago."

I wrapped the remainder of my roll in its napkin and regretfully returned it to the pile of food. My old favorites still tasted just as good, even now that I wasn't human. Sumay had mentioned this was a System effect, associating my new body's experiences to a memory matrix my mind could comprehend.

Still, the necessary internal organs no longer existed. I'd have to reach at least Master Class to fully replicate a human body. For now, to fake the process of eating solids, I had to use Minor Morph and create a pocket in my torso for anything my body couldn't absorb. Most fluids were easy to integrate, but solids led to debuffs to my Health whenever I had to store them until I could manually eject the residue.

"You're not going to eat any?" Tae Song shook his finger at me. "Just because a Polymorph can survive on fluids doesn't mean you're not allowed to enjoy a treat with the rest of us. Eat the bread, okay? Let's just enjoy it together." He shoved the roll back into my hand as I continued to hesitate. "I promise we'll eat the meat without you."

I had to laugh at his long-suffering tone as I reclaimed my portion. I might feel a little uncomfortable later on, but with each bite I felt more human than I had since the System changed my body.

Tae Song

Brilliant and familiar, the stars gazed down at me as I stood watch. Among them existed alien cultures and a myriad of worlds, similar to my favorite books and daydreams.

Rolled in a blanket on the platform beside me, Tae Song sobbed in the grip of a nightmare. He almost never slept in the shelters, saying he couldn't relax with everyone crowding together. I debated whether to wake him. These days, being awake wasn't much of a relief.

He jumped and reached for my arm. "Adrian? You're still alive?"

"Yes."

With a sigh of relief, he pulled himself up to keep watch beside me. I had Morphed my eyes to register the ultraviolet spectrum when night fell, and he had a Night Vision Spell. Even without a moon, his skin glowed to my eyes, revealing his oval face and straight nose as he glared out at the field. It might be better to ignore the glimmering traces of tears on his cheeks for now.

Together, we watched the mutated cockroaches feasting below. They'd attack any other creature attempting to sneak into their feeding grounds, giving us a chance to wake everyone up and get in position.

"I still can't believe we're using giant cockroaches as guards," he grumbled.

"Better them than us."

"True." He slumped against the wall and drew his swords. He'd once mentioned that holding them reminded him of the years he'd spent training with his father. "You can sleep if you want. I'm going to be awake anyway, and it's only an hour or so till dawn."

"I won't need to hibernate for another two days." It felt like my words would create an impassable wall between us as I spoke. "I'm too alien, aren't I? I wonder whether it's hard for everyone to be around me now."

"Hmm... Everyone changed. So what if your race is different? You're still you." His voice softened. "I feel like you becoming a Polymorph is a promise, in a way."

That was unexpected. I turned to face him, wondering whether I should ask what he meant.

Sumay floated higher. "Talk to him. I'll keep watch."

Noticing my hesitation, Tae Song shifted to face me. "You mentioned you don't have a gender now, right?" His narrow eyes seemed to pierce the darkness.

"Well, yes. It's part of being a Polymorph." This felt dangerous, like I was standing on the edge of exposing my greatest flaw. Even if Tae Song had always been more accepting of my oddities than anyone I'd ever met, I wasn't sure he'd accept this.

He lowered his voice until even my enhanced hearing could scarcely pick up the words. "It's like, if the universe actually has whole races without gender affecting their relationships, maybe there's a place where I'd fit in too."

"But everyone loves you already!" I couldn't understand how he could believe he didn't fit in when everyone had always admired him. That someone so popular chose to hang out with me had always felt like a rare error in judgement on his part.

"They'd reject me if they knew the truth." He curled in on himself, clutching his swords as if they were his lifeline. "I'm not normal."

I hesitated, unable to see his expression. His straight, black hair had grown long enough to hide his face. It didn't seem that long ago that the teachers had the energy to enforce rules on acceptable hairstyles.

There was a rush of motion below as the cockroaches encountered an invader. We tensed, but the creature was overtaken by the mob. I shivered. Without my toxins to cull their numbers below the control limits of Abuelo's Herder Class, even these low-Level swarms could wipe out the Fort within days.

The silence between Tae Song and I grew heavier as I reviewed our conversation.

"Tell him your secret, and maybe he'll feel safe enough to tell you his." Sumay sounded fed up with my hesitation. *"He's already accepted your physical changes. If you can't trust him now, then you might as well admit you think he's a liar for saying he values your friendship."*

Calling Tae Song a liar grated on me as she knew it would. "Ugh... fine!"

He jumped, since I'd accidentally spoken out loud.

Below us, the ropes of Rachel's hammock creaked. "Attack?"

I sighed. "No, it's nothing. Sorry. Sumay said something weird... Never mind."

"Okay then."

We listened as she settled back into sleep. Eventually, her breathing evened out as we stared over the wall.

"I... don't want you to hate me." I leaned in, keeping my voice low. "But can I tell you something I've never told anyone?"

Tae Song nudged my arm with his elbow. "I can't ever imagine hating you, Adrian. It's impossible."

"Uh… well. The genderless thing? I chose to change race because of it, whatever it is everyone else seems to know that makes them one or the other. My body just… it felt like puppet strings forcing me to be something I wasn't. I hated it." My voice trailed off, and I dropped my forehead onto my hands where they rested on the wall. "In spite of everything, it's such a relief to just be myself now. I can change the parts that bothered me before."

After setting his sword across his knees, he flung his right arm over my shoulder and patted the back of my head as if I were a puppy. "That's all? I thought you were going to tell me you killed someone or something."

"Not yet," I mumbled, thinking of Watson. "I hope I never have to either."

He chuckled. "It's strange to live in a world where that answer feels reassuring instead of creepy."

Forget trying to say things right. I had to get things out there one way or another. "I wanted you to know I trust you, in case you ever want to talk about your… thing. I can't imagine hating you either."

Raptor

A chilling shriek disrupted our conversation as a larger predator charged into the mass of cockroaches. The creature tore into them, clearly too powerful for them to take down.

"It looks like a velociraptor!" I yanked on the cord strung over Fort Tin, attached to a small bell by Mr. Sanders's bed, alerting our party back in the shelters.

"This had better not turn out like *Jurassic Park*." Tae Song leaned over the platform edge to wake Rachel and John.

We'd have to move outside to fight it off since neither the maze nor the walls were enough to handle a direct assault from something this powerful.

"It's crushing the cockroaches! Too dangerous. I'm going to lure it the long way toward the northern pit trap." I Morphed my fingers to increase adherence and began to climb down the wall.

"Be careful!" Tae Song leaned over the edge. "We'll be ready."

Cher's face appeared beside his, and I knew the rest of our party was close behind. Joachim would wake and buff them with Night Vision, and they'd run to the trap the short way. The cockroaches gave up the fight and scuttled back into hiding as I reached the edge of the maze. I hoped I could be irritating enough to distract the raptor from the Fort.

Half an hour later, I flattened myself behind a ledge to flash Minor Morph and repair the most recent hole the raptor had nipped in my shoulder. All the running and hiding reminded me of the early days when I'd been on my own. I glanced at my stats, noting the usual warning notification.

HP 75/490 MP 67/500

Warning! *Mass at 5% below optimal range. 6% debuff to Health and Stamina.*

Sumay swooped up the gully toward our destination. *"Run!"*

At least I had backup waiting. Even with Speed Boost for emergencies and my high endurance, the creature was far too close on my trail. Thankfully, its desire to make a meal of me blinded it to the party in hiding around the massive pit we'd dug a few days earlier. Dawn brightened the sky as I sprinted across a rigged slackline with the raptor nipping at my heels, the edges of my vision flashing with debuffs to Health, Strength, and more from losing too much mass to its attacks.

Its shriek of anger Stunned everyone but me when the twig-and-dirt cover over the pit collapsed, dropping it six yards onto sharpened stakes. I had coated them with blood thinner to increase their damage. I spent an anxious ten seconds waiting while everyone recovered, trying to think of what I could do to help fight it off. The raptor scrabbled at the wall, creating pockets in the earth so it could pull itself off the stakes. Just before it reached the top, a series of stuns interspersed with rifle fire blasted it back down, where Joe entangled it with a Vine Trap.

Tae Song and Mr. Sanders strained to swing a concrete platform into position, its base layered with jagged rebar spikes. The ramshackle tripod and pulleys creaked until someone released the catch and the platform dropped into the hole with a crash. Even this still wasn't enough to kill the raging raptor, which continued to struggle, its convulsions powerful enough to crack the concrete. Cher started to chain Smite every time it finished cooldown, hoping to drive the spikes in deeper before the lid crumbled completely. When it finally broke apart, the rebar remained embedded in the raptor's muscles, inhibiting its attempts to free itself.

By the time the sun rose, everyone had a chance to get in on the battle while the creature nearly managed to escape the trap multiple times. We won in the end, but various team members lost an arm, a few hands, and half a foot in the process, reducing our fighting force for the time needed to regrow their limbs. Combat Healer Joachim would have his work cut out for him when we got home.

A Quest update alerted me that I had received XP for warning of an invader before it breached our defenses, more for leading it away from Fort Tin, and a bonus for participating in a winning battle against a monster more than thirty Levels above my current party's average. I had finally reached Level 21, but it still wouldn't be enough power to protect everyone.

I couldn't help but wonder how much longer we could survive on too little sleep while fighting attackers like this. Sumay nodded in silent agreement with my thoughts as we watched Mr. Sanders climb down to settle for the basic loot. The body was too shredded and poisoned to retrieve much else. I helped poison it further, and we left the remains for scavengers before heading back to Fort Tin, hoping to arrive in time for breakfast.

On the way back, a mutated bush snatched at us with its branches. Thankfully, its last meal had damaged it enough that the fight was over quickly. Absorbing its Mana-rich remains boosted my mass enough to eliminate the worst debuffs.

Watson

Everyone's schedules shifted due to the injuries in our party, and the bustle that had arisen after our return finally died down. Chef Richards hovered over his stove, cheerfully whistling as he flipped pancakes for the second breakfast shift. I curled into a sunlit alcove beside the tin screen used to separate the dining area from storage, waiting out the cooldown so I could Morph.

The kids were playing Monsters and Magic between the tables while their primary guardian, Miss Angela, helped with peeling and chopping cacti for lunch. One waved two sticks in the air, jumping from one shelter roof to another and pretending to be Tae Song. A screaming match broke out over who got to be Cher until I intervened, suggesting they could both choose the Holy Warrior Class. Nobody wanted to be me.

I wasn't sure I wanted to be myself either. My torso had been warped into a lumpy mass by the cumulative effect of using Minor Morph to flash-heal on the run. I'd borrowed Tae Song's jean jacket to cover the worst of it, but I still felt alien and ugly. I could shift into Polymorph form anytime, but nobody would recognize me. Even though my stats and Skills were better in my new body, visibly showing myself as alien didn't feel safe. Since Morphic Disguise wouldn't allow me to repair my human form until four in the afternoon, I'd just have to wait.

Behind the screen, I heard Watson's voice drawing near. As usual, I tuned in, listening for something that might give me leverage to expose him. "We need to move these boxes to the side to make room for the next load of salvage."

I relaxed slightly. Even I had to admit his organizational skills were a big help these days, and this conversation wasn't worth my time. I almost tuned out until a familiar voice responded.

"I'll handle it." Tae Song's presence was a bit of a surprise. I had assumed he'd been sent back to guard duty so John could finally get some sleep.

Something clattered and the screen jolted. "You've been avoiding me, Tae." Watson's voice sounded muffled all of a sudden.

What? I jolted to my feet, then dashed around the end of the screen and arrived to see Watson cornering Tae Song against a stack of boxes. "What do you think you're doing?" I wanted to scream, but my throat had been warped too, so I could only speak just above a whisper.

Watson jerked back, stumbling dramatically. "I just tripped, so don't... Oh, it's you." He gave up on his terrible attempt at acting, and his eyes narrowed. He seemed to be calculating his chances of persuading me nothing was going on.

A notification flashed in the corner of my eye.

"He's using a Mental Healing Skill on you. It's meant to help people forget traumatic memories from what I can tell," Sumay reported. *"Your race is immune, but that is insidious!"*

Tae Song brushed past him and hurried toward me, his face tense with repressed emotion. "Let's just go."

I glared at Watson, whose face had already begun to smooth back into his usual mask. He must have realized from my expression that his Spell hadn't dealt with the situation because his brow furrowed and another notification flashed.

Unity failed: *(Congratulations!) You have not been persuaded that everyone should overlook minor differences in opinion (such as the right of teachers to sexually assault their students) in order to work together.*

The modified description had Sumay's fingerprints all over it, and I couldn't help but smirk. Watson's face twisted with frustration.

Sumay flashed into physical form in front of his eyes for a moment, making him jump and hopefully interrupting any other Spell he might have come up with. *"Get Tae Song out of here! He's vulnerable to this creep even if you're not."*

We ran down a narrow gap between the bunk shelters, agreeing on our goal without need for discussion. Moments later, we clambered up the side of our watchtower. Watson would never come this close to the walls.

John glanced at us as we pulled ourselves onto the platform. "Welcome back!" His face was far too young for the exhausted air of responsibility in his posture and expression.

I gestured toward his rifle. "We're both free for now. Why don't you let me take over and go sleep on a bed for once?"

If Watson hadn't had ulterior motives, Tae Song would have been assigned to the tower in the first place. John was far too tired to keep watch on his own. We watched in silence as he staggered toward the shelters. Sumay demanded we talk while she kept watch, but I hesitated to speak, uncertain of what to say.

Tae Song broke the silence. "You've never liked Watson much either. Even before you disappeared, I saw you cross the entire patio once, just to avoid walking near him."

"You're not the only person he's assaulted." I shuddered, unable to forget the memory of waking up in the dark with unexpected hands groping my skin.

"He hurt you?" Tae Song inched closer so it would be easier to hear me, but he kept his face turned toward the soccer field.

Going into the details after all this time felt like too much, so I skipped ahead. "They claimed I was lying and a fellow missionary would never touch me. Everyone thinks he's so wonderful, you know? My own parents said I was ruining the reputation of a good man as some kind of sick joke. They've always thought of me as a rebel, that God had cursed them with me in order to test their faith."

"That explains a lot, actually." He glanced at me and shook his head. "I knew something was going on. You were suddenly on extra work detail all the time and getting called in for disciplinary meetings for no reason I could see. I guess I can understand why you didn't tell me. I didn't say anything to you either, but still... Knowing might have changed things."

"I should have warned you about him before I left." It felt like the regret would crush me with its weight. "I'm sorry."

"It's not your fault. I didn't talk to you either." He turned away, but I could still see his ears redden with embarrassment. "It wasn't quite the same for me. Watson knew I was... uh... he saw me watching the guy I liked. He offered to be a substitute. He said I'd have to marry a woman one day since my parents would never accept it. He wouldn't leave me alone, and I... let him kiss me once on a bad day. After that, it was like I wasn't allowed to say no anymore."

My jaw clenched with anger. "What a creep!"

"For a while I thought I might as well just give in since I'd never find anyone else who would accept me. I'll never get to be happy, you know? My crush was totally into Cher. It hurt to watch them together and think I'd never have that… and then…" His voice broke on a muffled sob. "It turns out Watson scared my best friend away too."

His feelings were all too familiar, and Sumay murmured that Watson had likely preyed on us because of those similarities.

I decided to focus on a safer topic. "You liked Jeremiah? I can see why. He was a lot of fun."

Tae Song scrubbed at his damp face and sighed. "I can't believe he's gone."

We fell silent.

A familiar scent sweetened the air, and I scanned the horizon. "I can taste a *sur* coming in. I'm glad they got the rain barrels installed. At least we have covered shelters now and enough blankets for everyone when the temperature drops."

"So what are we going to do?" Ignoring my attempt to redirect the topic, Tae Song sheathed his swords for the moment. He settled his back against the wall so he could face me now that we were finished with our confessions. "I'm tired of Watson coming after me. I wish I'd never listened to him, but recently, even when someone sees him hanging on me, it's like they forget the next moment. And sometimes it feels like I should just give in and avoid making things more complicated since survival is what really matters. I just feel so guilty and disgusting all the time."

"That's a Spell." I frowned and reviewed my logs. "Apparently it's a group buff called Unity. It makes people ignore their objections and go along with a leader's plan for the sake of survival. From my perspective, he's essentially been Spell-drugging you… and everyone who sees him with you."

With the description in front of me, I understood how the Spell might even seem beneficial to some. "He also tried some mental-healing Skill on me that was supposed to make me forget what I saw."

"Why didn't it work on you? Everyone else just blanked out!" Tae Song slumped back, grimacing in frustration.

I shrugged, uncertain how to answer.

Sumay exerted herself to become visible. "Having a nonstandard mental makeup makes Adrian virtually immune to most mental and charisma-based influences." She spun in place, floating far too close to my face. "But don't get cocky! You're extra vulnerable to those who know how to manipulate Polymorphs."

Tae Song smiled at the rare privilege of seeing her, unconsciously reaching to touch her. She floated closer and brushed her forehead against his fingertips before vanishing again. He clutched his hand to his chest as though she'd given him a treasure.

"If he tells them I'm gay, they'll probably just assume I'm the real problem. They've already proven they can't imagine a Missionary might abuse his position. With his Spells, I doubt they're capable of helping even if they might be willing to otherwise." He groaned and bumped his head against the exterior wall as if trying to knock a solution out of the adobe. "I wish there was someone we could call in to help us!"

"Mr. Sanders is trying." My recently acquired understanding of our party leader's character had finally convinced me that I'd always had more support than I assumed. "He hinted that he and a couple other teachers were investigating my situation before. Then my parents called in and informed everyone I am the embodiment of evil.

"I ran away before I heard what happened after that, but…" I trailed off, regretting leaving even more than usual. "Others might have helped us too, before the System gave Watson the ability to literally brainwash them. I'm hoping we can find a solution when we get to a Shop, but they refuse to send anyone to search for it!"

Tae Song slumped against the wall and yawned, drooping with exhaustion now that the adrenaline had run its course. "We can't change the past. Let's just talk to Mr. Sanders and keep an eye out to see who else we might be able to trust. We need to figure out how Watson uses his abilities and whether anyone else sees what he's doing with them. We'll go from there."

"And, Adrian?" He rubbed a glimmer of tears from his eyes as he turned away. "Thank you for not judging me."

I patted his shoulder awkwardly, equally relieved that he hadn't assumed I was a liar. "Same here. Thank you."

I scanned the field for a moment to give him the chance to calm himself, then pointed toward the hammocks below. "Now that we have each other's backs on this, you need a nap. I'll keep watch."

Sumay hopped down to murmur something in his ear as I settled in to keep watch. I hoped she knew what to say, since I couldn't think of anything that might help him feel better. It was my fault for leaving him alone and vulnerable.

Journey

Soon after sunset, Mr. Sanders hurried toward our group after the nightly teacher's meeting. His grin radiated excitement as he pulled himself over the edge of the platform. Sumay offered to keep watch for a while as we settled in to hear his news.

"They agreed to send us out in search of the closest Shop!" He pumped his fist in a silent cheer. "At first Watson recommended we just send you, Adrian."

I tensed and glanced at Tae Song.

Mr. Sanders's eyes narrowed when he noticed our expressions. "It was obviously a bad idea to send anyone out alone. Everyone agreed we should send a small party and put me in charge. They left the rest to me."

"So, who's in?" I couldn't truly relax unless Tae Song was coming along.

"Adrian, Sumay, Tae Song, and..." He turned toward Rachel. "You, if you're willing. Your Shelter Spell will offer safety so we can stop to rest, and you three have decent teamwork since you all share responsibility for this watch tower."

Rachel nodded, wrapping her arms around John as he shook his head, his face twisted in silent protest. "I do want to help." She caught John's gaze. "And, John, maybe I can find out what happened to Mom and Dad."

John awkwardly hid his face against her shoulder. The poor kid was one of the few of us with a surviving family member close enough to rely on, and now we were taking his support away. Even if our mission was vital to everyone's survival, it couldn't be easy to accept.

Tae Song and I shared a muted sigh of relief when Rachel whispered encouragement to John. Watson's Unity Buff must have worked against his ulterior motives this time. We'd have to warn those we trusted to keep an eye on him while we were gone, but neither of us had noticed any signs of him targeting anyone else. Hopefully we'd be back soon enough to prevent him from causing more damage.

After giving us a few moments to accept the Quest to find a System Shop, Mr. Sanders continued. "We'll leave tonight. I don't want to give anyone a chance to change their minds. Chef Richards is putting together trail rations. Tae Song and Rachel, you need to help me load up the best of the loot."

He glanced in my direction. "Will you keep watch till Cher arrives? She volunteered, since Joachim is mostly done rebuilding her foot. After she gets here, you're in charge of finding backpacks and organizing whatever supplies Joachim has for us."

I nodded.

He climbed down, gesturing for everyone else to follow. "John, come along and say goodbye to your sister. In a way, she'll be safer with us than you are here, you know. We'll always be using stealth abilities, which means we can sneak past anything dangerous."

John didn't seem convinced, but passed me his rifle and followed obediently when they hurried to complete their preparations.

Cher arrived with only a limp and a mismatched pair of shoes as a reminder of her injuries. She pulled herself onto the platform and accepted the rifle from me.

I bit my lip, trying to figure out how to start. "I need to warn you about something before I leave, but it's a bit awkward to explain."

Cher gave me a keen glance, then sighed. "Is it about Watson?"

It took me a moment to recover enough to nod. Did she think I had an unfair grudge against him?

She grimaced. "He's been stalking Tae Song. I'm often on the same work group, so it's become pretty obvious even if the adults seem to mysteriously forget everything they see. I've tried to help wherever I can. He finally told you?"

"I wish I'd noticed earlier." Frustration surged as I realized that, even as his best friend, I seemed to be the last to know.

"Oh, Watson has been very cautious around you ever since you reported him." Cher noted my shock and sighed. "My parents heard rumors about the investigation and called to warn me to be careful. They asked me to encourage you since your parents are idiots, but you ran away before I could do anything."

"I... Wow! Uh... Thank you!"

She ruffled my hair and pointed toward the shelters where Tae Song stood waving to catch my attention. "We'll talk more when you get back. I'll keep an eye on everyone while you're gone, especially John. Tell Rachel not to worry."

I gave her a quick hug and swung off the platform, savoring the realization that she'd been supporting me all along.

About an hour before midnight, we reached Comarapa. Even knowing something had melted the entire valley, I still wasn't prepared for the sight. Everything organic had been reduced to a thin layer of ash that drifted past our feet, obscuring the road. Feeling exposed by the lack of vegetation, we moved in the deepest shadows, keeping watch for whatever may have caused the destruction. In town, the wind hissed around walls that had been shattered like flawed pottery in a kiln.

Whatever had happened had occurred within the first days of the System, before the school's scouts went searching for survivors in the area. We crept through, trying not to disturb the tomb-like stillness. Tae Song mumbled a brief requiem when we passed the charred field where we'd played soccer against local teens.

Once out of the valley, we took off our packs and hunkered down in the corner of an abandoned house to rest before continuing. Since the moon was new, Mr. Sanders was using his forty-five-minute Group Survival Spell to buff himself and Rachel with Tae Song's Night Vision. Every time his buff expired, we rested for the twenty-minute cooldown before continuing up the highway. As we continued, I could taste rain pressing in as the temperature dropped.

Eventually, Rachel began to stumble as she ran, clearly suffering due to lack of sleep. We needed everyone alert since our plan depended on our ability to remain undetected by the high-Level predators in the area. I jogged next to Mr. Sanders and asked where he planned to stop so Rachel could rest.

"There's a place in the next valley where I often camped, but we can stop anytime." He pointed up the switchbacks where the road disappeared around a curve. "Keep an eye out for a good campsite, since you can see farther than the rest of us."

Before I found a suitable place, we came around a corner and discovered a gigantic serpent, its coils spilling across the highway. We ducked back, keeping the mountain between us so it couldn't use its thermal vision to sense our presence. Sumay swooped ahead to examine it more closely and informed us it appeared to be digesting a large meal. It was unlikely to react to our presence so long as we did nothing to aggravate it.

Group Survival: Night Vision would run out in a few minutes, so we followed a game trail up the side of the mountain, keeping as much earth as possible between us and the serpent. Amid the rugged terrain, I found a hollow in the mountainside. The shallow hole was just large enough for everyone to crowd inside, and we were out of time to search for better options. Gesturing for the others to stay back, I used Environmental Barrier to compress the thorn bushes and cacti crowding the space. I stepped to the side to release the debris outside the hollow as Mr. Sanders used a Crafted plank from his inventory to scrape out a bench along the back so we could sit more comfortably.

As prepared as we could be, everyone crouched beside me as Rachel cast Shelter to cover the opening, muting magical signs of our presence and camouflaging our location to most forms of visual observation for the next eight hours. The Skill she'd chosen as a Perk created a two-person dome, scarcely large enough to cover the four of us even with the additional space granted by the hollow. We dug out enough of the wall so Rachel could lie down with her head on her pack, but there still wasn't much room after everyone wrapped themselves in blankets. I resigned myself to ongoing discomfort, thankful that at least my new body wouldn't cramp up or resent the cold like my old one.

In spite of her weariness, Rachel struggled to sleep. She claimed her Air Sense was reacting to the changing pressure of the incoming front, but I assumed the worry about leaving her brother behind was also keeping her on edge. Eventually, Mr. Sanders folded her into an extra tarp he'd brought, saying the additional insulation might help her relax. Either it worked or her exhaustion finally outweighed her tension, and she fell asleep.

The *sur* arrived in full force as the others slept. Rain seeped under the dome's edge and trickled down the wall, soaking my back and sopping into the blankets. I took the chance to absorb minerals from the muddy water as Tae Song dozed against my shoulder. Earlier, we'd agreed he should sit on my lap so the other two could have a little more space. Mr. Sanders didn't even seem to notice, which I hadn't expected given the school's many rules on physical contact. I'd even gotten in trouble for sitting back to back with a friend earlier in the school year. Maybe some teachers weren't as locked into the mission's rules as I'd always assumed.

As we waited for the others to awaken, Sumay and I reviewed our route, trying to get a sense of how much farther we'd have to travel to reach the Shop. She extracted the location name of Yuthupampa from the System, but it was unfamiliar to me and didn't show on the paper map we'd brought with us. I finally gave up on the pointless discussion since we didn't have enough information to plan.

Sumay floated off to watch for predators and read up on human history while I activated Meditation in hope of postponing the impending twenty-two hours of sleep my body would soon demand. When the other three woke up as the Shelter collapsed around dawn, I learned none of them were familiar with Yuthupampa either. We'd just have to keep heading in the direction Sumay's senses indicated, or at least follow the highway's zigzag climb to that point. After warming ourselves with steaming cups of coffee from a large thermos, we broke camp.

We ended up scrambling over the mountain through thorn bushes and along slippery game trails while the rain continued to fall. Even after an hour of careful climbing, Mr. Sanders still had to use Group Survival with Subversive Stealth so we could sneak past the final stretch of the serpent's tail where it curved along the highway. The steep slopes above had threatened to crumble beneath our feet, and a landslide would definitely betray our presence if the fall didn't kill us first.

I looked back at the serpent just before we rounded a corner toward a new branch of the valley. *"Reminds me of our first day,"* I sent to Sumay.

She laughed. *"At least we're not inside this one."*

I winced at the reminder. *"It feels more like a nightmare I had once than a real experience. Logically, I should have been panicking instead of wondering why I got a stupid Title. Is this indifference a Polymorph thing, or am I just broken?"*

"It's a Racial Trait, part of your nonstandard mental makeup that allows you to recover from traumatic experiences without psychological side effects." She brushed her head against my cheek. *"Pain and physical damage don't affect your kind quite so directly either, which is why you are able to keep moving even after predators take a few bites out of you. When you get a chance, you'll have to purchase the history of your people to learn more about yourself."*

"My people?" I nearly tripped over my own feet at the thought, and Tae Song gripped my shoulder to steady me. *"I'm an imposter at best, Sumay."*

She took off to float above us and sent a dramatic sigh. *"Not everyone is born into their true family, Adrian. Some families are chosen."*

"Well, it doesn't much matter if I chose them, does it? What matters is whether they choose me."

She dropped the subject, instead directing my attention to the fact that, with a mountain between us, we were finally beyond even the most extended possible sensory range of the serpent. *"You can start running again while I keep an eye out for danger from above."*

We made good time between breaks, at times hiding under Shelter while waiting to reactivate Subversive Stealth so we could sneak our way past increasingly higher Level predators. Late that afternoon, we reached a pass. Our map showed that a massive park curved up the back of an open ridge where the highway crossed to the next mountain. Sumay warned us the area was at least at Level 100 and connected to the Zone I'd barely survived when the System arrived.

The ridge between the mountains was scarcely the length of a soccer field, but we couldn't even see the cliffs on the far side through the heavy fog. In spite of feeling that nothing could possibly see us, we followed Sumay's instructions and crept forward with extreme caution once the mountain no longer stood between us and the park.

"Shelter! Now!"

At Sumay's warning, I waved a hand in front of the group and dropped it toward the ground. We dropped and huddled together as Rachel cast Shelter.

Sumay hovered beside me as she explained. *My scans picked up on something flying toward us, but it's not within my current knowledge base, so I can't say what it is or how powerful. It's from the park side, so it's better to assume you've been detected since the shared version of your Stealth is much weaker.*

Due to the need for silence, I was unable to tell the others and settled for pointing toward the sky and flapping my hands like wings. They nodded and pressed lower into the mud and grass.

We only had a half hour left of stealth remaining as something spiraled above us. At one point, it flew so close that the air from its passing gusted beneath the edge of Shelter. I'd almost given up on living when Sumay's sense of its presence began to fade into the distance. Even then, I waited to signal it was gone until we had to move or risk still being in the open when Group Survival inevitably dropped. We crawled beside the road in the mud until long after we had crossed behind the mountain again.

Late that night we decided to rest in a dusty, undisturbed farmhouse built against a cliff near the road. Whoever had owned the place must have abandoned it or died in their fields when the System arrived. Unable to trust the adobe walls and straw roof to block System-enhanced senses, we once again crowded into the least exposed corner beneath Shelter.

Thankfully there was a musty straw mattress we dragged off its rickety iron frame, and a few heavy, wool blankets so the others wouldn't have to use their soaking-wet coverings from the previous night. I hung our own blankets to dry over the empty bed frame. Even with their ever-increasing stats, I noticed the others were suffering from the constant cold and damp. They huddled in their blanket cocoons and clutched mugs of lukewarm coffee, wistfully agreeing that building a fire was too great a risk as they sipped the liquid. My own body seemed to adjust naturally to the ambient temperature, though I had yet to test myself against true extremes. I felt none of their discomfort.

Sumay popped into visibility in the center of our huddle. "It looks like we're about two-thirds of the way there."

Mr. Sanders nodded. "We survived the worst of it. From what we know, the next valley won't be quite so high Level. For now, let's rest and regain our strength. Silence is safer."

Everyone nodded and Tae Song settled against my side, tugging the edge of his blanket to cover me as well. I almost protested, then realized this was another moment like sharing the bread, where accepting would reassure him. I gave in and waited till he fell asleep before tucking the blanket more securely around him.

Over the previous weeks, I had begun to realize that even frequent evidence of my physical differences wasn't always enough for my friends to remember I was no longer human. Sumay suggested I should remember the thought whenever I felt like depressing myself by believing I was too alien for anyone to tolerate being around me. Her words followed me into the stillness as I activated Meditation.

We spent the next morning climbing around landslides and hiding whenever any of us sensed danger nearby. Around noon, I fell into a daze, following the others without much thought.

"Adrian?" At first I couldn't focus on Sumay's voice, but her tone sharpened. *"Adrian! Wake up!"*

I snapped alert and found everyone had stopped and crowded around me.

"What's wrong? Are you hurt?" Mr. Sanders studied me with a concerned expression.

I shivered when I realized how dangerous it was to push myself. I couldn't put off hibernation much longer, even if we had to find a location to camp before we found the Shop. Seeing how I was struggling to frame my thoughts into words, Sumay manifested and explained the situation.

"Ah." Tae Song shook his head. "It's one thing to know you hibernate once a week and another to actually see you staggering along like I do after only sixteen hours. I'm so used to you being alert, no matter the time, that I forgot you'd need sleep soon."

"I've been using Meditate at night, hoping it would help me stay awake longer." I shook my head, trying to think how to explain. "My body just won't sleep, then suddenly it's the only thing I can do. I can push myself for the rest of the day, I think, but I can't put it off much longer. I'm sorry. Maybe I shouldn't have come."

Rachel laughed in my face. "If you think we'd have survived this long without you, think again. Subversive Stealth is the reason we've made it this far."

Everyone nodded.

"And Group Survival, Shelter, Night Vision…" I added. Based on their expressions, it obviously wasn't worth the energy to argue.

Rachel smirked in triumph when I gave up and gestured toward the road ahead. "We're so close. From what we know, I'm pretty sure the Shop is in the next valley. Let's hurry."

Sumay made her voice audible to everyone. "That's actually the reason I wanted to catch your attention. There's System-built town ahead, and you'll find the highway has been upgraded once we reach the valley. We need to be cautious. Not all cultures play nice with humans."

"Let's hope they're friendly, but it's something to discuss later. We need to find a secure location first." Mr. Sanders gestured, indicating our vulnerable position.

We refocused on the task of sneaking forward. Tae Song took charge of me as we continued on our way, checking in regularly to make sure I was still functional.

We had found the borders of the alien-owned land and were under Shelter, attempting to gather more information, when Sumay noticed a band of warriors hunting in our vicinity.

"They're of the Beoheva, which is one of the safest of the Great Family conglomerates we could have run into. Their motto translates to something like 'Nurturing the soil is the best way to guarantee a repeat harvest.'"

We had finally decided to walk openly along the highway when Sumay suddenly became visible. "Run. There's something beneath you!"

I hurried to follow the others only to find that a root had twined around my ankle while we had been talking. In the time it took to untangle myself, the creature at the other end realized it had located something edible. It fully broke stealth to snatch me as the others shouted a warning.

Normally, I'd have activated Speed Boost immediately and easily avoided its grasp, but my reactions were slowed by exhaustion. Intervening objects shattered against my torso as it yanked me toward the center of its trap. I felt a tearing sensation as Hibernation activated, erasing the world around me.

Beoheva

I awoke submerged in a bitter nutrient bath with a metallic aftertaste that was somehow still the most satisfying and easily absorbable substance I'd encountered so far.

> **Hibernation Complete!** Your next hibernation will begin in 146 hours.
>
> **Warning!** Mass now 75% below optimal range. 90% debuff to Health and Stamina.

Sumay sent me a quick mental brush of relief, then reassured me everyone was safe. I was now under the care of the Beoheva, though all they could do was provide nutrients so I could rebuild mass at this point. Our group's assigned liaison, Vaone, would lead me to our group once I had healed enough to emerge.

I raised my absorption rate to the maximum and drained the last of the nutrients from the fluid. Most of my body was missing when I Scanned myself. I'd never lost this much mass before. Maybe I could try Morphing and end up with a miniature body though.

Sumay interrupted my thought process. *"Please don't try to Morph until you reach at least 75 percent mass! You'd have a basic, functional body at this size, but the Health and Stamina reductions mean you'll die if someone steps on you. They're adjusting the monitor to adapt to your new absorption levels."*

I resigned myself to the wait. Even with System-assisted healing to support the natural process of re-growing my body, it would take hours to rebuild enough mass to restore my usual size. A fresh surge of nutrients swirled around me. I settled in, requesting an update on what happened while I had been out.

It turned out the creature had ripped me apart. Tae Song managed to cut off the tendril that had grabbed me, but by then, we were at the center of the trap and he couldn't both fight off the monster's roots and carry me to safety. Rachel's Eye of the Storm had shielded us just long enough for the Beoheva hunting party to arrive and cut the core of the Subterranean Plant Elemental out of its cave.

They then rushed me to the clinic, looked up Polymorphs in their data, and submerged me in nutrient fluids so my body could rebuild itself while I was in Hibernation.

Sumay had been checking in on everyone while I was unconscious. Apparently, The Family were excellent hosts. They had offered our party a suite in their Welcome Center, where my friends were now recovering from the journey. However, they had yet to permit anyone to enter the Shop, explaining that they preferred to negotiate access for everyone at once.

Sumay scoffed at their explanation. *"They're studying us. Don't take what they offer at face value, Adrian, whether high or low. The Beoheva are known for always testing for wisdom, skills, and intelligence. They don't consider it cheating when someone willingly accepts an agreement that is less than ideal."*

Since the tank was completely opaque, I could only lie there in the dark. I spent the time reviewing records of the attack and figuring out how I could have done better. Sumay regularly left to update everyone on my condition, while I tried to be patient.

You have reached 80% of optimal mass.

Warning: *You have reached your absorption limit. Ingesting additional material will no longer improve your Health and Stamina due to overloading the ratio of fully established tissue to partially transformed matter. 50% debuff to Toxin Resistance due to 50% non-integrated matter. Complete integration will take 12 hours.*

Apparently speeding through rebuilding my body had limits. I was still 20 percent too low, but I'd have to regain the rest later. Purge ensured there was no residual poison in my channels. Morphic Disguise restored my human form as Sumay left to alert Vaone. It took several long minutes before the top of my temporary coffin finally flipped open. I sat up, ready to meet my first sentient alien.

"They look like a living Jizo statue!" Thankfully, I managed to control my excitement enough to merely send the thought to Sumay. I'd spent days reading articles on the Jizo a few years before, and the idea of the mystical monk who had become a protector of children had stuck with me.

Vaone swept forward, prepared to hand me a robe as I climbed out of the tank. They paused when they noticed my faux clothing and tossed the fabric into a nearby alcove. My reduced height meant I stood face-to-face with them. They had a calm, rounded face and a bald head with skin the color of limestone. Their monk-like robes, drooping eyelids, and large ears only reinforced my first impression.

I grinned. "Thank you for taking such good care of me!"

They replied in surprisingly fluent English. "We offer healing to anyone who reaches our land after surviving the high-Level zones surrounding us." They gestured toward the arched door. "I am Vaone. I will lead you to your friends. They are eager to see you again."

"I'm Adrian. Thank you! I can't wait to see them too." I glanced around the room, disappointed by the lack of visible technology. Narrow, curving lines of what appeared to be glowing stone were embedded into the upper walls, illuminating the space with a soft, silver light. The rounded room contained several arched alcoves with raised platforms made up with beds, though only the one behind me contained a tank. There was an extra mattress, pillow, and blanket folded on a raised shelf, also inset into a wall.

Sumay pointed her beak at where Vaone waited by the door, and I realized I'd gotten too caught up in my observations. "Sorry. I've never seen a room like this. It's very cozy!"

After a brief nod, Vaone turned to lead the way down a long hallway.

I tried not to slow down as I continued to stare at everything we passed. These people seemed to avoid sharp corners or straight lines; every surface was arched and curved. Even the floor sloped upward. If the hallways hadn't been designed to accommodate extremely large individuals, it would have been easy to assume I'd awakened in a hobbit warren. The colors made me think of a painted desert since they'd coated the entire hallway with striped layers of what appeared to be clay and sandstone. We passed widely spaced, arched doors with surfaces carved in unique, stylized patterns. There were no windows.

I glimpsed a few more Beoheva, similarly bald and robed in earthy tones, with no apparent indicators of gender. It felt like they were purposely ducking out of sight before we passed them. Sumay informed me the place was built on a rising spiral. Our seemingly unending path circled upward a few levels within a cone-shaped building.

Our guide finally stopped in front of one of the doors. "Inform your party that a casual appointment with the Vizier has been scheduled now that you have awakened. Someone will come for you an hour after lunch."

"The Vizier?"

Vaone bowed slightly. "We are honored to have a new Vizier in charge of this endeavor. The development of a new Dungeon World must be managed wisely, so The Family sent one of their own."

"Don't ask! It's considered an insult not to research this yourself." Sumay jumped in before I could embarrass myself. *"The Class of Vizier is only available to an official representative of the core Family government. They must believe Earth will be very profitable. This town is only a small part of their holdings on Earth if they have a Vizier in charge."*

The door opened suddenly, and Vaone nodded in farewell before turning and walking briskly down the curving hall.

"You're here!" Tae Song pulled me through the entry. Beyond him, the room was filled with sunlight pouring through a large, balcony window on the opposite wall. He measured me against his shoulder. "You made yourself a lot shorter this time!"

"I'm still missing twenty percent mass. It turns out it can be unhealthy if I rebuild too much at once." I smiled as he pulled me toward Rachel and Mr. Sanders, who were standing in the center of a sofa shaped like a concave donut with a slice taken out of it. It formed a comfortable window seat, piled with extra cushions. "Hey, guys! Miss me?"

Rachel shook her head. "I'm glad you're alive. I don't think a human would have survived that, not even with our Levels and fast healing."

I moved to the open section of the sofa across from Mr. Sanders. "Hibernation shuts down my system, which stabilized me. Then the Beoheva put me in a nutrient bath so my body could initiate repairs while I was unconscious. I wouldn't have survived without that kind of support."

"We'll have to learn how to create a nutrient bath for you, but that's for later." Mr. Sanders ruffled my hair before I could dodge him, then he settled back where he'd been sitting before I arrived. "It's good to see you, Adrian!"

Sumay draped herself over my chest as I sank into the surprisingly soft surface of the sofa before responding. "I'm glad you're okay too. I thought we were all done for and it was all my fault."

Rachel shook her finger at me. "I don't think getting caught by an underground monster is something to blame yourself for. It was so sneaky that Sumay only detected it after its tendrils broke the surface beneath us!"

Tae Song settled next to me. "We can talk about it later. For now, they said they'd meet with us once you woke up, and we need to decide our negotiation strategy."

"Oh, that reminds me!" I tried to sit up straight, but the cushions gave way under me. "Ugh, this thing is going to eat me."

I gave up and tucked my legs under myself for better leverage as the others laughed at my awkward flailing. When they finally settled, I returned to my interrupted thought. "Vaone told me the Vizier would meet with us after you eat lunch."

"Good to know!" Mr. Sanders leaned forward. "You'll have to speak for Sumay, since she can't maintain audio long enough to explain what we need to know."

I sighed, resigning myself to playing parrot as Sumay gave a summary of the Beoheva culture. "In the end, they're only dangerous if we start it. They destroy those who attack or cheat them. If we're useful as a business connection, client, or employee, they'll take good care of us. The worst that will happen is being sent home. Even then, they'll more than likely allow us to use the Shop since we have items of value to trade."

Rachel settled back against the cushions. "They've taken good care of us since they told us we would be their guests until Adrian recovered. This suite is as comfortable as a four-star hotel, though you never know… Maybe it's just the basics for them. I get the feeling everyone we meet is waiting for this Vizier of theirs to decide our status."

Something chirped near the door. Tae Song extracted himself from the couch and retrieved three covered trays from a compartment in the wall.

Rachel accepted her tray and crossed her legs as she tried to find a comfortable position to eat. "What I can't understand is why there are no tables. No kitchen either. Just the food delivery cabinet and these trays. I've been eating sitting on the floor since the sofa is too awkward."

Sumay hovered over my head and spoke audibly so everyone could hear. "If you're wondering how the Beoheva manage, try reclining and eating like the Romans of your history. The trays rest in front of you and you prop yourself up with cushions."

Everyone shifted position to try her suggestion.

Mr. Sanders raised an eyebrow. "I suppose this explains why our meals have consisted of foods that are easy to pick up and eat."

As we continued to discuss the Beoheva, the others eagerly consumed an assortment of finger foods. Most were unfamiliar, though I recognized the small empanadas. I wondered if they were trying local recipes or if the Beoheva happened to have a similar pastry in their culture.

The others finished eating and brushed their crumbs onto the trays. While setting them back inside the compartment, Tae Song found four sets of robes with a note explaining they were "appropriate attire for the occasion."

Sumay translated. "You're wearing rags, so let's get you cleaned up enough to be seen in public."

Everyone chuckled awkwardly when I shared that comment, then hurried to get changed. There was a yellow robe in the pile, perfect for my new size. I flung it on over my faux clothing, trying to get the hang of how to wrap the brown, fabric belt. Sumay ended up having to coach all of us through the belt wrap, since it wasn't as simple as it appeared. We settled in to talk until a chime sounded at the door.

Mr. Sanders opened it. "Is everyone ready?"

We hurried to join Vaone, who offered a brief bow before turning to lead the way.

Our long-awaited meeting ended up feeling rather anticlimactic. The Vizier was seated on a raised stool and wearing elaborate gold-fringed robes. A large, round table at about counter height stood in front of him, and to either side were guards in decorative armor.

Vaone stopped halfway to the table and formally bowed toward the Vizier, then turned and gestured for us to approach. "The Vizier welcomes you! No need to be formal. Stand on this side of the table, and we'll discuss your situation."

It was difficult not to feel a need for formality even in this supposedly casual setting. Sumay made a quick suggestion, and I stopped before approaching the table and bowed as formally as I could without having practiced the gesture. The others caught on quickly and bowed as well.

"Greetings, Vizier. We are grateful for your hospitality. I'm sure you are very busy, so thank you for meeting with us in person." I parroted Sumay's words, since I'd gotten stuck on worrying whether I'd bowed correctly.

The atmosphere in the room shifted immediately as the Vizier examined me with a keen interest that seemed out of place on their otherwise cherubic face. A memory of rows of smiling, stone statues, decorated with baby garments, popped into my head. I had to fight back the urge to laugh.

Vaone smiled slightly and gestured for us to move toward the far side of the table as they stepped to stand halfway between the two groups. "Now, please allow us to become acquainted with you. Who are you, and why have you come?"

Mr. Sanders briefly introduced each of us before explaining that we represented the remaining survivors from the school. He mentioned how we had brought what we'd hoped were the best drops from the monsters we'd fought and that we had sneaked through even higher Level zones in hope of finding a Shop so we could attempt to expand our Safe Zone and resupply.

Sumay pointed out that the Vizier seemed especially interested at the mention of the Fort and the fact that we were a boarding school before the System had arrived, even though they remained silent.

Instead, Vaone was the one to ask, "How many of the children survived?"

Even the Vizier bowed slightly in their seat on hearing that fewer than 40 students of the original 109 had survived.

I had grown numb to the grief most of the time, but their acknowledgement of our losses made them feel overwhelming once again. I shivered as the memories rushed over me. Tae Song's shoulder pressed lightly against mine in a quiet gesture of support.

After requesting more details, Vaone turned toward the Vizier as if awaiting a decision. Sumay noted a quick hand signal, though for all we knew they were having a lively telepathic conversation. Finally, they turned to look at Mr. Sanders once again. "You may officially make your requests, Brave Ones."

"Excellent!" Sumay fluttered her wings in excitement. *"They only offer informal Titles to those who impress them in some way."*

Mr. Sanders bowed his head. "We merely hope for access to the Shop, Vizier. We appreciate your willingness to accept strangers as guests. Also, we thank you for ensuring Adrian's survival."

"Access to the Shop is granted." Vaone's eyes flickered toward the Vizier for a moment before giving a brief nod. "We would reward you further. Do not accept immediately, since the process will be distracting." They waved a hand, and a notification popped up.

> **Hidden Quest Complete:** *You have managed to impress the Vizier with your behavior and your story of survival against all odds. You are now listed as Level 1 Commercial Partners of the Beoheva Family.*
>
> *As a reward, you have received the Basic Beoheva Business Information Pack, which will be installed on confirmation of your acceptance. This Skill pack contains the Basic Trade Language; Basic Agreements, Legalities, and Terminology; and The Basics of Social Conduct. You may also request information on employment opportunities and other services from The Family representative assigned to you.*

Sumay fluttered urgently on my shoulder as I finished reading. *"Pay attention!"*

Suddenly, I realized the entire group, including the Vizier, was now looking at me. This time, the Vizier themselves spoke. "Greetings, Rebel Within. We are honored by your visit."

I jumped and stared at them at the mention of my Title, having forgotten it might be important. After an admonitory peck from Sumay, I managed to bow and parrot her reply. "Greetings, Vizier. The honor is mine. I am grateful for your assistance or I would not have survived to be here." I could feel my friends' eyes on my back and wondered whether they'd be upset that I'd kept my Title a secret from them.

"Someone will meet you within the Shop to discuss an opportunity with you, Rebel Within. You have interested us greatly. May our connection be profitable." The Vizier rose to their feet.

We all bowed with Vaone as the Vizier left with their guards.

Vaone led us back to our door and held up a hand before we could enter. "Preparations must be made. I will return to guide you to the Shop in an hour."

"Your suite will remain available until you are prepared to return to your Fort. If you are willing to wait, we will soon send a party down the highway to assess the value of our territory near there. You may travel home with them if you wish."

I wondered why they always sent a guide as we entered the room.

"We are not yet trusted enough to wander unsupervised." Sumay swooped over my head and became visible, making Rachel jump in surprise. "This is a very good beginning! The information packet they gave you will be useful even outside The Family."

Sumay suggested we sit before confirming acceptance of the Skill pack. Apparently, we wouldn't merely be studying the information but actually downloading knowledge into our minds. I settled into the sofa and accepted the reward. My head felt the same way as it had after I'd studied all night with only a flashlight, so I closed my eyes, hoping the sensation wouldn't last too long. I blinked slowly when the rush of information settled and the odd sensation receded.

I instinctively checked the formalities of meeting the Vizier and shuddered. Sumay's prompts to bow had allowed us to pass the lowest possible bar of civility. Thankfully, the Beoheva seemed to understand the obstacles to intercultural communication and hadn't taken offence at our lapses. It also appeared that the Vizier wouldn't have bothered meeting with us themselves had it not been for my Title.

I winced at the memory of receiving the ironic notification that I was now Titled Rebel Within as I had sat in a tunnel deep underground. Surrounded by the decomposing remains of the creature that had eaten me whole, it had felt like salt on my wounds. I had done my best to ignore the notification in spite of Sumay's congratulations.

Mr. Sanders had finished absorbing his Skills as well and now sat studying me. He leaned forward and rested his chin on his hands when I met his eyes. "Just so you know, I've been aware of the Title since you returned. My Insight Skill allows me to see these details. However, you've been through a lot so I didn't ask about it. May I ask now? How did you get a Title?"

The others turned to stare at me expectantly, and I sighed. "I was only Level 2 at the time and still trying to escape the national park beyond the mountain where I'd decided to camp out until the school stopped looking for me. The rainforest had become a Level 100 zone. Anyway, a tunneling monster with a head like a shark and the body of a snake easily swallowed me in a single gulp. I was still too low Level and inexperienced to hide properly."

Rachel gasped. "How could anyone survive that?"

"I can still breathe when immersed in fluids and I'm immune to toxins, including digestive enzymes, as long as I'm alive." I hesitated. "Still, I'm not entirely certain myself. The details of the experience have gone foggy. Apparently, the Polymorph race instinctively protects its sanity by reducing access to memories of traumatic experiences.

"Sumay tells me that I managed to use the creature's own enzymes against it by clawing through the lining of the throat and using a blood thinner toxin I'd picked up earlier to prevent it from healing itself. I still don't fully understand how I managed to not only survive but kill the creature. Apparently, the System found the unexpected success of my frantic attempts to escape worth noting, and voilà! A Title."

Tae Song patted my knee. "Well, I'm glad you survived, Rebel Within!" He grinned. "I like it!"

Worming my way deeper into the sofa, I considered hiding behind a cushion. Being called a rebel had always been a precursor to punishment both with my parents and at school. I had hoped nobody would ever find out even though the System thought I was one. Being a rebel was a terrible flaw, not a cool Title or something I wanted for a nickname.

Mr. Sanders sighed at my reaction. "I know the Mission tends to be harsh when it comes to those who think for themselves, Adrian. Keep in mind that you were dealing with a kind of system back then too. The school just wasn't willing to blatantly explain its biases, definitions, and influences at every turn the way the current System does."

He slipped smoothly into lecture mode. "Some people follow systems and rules because it's easier to just do what an authority tells you to do than it is to truly process a situation. It takes time and effort to research the influences that create context and affect others' choices. As a result, the label of a rebel has been applied to thousands throughout history. It is only later that many of those stories of rebellion were revisited and reinterpreted. We frequently call them heroes, but that's not how they were seen by those who didn't appreciate the way they exposed the flaws in their societies. Even the Bible was primarily written by rebels."

Sumay became visible long enough to offer Mr. Sanders a vibrant, "Thank you! Adrian needed to hear this from a teacher."

Mr. Sanders coughed. "Er. I apologize for dropping lecturing you. I simply hope you won't be too hard on yourself, Adrian."

I managed to endure the resulting awkwardness until Rachel took pity on me and diverted everyone toward another topic. After closing my eyes, I pressed my face into a cushion and tried to think. I wasn't certain what to do with the thought that being a rebel might be a good thing. It felt like I accidentally dug my way out of a cave system I'd been buried in my entire life and found myself standing in the center of a vast plain—exposed, directionless, intimidated, and, for the first time, free?

The door chimed, and Mr. Sanders hurried to greet Vaone as I opened my eyes. It seemed everyone had heard the news that we were now considered more than mere savages. A bustling crowd of Beoheva and other aliens moved through the hallways. One even looked similar to the Diva Plavalaguna in *Fifth Element*.

Because we were finally on our way to the Shop, I tried not to get too distracted by the fact that I could now understand the casual conversations of people around us. Even so, it was obvious I was missing a lot of nuance. The information packet was apparently the very basics. I already knew I wanted more.

Negotiations

After touching an orb, we found ourselves suddenly standing in a Shop that matched the building we'd been visiting in shape, decoration, and colors. The only new element was a small, raised garden with a fountain in an alcove along the wall.

Sumay, now able to remain visible somehow, offered to take charge of haggling for better prices on our loot. It was the first time I'd seen an enthusiastic Beoheva. The shop keeper gesticulated wildly as Sumay countered their initial offers.

She soon called me over to telepathically explain every transaction in detail. I tried to notice the clues that would help me know when someone was testing to see whether I was a worthy trading partner. The others retreated to a smaller variation on the circular sofa to explore possible purchases as they waited. We finally cleared even Mr. Sanders's massive extra inventory of its last item. By that point, I managed to raise my new trade Skills by three Levels and my respect for my companion even further.

All together, we earned enough Credits to purchase the central plaza of the school and the four buildings surrounding it. This was only possible after a 50 percent discount for previous occupancy, combined with Mr. Sanders's 10 percent off for being a school administrator. At least we could now move into two of the smaller dorms. Our dining room and kitchens were also inside the Safe Zone, along with several classrooms that could be repurposed into residences.

With the remaining Credits, Mr. Sanders dove into choosing additional purchases and comparing the cost of building upgrades. His Skills were customized around managing supplies for the school, so he was in his element. He'd already delegated a couple thousand Credits to each of our fighters, including those back at the school. He explained that it would benefit the community for us to invest in ourselves and that, in the future, he would insist on splitting the profits. Everyone would also receive notifications and know we had reached a Shop.

My inventory had long been crammed full of rare loot from my initial struggle to rejoin my friends. I hadn't trusted anyone to remember the income wasn't a community resource, since everyone else had donated their loot to the school. Now that it was my turn to sell, I hesitated. What if I earned enough for another building? Would everyone understand if I chose to spend my income on a Spell to block Watson's influence and expose him?

Rachel and Tae Song were both immersed in figuring out what they'd buy with the Credits Mr. Sanders had given them, and I felt relieved that they wouldn't be watching. This time, Sumay had me take the lead and only offered suggestions. In the end, I earned a tidy sum of forty thousand Credits.

It only took a moment to switch to purchasing once we were through.

Sumay swiftly sorted our options by what we knew of Watson's Skills. "We need something that prevents or counters both Charisma influences and Spells that affect the mind."

She flicked three choices in my direction as the Beoheva in charge of the Shop now stood back and observed with calm detachment. Here, prices were fixed by the System and nonnegotiable.

"The first two are lower impact but what we can afford. Neither Spell is guaranteed to be completely effective, but they might work, and at the very least everyone will be slightly less affected by his buffs and Spells while the Spell is active."

Sumay pointed her beak toward the final option. "If you can persuade anyone else to contribute, this would definitely prevent him from manipulating everyone long enough to figure out how to handle him. As a bonus, it would also block certain Skills and Spells during battle."

Advanced Con Containment: *A vital Skill for law enforcement. Prevents the target from using charisma and mental-influence Skills and Spells for up to five hours.*

After reading the description, I turned toward Mr. Sanders and realized he'd already been listening in on our discussion.

"I can't contribute. I'm sorry." He shook his head. "There is too much needed to ensure basic survival for everyone right now. Righting the terrible injustice that has been done to you is something we are capable of resolving, even without Spells. It will just take longer for everyone to understand the need for action. I promise I won't give up until we find a way to ensure they deal with Watson."

I sighed. "It's all right. I already knew it would be too much to ask."

Even the full amounts both Rachel and Tae Song had received wouldn't have been enough to make up the difference. I glared at the remaining options, trying to resign myself to spending all my Credits on something that wouldn't solve our problem. There was nobody left to arrest the man or try him, but I wished I could find some reliable authority outside Watson's mental influence. It would be best if I didn't have to kill him to protect everyone.

Sumay flicked a wing toward Vaone, and I realized they'd been waiting for me to glance in their direction. They directed me through a door that had appeared in the far wall. "The meeting the Vizier mentioned has been arranged."

Once again, the decor was very similar, and I wondered whether it was a signature look for the sake of marketing or a cultural design based on the Beoheva planet of origin. This time, however, the room was empty aside from a table full of refreshments in the center of a traditional, rounded sofa. An array of tiny cups sparkled with a variety of liquids in all colors.

Vaone directed me to sit but remained standing outside the sofa's circle. "You will meet the individual of whom the Vizier spoke. We await their arrival."

A few minutes later, a flamboyantly dressed Beoheva burst into the room, clearly scandalizing Vaone. Vaone stiffened at the sight. Their iridescent robes gaped open in a way that The Basics of Social Conduct proclaimed would be insulting to anyone other than the most intimate of friends. I stood and bowed, admiring the brightly colored fan of feathers and flowers balancing precariously on their head. Whatever had I gotten myself into, it seemed interesting.

They turned to face me and proclaimed in English, "I am Genius!"

Even Sumay was unable to discern whether this was, in fact, their name or a self-description.

They noticed my confusion and clarified. "You may call me Genius. This human term suits me!" They languidly reclined on the sofa and gestured grandly at the table. "I have arranged for refreshments that should appeal to you, my dear Rebel Within. While you savor them, listen and consider my offer." They claimed one of the cups and tilted their head as they waited for me to do the same.

I took a cup filled with a pale-blue liquid with bubbles and sipped cautiously. The flavor was much clearer and sharper than anything I'd sampled before. "It's very good!"

"Of course! It is the fermented juice of a rare blueberry variety that only grows near mountain mineral springs. It is both nutritious and delicious!"

"Nobody would ever claim that randomly absorbing bushes and cacti—that happen to cross your path—develops a refined palate, Adrian." Sumay preened her wings. *"Of course this tastes better!"*

"Good point. I haven't had the chance to experience tastier fluids." I finished the juice and set the empty cup on the table.

"Excellent!" They nodded, obviously waiting for me to claim another cup before explaining the reason for our meeting.

"I am an Entertainment Producer!" They paused dramatically.

"Of course! And a stereotypical drama queen as well." I wondered why Sumay sounded offended until she allowed me to view the constant barrage of notifications that said I had resisted mental influences.

"Okay, I'll be careful. Now, shh. Let me listen!" This flamboyant individual personified the boldness I'd often wished to have.

They summarized a flattering description of a brave adventurer surviving against all odds. I only recognized this hero as myself because they had directly explained they were talking about me. The fruit juices were much easier to absorb than the myth Genius was spinning. The flavors filled a hunger I hadn't even realized existed. I continued to sip slowly, savoring each drop, as they continued to expand on the concept.

It became clear they were laying out the framework for some kind of play or movie based on an extremely skewed interpretation of the events leading to receiving my Title. Sumay mentioned they had probably purchased a summary of my experience from the System, since they knew details even I hadn't known.

Eventually, Genius finished circling and came to their point, sitting up and taking on a recognizably formal posture. "And so we wish to purchase your story for fifty thousand Credits."

The amount was enough to stun me into silence. I could expose Watson and still help purchase supplies!

"Think, Adrian. The first offer is a test." Sumay didn't seem inclined to speak out loud, leaving me to figure out how to react.

"Can you explain the process? You already seem to have access to everything that happened, so I'm wondering what the payment is for." I was pretty sure I sounded like an idiot.

Genius gestured as though flinging an invisible ball. "Here is the contract." A box popped up in front of me, and they sipped a golden juice I hadn't tried yet.

Sumay read the details through alongside me. *"They're asking you to give them your own memory files, you know. You're going to be visible to a lot of people if you do this. You dislike your Title, and they've made it the central feature of their marketing plan. Your race change might also bring up social elements you haven't considered. This is an established company with a big name, so the amount they're offering seems low given the exposure you'll be facing. I'm still not sure why they're even asking you in the first place! They have all the power here, and it makes me nervous."*

While the thought made me wince, the Credits were a huge lure. At the same time, I didn't want to pull anyone else into the consequences of my choices. By the time we reached an agreement that protected the school and my friends from exposure, I felt like I'd been pulled through a wringer.

Sumay continued to suggest I should hold out for a higher amount, but Genius had already tripled their offer. I couldn't help but feel like I'd won the lottery in spite of her warnings. I'd receive enough Credits to ensure I could counter Watson's manipulation, and that was all I cared about. An overly dramatic presentation of my struggle to survive and make my way back to safety when the System had arrived would have very little effect on my life. After all, I lived in the "isolated wildlands of Earth," as Genius had phrased it. There was nothing important about me, and I worried they might not even make back the Credits they were paying.

Sumay begged me one last time to at least request a day to think it over or demand legal counsel before signing, but I knew I'd hate myself if they changed their mind. The ability to block Watson's power was on the line.

After a formal exchange, a new notification glowed in front of me, showing an incredible increase in my personal fortune. I had to work hard to focus and bow formally to conclude the meeting instead of jumping for joy.

Having accomplished their goal, Genius rose from the sofa and examined my face, this time without the overt drama. "You have potential as a negotiator, so I will give free advice. It is in your best interests to require the attendance of your own legal advisor before you agree to contracts instead of attempting to create your own agreements within a system you don't fully understand." They bowed slightly. "Next time we meet, I expect you to be more of a challenge, my dear Rebel Within. I will be observing your progress."

Resuming their persona, they swept out of the room. I collapsed into the sofa, simmering amid an odd mixture of triumph over my sudden windfall and worry over whether I had failed to protect myself in a way that might come back to haunt me. Finally, I put the internal debate aside and focused on my new ability to protect everyone. As I settled down, I realized Vaone had vanished at some point during the negotiations and had only just returned.

They nodded formally. "Do you wish to continue shopping? Your companions have completed their transactions and returned to the suite if you prefer to join them there."

I returned to the main Shop to make the one purchase that was most important to me, then purchased Sumay the upgrade she'd been wanting so she could access more detailed information and detect predators more easily. Even after paying for both, I still had Credits left to help with purchasing supplies.

As I followed Vaone back to the suite, I wondered whether the others would be upset with me for spending so much without asking their opinions.

Eventually, Sumay grew weary of my mental flagellation. *"Stop it. You're not obligated to make every decision by committee. You've earned every one of the Credits you spent, and you could waste every last Credit on Guaraná and fantasy books, and nobody would have the right to complain. Get used to being an adult, Adrian. You'll need that confidence to deal with Watson."*

The others were relaxing on the sofa, immersed in their screens, as I let myself in. Outside, the sky was already dark.

Tae Song glanced up and gave me a relieved smile, patting the cushions beside him. "They told us you were meeting with someone about that offer the Vizier mentioned. How did it go?"

I tried to shrug off my fears and moved to sit between him and Rachel. At least he would understand my choice, even if nobody else would.

Mr. Sanders's face was tense as he gestured at his screen, and he jumped when I walked in front of him. "Adrian! You're back!" Obviously, he'd been intensely focused on whatever he'd been studying.

Rachel blinked back tears and looked up at me over the edge of a cushion. "I hope you have good news. Please, please have good news! I don't think I could handle anything else today."

"Are you guys okay?" Something must have happened after I left, since they hadn't been this gloomy before.

"I looked up the families of everyone at the Fort." Mr. Sanders's voice faded, and he shook his head. "Not many survived."

"It's only me and John left." Rachel's voice caught on a sob.

I sat beside her and leaned to offer her a hug, not knowing what to say. She burst into salt-flavored tears and curled up against my shoulder. Feeling helpless, I turned to look at Tae Song.

"My parents are still alive." He was obviously relieved but still looked hesitant. "Uh. There's no way to say this easily… but your family is dead too. I'm sorry."

I blinked. "I expected so. They were in the middle of an extremely high-Level zone. They wouldn't have accepted the System's suggestions since it doesn't mesh with their beliefs." I could see Tae Song had expected more of a reaction. His love for his parents would have made similar news as devastating to him as it had been for Rachel.

"Uh, you see, my parents always hated me. Maybe I should feel sad… Maybe I'm a terrible person… but …"

"It's okay to feel relieved when someone can no longer abuse you, Adrian." Mr. Sanders sighed. "They caused you far too many wounds while they were alive, so it's not surprising they didn't leave much of an injury by dying."

For some reason, the fact that he understood made me wish I could still cry. Polymorphs don't have that kind of physical reaction to grief, however. I shivered at the intense rush of emotions and leaned back into the sofa as Rachel's sobs began to slow.

It felt important to explain. "I finally realized I'd never had parents when they didn't stand up for me against Watson. I ran away from school because it hurt so much. But now? Now I've lost people who actually cared about me. Our friends died defending us so we can keep on living. That's what means the most to me, you know?"

Tae Song's face dropped against my shoulder and his tears combined with the flavor of Rachel's. Tasting their grief, I couldn't stop shivering as salt soaked into my skin.

Eventually, Mr. Sanders sighed. "Let's focus on the present. Tell us about your meeting, Adrian."

I explained the meeting with Genius at length, then quickly described my purchases. "I wanted to offer you the rest to help with supplies." I fell silent, waiting for Mr. Sanders's reaction. At some point during my story, Rachel had pulled away and was now wrapped around a cushion instead. Tae Song seemed to be on the verge of sleep against my shoulder.

"Huh." Mr. Sanders examined me closely and finally shook his head. "It's ironic that your Title will suddenly become so very public after hiding it for so long."

"You need to purchase the knowledge you'll need to deal wisely with our alien neighbors, Adrian. Make sure you're prepared to protect yourself both socially and physically. After you have what you need, then I might accept a portion of what remains to help provide for the school." He shook his finger at me. "I won't take your word for it. Only Sumay's will do."

Sumay burst out laughing. *"He's got you there, Adrian! No generous self-sabotage for you!"*

I shook my head, but Mr. Sanders interrupted before I could speak. "It isn't selfish to nurture your own strength, Adrian. Those who don't understand the importance of this task usually fail in their attempts to care for others."

Tae Song poked me in the side. "Shut up and just nod your head." His voice slurred slightly with drowsiness. "If you insist on letting us spend your money, we'll just spend it on you. Now let me sleep so I'll be awake to supervise your shopping excursion tomorrow."

Rachel chuckled at his words and curled up with a cushion beside me. Even Mr. Sanders merely stretched out where he'd been sitting and propped his shoulders on a pile of cushions. "Lights out." Surprisingly, the lights actually understood his spoken instructions, and the room went dark. None of them seemed inclined to retreat into the cozy alcoves to sleep in their own beds.

I watched the stars spin outside the window. *"Sumay, I think I might understand what you meant about choosing family."*

She snorted, looking up from whatever text she'd been reading. *"It's about time!"* She draped herself over a cushion and waved a wingtip in my direction. *"You were trained to be so certain that nobody could possibly want you that you didn't even notice we had all adopted you long ago. Now go Meditate or something. I just found a hilarious theory about how the world is secretly flat, and I plan to read everything I can find on the topic."*

The next morning, with everyone crowded around offering opinions on my options, I felt like I'd been dropped in the middle of a circus.

"You definitely need *Health and Well-Being for Polymorphs*, Adrian." Tae Song was having far too much fun pulling up anything with the word Polymorph in its name.

Rachel selected *The Mystical Secrets Behind the Success of the Beoheva* and pushed it into the stack of possibilities as well. I groaned at the title and eliminated it, then glanced to see whether Mr. Sanders might be willing to save me. He noticed my pleading expression but shrugged and looked away to hide his smirk.

Eventually, Sumay stopped laughing at their craziness and took pity on me. *"Here's what I recommend."* The massive pile shrank to a manageable level, and I sighed in relief, taking a look at the first item on the list.

Polymorph Childhood Education, Life Skills & Survival Pack

A collection of skills and basic information that most Polymorphs learn as children. It is useless to most, aside from freed slaves, the mind-broken, feral wanderers, and others who have been deprived of their birthright.

Sumay refused to meet my eyes after I read the description. I couldn't argue with her logic though. I needed to figure out how to make the best use of my new body since I'd managed the changes mostly by using Morphic Disguise to make myself as human as possible.

In the end, I left the Shop with a stack of new Skills, including *Intermediate Beoheva Business Skills & Culture; Countering Manipulation Techniques;* and *Basic Bartering & Negotiations.*

I was also wearing a new Mana-fueled, arm-mounted, variable-projectile launcher as well. Sumay had strongly suggested it as the most cost-effective solution to my need for some kind of weapon, along with the Skills to aim accurately and craft projectiles. This way, I could restock without access to the Shop. Everyone insisted I should wait and spend the pitiful remainder of my windfall on upgrades for Fort Tin or the school's new Safe Zone when we got home.

Justice

The next day, I found myself crowded into one of the two armored transports assigned to the survey team. Vaone, who seemingly had been permanently assigned to our group, sat nearby. Even with Survey Spells slowing us every few kilometers, they claimed we'd be at the school within a few hours. Since the transport had antigrav and didn't need to follow the many curves of the highway, we could have arrived within fifteen minutes.

My cramped position in the corner couldn't muffle my excitement over the first mechanically advanced technology I'd seen. Many System conveniences seemed to be fueled by ambient Mana, which meant they didn't always have a space-age aesthetic, but this transport could have been lifted straight out of a *Star Wars* movie.

Suddenly, Vaone sat up straight and spun to face us as everyone on board surged into a flurry of preparation. "It seems Fort Tin has fallen under an attack. Our battle group will drop first to clear the way. I will join you to meet with the survivors and help coordinate your defenses."

I jumped to my feet in a rush to run and help, then had to wait for an excruciating ten minutes until we settled to the ground and the ramp finally lowered. I paused in shock at the blackened rubble in front of me. Tae Song and Mr. Sanders pushed me forward. The bunk shelters were smoking, I hoped because someone had followed through on the plan to use them as a firewall in an emergency. Thankfully, the main buildings still remained standing, and I could see rifles poking out of the shutters. Two armored Beoheva warriors stood guard near the shattered doorway, stomping on a still-twitching body of a massive Milliscorpion. It was even larger than the one our party had killed only ten days before. A similar corpse lay draped over the cooking shelter, and the sounds of battle continued behind the building.

Mr. Sanders hurried forward with Rachel close behind him. I could only hope John had survived. I let Tae Song guide my steps as he moved to walk beside me. Better to just face the worst and get it over with. Vaone followed silently, their alien presence both intrusive and reassuring. The sounds of battle grew louder as we approached the building. More warriors ran to the side, their weapons raised. I hurried to get inside, knowing I wouldn't be of any help in the attack.

Tae Song began to turn, but Vaone caught his arm. "Our warriors have the problem handled. Your time will come. Introduce me to your people for now."

The Fort was dark due to the heavily shuttered windows. In the stream of light through the doorway, I saw groups of people huddling together. Too many were missing limbs. Rachel had already found John propped up near the door and was now stroking his hair as she gazed at his missing legs in shock.

Ms. Jaine and two other teachers hurried forward with Mr. Sanders close behind. "Thank you so much for assisting us in defending the Fort."

Stepping forward, Vaone gestured for me to join the group. Tae Song had already moved to join Rachel, and I reluctantly turned from my friends, wondering what I could do among the adults.

Vaone bowed slightly to Ms. Jaine. "I would do more, but I will need access to do so. The Family is prepared to purchase this Fort from you at a reasonable price. We planned to set up a guard post in the area even before knowing there were children to protect, but now the matter has become urgent."

I hoped they would accept, since we didn't have enough resources to shield the new Safe Zone now that we'd bought it. I'd been worried about how we would guard both areas even before the attack, and now we'd lost even more people.

Ms. Jaine glanced at Mr. Sanders, then shook her head. "It's not as though we have a hope of defending ourselves without enough credits to shore up the defenses on our new property. If we accept, will you help us clear the school Safe Zone so we can move soon?"

Vaone gave a firm nod. "When the security and protection of children are at stake, The Family is generous. We offer one hundred thousand Credits, which is what the Fort would be worth if it were not currently under siege. We govern this entire area, and the Fort will be tasked with securing safety for those who live here. This includes clearing your Safe Zone as long as you maintain your Commercial Partnership with us."

Sumay made herself visible. "This is a very generous offer by any standards."

Ms. Jaine sighed. "Give us a few minutes to discuss it. If you'll wait here, we'll return shortly." The teachers picked their way across the room, discussing the offer in low voices.

I turned to Vaone. "Thank you for your generous offer."

Their face tightened as they looked around the room. "We do not expose our children to such overwhelming dangers."

Eventually, Vaone must have received a message because they gestured for me to follow them back outside. "The area is secure for now."

Soon after, the teachers joined us. This time Watson was with them, his face tense with frustration. I took the opportunity to try Con Containment for the first time. My Mana dropped by four hundred, and I wondered when he'd notice that his abilities had been locked down for the next five hours.

Unsurprisingly, everyone agreed to sell the Fort. There were too many obvious benefits with our survival on the line, and the Credits would help them upgrade defenses on the new Safe Zone.

Vaone formally completed the transaction, and we watched in shock as the entire area transformed in moments. The broken walls reformed and thickened into a two-meter-high walkway around the perimeter. A long, curved building with multiple doors took shape on one side. Above us arched a shimmering shield. Beneath our feet, the rubble melted away, replaced by what appeared to be a ceramic patio. I turned back toward the original building, which remained unaltered. It looked dingy and out of place in contrast to the flowing design of its surroundings.

"Your building will not be altered until everyone has been moved into the new barracks. Our floor plan is too different from the current layout to upgrade it safely while occupied." Vaone nodded before turning away. "I will be in the transport if I am needed."

I bowed formally alongside Mr. Sanders as the rest of the adults looked on.

Watson's frustration had developed into a simmering rage. We barely made it through the door before Watson turned on me. "You may have saved us for now, but you have stolen our freedom in the process, you traitor! They're already taking away our abilities and planning to enslave us."

Mr. Sanders pushed between us, knocking Watson back a step. "I take it you've realized you can't use your Spells anymore? Did you really try to manipulate our benefactor, or were you attempting to control our choices instead?"

"You all agreed it is my job to ensure we remain united and organized as a team, working together to ensure our survival! Why are you suddenly questioning me as if I am in the wrong for doing what you yourselves asked of me?"

Ms. Jaine stepped forward. "My Skills are currently working just fine, Watson, and I have seen no evidence of betrayal. We agreed to do what it takes to secure our safety. Adrian had nothing to do with this decision. What is going on with you?"

With a sigh, Mr. Sanders leaned back against the wall. "I thought we'd postpone this discussion until after we take care of moving everyone over to the barracks. Still, I suppose I can summarize for now. First, Watson has been using his Skills to assault our students and cover up the evidence. Second, Adrian purchased a law enforcement Spell that will temporarily prevent Watson from using his Skills and Spells so he can't manipulate anyone."

He turned toward Watson. "The block on your abilities has nothing to do with the Beoheva. It's a necessary precaution. I completely support limiting your abilities until we can sit down and review the evidence Tae Song and Adrian have gathered."

"I've done nothing wrong!" Watson sneered at me. "I can't believe you'd accept the word of a rebellious child when you know how much I've sacrificed to help everyone."

Mr. Sanders sighed. "You really don't understand, do you? There is no such thing as a secret anymore, Watson. The System records everything we do. We all have access to our own experiences. With enough Credits, anyone's records can be bought. When I looked into it, even I have witnessed questionable behavior toward Tae Song, actions for which I would usually have immediately brought you before the committee. Yet for some reason I forgot these events occurred until I ran a specific search for them."

The expressions of the teachers varied, from Miss Angela's intense concern to Mr. Pots' firm solidarity with his longtime friend. Most just looked overwhelmed at this new complication on top of the tragedy of the attack. A heated conversation broke out, and I couldn't figure out whether they were more offended at the accusations against Watson or the fact that the System was so invasive as to record everything.

As their voices began to rise, Tae Song interrupted. "We could use some help moving to the barracks. They have bathrooms and food over there and enough beds for everyone. Besides, I think Liaison Vaone would appreciate upgrading this building as soon as possible so they have a place for their own people as well."

Ms. Angela immediately turned to gather the younger kids, who were the only ones who had made it through without a scratch. Her shirt was shredded and bloody on the back, though she'd already healed.

As I helped move our few remaining supplies, I learned we had lost another seventeen of our friends. Cher was among them. She was stung while carrying John to safety, and Joachim hadn't been able to counter the poison in time to save her. I ended up claiming the alcove next to John, and I huddled there listening as he and Rachel cried together.

I found myself wordlessly shivering with grief as Sumay murmured comfortingly. It felt as though I'd been trapped in ice. Eventually, Tae Song found me and pulled me out into the sunlight next to the transport.

Sumay showed herself briefly, hovering face-to-face with Tae Song. "I'm leaving Adrian to you for now. I'll be back soon."

He bowed as though she were offering him a great honor. "I'll be here."

I sighed as his words mirrored the painful thought that had been drilling into me all afternoon. "If only I'd been here, I could have saved Cher." I dropped to the ground and stared up at the cloudless sky.

"You know 'if only' is just a dream." Tae Song settled next to me. "We'll help others in honor of her memory."

We sat in silence for a time as I refocused on trying to solve the problem lying ahead of us. "What are we going to do about Watson?" I winced at the memory of Watson's reaction to my Skill. "He's furious that I can shut him down with Con Containment, and several of the adults still aren't sure who to believe. I overheard them talking, and the things my parents told them still undermine me as a witness.

"Since you're my friend, some are jumping to the conclusion that I've somehow corrupted you. Mr. Sanders and Miss Allison have seen enough to believe us and are on our side, but the rest are overwhelmed and confused."

Tae Song settled his swords across his knees. "I'm not sure what they'll do even if they do acknowledge he sexually assaulted us and abused his power to manipulate them. Kill him? Even kicking him out is equivalent to a death sentence. Imprisoning him would be a burden on the rest of us when we scarcely have enough people to protect ourselves. We're basically cut off from justice even if they agree he did wrong."

A new voice broke in on our conversation. "Justice resides with The Family of the Beoheva and arrives with us when we claim new territories. Since you are Commercial Partners, I can represent you. Only keep in mind that, once we become involved, our justice is enforced by the System, without exception."

I spun in place, surprised to see Vaone standing nearby.

"Vaone is your ally in this." Sumay landed on my shoulder. *"I decided it was important for them to know the difficulties you are facing and told them of the problem before bringing them to you in time to overhear your conversation."*

I nodded at Vaone. It was too late to debate Sumay's decision, and I had to admit I couldn't think of any other solution aside from becoming a murderer.

"Join me, if you will." Vaone smiled slightly. "I prefer not to sit on the ground."

We scrambled to our feet and followed them into the newly remodeled central building of the Fort, now a curved, trilevel cone with a ramp spiraling up the exterior to a platform at the top. The second level contained a large, round room with a stone table in the center, reminiscent of the room in which we had met the Vizier.

"I'll call Sanders and the rest." Sumay didn't wait for me to agree before swooping out the door.

Vaone examined us for a moment. "First, let us discuss how best to protect the two of you from those who may not understand your choices. We wish to hire Tae Song and any others who are suitable as guards, to be stationed here at the Fort.

"Adrian, your unique abilities are useful to us as well, though you will primarily be exploring our lands in search of Dungeons and nests. As employees of The Family, you will live in the barracks, receive a weekly income, and work alongside our mercenaries to secure the area. Your primary tasks will be to locate resources, cull predators, and guard the Safe Zones within our territory. Are you interested?"

Tae Song and I glanced at each other, then nodded firmly. "Yes."

"We'll negotiate the details later. Understand we would have made this offer even without these circumstances. However, even if these people choose not to accept our judgement regarding this Watson, you will no longer be under their influence."

Vaone's eyes glinted with anger. "Those who prefer to debate blindly rather than seeking out information that easily enables them to know the truth have not earned the right to be responsible for guarding the young!"

"I agree!" Mr. Sanders stepped through the door, closely followed by the rest of the teachers.

Watson was looking a little too smug. I realized my Skill had worn off and quickly refreshed it. Moments later, his expression shifted from arrogance to fury. Had he really assumed I would let him use his abilities in this situation?

"We should deal with this later! We need to clear out the Safe Zone and move everyone into the dorms. This is a waste of our time." Mr. Pots stood beside Watson as the others arrayed themselves around the table.

Tae Song stepped forward nervously. "I know you're concerned about the monsters outside, but those are easy to recognize and to fight. I'm more worried about a monster among us. How can I protect myself and my friends when you don't take this threat seriously?"

Vaone glanced around the room. "Do you accept that as Liaison of The Family, everything I observe of your behavior will affect my decisions? I am the one who decides on trade privileges. I decide on the level of support and protection we offer your community. Think carefully where you stand. Sexual assault is not a crime taken lightly among the Beoheva."

When nobody objected, Vaone masterfully took charge of the room. They led everyone step by step through intense questioning, clarifying the sequence of events since I had spoken up, before the System had arrived.

By the time he linked everyone to the records of Tae Song's interactions with Watson, most of the teachers had already shuffled away from Watson's side of the table. A series of nauseatingly manipulative interactions played out in front of us. Eventually, even Mr. Pots stepped away, unable to overlook the evidence that shattered his trust in the end. For once, Watson seemed unable to find an excuse and stood silently, his eyes narrowed.

One of the warriors who had arrived with the transport appeared soon after to remove Watson from the room. He exploded in fury, and the sound of his ranting trickled back through the open door. "They manufacture lies using this cursed System, and you just swallow them whole? How can you trust these demons?"

His voice faded in the distance as everyone slumped wearily. Realizing that nobody was prepared to take the lead, Mr. Sanders finally hustled the teachers from the room before turning back to study Tae Song and me with a shake of his head. "I'm sorry this didn't happen sooner. I should have pushed harder when you first spoke up, Adrian."

Tae Song slumped against the wall beside me, seeming as emotionally drained as I felt. I hesitated a moment, fishing for the right words. "It's like you said. Everyone was trapped by the old system in the same way that we're stuck with this new System. It just wasn't as obvious. I'm just relieved there are ways to prove the truth now, and that it's finally over."

"My wife and I loved being dorm parents, since we couldn't have children of our own. She would have been proud of you both, just like I am." Mr. Sanders's voice cracked, and he patted my shoulder gently before walking into the shadows beyond the door.

As he left, Tae Song dropped to the floor and scrubbed his face. "I don't want to sleep in the barracks tonight. I'm sure they'll soon start judging me for being gay."

Vaone moved to the door, then turned and nodded. "We'll complete our negotiations in regard to your employment tomorrow morning. For now, rest here. I understand you find our gathering circles comfortable." As they spoke, the table sank into the floor and a familiar sofa arrangement slid out from a wall to take its place. They stepped out and the door closed behind them.

Sumay settled on my shoulder as I offered a hand to help Tae Song back to his feet. We dropped into the sofa with sighs of relief.

"I guess we can consider ourselves officially graduated now that we're going to work for a living?"

He laughed. "I could never have imagined we'd be jumping at the chance to work as guards."

"At least I've got friends to face it with me." I slumped back against the cushions and sighed.

"I can't imagine it any other way." He flopped to the side against a cushion and craned his neck to look at me. "As far as I'm concerned, we're family, you know."

I turned to rest my head on the same cushion and stretched my feet in the opposite direction. "I feel the same way. Maybe we can adopt Rachel and John too."

He yawned. "And Mr. Sanders. I think he wishes he'd been your dad."

"Maybe... huh." It was too much to think about just now. "Go to sleep already. We can talk about this more later." Whatever lay ahead, I'd just have to do my best to prepare myself.

I opened one of the books Sumay had insisted on, *Inside Polymorph History and Culture*. It was time to explore this new life. Maybe one of these days, I'd find the courage to show Tae Song my new form.

Name	Level	Adrian	21	Class	Toxic Apothecary
Race	Polymorph (A)	Title	Rebel Within
Health	500	Stamina	500
Mana	520	Mass	60 (55-75 optimal)
Strength	31	Agility	32
Constitution	55 (-5)*	Perception	25
Intelligence	52	Willpower	36
Charisma	15	Luck	15

Skill Descriptions

Skill	Description
Subversive Stealth Skill	Hide from localized System Scans, Spells, Skills, and Senses.
Chameleon Skin Skill	Superficial skin alterations to merge into the environment.
Danger Sense Skill	Warning of immediate danger & direction of origin; improved chance to see through stealth.
Speed Boost Skill	Temporarily increases speed.
Morphic Disguise Spell *	Design & save 1 full body design/10 levels. -5 to Constitution while in any Disguise affecting more than 50% mass. (Polymorph Only) 24 hr cooldown & affected by Minor Morph cooldown.
Minor Morph Spell	Design & save minor modifications under 10% mass. Up to 5 saved traits/10 Levels (Polymorph Only) 8 hr cooldown after affecting more than 30% mass.
Environmental Barrier Spell	Absorb nutrients and trace Mana by crushing the juices from nearby plants. Creates a weak armor layer from the pulp. Running out of Mana before releasing the residue results in shredded skin. (Polymorph Only)
Dimensional Lab (Perk)	A dimensional space designed to store and process chemicals; Spells: Identification, Breakdown, Recipe Record, Experimental Blending, and Creation; Spells only available within laboratory. Note: Initiates Apothecary Class; Rare "Toxic" variation is only available to Polymorphs.
Scan	Research the properties of substances and systems to inform replication via morphing.
Racial Trait	**Description**
Remorph Skill	Easily return to unaltered Polymorph body, resized according to mass. Heals damage, aside from suboptimal-mass debuffs.

Body Morph Skill	Alter appearance naturally by using a practical, practiced understanding of physical traits & the qualities of the tissue. DNA based replicas become possible with skill mastery.
Optimal Mass	Optimal mass determines the scope of potential transformations. Morphing into shapes outside of optimal mass range comes with increasing debuffs.
Non-Standard Mental Makeup	Gives a high resistance to traditional mental and charisma influences. Reduces access to memories of physical pain and torturous experiences. Highly susceptible to manipulation by those who have experience/Skills/Spells for dealing with Polymorphs.
Absorb	Draw in Mana, air, and nutrients via direct contact with fluids or atmosphere.
Hibernation	Stay alert up to seven days, followed by 22 hrs of hibernation.
Toxin Resistance	Unaffected by most toxins.
Purge	Filter toxins from blood/living tissue in self (& others when combined with absorb). A necessary first step before switching secreted toxins.
Toxin Production	Create and secrete a single toxin based on a tangible sample.

Intermission Five

"Interesting. I'll let Lord Roxley know. But in the short-term, the Boheva and their wards are of little consequence to us," Vir said, dismissing the note. "As for the race changes, I believe many will come to regret those choices in the end. Perhaps not this one... but most."

"Like Tim, because he doesn't feel human anymore?" Amelia's eyes narrowed in suspicion.

"And is not really of the other species, yes," Vir said. "It is not as simple as purchasing a gene wash to be another species. Culture, beliefs, experiences are not something the System can easily provide."

"But it can."

"For a price. And only as an informational download." Vir shook his head. "A dog given sapience is still a dog in the end. A human changed into another race might, biologically, be of that race, but they will not think like them. Not yet. In time, some of their behaviours might reflect their races. It can be as simple as a preference for sunny spaces or open accommodations, but they will not be of that race.

"Galactic experience has shown that such drastic changes are rarely to the satisfaction of those involved. In fact, many decide to change back eventually. Others, find themselves in their own communities."

"Huh." Amelia leaned back. There were parallels to pre-System life, of course, but those parallels were only surface deep. Still, it was something worth considering and raising. A new factor to watch for, especially as the children who grew up in the apocalypse neared their age of majority. More complications.

For a time, the pair worked in silence, going over the documentation. Occasional new stories arose, were debated and filed away. It was one other file that sent shivers down her back. A reminder, of the kind of world that they had survived. The destruction that they had all seen. And barely escaped.

Overture to Obliteration

by L.A. Batt

[*Author's note: This story contains Te Reo and Māori words and phrases. For a simple description and pronunciation guide, please refer to the section at the end where each of these words have been listed in the order they are mentioned. Thank you for reading.*]

I'm dead.

Well, not really, but with all that's happened since the System kicked in ten months ago, turning our lives into some kind of messed up role-playing game, it's been easier to get through the day if I think I'm already worm food. As the old saying goes, the lower your expectations, the less you're let down.

You might be asking yourself, what's a win look like for this joker? If I'm being honest, all I want before that final nap is to listen to some actual music again. Gods, how I miss music.

***

I scream as my jacket and chest are mauled by three razor-sharp claws, dropping my health from near full to just below half. Are you serious? That was my favorite gods-damned jacket. Now I'm pissed. I scramble back while fumbling down a health potion. Mid-gulp, I narrowly avoid a follow-up strike from the Kiwinuipāhue's massive beak.

"Oi, Nate! You right?" Jason—sorry, *Jase*—my remaining party member calls. I ignore him for the moment. "Yeah, you look all right. I'll, uh, stay over here. Yell out if you die, 'kay?"

Being a Level 25 Barkeep he doesn't have any offensive skills, save a few melee moves he picked up from the Shop for dealing with the odd roughneck. Honestly, he's only out here for the free XP. Well that, and to act as a second pair of eyes while I hunt.

"Mother…" I leap aside, dodging another leg attack. The wounds across my alabaster skin stretch, itching as the health potion does its trick.

"Fucking…" When I roll to the right, the overgrown fowl rushes past, blasting through the trunk of a tree, throwing wood chippings, dirt, and foliage into the air.

"Killer…" *Shit!* I stumble back a few steps. With all the debris flying around, that swipe came a bit too close.

"Kiwis!"

I finally find my moment and plant my feet. As the Kiwinuipāhue comes at me, I renew the activation for Warrior's Rage, temporary boosting my strength by four, and thrust the tip of my spear straight through its right eye and into the dino-vampire-bird's cranium.

As the Kiwinuipāhue spasms, I hold fast, continuing to allow the adrenaline from the fight to bubble inside me. Finally, I see the glow of its remaining red eye go dark and feel its body go limp. These pricks have tricked me before though, so I wait a touch longer to make sure it's dead. A moment later my tension disappears a touch as the System message I've been waiting for appears.

Quest Updated: Cull the Bloody Plunderers (Repeatable)

Kill the roaming flocks of Kiwinuipāhue that have taken up residence in and around Maraetotara and the Nga Tapuwae O Toi Track.

Kiwinuipāhue Killed: 14 of 20

Nice. One kill closer to those sweet, sweet quest completion experience points.

After wriggling the spear free, I check the body for loot. Then I see them. They're exactly what I've been spending the last few months out here collecting.

"Boo-*ya!*" I scream, jumping with joy.

Oops. Remembering where I am, I crouch, listening for any signs of movement.

"How'd'ya go? You get them?" Jase asks. "Can we head back'ta town now?"

Taking a moment to calm down, I reply in a softer tone, "Yeah, man, that, oh man. Haha!" I laugh, still unable to believe my luck. "This haul should actually tip me over my target."

I do a few mental calculations while scrolling through the System logs, and a stupidly large grin forms on my face.

Items acquired

1x Kiwinuipāhue corpse

1x Kiwinuipāhue beak

6x Kiwinuipāhue claws

2x Gastrolith Greenstone

The beak and claws should make for decent trophies I can use to boost my attributes using the Trophy Hunter skill. My last lot broke days ago, so these replacements will make things easier going forward. The real jewel though... well, I only started the day with the hopes of finding enough loot to push me a little closer to my savings goal. But now, thanks to these rare greenstones, I'll finally be able to afford an entry level *Audiblic Split-Mind Implant*, with the module titled *Audio from Earth - The Complete Collection*.

The first device, that one's installed in your head. It allows you to store, play, and perfectly focus on two sources of sound at the same time. *An elegant companion for a more bloodthirsty age*. The second's a library of every piece of recorded audio the System was able to gather from our world. Yep, the add-on contains every single news report, podcast, secret phone recording, and piece of music from Earth's digital history.

And I'm about to own. It. All.

I found these beauties in the Shop shortly after the Vaaharu turned up. The Vaaharu, see, they're this weird-looking race of upright cat-humanoid creatures that rocked up and laid claim to my hometown, Whakatāne, then gave us access to the Shop. Well, it's not like they did that last part on purpose. Having the Shop there just made what they were planning to do easier.

Once they were done setting themselves up, they went around hiring anyone willing to work for food and a little security, then enslaved anyone who pissed them off. Next thing you know they're using our access to the ocean for a food-gathering operation to feed their settlement in Rotorua.

A lot of people were ticked off about all this. Whatever. New world, new rules. That shit happened a week or so after the System took over our lives, and that's going on ten months now. Since then, while everyone else has been buying up the buildings around the Whakatāne High School and Kopeopeo—or trying to get what's left of their whanau, err, *family* out of slavery—saving for these two marvels has been my one and only driving force. The thought of being able to listen to my favorite bands again sends cascading waves of joy through me. Just once more before I die.

After throwing the loot into my inventory, I close it and look at the cloud-filled sky. Pretty sure there's a few hours of light left.

I look over at Jase. "While the hunting's good, wanna try for a few more?"

A look of dread crosses his face.

"Besides," I say, flourishing a hand before pointing at him, "I may have blown past my target, but we still need to eat, and you're coming up on a year in this hellhole with only the ability to slap around a drunk. We need to get *you* some decent combat skills."

"C'mon, man, everyone else has already head back, and these Level 50 zones freak me out. I only stayed 'cause it's good XP when it's just us, but I sure as hell don't wanna be 'round when the grownups of that flightless fucker turn up." Shuddering, he continues, "I really don't want them following us back to town, bro. There's so few of us left. Last time one snuck by the guards, six people were killed in their sleep."

"Mmmmm, but—"

"Shrivelled up like raisins, Nate!" he says, emphasizing his point with his fingers. "Their faces were all screwed up like they were in agony but couldn't do nothin'. They didn't even get a chance to fight!" I look back, still unconvinced, and he gives me a serious glare. "You know they almost got El—"

"Ahhhhh! Okay, fine!" Throwing my hands in the air, I groan loudly in annoyed resignation. Then rounding on him, I thrust my finger in his face. "But dinner's on you when we get back."

Scoffing, he says, "Pfft. It's my bar. It's almost always my shout."

"Ha!" I say as I walk toward town. "True that! But this time I've got an excuse. After a visit to the Shop I'll probably be stone broke."

"Didn't ya just sa—"

"Besides"—I grin mischievously—"who's to say we don't run into something on the way?"

***

Growing up in this retirement village of a town, I never thought I'd be here in my thirties, let alone be stuck here when shit went post-apocalyptic. To be clear, it's not as if any bombs were dropped or viral outbreaks occurred. No, we basically caused the annihilation of the human race all on our own, or so the various aliens we've encountered love to remind us.

All we had to do was follow one simple rule—*treat guests with respect*. Or something like that. Unfortunately, that's a little hard to do when no one tells you the rules. Then again, maybe slicing open the first extra-terrestrial you come across isn't the best way to introduce yourself to the galaxy. Thanks, America!

I kid! I'm sure we'd all have done the same thing. Well, maybe not Canada. Or Iceland. Or us here in little ol' New Zealand, but who's to say? Guess it'd all depend on where they landed, and who they talked to, *and to be fair*, they really should have done some homework before being all like, "Oh, 'ello, gov,

I'm from the Galactic Council, this is the System, and your world is scheduled for demolition."

Okay, so obviously I wasn't in the room when they took the guy hostage and gutted him alive, but growing up on a healthy diet of Douglas Adams, Monty Python, and Phil Janes (*The Galaxy Game*, great book, highly recommended), I can only assume that's how it went down.

On the surface, you'd think I'd be having a blast. Hell, I'm sure my teenage self would be going out of his mind with happiness. Slaying monsters, meeting aliens, scoring loot, levelling up, and getting the babe (because that's what the story says will happen.) Yep, what's not to love about having your whole world be turned into a role-playing video game? Oh right, all the death, destruction, general loss of life, and the fact that *this. Isn't. A. Game!*

Sure, we have an inventory, pop-up windows, Skills and spells, but *there's no campaign*. There is no epic story, no plot-armored companions or loved ones, and certainly no respawns. At least not for us sentients. Any moment could be my last. One wrong step, one missed attack, one unexpected monster spawn, and *poof,* it's lights out. Just like damn near the entire freaking planet. Shit, man, there're only a few thousand of us left round here—not including the cats, that is.

Man, I just want my music. Please let me live that long.

***

The walk back to town is mostly uneventful. Only one group ambushed us. A couple of Flametails came out of nowhere as we were leaving the bush trail at the base of Mokoroa. These mutated former fantails, now with two-meter-wide wingspans, leave a trail of roaring blue mana flames as they fly, and as you probably guessed, they use fire attacks. How they don't burn down the countryside is beyond me. Quirks of the System, I suppose.

Jase assists this time, pouncing on them to deal the killing blows after I finish instilling fear, stunning them with my level 1 skill in War Thunder. Downside to this final scuffle of the day—no decent loot. Plus side—the meat will still sell, so at least we managed to cover a light celebratory feast.

We part ways at the War Memorial Hall. Hoping to get more bang for our buck, Jase wanted to try flogging the Flametails off to the community hunters before making his way to the Shop. Meanwhile, I wander along Commerce Street, heading for the central business district.

Along the way I pass several groups of people reeking of fish. They're workers coming from the makeshift factory down near the Information Centre, over where access to the Shop was set up. My guess is that the Vaaharu set up their little operation there so they could get the packaged food into the Shop quicker. Pretty smart of them to do that. Gave them plenty of automatic safe zones to fish from, and they only had to buy up a few of the buildings across the street to make their entire living area and workspace a monster-spawning-free space.

Rather than go directly to the Shop, I head toward my place to freshen up and replace my torn clothes. Won't help me to look like a right mess in front of our *alien overlords*, especially when I live less than a five-minute stroll away.

As I walk, I get to thinking. Now that I've got enough for the audio equipment, I wonder how much it would cost to repair my jacket, or better yet, upgrade it? I figure before I make any rash decisions, I'd best check my skill sheet to see what I'm working with:

Status Screen			
Name	Nathaniel Atkinson	**Class**	Kaikiko Toa
Race	Human (Male)	**Level**	37
Titles			
Kai Taua, Pyrorational			
Health	470	**Stamina**	470
Mana	320	**Mana Regeneration**	78 / minute
Conditions			
Exhausted			
Attributes			
Strength	86	**Agility**	51
Constitution	47	**Perception**	51
Intelligence	32	**Willpower**	83
Charisma	22	**Luck**	21
Class Skills			

Haka (Level 1)	Haumia's Trap (Level 1)	Te-koha-o-Tū (Level 1)	Warriors Rage (Level 4)
Tāne's Sight (Level 1)	Trophy Hunter (Level 1)	Heart of the Warrior (Level 1)	Rehua's Light (Level 1)
Meteoric Strike (Level 1)			
Additional Skills and Spells			
Instantaneous Inventory (Maxed)			

So weird how the language jumps around. Today it's Kaikiko Toa, tomorrow it's Vengeful Warrior. Hell, some of them aren't even proper translations. Cool as it is, it's not like Haka actually means War Thunder. I really wish the System would make up its damned mind. If it even has one.

Fuck, I don't even really know what the System is, other than it's what creates the floating blue screens, stats, and monsters… and don't get me started on that impossible *What is the System* quest. Been sitting in my Quest Log for months and hasn't progressed an inch. *Ugh.*

Looking through my stats, I could probably do with a few more offensive and movement Skills, but for now, I feel pretty rounded. Honestly, I'd rather not spend my credits on them at the moment. Picking up the Instantaneous

Inventory was painful enough on my wallet. Thankfully it was totally worth it, what with the number of weapons I go through during an average day of fighting. Summoning items from my inventory with only a thought and being able to quickly collect loot without having to open System windows every time really does improve my ability to kill things. Hmmm, now that I think about it, that's kinda morbid… maybe I need to take up cooking?

Going over my inventory one last time, I see the proof of my efforts these last few months. I've got several stacks of the rare greenstones, a pile of random monster drops, another dozen low-quality steel spears, and just over a hundred thousand credits.

It feels nice to know that I'm so close to completing my goal. Guess I'll have to come up with a new one? Suppose I *could* do with some armor. Once the implant's been hooked up, that is. Not to mention that since day one my weapons have been cobbled-together pieces of crap—I mean, scraps from the hardware store—so, hmmmm, I wonder…

Turning into Canning Place, I pass the back of the bar Jase bought from the System and aim for my one-bedroom hole-in-the-wall above the old kebab place. Maybe I could finally look into buying this joint from the System.

Lost in thought as to what I could be spending my hard-earned credits on, I begin the jiggle work to unlock my door. Then, coming from the direction of the bar, I hear a soft padding of footsteps.

As they slowly grow in sound, a woman's voice calls, "Nate. Naaate! Wait uuup!"

I turn to see a fallen angel—Ellie godsdamned Hughes. Looking at her, I want to see the girl I knew and loved. Someone healthy, laughing, and always up for an adventure. I remember her curly brown hair flowing in the wind, one hand clamping down a floppy wide-brimmed sun hat as she catches the hem of her dress with her other, all while dancing among the shallow waves. I want to see that, but all those memories are shattered the moment I lay eyes on her.

Her hair looks like bird's nest. Sunken eyes, pale skin, and loose-hanging clothes scream of someone throwing away their chance at a new life. It completely baffles me. You have to be seriously dedicated to look that bad in a world where most issues disappear in less time than it takes to cook a pizza. Then again, who am I to talk? At least she's doing what she enjoys while working on her *accidental* suicide.

Walking inside, I say over my shoulder, "Go away, Ellie. We're done. You messed up. I want nothing to do with you. Goodb—uh... "

I'm too slow, and she manages to sneak an arm in before I get the door closed. "Wait, pleaasse, c'mon, I know you got some cash stored away." She's shaking a bit. "You and ya mates are always off playing in the woods. I just want, ya'know, a little something to help." She looks at me, makeup running and the bags under her eyes showing clearly, desperation written all over her face. "I can, I can do something for it. *Anything*. I just need a few hundred creds, *that's all*."

Her words spill out in a slurred mess as she tries, and fails, to force herself through the crack. Watching her struggle, I say nothing. After a few more attempts she gives up, and just like that she slumps to the ground, passed out, one arm inside, her face leaning against the edge of the doorway.

I feel guilty, revolted, and nauseated. Why'd she turn out this way? Why'd someone who'd just become a junkie in this new world get to live while so many didn't? Why didn't she let me help when all this started? Why'd she...

Reality snaps back, and I'm looking at the hollowed out mess of a woman I once loved, lying on the sidewalk.

"Jesus. What's wrong with you?" Looking closer, I call upon the god of forests and birds to activate Tāne's Sight, and as I read the System message I'm shocked to see just how close to the edge she really is.

Status Screen			
Name	Elise Hughes	**Class**	Ranger
Race	Human (Female)	**Level**	6
Titles			
None			
Health	20/110	**Stamina**	5/110
Mana	0/240	**Mana Regeneration**	4 / minute
Conditions			
Fatigued, Depressed, Addict, Mana Withdrawal			
Effects			
Hel's Breath - *Euphoria, +40% Perception, -40% Constitution, 50% Reduced Healing*			

Loki's High - *Negative-Memory Block, +40% Intelligence, -40% Willpower, 50% Reduced Mana Regeneration*

Curse of the Undying Wraith - *Perception Amplification, Insomnia*

Overdosed - *Persistent Damage Over Time (10 damage / minute)*

Attributes			
Strength	13	**Agility**	26
Constitution	11	**Perception**	31
Intelligence	24	**Willpower**	4
Charisma	12	**Luck**	9

"Jeez!" Acting quickly, I drag her inside and get her on the couch.

Calling upon the star god, I use Rehua's Light to heal her for one hundred hit points. It's not powerful enough to purge her body of the toxins or get rid of any of the many debuffs affecting her, but it buys some time. I slap her face a few times until she comes around.

"Whaaaa? Go 'way," she slurs.

"Ellie. Ellie, wake up." I slap her again. "You almost died, and you're still being affected by whatever you took. You need to go to the Shop and do a proper cleanse."

Fed up as I am, I try to stay polite while pushing down the fear and anger I'm holding onto for her. I feel a little sick, thinking of what might have happened had I not come home when I did.

"Mmmi'cnt," she manages to burble.

"Why, Ellie, why can't you?"

"Cats banned me," she says, this time easier to understand.

"You need to get a body purge. Did they say for how long or what you need to do for them to let you back in?" A bit of my worry and frustration leaks out.

Rolling away from me and pushing her face into the cushions, she mumbles, "Noooo, they just don't like me."

My mixed emotions surface again as I mumble, "Can't imagine why."

Ugh. I shake my head. No, that line of thinking isn't getting me anywhere. Damn it. Why today? How the hell am I supposed to handle this?

"Ellie, I'm going to go to the Shop to see if there's anything I can get that will help. Do you have any money or equipment I can use?" I say, but don't expect or receive a response beyond some snores.

Fine then, it'll just go on the tab. This better not hamper my plans. I regret that line of thinking as my eyes burn and I taste bile in the back of my throat. Damn you, Elise.

I quickly wash my face, change my shirt, and cast another shot of Rehua's Light as I rush out the door to the Shop. Should have just under 20 minutes before I need to heal her again. I really hope I can get there and back before she runs out of time.

***

Arriving at the foot of what was once the Whakatāne Information Centre, I can't help but notice the energy in the air as the Vaaharu and their evening workers complete their tasks. The entire area smells of seafood. Their fishing and prepping-for-transport methods look as though they came straight out of a fish factory. Then again, considering they've remodelled the old pathway to suit that purpose, the comparison is more than apt.

While I race up the stairs, I take a second to appreciate that the mud and debris that constantly filled our river is gone, leaving behind a crystal-clear thing of beauty. It's brimming with so much life that the Vaaharu barely ever take their reinforced, System-registered boats out to tackle the larger sea life. Although, when I think about it, I suppose they'd rarely want to, what with the Dungeon World mutations not only affecting the land creatures, but also those in the water. Seriously, who knows what kind of creatures are waiting just off the coast?

As I pass through the Info Centre's doorway, I vanish from the real world and find myself transported to a fancy retail setting. Luxurious couches and coffee tables make a pathway to the counter. The walls are lined with opulent shelving, and lights point perfectly at a selection of equipment, armor, vehicles, and more that's far outside of my price range.

Making my way toward the empty counter, I notice today's attendant float out from the rear entrance. It's a creature I've had pleasant enough dealings with in the past.

The best way I can describe it, is that it looks like a messed-up turtle that has the tail and fins of a shark, wearing the top portion of a three-piece suit. I've always thought of it as a Turark. Never asked or scanned to see what race it is, as I figured it might notice, and it may come across as rude—seeing as I'm in a hurry, I see no reason to indulge that line of thinking.

"Hi," I say before the assistant gets a word in. "I have some *really* stunning bits and pieces for you today, and I'd love to see what you have in the way of body cleanser Skills or items like that I can take with me as a gift for a friend."

"My, my," the Turark's beak snaps open and closed, its voice sounding like someone chewing on a mouth full of gravel. "Don't *we* appear to be in a rush today? Must be a hell of a catch to have you wanting to spend so quickly on something so special."

The fiendish salesman has seen straight through me. Today just isn't my day.

Flustered, I cough lightly while waving. "Psh, me, in a rush?" In an attempt to gather myself, I gesture with enthusiasm. "No, no, no, no rush, just excited to get these beauuuutiful gems off my hands and into your gorgeous fins."

"Flattery will get you everywhere, Mr. Atkinson," it coolly replies as it floats a little closer. "Now let's see what it is that you think would suit me and mine so well."

Opening the Shop system tabs that allow me to show what I have to offer, I prepare myself to make a deal. I drop the loot from today, along with a stack of sixty gems and a bundle of other items I've been hoarding for my upgrades.

"Well, well, well," the Turark says after going through the list. "This is a tidy little present you've brought me." Its eyes roam me, looking for a response—which I hope I'm not providing. "I can offer you... thirty thousand credits for everything. How does that sound?"

It sounds like I'm about to get screwed is what it sounds like. I've been scrimping and saving for months. I've forgone repairs, and I've been living in a non-registered house for almost a year. This haul should have been enough to get me over the 160,000 creds I need for the audio implant and module, leaving me plenty to live off for a while. Instead, its offer leaves me over twenty thousand *under* what I need for just the gear.

"Interesting," I say as nonchalantly as I can. If he wants to play the ridiculous offers game, I can do that too. I bring up the Shop screen and spin it around to show the item I'd *like*.

Skill: Fortune's Flush

Instantly recover user from all status effects (no limit). Performs a full body purification. Grants 24 hours immunity to negative statuses and toxins.
Cost: 300 Mana
Target Cooldown: 30 days
80,000 Credits

"I was thinking more along the lines of the Fortune's Flush skill, plus sixty thousand credits. That should make us both incredibly happy."

And with that, our session of haggling begins.

***

That did not go my way. Well, not entirely.

After a few minutes of back and forth, I'm sure it could tell I needed to be somewhere. All I managed to get was enough credits for the audio gear, with no room for error, along with a purification pill. As I'm in a rush, I forgo the purchase of the equipment. So, while I'm a bit miffed at the outcome, I'm excited for my next visit.

The pill I successfully bargained down for will do the trick as far as purging Ellie's body of the toxins and most of her negative conditions. Thankfully, this includes the overdosing effect. Unfortunately, it won't do anything for her other debuffs. I suppose she'll have to let those work their way through her system.

With the transaction complete, I sprint home.

***

Getting back with but a hair's breadth to spare, I notice that the door's open, and hunched over Ellie is a hooded figure. Who the fuck is that, and what the hell is he doing? I seriously don't have time for this.

"Oi! Mate! Back the fuck off right now and maybe I won't hurt you for busting into my place and disturbing my friend," I blurt while loading up my Skills for a fight.

Moving closer, I realize, using Tāne's Sight, that any efforts to fight him would likely be futile. All I see are question marks. Not even a name or race.

Standing with a casual grace, the mysterious stranger surprises me by raising his left hand and producing a key. That's—that's a key to my flat. Not many know where to find my spare, and while it might be easy enough to locate or create such a thing with Skills or spells, I recognize the jawline and build of the person holding it as he slowly turns to face me.

"O? That you?" I say, a little shocked to see who I believe is a friend from the old days.

He replies as he removes his hood, "Kia ora. Hey, bro."

"Hah, holy shit!" There's a touch of excitement in my voice as I clasp his hand and shake him by the shoulder. "Otiniara motherfucking Matetu."

My mind's awash with happiness from seeing one of my best mates. Otiniara had been out of town when everything went down, and after all the friends and family we—no, that's a lie. All those I'd seen taken from *me*—I'd never had the heart to look up people in the Shop.

"Damn, man, I never thought I'd see you again." Shaking my head, I continue in a rush, "Where, how, why, but… oh, shit!"

I suddenly realize I haven't given Ellie the purification pill. I fall down to her side and reach to wake her, but O places his hand on my shoulder.

He says, "It's all right, man. She's good now."

Looking up, I see the honesty in his face.

His eye twitches a bit as he continues. "I saw her through the window when I rocked up, and could see her health dropping. I remembered you used to hide a key in the tree across the road, so I let myself in. You almost lost her, man."

Looking at Ellie I say, "Lost her months ago, O. We were both fighting to save a memory." I take a quick glance with Tāne's Sight and can see that all her status effects and debuffs are gone. All except one condition that's listed as a question mark. "Holy shit. You must have some crazy powers man. How'd you do that? And what's up with the effect?"

Otiniara's left eye twitches again as he replies. "I—it's been a rough trip, man." He looks away from me. "Was forced to pick up some tricks along the way." Looking at Ellie, he continues. "I didn't see a pop-up telling me that this is a Safe Zone. You know you have to buy the place to stop the monster spawns, ay?"

Feeling a little rebuked, I say, "Yeah. She collapsed in the doorway as I got home. The Shop's just down the street, and she's been banned from it, so all I could really do was hope she'd be okay for the few minutes I was gone." I add a bit of a smile to my words and slap O on the back. "If I'd know you were coming, I could have saved myself some coin."

"Ha! You hinting that the drinks are on me?" He laughs as he falls into a chair and sticks his dirty boots on the dining room table. "There even a place to get on the piss round here anymore?"

***

A short while later, we're dropping Ellie off in a chair at Jase's bar before snagging a table for ourselves and getting the lay of the land.

"Hm, pretty busy," Otiniara says while looking at the various groups around the bar. His gaze falls on a group of battle-worn ladies in the back corner of the room.

"That's the Coastlands Quartet," I say, interrupting his ogling. "They're a group of high school teachers led by our old PE teacher, Mrs. Terrell. They all took warrior and hunting classes and have been working on getting the other side of the river clear of monsters."

With a look that speaks volumes, he says, "Nice. They all look to be in their thirties. Seem pretty flush too."

"Heh, yeah, so I'm gonna assume you mean levels. The highest over there is Mrs. Terrell at 39. Pretty sure she's the highest in town. When she hit Level 30, the four of them went dutch on the golf club out by the airport. Turned it into a place where people can test their Skills and spells without pissing anyone off. Takes a bit of work to get out there, but last I checked, they were setting up cages and rounding up low-level creatures to help level people up. Been a while since I went out that way though."

"Chur." He shifts his focus to the bar then over to the pool table. "Didn't this place used to be called the Quarthouse?" I notice his eye twitch again as he checks out the state of the game.

Half watching the game, half looking for a staff member, I say, "That was before the entrance was knocked down by some sea creature that stormed through town early on." I catch the waitress's eye and smile while indicating that we want a few drinks. "After Jase bought and finished doing up the place, he christened it the Pub. Pure creativity 'n class, that one."

"No shit. How's ol' Jase doing?" he says, eye twitching again.

"You'll see soon enough." I look around, expecting him to walk through the door. "Should be here any minute. Bastard owes me a feed."

I grin as Ngaire, the Pub's all-in-one chef, waitress, and part-time manager drops two handles of frothing amber liquid on the table.

"'Fraid we're all outta ya favorite, Nate. All's we got is the bird or the lion, and I've neva seen ya have the red, so Tui it is." She pulls a pen and paper out of thin air. "You boys want—" She stares at O. "Otiniara... is—is that you?" She doesn't wait for a response and falls atop her unsuspecting victim. Wrapping him in a tight hug, she softly sobs. "I-I didn't think I'd ever see you again, and after your sister... oh God! Your sister! I'm so sorry, she... umm. I'm sorry." Then she grips him tighter and quietly cries.

Hugging her back, he says in a soft tone, "Hey, hey now. Tumeke. It's'all good. I found out a while back, but cheers for saying it." Slowly releasing himself, he places a hand on her forearm, smiles, and looks her in the eyes. "It's good to see you, Ngaire."

Interrupting their moment, I cough. "Well, looks like you might be a popular one tonight." I get a half-hearted glare from both of them. "Ha. Well, we were just about to do a bit of a catch-up. Did you want to join us?"

"Can't. Jase hasn't turned up yet, and when he does, he'll probably be clowning around with you two."

"Yeah, sounds about right." I cross my arms in a mockingly serious manner while nodding. Then looking at her, I throw on a sly grin. "Weeeelll, if you aren't joining us for a powwow, could ya find it in ya heart to bring us over a few bowls of hot chips and a couple'a burgers each? Maybe something for the comatose one over there too." I indicate Ellie. "It's been a long day, I'm starving, and no doubt she'll need something when she wakes up."

Ngaire looks slightly concerned as she looks from us to Ellie, then she also crosses her arms, but in a more serious manner. "'n how exactly are you paying for this?"

"Jase said—"

"No, not tonight you cheapskate." She slams a palm on the table. "Not without Jase here to back you up."

"Oh, c'mon, Ngaire, it's O's return party, and Ellie almost died."

"I'll sort *Elise* out when she wakes up." Smiling at Otiniara, she says, "O, your meal's on the house." A heartbeat longer than necessary later, her stare turns to daggers as it falls on me. "*You*, I wanna see hard creds before I leave the table."

I place my hand over my chest. "Ngaire, you wound me. Whatever gave—"

"No," she says, one hand on her waist, the other hovering inches from my face, "Credits. Now." Then she flips her hand over, palm-side up.

I show her my best puppy dog eyes before caving with a sigh and summoning enough for the meal, dropping it in her hand. "Fine, here's—"

"And the drinks." Her hardened eyes don't break contact with me, and she emanates an aura of heat.

I drop a few more credits. "You'll have me sleeping on the streets at this rate."

Sliding the credits into her inventory and jotting down the order, she says, "Might as well already be on them. Hell, they're probably safer than that hovel you call a flat. You bought it yet?"

This time O chimes in. "No, he hasn't. Was givin' 'im grief 'bout it when I turned up this arvo. Was hoping to ask him about it now."

"Well then," she says as she magics the pad away and turns to leave, "suppose I'll leave you two ta have a bit of a chat. Back in a bit with ya kai."

She walks off, giving us a wave over her shoulder before slowing a touch and doing a half turn, giving O a warm smile, and glaring at me.

"Salt of the earth, that one. Perfect partner for Jase," I say, glancing at O.

"Business partner?"

"Ha! As if that's ever stopped you." Then I turn to him with a deadpan face. "But seriously, please don't fuck this up. I like eating here, and she'll take it out on me if you hurt her."

"As if I would," he says, smirking. Then he shrugs as he gets comfortable. "So anyway, I know it's been the end of the world 'n all that, but what's the deal with you and Ellie? Weren't you two, like, a thing? And what's with your class? What made you choose a Māori one? And why don't you own ya place yet? And while I admit, the title *Pyrorational* is pretty cool, why on earth are you known as *The Eater of War Parties*?"

"Hold up," I counter. "How the hell did you get back here in one piece? Weren't you in Auckland? And why can't I read your class or stats? And what's up with that badass healing spell?"

"Yeah, nah man," he says, left eye twitching hard as he shakes a hand. "Kai Taua. Eater. Of. War. Parties. Explain."

"Okay, but you mind if we have our feed first? I'd rather not go into detail on an empty stomach. Probably won't be able to eat afterward."

"Fair enough." He looks at the pool table. "Table's free. Want a game while we wait?"

"Sure."

***

Three games of pool, a half dozen drinks, and a table of food later, we've got a few more beers in front of us as I'm about to start my story.

I blurt, "Hey, Ngaiii! What's up with the drinks tanite? I'm actually starting ta feeling it."

"New skill!" she screams across the room. "Called Lightweight. Reduces resists on people I serve my drinks to. Basically lets ya get drunk easier."

A few people cheer, causing a chain reaction across the pub.

"*Nice!*" I call back over the racket before emptying my drink, then sliding the empty glass upside down across the table. Picking up another, I turn to O. "You grow up thinking that when the zombie outbreak happens, you'll be ready. Ya know, like, out of everyone you know, you're the one with the plan. You'd drop what you're doing and race to the hardware store, pick up everything you need to survive. Then once the place is all boarded up, you make your way over to the supermarket for supplies. Or something like that.

"Turns out that when the world fell apart, I was fast asleep." I can see a smirk appearing on O's face. "Oi, don't look at me like that, it was like two a.m. I totally missed the initial notice and almost slept through the entire prep hour."

"Fuck," he says.

"Fuck's right. So, what'd I do when I woke up with a glowing blue square flashing in my face? Same as most other people, I guess—stopped thinking and freaked out. Nothing was working. Computers wouldn't turn on and I couldn't call my family. So I decided to run across town to my granddad's place."

I shift in my seat, then look down into the mug of beer I'm grasping tightly with both hands. "Looking back, I suppose that was a good, wholesome, family-first thing to do. Gotta make sure they're all right before taking care of yourself. But I seriously wish I'd thought a bit more before rushing out the door at a quarter-to-three."

"Yeah, that was pretty stupid" O says mid eye twitch, "But what about your class? Why'd you choose Kaikiko Toa? What's it do?"

"I'll get to that soon enough," I say, a little annoyed that he isn't letting me just tell the tale.

"Anyway, so the streets were pitch-black and it was hosing down. A few drunks were stumbling around outside the Quarthouse, and the homeless guy who lives under The Rock tried to ask about what was going on. I didn't care, I just ran. I had to make sure my pop was okay."

"Your Pop? You mean your Grandad?" He asks, as if he's never called a person by two names.

"Huh?" I say a little surprised, "Oh, yeah, I call him both, so sue me. Mind if I get back to the story?"

"Sure." He says with a shrug, "Just making sure." I take the moment to down some liquid.

"Honestly," I say as I wipe my mouth, "I should be dead. Idiot that I am, I turned up without any kind of a weapon. Didn't even think to stop at Mitre 10 as I ran past. Oh, and in case you hadn't realized yet, I hadn't spent any time looking over my class options, so I didn't even have any Skills."

"Hold up," says O, shaking his head in disbelief. "You're telling me you *didn't* choose your class, or assign your Skills yet?"

"Yeah," I reply before taking a sip. "I didn't know anything about the System at this point, hell, I was still surprised at how quickly I made it across town. The pain in my leg from busting my tendon a few years ago? Gone. But I didn't even notice this until I was walking through the door and I'm greeted with a familiar but completely unrecognizable face.

"My granddad, the frail old ex-navy man I'd come to rescue, who'd been plagued with dementia and spent the last few years slowly wasting away, he's no more. Standing in front of me was an imposing figure. Strong, certain, proud, and dressed to the nines in his formal suit. World War II and service medals pinned to his chest, bugle in one hand, a machete in the other. It was breath-taking.

"Turns out, about fifteen minutes after the System went live, most people's issues were fixed by the automatic health regeneration. Which meant that all the old war vets and Returned Service Association members in his retirement village were suddenly healthier and more alive than they've been in years—hell, in decades—and they were all staring at a message telling them that their friends, family, country, and world are in danger."

I stop and take a drink. O doesn't say anything this time, but I notice his eye twitching again and it's starting to bug me. Gotta remember to ask about that after this.

Setting the drink down, I continue, "So yeah, first thing he does after letting me in, Pop points me toward my aunty, who thrusts a few chef's knives and a sharpening steel rod at me, obviously expecting me to get to work. Meanwhile, Granddad's outside blasting the 'Reveille,' making sure the whole neighborhood's awake and directing people to gather by waving his blade.

"Just like that"—I snap my fingers—"close to two hundred of us are huddled in the middle of Pohutu Street, rain coming down hard as we pass around sharpened shovels, gardening tools, and kitchen knives before we make our way somewhere more defensible."

At this O leans a bit closer, as if trying to pay a bit more attention.

"Again, none of us think to go to the hardware store or even the supermarket. All these people, and the best thing we come up with is to head toward the Mataatua Reserve and the Ngāti Awa marae across the road. I guess we thought that maybe that area would be easier to defend, what with the river and reserve on one side and the steep side of the hill on the other.

"Once the prep hour was up, we didn't even make it a block before the monsters caught up with us." Memories of the night cause me to shrink into my chair a touch.

"It was like some kind of horror movie. There we are, wandering the streets with only a sliver of moonlight guiding us... I felt lost. Darkness seemed to be swallowing me, and obviously that's exactly when shit hit the fan."

"All around us, I hear these sloshing *thumps*." I sit up straight and slam my open palm on the table a few times, causing a few people to turn our way. I pay them no mind and keep going. "Then someone near the back screamed. Then another, and another, and suddenly we're no longer a reasonably structured group. No, now we were a warbling mass of jelly haphazardly flowing through the streets and slowly losing more and more of our body as we ran." As I say this, I pour some beer on the table, and watch as it pools together, then swipe at it, sending the liquid flying. O leans back, watching the beer hit the floor as he takes a drag from his own handle.

"Screams were coming from everywhere," I say, continuing the story. "We still had about fifty people in the group, and my granddad was leading the way with some of his RSA buddies. I was as good as useless. I'd only been a salesperson before all this. Spent more time with games and music than with exercise or fighting, but my pop, even as a Level 1 Naval Officer, he was a beast." This catches O's attention, and I can see him focus again as he sits a little straighter in his chair. "My guess is he had that class offered 'cause he was a chief petty officer when he left the navy. Whatever the reason, he was leagues ahead of pretty much everyone.

"Wouldn't find this out until later, but it turns out we were basically guppies swimming in a pool of frogs. Most of the town started as a Level 10 zone, so while that's pretty low, it was a freaking mountain when we were just starting out. Yet there he was, this man who never bragged about his time in the service, who'd take me out fishing, who taught me the need of a soft touch when playing pool, and who I'd been forced to spend the last few years watching lose his memories and motor skills, there he is in front, leading the way and carving up every last mutated weta, centipede, and goblin he came across.

"He's the one who got us to the marae. He's the one who coordinated with the Ngāti Awa Iwi members held up there. He's the one who organized building the fences and defensive structures around the area. He's the one who saved not only me and my aunt, but hundreds more that night, and he's the one who got stronger as he kept going, time after time, into the miserable night to look for more people to herd back."

Stopping again for a drink, I look at Otiniara to see if I can get a read on what he's thinking. He's definitely paying attention, but all I really get is a slight twitch of his eye as he too takes a drink. Weird. I guess I was expecting him to have more to say.

Putting my drink down, I get back to the story. "Mmmm, so the sorry sight I was, my main contribution that first day was to help fend off waves of massive crabs, land-walking jellyfish-like creatures, and a horde of ants, all while successfully looking like a drowned rat guarding our makeshift gates. I may not have been a hero, but me and the guys at the gates fought all night with no time to rest or look at our stats, all while more and more people were brought into the fenced-off area.

"I tell you what though. The moments when we were standing there at the gates of the Ngāti Hokopū marae, fighting side by side with my granddad, I'd never loved him more or been more proud of him."

I stop again, this time to take a breath. The noise of the bar bounces off me as I reflect on that day and wipe my reddening eyes. After a few minutes, I down the rest of my mug and get started on the next before getting up to go to the bathroom.

***

Stumbling back a few minutes later, I can see that the bar is full, Ellie is still fast asleep at her booth, and having downed another beer O's just watching the crowd. Sitting down at the table I start things up again. "Good to keep going?"

"Yeah man. Go hard, I'm all good." O says, shifting to get relaxed as he prepares to listen again.

"So, after that first night of hell the number of spawns slowed to a crawl around midday, and people used the time to start breaking off for food or taking a few moments to themselves, trying to digest everything that'd happened." Remembering the next part I look away from O. "In my stupidity, not even really thinking about it, I went off with a bunch of blokes from the wall to raid the various pubs. We just wanted a drink. Didn't say goodbye, didn't tell anyone where we were going or when we'd be back, just left a handful of people to watch the gates and headed for town.

"We ended up at the bar down the road, the Craic. A lot of us were pretty broken up about how many people we'd lost, and we drank a bit more than we probably should have. I passed out around three p.m. and didn't wake up until I felt someone shoving me a few hours later. Turns out that while we were getting drunk and sleeping, more monsters showed up and attacked the marae."

"Shit," says O as he leans forward, resting his crossed arms on the table, eyes focusing just before the left one twitches.

Nodding to his response I continue, "The guys had already left to help. I was the last to leave. I tried to catch up, but I was still a little drunk. As I came round the corner, I saw the others just hitting the gates as my pop and a handful of RSA, Ngāti Awa, and a few people from the marae fell through our fencing. Right behind them were these huge half-man-half-snake-looking creatures wearing opal and gold armor. Most of them were holding spears or bladed polearms, but the biggest was holding some kind of thick battle axe."

Resting his elbows on the table and clenching his fists, I can see an intensity in O as he focuses on this part of the story.

"Our side had actually been doing a pretty good job. They managed to take down several. But it didn't last long. The guys, and most of the others, were ripped apart in under a minute. All I could do was watch in horror as person after person fell. Soon it was just my granddad standing up to them, and before I finished psyching myself up, the axe-wielder sliced off my granddad's legs, and another put a spear through his chest—all while I cowered in fear."

I take another swig of my drink as the memories make me feel anger and resentment toward myself. Slamming the beer onto the table I see O jolt back as I accidentally break off the handle and send the cup flying. The drink spills and the glass smashes. *Fuck.*

"Oi! What's going on over there?" I hear from the bar.

"Sorry, Ngaire, I'll pay for it. Can I get another?" Collecting the broken glass, I wipe the spilt beer off the table with my shirt as best I can.

"No. You're on water for a while. You can have more when Jase turns up," she snaps while walking over with a jug and two clean glasses.

"Thaannksss, Mum," I say with a bit of a slur, squinting as I give her a grin.

"Yeah, sorry, Ngaire. We'll try not to break anything else," O says.

Looking at him, I remember what I was talking about, and my smile fades. "Okay, where was I?"

I pour some water and drink a full glass before continuing. "Right, so my pop and all the guys I'd been fighting and drinking beside are dead, I have no idea if my aunt or anyone else in our little refuge is alive, and I'm blaming myself for not being there to help. Meanwhile I'm running back the way I came like the little shit I am."

O looks at me sadly, and his eye twitches a little. "So how's this explain your class and those titles? Offense meant; you're not coming across in the brightest light right about now."

"Mmmm…" I look down and take another sip of water. "Can't disagree. I was *not* a shining ray of light in our darkest hour that's for sure." Looking up, I say in a harsher tone, "Listen, if I could trade my life for my granddad's I would. He was the hero, he should be here, but that's not how the world works. All this bullshit happened, all the best and brightest died, and I'm one of the pathetic fools who didn't. Now do you want to hear the rest or not?"

Raising his hands in defense, he says, "Geez! Fuck, yeah, man, shit, trust me, we've all had a rough go, I just… I'm sorry. What happened next?"

"Well, instead of running back to the marae, I did one of the things I should have done when all this started, and I headed to Mitre 10. Figured I could find something that might be able to help."

"Waitwaitwait," he says, shaking his hands and head. "I know I just asked, but you haven't said anything about your class yet. Have you still not done that at this point? How did you go almost an entire day with a freaking class? And how didn't it come up?"

"We had a lot going on, and I just… man, I'd only had like two hours sleep, *and* I woke up late. I never had a chance to take it all in or go through the options. Besides, we weren't really talking as we drank. Shit, will you just let me finish this?"

"Yeah, man, okay, sorry. Please, continue," he says, resting his arms back on the table.

"Okay, so, hardware store. I made my way back to Mitre 10, and I don't know shit about how to make a gun, or explosives, or any of that. But I knew wood burns, knives cut, and that I should probably try a stealth approach if I wanted to stand a chance."

"Wait, you wanted to go back? I mean, you literally saw everyone get killed. Surely you knew—"

"Dude, seriously, I wasn't exactly in a clear frame of mind. All I could think about was paying them back, and I guess seeing if anyone was still alive.

"To do that though, I thought it'd be best to try sneaking in, and if possible, creeping up on them to take them down quietly. Did I know about perception, listening Skills, or spells? That would be a resounding *no*, but as I said, I was an idiot.

"I ended up taking a bunch of stuff. Some safety glasses, a pair of black overalls, gloves, steel-capped boots, a bag. Also grabbed a few more blades, some binoculars, and a few survival bits and pieces. Last lot of stuff though, they were for burning things down. A handful of lighters, a hose, tons of rope, a twenty-litre fuel canister—which I filled up by siphoning gas from a car along the way back.

"By the time I'd finished stocking up, night was falling again. I figured I'd best scope the place out, so I snuck into the fishing club across the road from the marae, and from the balcony, I took a look to work out how many there were, where they were located, and whether or not I could see any humans alive in there. There weren't. They'd piled the bodies off to the side, and that just made me angrier. Not only had they killed my granddad, but they'd also killed my aunt, all the other war vets, and everyone we'd been able to gather down here. It was a godsdamn massacre. I was seething. All I could think was that *they were going to pay*."

Perhaps sensing that the story was about to get heated, I notice the focus return to O's eyes as he lifts his arm to rest his head on his clenched fists.

"A number of the snake people had cleaned out the main building and were using it as some kind of base, or nest, or home—I'm not sure what they'd call it. But there were less than a dozen scattered around the area on guard, and none of them were near each other.

"It took me two hours to sneak up on the first one I killed. I have no idea how or why the System allowed me to do that, or why it never detected me—because I've no doubt it was a higher level than my no-class-chosen, no-stats-allocated ass—but such is the way of things."

I see O move as though he wants to ask something, but he closes his mouth and nods for me to continue.

"When I finally managed to get behind it, I heard its light breathing, saw its scales shifting, expanding, and contracting as it breathed. It was surprisingly easy to slide a blade into its unsuspecting mouth to stop it from making a noise and use a second to slit its throat. There must have been some kind of sneak bonuses applied, because since then, I've rarely had as simple a kill." I look down at this point and take another drink of water.

"All in all, it took until around four a.m. to take out each of the guards. In all that time, no one from inside had come out. I made my way around the outside of the building as quietly as I could, closing all the windows and tying the doors shut. After pouring gasoline around the building, I lit the place on fire and made a bonfire out front."

Remembering all this causes my chest to tighten for a moment and I stop to collect myself before taking a deep breath and continuing. Eyes wide, knuckles white, and jaw clenched, I can see O has his full attention on me now, and can tell he knows I'm about to get to the part of the story he seems to be most interested in.

"As I waited, I cooked the meat of some of the snakes. I hadn't eaten anything since the evening before everything started. I thought they were just monsters, and well, to be honest, I wasn't really thinking about it. In hindsight, I guess I just saw them as massive snakes, and to me, snakes are edible, so surely I should be able to eat this meat if I cooked it well enough.

"Sitting there in the early morning of the second day of our integration into the System, eating snake-monster meat, waiting, and watching for anything to rush outside from the now fully engulfed building, I heard the cries coming from inside. Then the banging on the doors as whoever was inside tried to escape. Smoke billowed out of broken windows and the holes that formed in the roof and walls."

Ashamed and angry, I look away. "I just sat there, chewing. Blade in one hand, a fistful of charred meat in the other. I watched the fire until the last of the screams died out."

Looking back and shifting in my seat to get a bit more comfortable I say, "That's when I finally took notice of the noises coming from the System. Apparently, I'd been receiving messages and notifications the entire time, and only now did the System deem it necessary to force me to open them, so I did.

"One of the notifications told me I'd gained two new titles for *worthy* acts. The first was Kai Taua, and the message read—hold on a sec, I'll bring up the title itself." Opening the Titles system window, I brought up the Eater of War Parties title and read its description.

Kai Taua

Not many have what it takes to slay and kill an entire war party of sentient beings many times your level, but you're the exception to the rule. Not only did you singlehandedly wipe them out, but you dined on their flesh as you watched their women and children suffocate and burn to death. You are a ruthless one, aren't you?
Gain: 15% increase to damage against all sentient creatures you consume the flesh of. Reputation changed with select groups.

Opening the second title, I read that one too.

Pyrorational

Some love the smell of fire and are obsessed with watching the world burn, but not you. You quickly and skilfully plotted and enacted the arson of a building full of innocent sentient beings many times your level and did so in a manner that meant they could not escape their fate. With a mind as logical as yours, no one could mistake you for a maniac.

Gain: 30% increase to Fire Affinity.

Reputation changed with select groups

Otiniara stared at me with a look of... not quite horror or disgust but certainly pity. "Innocents? Women and children? Fuck man, those are some twisted titles."

"Yeah, they are. It wasn't a good night. I can't say for certain I would have let them go had I known they were sentient aliens. Who, by the way, it turns out are called Volatarians. I mean, c'mon, they'd just killed hundreds of people on one of the worst days in human history, and here they were sleeping in our beds while the world was being taken over by aliens and monsters.

"Although I can definitely tell you that very little of that meat stayed in my stomach after I read those titles." Taking another full glass of water, I have to steady myself as I feel nauseated remembering that night.

Watching me with a subtle twitch in one of his eyes, O says, "I'll bet. I guess that kind of explains how you got the Kaikiko Toa class too?"

"Pretty much. Kaikiko Toa, the Vengeful Warrior. The System informed me that after completing a hidden quest, one of the rewards was the ability to choose this as a unique class. Well, choose isn't exactly the right word, the System assigned me the class, seeing as I had yet to choose one, and considering I had spent the last day and a bit killing, or helping to kill, creatures with actual levels, all those experience points instantly shot me up to Level 10."

"And the loot?" asked O.

"From the snake people? Yeah, after allocating my Skill points and reading what information I could, I went around and looted everything. But seeing as how I didn't exactly have anywhere to sell it and that the weapons and armor didn't suit me or my stats at the time, I simply stored most of it in my flat until the Vaaharu turned up and gave us access to the Shop. That's how I got to thinking that I'd be able to afford the gear I want, which is also why I haven't turned my place into a safe zone yet."

"Aw yeah. What's this gear that has you so excited you can't be bothered with personal safety?"

"Music."

"Huh?"

"Music," I say again, giving him the simplest and most straight-forward answer possible. "First is an implant, then a module with all of humanity's music on it. The implant is only a basic model, but together, they're still gonna cost a small fortune. And *they* are what I've been saving for." I give him a smile. "Pretty sure that answers all of your questions. How about you start answering mine?"

"Huh? Hmm, right." He shifts from side to side in his chair. "What about Ellie?"

"What about her?" I say, slouching in my chair and crossing my arms, not wanting to get into it.

"C'mon, man. What's up? You two were good together."

"Until we weren't." I humph. "Not everyone adapted to the System, or they're still adapting. Whatever."

"Mmmm, you sure that's all? Feels like there's more to it than that," he says with a cocky expression.

"Yeah, months more," I retort with a touch of anger as I sit up straight. "But fine. Short answer is we met up the day after everything went down at the marae. She'd hidden with a group over at the Rex Morpeth Park Soccer Club. They'd barred the doors, frantically killed the few things that managed to spawn inside, and hadn't left.

"Things were as fine as they could be for the first month, but I could tell she was becoming more and more depressed. She refused to come out and level up, and she hung out more and more with the freeloaders at the high school. Then while I was on a trip to Ōpōtiki to look for survivors, she got hooked on some Shop-bought-but-locally-duplicated drugs and cheated on me with her dealer when she ran out of credits."

"Daaamn," says O.

"Mmm. Yeah. I found out, but not before trying to help her get off them. She wouldn't, or maybe couldn't listen, which is odd, considering the perception increase they gave her, but whatever. We got in a fight, she told me she'd fucked her dealer friend—who, by the way, had genetically altered herself via the Shop, turning from a her to a him—and I broke it off. Seeing her on my doorstep today, which was less than half an hour before you saw her, was the first time I'd really talked to her in probably six months, and now can we *please* move on," I say as I shrink back into my seat.

"Fuck, man. That's rough. Gotta say though, didn't know the Shop could do that. Think there's still a chance for you two? I mean, she *is* technically completely clean now."

"Mmmm, so A, neither did I. But where there's a will there's a way, I guess, and B, not likely. I've zero doubt she'll be back on them the second she wakes up, especially if all it takes is a booty call with her new *boyfriend*, and I doubt she cares enough to want to. So, fuck her."

From behind me, I hear the scuffing of a chair. As I turn, I see Ellie's hair as she runs out the door of the Pub. *Well, that's just great.*

"Couldn't have warned me that she was awake?" I ask.

"Didn't want to ruin the surprise if you thought there was a chance. Although, I guess there isn't, so…" He shrugs and winces. "Plus side, your guess was mostly right?"

"Fuck you." I take another drink of water. "Well, she's gone now. If she comes back, she comes back. I'm not chasing after her, not tonight, and I don't feel like it's my job to. We fixed her. I spent my hard-earned money on a cure—which you so kindly made redundant—and I have no obligation to her. If she wants to come back, she's the one who'll have to come crawling on her hands and knees and with words made out of pure godsdamned gold." I finally turn back to O. "Ohhhh, okay, now you. Quit dodging the questions. I laid my hand on the table, it's your turn."

"Uh huh. Okay, fair 'nuff. But let's get a few more drinks. My shout this time."

***

Getting ready to tell his tale O stretches as he rolls his shoulders then takes a swig of beer. "Right, so you know I was up in Aucks, ey? See, I'd been running with this lot working outta TAPAC, The Auckland Performing Arts Centre. We'd been doing this vampire-rock cabaret, and the shows usually ran 'til about two thirty, meaning we didn't usually get out of there 'til three. So when the System happened, I was onstage and in the middle of pretending to suck the blood out of one of the guests as one of our final acts. All of a sudden, everyone is freaking out because of these floating blue System messages.

"I had a few solid options but ended up choosing the class Creative Conjuror. I literally get to fight with the power of music and art."

"That's fucking awesome!" I say as I excitedly sit up straight. "Do you have to use actual instruments, or are they made magically, or what?"

"Actual," he says as he scratches his head. "It's more like, I can channel magic through the instruments and art, but because I can sing, my vocal cords count as a weapon, so I'm rarely without one, especially with the auto-regen."

"Nice," I say, nodding in affirmation before having a sip of beer.

"Yeah. But that's not the story. Turns out working across from the zoo when a ton of mana is dumped on the world isn't such a good thing. As soon as that first hour was up, we were swarmed by tons of rapidly evolved animals from the Auckland Zoo."

"Fuck," I say as I cough on the beer I just swallowed.

"Not yet. See, most of animals that came our way were under some kind of mind control spell. At first, we thought they were just swarming monsters, but then someone worked out how to read basic stats and conditions of monsters, and we found out they were being controlled. Then it turned into a game of *Where's Waldo?* with Waldo being the person or creature pulling their strings.

"Fun fact," O says, pointing a finger at me. "Being a magic user who attacks the mind, I actually have fairly decent resistances to mental magic."

"No shit? Me too!" I say, puffing my chest out in surprise. "Something to do with my anger and sense of vengeance being too powerful for most mind attacks, so I get, like, fifty percent resistance or something. Don't really come up against those kinds of things, so I'm not sure how effective it really is." As I say this, O's eye twitches. In my foggy state, I try again to remind myself to ask what's up with that.

"Well, if my twenty percent is anything to go off, you should be fine. Anyway, a few bloody fights later, one of the guys who'd been a guest at the show works out where the caster is, and we all work our way through the monsters toward them.

"Cost us twelve people from our group and who knows how many people who just happened to be on the streets at the time, but we finally found out that the one in control was this heavily altered tuatara that had grown to the size of a horse. This thing was massive. The tiny bumps on its back had morphed into this fluorescent blue mohawk of sharp spines that ran right down its back to its tail. But as weird as that was, you know how they have that third eye? Well, it had grown to be, like, twice the size of its other two, and this fucker was throwing around mental magic like there was no tomorrow... which I guess isn't too far from the truth."

O stops, eye twitching as he skulls a full tankard and belches. "'Scuse me. So um, yeah, this new tuatara also has a new name. The status screen said it was called a *Manawatara*, and as more and more people were killed, it grew in power. Before we could reach it, it turned its actual sight on us, and then I'm basically fighting by myself, as I and, like, two other people manage to resist its mind control powers.

"The... well, the next few hours sucked. The Manawatara chased us across town, and it kept adding humans and monsters to its horde that it would send against us. We were all exhausted from hours of running and fighting. I'd managed to cast Dispellere, this low-level dispel magic spell I had, on a bunch of people, and we were making a stand on the Auckland Harbour Bridge. I couldn't even tell you how many the Manawatara was sending after us, but the entire road for as far as we could see, stretching right down the motorway and covering the entire area around the harbor, it was just a sea of creatures and humans, all being mind-controlled and all coming for us."

He takes a drag from another handle of Tui. Then he takes a deep breath and sighs. "I killed a lot of people that night. I couldn't count them. I couldn't dispel the mind control effects on enough of them, and for those who were too weak against the attack, they were taken over again pretty quickly.

"Turns out that, like you said, the System has a pretty fucked up sense of… I dunno. Humor? Obligation? Respect? Whatever it is, it's messed up. I may not have been able to count my kills, but it did, and…" He pauses, obviously wanting to say something but can't quite get it out. Then his eye twitches and he starts back up. "Mmm, well as night was falling on the first night, there was still no end in sight. I was the only one left, and then I either messed up or was really lucky, because I slipped and was hit hard. The force threw me over the side and into the water under the bridge.

"When I woke up, I was on a sailboat. This sailor, who'd taken to the ocean as soon as the message hit, he'd seen me fall and picked me up. I must've only had a sliver of health left when he did because he was surprised I came to at all. We ended up in Fletcher Bay, and I slowly made my way back here via Tauranga."

"Seriously, that's it?" I say, a little shocked at the brief summary. "So why can't I read your Skills? How'd you get rid of the status effects on Ellie? Were you given a title? And are you telling me that there's a mind-controlling tuatara the size of a small car gathering forces in Auckland? Also, how's Tauranga? I still haven't heard from my sisters and haven't had the guts to look them up in the Shop."

"Tauranga's pretty much gone, man. At least, I don't think there are many people left there. If there are, they're either incredibly lucky or exactly the opposite. The Mount and Papamoa are a freaking wasteland. When I was making my way through, I had to take a pretty wide arc and move quietly. There's now this massive hole, or I guess a cave, in the side of Mount Maunganui, and it looks like a dragon's decided to make its home there. You'll never guess what the people in Te Puke are calling it."

"*No.*"

"Yeah—Smaug! Ha! *Lord of the Rings* and *The Hobbit*'ll haunt our lands forever!" He lowers his head, acting a bit more somber. "Uh, but yeah, as for your sisters, sorry, bro, I uh, I didn't see them."

"Nah, that's... yeah, nah, 'sall good. I'll um. I'll look them up at the Shop in a few days. Once I've cleared my head 'n shit." *Almost lost it for a sec.* Letting out a deep breath, I continue. "But yeah, the news of monsters with mind control powers and that there's a dragon within a hundred ks of here is pretty terrifying. Although I'm a little surprised it didn't take up residence at Mount Ruapehu. Wasn't that used as *The Lonely Mountain*?"

"True that. But I guess they don't like living in active volcanoes?"

"Mmmm, yeah, I can see that. So your class and the spell? Did you use that Diseplla-something to fix Ellie?"

"Pretty much. I have Dispellere, and when I use it alongside another spell, Golden Harmony, while having Unrestrained Grandeur cast, I can pretty much cure a target of any negative status effect. At least anything I've come across that's under an Advanced Class skill in rank."

"Advanced? Can't've seen many high-level Basics, let alone an Advanced, in New Zealand. What the hell level are you, cause there's no way you're an Ad—"

"Yeah, nah, still Basic, still a Creative Conjuror, but not for much longer." A grin slowly forms on his face. During this transformation, his head tilts slightly down and toward me while his eyes narrow, a wicked laugh bubbling as if he's channeling a mocha-colored Joker. Letting out a low dark chuckle, he says, "No, noooo, not Advanced yet, but almost. I'm just about Level 48, and if all goes well, I should hit the Advanced Class I'm gonna go for, Virtuoso Thaumaturge, sometime in the next few days."

"Next few wha? Holy fucking shit on a stick. What the fucking fuck? How the fuck. *Fuck!*"

"I'm sure there are classier ways to say all that, but yeah, it's pretty nuts."

"Nuts is an understatement, you overpowered prick! You've gotta be one of the first to hit that on the whole fucking planet! I'm only Level 37, and I've been going at it hard since the first week."

"Yeah, it's been a ride. As for hitting Advanced first? Probably, not sure. It's not something I've looked up. Just been doing my best to get back to Whakatāne. Which actually brings me to another topic." Then sitting up a little straighter he says, "I've got a quest, and I'd like your help."

"Huh? A quest?" I say as I take another drink. "This the one that'll tip ya over? Why would you need my help? You probably have more power in your pinkie than I do my entire left arm."

"I guess it's more a numbers thing?" he says, waving away my comment. "Anyway, I need to head out to Whale Island tomorrow. Was hoping you'd want to come along. Should be some good XP," he says with a grin.

"Fuck, man." Sitting up I start shaking my hands and head in the negative. "Yeah, nah, listen, anywhere else and I'm there. But that's twelve kilometers of open water, and there's no fucking way I'm going that far on the boats we have. Who knows what hell's mutated down there? Sorry, man, I'd literally help any other way, but I can't. Maybe I can introduce you to the Vaaharu? Maybe they have a party that'd be keen, or maybe they have some crazy nutters they can call over from their main base in Rotorua?"

"Nah, nah, tumeke, it's all good, man, sorry to ask. How about we just get our drink on and maybe see if you can introduce me to that Coastlands clique?" With a wink and a smile, he sways to his feet and activates one of his spells that seems to amplify his voice, or make me hear a quiet echo in my head. "Ladies and gentlemen of the Pub! Drinks! Are on me!"

***

I wake up the next morning with one of the worst headaches of my life. How is it, with an automatic regeneration ability, that hangovers are still a thing? Hello? Anyone? Of course, why would anything be listening to my thoughts?

With blurred and aching vision, I check my status and see that I'm no longer Exhausted, which is nice and a little terrifying. That would mean I've had a full night's sleep. I either did so in a Safe Zone or passed out in my bed, where I could have been attacked by a random spawn at any moment. *Fuck!* What the hell happened last night?

Rubbing my eyes, I focus to see that I am indeed in my bed, and thankfully... *really?* Whatever. There's no one beside me and no mysterious clothes scattered across the room. There's also no sign of monsters, monster corpses, or Otiniara. Again, what the hell happened?

I remember playing pool, having dinner, drinking, talking about our whos, wheres, and whys, finding out about dragons and a mind-controlling beast, then... talking with Sue and Pearl from the Coastlands Quartet, and... a fight? With someone? I think? Then... well, that's it. Shit. Ngaire's new skill must really pack a punch. I don't think I've been blackout drunk in years, let alone since the System kicked in. Hell, I didn't even know you *could* get that drunk under the System. That lady has opened up a whole new world to us. *Gods bless her.*

Guess it's time to have a feed and work out what's happening. Didn't O want some help with going to Whale Island or something?

***

"You've got some nerve showing up after the crap you pulled last night! And where's that prick of a friend of yours? O! O, get your butt out here now!" Ngaire screams from behind the counter at the Pub.

"Shhhh, please, indoor voices," I say with a look to match the pain I'm feeling. "Now what's this about me doing something?" I slouch into a chair at the bar and rest my head on my arms, indicating for Ngaire to make me some coffee. "Also, I don't know where Otiniara is. I don't remember seeing him since last night after... maybe talking with the... oh."

"Oh? *Oh?* Do you remember something?" Ngaire says with a fire in her eyes that could cause the sea levels to rise.

"Nothing major. Just that O was talking to one of the gi—um, teachers from Coastlands, I don't remember which one, and um, I can't remember anything past that." I can't look at Ngaire, so in some misguided attempt to hide from her reaction, I snuggle further into my arms.

It doesn't help. Words aren't the only thing that can hurt, and I'm suddenly sorry I asked for coffee.

Leaping to my feet, I cry in pain. "Come on, Ngaire! That hurts!"

"I'll *that hurts* you."

"And now I'm all wet."

"You—"

"But at least I smell like coffee," I mumble as my auto heals do their trick, and I slurp up the liquid from my shirt sleeve.

"Disgusting," she says and begins brewing another pot.

Mumbling with a mouthful of shirt, I reply, "Isshhhh yyyorrr fffaaalltt, iissshhhn iiitt."

Not looking in my direction while throwing bacon and eggs into a frying pan, she says, "Don't speak with your mouth full, ya idiot. Now is that all you remember?"

"Uh huh."

"Nothing about running into a certain lowlife POS who might not be too happy about his favorite customer suddenly being clean?" I hear the smirk in her voice, but I can't tell if it's an angry smirk, a teasing smirk, or something else. But if what she says is true, I might want to leave town for a while.

"*No.* Did something good happen? Or something bad?"

"I'm guessing you didn't see the damage across the street then? Or the fact that *I no longer have a pool table!*"

Oh boy, that last one had venom.

"What happened to the pool table? And…" I shift my gaze outside and see a hole in the front of what used to be the entrance to the Credit Union Bank, which is now a collapsed wreck, made all the more impressive with the inclusion of a handy new skylight. "Fuuuuuck me."

"No thank you, but *that* is apparently what happens when a childlike drug lord pisses off someone nearly three times his level. Which, by the way, did you know that Otiniara's almost a freaking Advanced Class?"

"Uh, yeah, I did know. Found out last night before everything went fuzzy. I didn't have anything to do with that, did I?"

"Oh no, honey." Is that anger or is she mocking me? It's too early, and I'm hurting too much to tell. "That was most definitely because of you." She slides a plate of heaven across my arms to rest under my nose. "Now eat before I beat the seven living hells out of you for going off at Ellie right before you started a fight with the bitch-King of Kope."

Mouth full of bacon, words spill out before I get a chance to think. "Did I seriously start'a fight last night?" After swallowing my food, I try again. "Sorry…" I wipe my mouth, "Did I seriously start a fight with Sam? What on earth would make me want to do that? And last night of all nights?"

"Says the guy who beat the snot out of him. You must have been wanting to do that for a while, because when the gloves came off, he was almost dead before anyone thought to stop you." Glancing away, she looks a little chastised. "Not that many would, I suppose. Those drugs he's been throwing around have been causing nothing but trouble, then again, after last night…"

"That bad, huh? Think I'll see him again?"

"Nate, you're lucky to be alive. When no one came to his rescue, he pulled some buff outta his inventory and suddenly he's hulked out like no one I've seen before. That's when a certain someone stepped in and used their super-duper spells to send the fucker to the bank for a fast withdrawal—*using my damn pool table.*"

"Yeah…" I look back toward the old bank again. "He didn't come back? And what about Ellie?"

"Sam went flying into next week. I doubt we'll hear much from him for a while. As for Ellie, she ran off before I could stop her. Although I gotta say, she was looking more like her old self, which was a surprise."

"She's got O to thank for that. I ran down to pick up a purification pill because she's been banned from the Shop, meantime he sallies up and purges her in less than two shakes of a lamb's tail." I finish another mouthful, then keep going. "Must be nice to have power like that. Speaking of which, you sure you haven't seen him this morning? Also, where is everyone? Today's a work day, isn't it?"

"It is, and Jase didn't show up last night either. I was thinking about going by his place later today to see if something's the matter, but my other girls haven't shown up. I've been expecting the morning rush of dock workers for the last half an hour, but all I got was you."

"You think something's up? Want me to check things out?" I say, a touch of clarity finally breaking through the fog of a morning-after.

"Might be an idea. Maybe see if you can find Otiniara and whoever he shacked up with last night?" Felt the negative feelings that time.

"Sure thing, Ngaire, and um, sorry," I say quickly as I stick the last piece of bacon in my mouth and rush out the door.

***

Making my way toward the War Memorial Hall, it's obvious how quiet the town is. I mean, it's usually a lot quieter these days, but this atmosphere has an extra layer to it. There's literally no one else on the street, and I'll usually pass at least one other person.

Arriving at the hall, I see that the Hunters Market is completely barren, nothing but empty beds and a few half-eaten meals. "What the hell is going on?"

Putting a bit more of an effort into my run, I sprint to the Shop. Once again, I'm struck by the lack of people. Down here however, at least a dozen or so Vaaharu are huddled about, talking with exaggerated movements.

As I walk up to them, the closest spins toward me. "You, human, where are our workers? They are late, and some of our vessels are missing."

Shit. "Hold up, man." I don't really know how to properly address a Vaaharu as I've only dealt with them on a few trading occasions. "I, um, listen, that's why I'm down here too. I can't find anyone."

They look at me as though I'm about to become their lunch.

"I, uh, hey, so you said your boats are gone? How many? Do you have any way to track them? Or have you seen anything else that you've thought was strange?"

Scowling at me—or at least what looks like a scowl—the one closest says, "Do you think we are stupid human-monkey children? We have scanned and know the vessels are heading toward the land mass designated as Moutohorā."

Whale Island? Hmmmm. That's where O was going, but he wouldn't...

"I also saw a large swarm of creatures in the ocean this morning while I stood on my balcony," another one says, this voice sounding less hostile.

"Where? Would you be able to show me?" I ask.

"Show you? A human? We do not allow non-registered humans into our buildings," the first one says.

"Come now, Flaxish, this one is trying to assist us in finding our lost property and stolen vessels," a third one says.

I do a subtle double-take as they say property and vessels as though they are separate things… ohhh, yeah. Slaves.

"Fine. But he must be leashed."

"I'm not being leashed! But if you'll let me go up there and check what I think is happening, then maybe we can work something out."

The first one, whose name I now know is Flaxish, glares at me, but he is cut off before he can speak.

The second one says, "Thank you, Human. I am Walkune. Please, follow me."

Then it runs into the nearby apartments. I follow as it sprints up the stairs. Did they never think to get the elevators working?

Upon reaching the top, I pull out my binoculars and look at the waters between the Whakatāne Bar and Whale Island. At first, I can only see what looks like crashing waves. Then I realize that in the middle of the ocean, I see what looks more like a gathering of fish jumping in and out of the water… or a large group of creatures swimming.

Zooming in a little closer, I see several boats full of people *and* monsters. Swimming alongside the boats are hundreds, maybe *thousands* of people and creatures, and none of them doing a thing to stop the sea creatures from biting, chomping, and in general dragging them under the waves. In the center of all this is a single unharassed boat, carrying the thing I was fearing most—a lizard the size of a horse, with massive, fluorescent blue spines running down its back, and beside it is my friend O.

***

"Welcome back, good sir, welcome, welcome!" the Turark greets me.

This time I take a moment and scan its basic stats.

Name: Frolik'va'naush
Race: Raluagief
Class: Spirit
HP: n/a
Mana: n/a
Titles: None
Conditions: Slave

Huh, well, I can honestly say I'd never have guessed any of that. "Frolik, my man, good to see you. Let's get to spending, shall we?"

Having worked out where the vessels and their... *workers* are, I made a deal with the Vaaharu that I'd be rewarded ten thousand credits for each vessel I bring back, and two thousand for each slave. They've also set me up with a fifty thousand credit investment so I could gear up.

I feel a little mercenary about bringing back slaves, but if playing a knock-off Boba Fett gets me what I want, then I suppose it's something of a win-win. Maybe I can look into ending slavery when I have a few more levels under my belt. Maybe a few more than a few more levels.

Then again, what is it exactly that I'm after here? Am I trying to save people? My friend? Kill the mutated tuatara? I thought I just wanted to listen to some music, which by the way, I have to skip *again*.

Whatever. Right now, I have a mission to travel across the ridiculously dangerous twelve kilometers of open water to save a few vessels and several groups of indentured humans, all while dodging sea monsters and any other creatures the Manawatara has dragged along on its journey. Fuck it, let's get to spending.

***

Eighty-two minutes and slightly more than ninety thousand credits later, I emerge from the Shop not only feeling better but looking it too. Since this was one of the first times I've used the Shop for more than restocking the absolute essentials, I finally picked up something I've seen and heard others rave about—the Human Genome Treatment. It's an individually tailored treatment to fix and optimize a user's genetic code, repairing any damage and errors due to aging or radiation, while optimizing a few other things I don't care to read about.

As for gear, I grabbed some kind of a fancy space-age one-piece suit of skin-tight armor that lets me move freely, all while hugging a touch *too* well—especially now that I've taken the Genome Treatment. I pay a little extra for the add-on that allows me to manipulate the colors and mess around with digital patterns and designs at will. Now I can cosplay Iron Man one day, and Nightwing the next. Yay!

For weapons, my class works great with Fighting Staffs, Bladed Fighting Staffs, Poleaxes, Short Spears, Long Spears, and Clubs, so I picked up one of each—just in case I feel the need to switch mid-battle. I also chose a nice selection of grenades. Variety *is* the spice of life.

To complement the weapons, I grabbed some instant-knowledge about the staffs, spears, and clubs. They cost a pretty penny and don't give me muscle memories, but knowing the moves will still take my fighting skills up quite a bit—particularly since I've mostly been brutishly swinging metal cut-offs and broken branches the last few months.

I considered picking up a gun too, but instead I went for the ability to Fly. It costs a ton in mana, but I figure if I'm traveling across the ocean, then I'd rather be able to zip away from a sinking ship than go down with her.

The last items I picked up weren't armor or a weapon, but a scanner implant and a rebreather. Now I can breathe underwater for up to two hours without surfacing, and for the low, low cost of thirty mana per use, I can run a scan of the area around me in a one-hundred-meter diameter to determine the number of and types of nearby creatures. This will prove invaluable as I attempt to infiltrate one of the most instant death locations I've ever visited. Hmmm, better stock up on health and mana potions too.

***

Being the ever-so-benevolent beings that they are, the Vaaharu are allowing me to use one of their remaining vessels. I can't fly the entire way, as I'd run out of mana in about twenty minutes, and if I did manage to squeeze out that distance, then I'd have to worry about not having enough mana left to fight whatever I encountered either along the way or when I got there. No, using one of these fancy mana-powered boats is the best move.

Gliding through the surf as if it's not even there is a new sensation for me. When coming over the bar in a pre-System boat, the waves could be pretty rough and you had to watch out for rocks. Now? It's as if the water simply makes way for the boat. As for the little islands of rocks? The water is so clear that maneuvering around them is child's play.

As I make it past the bar and into open waters, the clarity remains the same but the depth becomes an issue. Light only passes through water so well, and while it *is* still crystal clear, due to the ever-increasing vertical slope, soon I can barely see the ocean floor. Then just like that, I can't. Truth be told, being able to see so deep into the water is not doing anything good for my nerves. Below me are swarms of fish that look tiny but obviously aren't, as I can quite plainly see that they are several dozen meters below the surface. *Please don't notice me. Please don't notice me. Plea…*

They notice me.

"C'mon, you space age hunk of junk! Can't you move any faster?" I plead, searching for any kind of imaginary button that says *Boost.*

Looking over the edge, I can see that the fish are hurtling straight for me, so I cast Warrior's Rage and Heart of the Warrior, then I get ready to cast War Thunder the moment the creatures come within range.

Now!

As I activate the skill, a ghostly group of Māori warriors fade into existence. They float around and alongside the boat as it speeds along. Once they've all appeared, they line up, stamping their feet and smacking their arms and thighs. Each *thwack* sends a booming echo across the ocean as they chant a threatening mana-enhanced haka.

"KA MATE! KA MATE!"

I add my own moves and voice to the thunderous chorus while keeping an eye out for any changes in my enemy's direction.

"KA ORA, KA ORA!"

I quickly see the oversized fish scatter. However, in the distance, a fin the size of a building slowly makes its way out of the water. Heading toward me.

Screw this. I stop the haka mid-cast, dispelling the warriors and bringing the vessel to a stop. Activating Fly, I leap into the air and move toward the incoming threat. Once I'm close enough, I activate Tāne's Sight to get a look at what I'm up against.

Megalodon

Level 71

HP: 32,962

Mana: 10,675

Status: Hungry

Well shit, that's literally a Megalodon. That is both terrifying and awesome. I can't help but wonder if it's been here the whole time or if it was just a normal breed of shark before all this. No matter, I am *way* out of my league with it and hanging around here is suicidal. So, I simply fly toward Whale Island, leaving the death-beast beneath the waves.

Once I feel I'm out of range of the Megalodon, I stop to allow my mana to recharge, treading water whenever the ocean appears clear of anything potentially hostile. That plan works—right up until it doesn't.

With less than a hundred meters to go before I reach land, in an area of water I was sure looked safe to recharge in, I find myself struggling to free my arms from tentacles that seem to appear out of nowhere.

No, nonononono, fuck me no. This is literally the thing I feared most about coming out this far. Something able to grab onto and pull me under the waves. Pure nightmare material.

I feel my air supply running low as one minute, then two goes by. I'm wriggling and trying to shift my arms away from the limbs that have me wrapped up. I can feel as each of the suction cups detaches and reattaches itself as it slowly tightens its grip.

Panicking now, my mind simply can't come up with a way to escape this. As my vision darkens around the edges and the last of my oxygen bubbles out of me, I have a thought. If I can summon items from my inventory directly into my hands, maybe I can do so right into my mouth?

I try to focus with everything I have, all while doing my best to not suck down a lungful of saltwater. My chest is burning, my head is throbbing, then it appears. *I did it.* My rebreather is in my mouth! I suck in as deep a breath as I can, but the tentacles are still restricting my movements.

Now that I can breathe, I take a moment to inspect my opponent.

Greater Architeuthis

Level 67

HP: 25,842

Mana: 6,718

Status: Annoyed

Annoyed? Well try to imagine how I feel, ya great dolt. Considering my position, I can't help but wonder if my performing the haka earlier actually drew the giant shark toward me.

Activating Warrior's Rage to increase my strength by several times, I'm able to free up my chest and take a few deep breaths. Then, when I feel my chest is full of air, I store my rebreather with Instantaneous Inventory and activate War Thunder, hoping that the Megalodon hasn't given up the hunt and that the effects of the skill will reach it.

The maneuver does *not* go over well with the super-giant squid creature, and as I replace the rebreather I see that its tentacles are moving me toward the creature's enormous beak. *Jesus H. Christ!* I panic again and try to force my way free by summoning, storing, and resummoning my pole axe in an attempt to slice the tentacles by using its own pressure against them.

The beak snaps open and closed as it moves me closer and closer. The water around me becomes a haze of red as I manage to create tears in the tentacles. Then moments before the beak closes down around me, I see the gaping maw of the Megalodon fade into view from the black of the ocean. A moment later, it closes down around the Greater Architeuthis's head.

All of a sudden, the tentacles engulfing me are gone and I can move. Staring in horror at how close the jagged teeth of the shark came to me, I summon, activate, and drop several grenades around the squid, then I move as fast as I can to the back of the beast.

At the shark's back, I give a shout to the god of war and activate Tū's Gift, increasing my weapon damage, and attempt to carve into the rock-hard skin of the creature with my poleaxe. Before long, a pair of tentacles surrounds the body of the shark. Moving out of their way, I hear multiple *thumps* from within the shark. *Sweet.* It appears as though the shark swallowed them while attempting to chow down on the squid.

Looking at the stats for both creatures, I see their hit points are dropping rapidly, and I have no idea which one will come out on top. Although my bet would be on the Megalodon.

Crawling with all my strength along the shark's head toward its eyes as it thrashes through the water, I notice the surface is quickly coming upon us. We burst through and I'm flung into the air, away from the fight, as the shark brings both creatures out of the water.

Activating Fly, I stay near the colossal foes as I consume a mana regeneration potion, then I activate Meteoric Strike. Modes of red light surround me and cast massive circles upon the ocean and monsters fighting below the waves. Then a ginormous ball of flaming rock, followed by six slightly smaller balls of flaming debris, appears from a cloud of purple and black void and hurtles toward the space I've targeted.

The attack smashes into the ocean, and chunks of meat, rock, and bloody water are thrown into the air. Neither of them are dead yet, but that attack brought them both to below two thousand hit points. I deactivate Fly and swan-dive back into the fray.

It takes another few minutes of avoiding shredded tentacles and flapping fins, but together, the squid and I deal enough damage to kill the Megalodon. However my fight isn't over just yet. With less than five hundred hit points remaining on the Greater Architeuthis, it now tries to run away. I cast War Thunder again, stopping it in its tracks and giving me enough time to renew both Warrior's Rage and Tū's Gift. Then I deal a final blow to the creature's face, cleaving what's left of its head in two and bringing this battle to an end.

Items Received

1x Megalodon corpse

12x Megalodon Teeth

1x Megalodon Fin

1x Greater Architeuthis corpse

1x Greater Architeuthis Beak

2x Greater Architeuthis Tentacles

52,621 Credits

Congratulations! Level Up x3

You are now Level 40

Fuck yes! Level 40! Holy shit, this fight with the Manawatara might not be so *ohmygod-ohmygod-I'msogonnadie* anymore.

Side thought, where the hell did the credits come from? Is that from the people and sentients these two have eaten? Wow, that's messed up.

Also, gotta say, I'm a little gutted that I didn't get a title for soloing two really powerful enemies, but I guess that's not *that* an uncommon thing in this new world... which is also pretty messed up. Plus side though, the beak and teeth should make for decent trophies, once I get them all tidied up. I can't believe I forgot to equip my Kiwinuipāhue claws again.

Allocating my Skills and stat points, I take a look at my updated character sheet:

Status Screen			
Name	Nathaniel Atkinson	**Class**	Vengeful Warrior
Race	Human (Male)	**Level**	40
Titles			
Eater of War Parties, Pyrorational			
Health	500	**Stamina**	500
Mana	320	**Mana Regeneration**	84 / minute
Conditions			

None			
Attributes			
Strength	92	**Agility**	54
Constitution	50	**Perception**	54
Intelligence	32	**Willpower**	89
Charisma	23	**Luck**	23
Class Skills			
War Thunder (Level 1)	Haumia's Trap (Level 1)	Tū's Gift (Level 2)	Warriors Rage (Level 5)
Tāne's Sight (Level 1)	Trophy Hunter (Level 1)	Heart of the Warrior (Level 1)	Rehua's Light (Level 1)
Meteoric Strike (Level 1)	Warriors Resolve (Level 1)	Shroud of the Fallen (Level 1)	
Additional Skills and Spells			
Instantaneous Inventory (Maxed)	Flight (Level 1)		

So, I now have Warrior's Resolve, which gives me a tidy boost to my perception, luck, and—most importantly for this upcoming fight—willpower. The mana cost hurts, but thankfully I'm currently flush with mana potions.

The pièce de résistance however, and the skill that will hopefully let me clench a capital V, is Shroud of the Fallen. This covers me in a shield that has the strength equivalent to the health of all those I'm seeking vengeance for.

It'll cost me almost all my mana and I'm going to get pretty close to earning that splitting headache that is mana withdrawal, but if I can pull this off, maybe I can go… without hearing Gorillaz, Kora, or Matchbox Twenty again…

All right. Enough of that. Let's get this little adventure over and done with.

***

Scanning the ocean between the island and the coast multiple times, I can't see any sign of predatory life, so I assume the fight between two higher levelled creatures and the scent of their blood must be enough of an indicator that there's trouble around, and everything has scattered. That suits me just fine.

Not expecting to run into any more trouble on the open water, I fly back to my borrowed vessel and get it heading toward Whale Island again. While I travel, I tidy myself up and have a bite to eat.

As I'm about to reach the island, I slow the vessel down so I can see if anything's waiting for me. Using my binoculars, I see a group of about a dozen humans and several creatures guarding against eventualities like me.

Opting to not engage the innocents, I push down my anger and take the boat closer to the cliffs. There's no shoreline, but I simply fly over.

After I land and make my way across the island, I activate the scanner and see groups of people and monsters all over the island. But eventually I see the blue glow of my target in a rocky area inland from Sulphur Bay.

Coming down quietly from above them, I land in a tree and notice that in the group surrounding the Manawatara is not only Otiniara, but also Jase, Sam, Ellie, and three of the Coastlands Quartet. Behind the mutated beast is a pile of human and creature bodies. None of them are moving, so I can only assume these are people and monsters that have either been killed to use as food, or they're the ones who didn't make it all the way and were added to the pile after having washed up on the island's shores.

Anger, along with a hint of humiliation and betrayal, strike me. How long has this creature been subduing people around here? Was it only after O turned up? And more importantly, how am I going to deal with this?

Scanning the area again, I look for the highest-level human I can find, and eventually I find her guarding Boulder Bay beach. Mrs. Terrell, the fourth of the Coastlands Quartet, is just the person I need to help save everyone.

I make my way over to the area behind where she's stationed and hide in another tree. Calling on the god of uncultivated food, I cast Haumia's Trap on the ground out of sight of the others in her group and just within the bushes below me. Now that I've completed what little prep work I can do, I throw stones at her until she comes over to investigate.

Sometimes the simplest things work like a charm. The second she searches the bushes, the trap snatches her and I make my move. Slipping to the ground, I close my hand over her mouth while dropping in the purification pill I'd purchased for Ellie. Then tilting her head back, I force it down her throat until her eyes go wide with what I assume is shock, revulsion, and fear. In short order, she stops struggling.

Using Tāne's Sight, I can see that the question mark conditions are no longer affecting her. Slowly letting her go while helping her out of the trap, I cast Rehua's Light.

"Mr. Atkinson," she says, brushing herself clean and casting her own healing spell, "thank you for your help, but what are you doing here? You are in a lot of danger, there's—"

Before she can say more, I interrupt. "Yep, know all about the mind-controlling lizard. It has my friends, not to mention a few thousand people and miscellaneous monsters, under its spell." I wait a moment to be sure she heard me before continuing. "What I need from you is a distraction. Other than me and Otiniara, you're by far the highest-level human on the island, but based on the fact that I just released you from the mind-controlling spell, I'm guessing you don't have much of a resistance to mental attacks."

I wait for her nod to indicate that she's following along.

"Well I do, and I think we can save most of the people here if we work smart," I say. "By now, the Manawatara will know you've gone rogue, but if we're lucky, it doesn't know how or why. You need to knock out as many people as you can and get them on the boats, while killing as many of the creatures as possible. Meanwhile, I'll try to get past its guards and take out the beast itself."

Her eyes go wide with the task I'm setting her, but she nods in acceptance. Huh, weird, telling my old PE teacher what to do, but again, that's our new world... hope I pass this test.

***

Sneaking back toward the lair of the mystical tuatara, I see that a number of its guards have left to deal with the distraction. However, Otiniara, Ellie, and Sam are still there. I can't see Jase or the other girls from the Coastlands team, and I can only hope they haven't been killed and aren't able to take down Mrs. T.

Before launching my plan, I look at the stats of the Manawatara so I know how much damage I have to do.

Manawatara
Level 88
HP: 42,581
Mana: 259,122/ 617,286
Conditions: None

On the one hand, I'm scared shitless. This thing is *so* much higher in level than me, and it has guards—who, by the way, I don't want to harm and I don't want harming me. On the other hand, forty thousand or so hit points is totally within my ability to accomplish, especially with my newly allocated and acquired Skills. I might just be able to pull this off.

Deciding that the element of surprise is my best bet, I load up all my body and weapon buffs, then drink a mana potion, and attack.

First, I cast Meteoric Strike. Before the flaming chunks of rock materialize above us, I'm already drinking another mana potion and focusing on all the people this monster has killed. My rage and determination hit an all-time high, and I cast Shroud of the Fallen as I leap through toward the beast. The glow of the shield encompasses me as I land a critical blow with my poleaxe atop the Manawatara's head, then the rain of molten fire crashes down upon us.

For a solid minute, all around me is chaos, flames, and earth being blasted apart. I keep my attack going against my target as I deal hundreds, and occasionally thousands, of damage per swing. Shortly after the final blast of the comets fades away, O, Ellie, and Sam are aware enough to know what's going on, and by then I have the Manawatara's health below twenty thousand.

Ellie screams with rage and fires arrows at me. Sam downs one of his elixirs and bulks out to be what looks like five times his original size. His clothes are ripped apart and he smashes the ground to create boulders to hurl my way. Out of the corner of my eye, I see Otiniara casting buffs on his party before beginning a chant that generates a crazy-looking ball of black light surrounded by yellow pulses of power.

Shroud of the Fallen Shield Status
HP: 42,354/ 76,503

"You know, I did try to get you on my side," O says between verses.

Meanwhile, Ellie with her bow and Sam with his boulders rain down long-range attacks as I hack away at the Manawatara. Its writhing body twists and thrashes in pain beneath me. *Just a little longer, shield! Please hold out a little longer.*

Shroud of the Fallen Shield Status
HP: 37,726/ 76,503

Mid-attack, I reply to O. "That's." *Swipe.* "Not." *Hack.* "You." *Thunk.* "Talking." *Slice.*

The creature's hit points are dropping, but so is my shield. Along the ridge, I notice more people coming to join the attack. I can only pray that Mrs. T and the people she was taking to the boats are still alive.

Shroud of the Fallen Shield Status
HP: 28,321/ 76,503

"I just wanted to go home!" Ellie and Sam scream in unison, moments before Sam launches himself at me and drops ground-shattering punches against my shield. Each strike results in visible shockwaves that shake the nearby rocks and flora. Once again, in perfect, gut-wrenchingly horrific harmony, they yell, *"Leave me alone!"* THUD! *Ttthhrruummmm.* *"And die!"*

Shroud of the Fallen Shield Status
HP: 16,947/ 76,503

Swiping at Sam with my poleaxe, I yell, "Get off me, ya plodding oaf! Can't you see you're about to be killed by O's attack?"

Ellie's arrows strike my shield, some bouncing away harmlessly, but Sam is also getting in the way of them, resulting in several protruding from his back and slowing him down a touch.

"I said, *fuck off!*" With all the strength I can gather, I strike Sam as hard as I can, slicing off an arm and removing a chunk of his left leg as I send him flying into the group of people who had just joined the fray.

Shroud of the Fallen Shield Status
HP: 5,292/ 76,503

"You're too late!" O says. "This is going to kill you. Even if you deal the final blow, this will still wipe you from existence!" Then he launches his roaring balls of electrified darkness at me.

I yell, *"Go to hell, you mind-fucking piece of—"*

The Manawatara screams in agony, its health almost completely gone. Just as I'm about to see it hit zero, O's attack strikes us both.

Otiniara Pio Matetu's attack Overture to Obliteration deals 5,785 points of damage.

Shroud of the Fallen Shield Status
HP: 0/ 76,503

Fire and hell rain down on us. The Manawatara is cooked to a crisp in less than a heartbeat, and I'm tossed around like a ragdoll in a flaming hurricane. This is the most pain I have ever experienced.

As the spell's universal orchestra plays, I feel my body being ripped apart at the molecular level. The torture lasts for only a moment, but to me, it's as if I've experienced the annihilation of every star in our universe, had them explode around me, then had the energy from each one crash into my core over and over and over until they'd managed to form new orbs of light and form their own ecosystems once more.

That is to say, to me, the pain felt as though it lasted an eternity.

When the flames subsided and the dust settled, I was still there. My body felt, and probably looked, as though I'd fallen into a volcano. Charred skin fell away to expose boiling blood and roasted bone. One of my eyes had burst, and while my ears were damaged, I could still make out the odd sound through the persistent ringing. I found myself unable to speak as I no longer had a jaw, and only my right arm remained attached. But I was alive. Sure, I only seven hit points left, but I was alive.

Slowly rolling to the side, I faintly heard sobbing, then there was the barest amount of pressure on my chest and head. It seemed most of my nerve endings had been fried. Beyond the subtle crying, I heard a tortured scream—

long, deep, and what felt unending. Soon my hearing faded, my sight grew dim, and finally true darkness greeted me like an old friend.

***

I woke up several weeks later. Apparently due to my ocean battle before I arrived at the island, the Vaaharu's vessels returned to Whakatāne without any encounters. Mrs. Terrell didn't make it, but her efforts had taken out over half of the more dangerous creatures and she'd gotten several dozen people knocked out and placed on the boats. Other than her and those who were killed before I arrived, we lost around two hundred people to monsters after the effects of the Manawatara wore off. Still, that meant we'd saved over two thousand people.

As for me, the Vaaharu wouldn't pay up unless I woke up, and in the meantime, due to the upfront payment for gear, they considered me their property. It apparently took quite a bit of negotiating on Ngaire and Ellie's parts to get my limbs and lost pieces repaired. Even then I wouldn't wake up, and they simply had to wait me out.

Ngaire and Jase seem to have taken this experience to heart, and they now co-own the Pub. Jase moved in with her the week before I woke up.

Ellie and I... what can I say? I still don't fully trust her, but she stood by me after the fight and hasn't touched any substances since O cleansed her. I heard from Ngaire that she even threatened to chop off Sam's third leg if he came round again, so yeah, maybe I'll give her another shot. Toxic as our relationship has been this past year or so, it's possible we both had a bit of adjusting to do.

Otiniara has yet to recover. He was under the Manawatara's spell the longest, and didn't take well to the things it had made him do. Turns out the whole eye twitching thing happened any time the Manawatara used its mind control abilities on people O was looking at. With the number of times I saw it happen while he was talking with me... Geez. Maybe if I'd checked my notifications more I'd have noticed the failures and been able to do something sooner... or we'd all be dead, who knows.

Thinking about the psychological ramifications of all that, plus the fact that when I was finally able to check his stats with Tāne's Sight, it said he had the title Whakaheke Tangata, or Slayer of Men—well, I kind of expect him to be out of the game for a while, and haven't been pushing him to come out hunting with us. Hopefully all he needs is a little time.

I own a new place now, with multiple rooms, power, hot water, decent walls, and security. Everything I could need—except one thing. *Music.*

That brings me to today. I'm free and fixed. My medical bills cost over a hundred thousand, but thanks to the help from some of the people I saved, I only had to cover about sixty thousand of it. That means that after the medical fees, buying the house for me and O and maybe eventually Ellie, on top of repairing and restocking my weapons and armor, plus the pay-out from the Vaaharu bounty quest and the massive loot drop from the giant shark and squid fight, not to mention the loot from the Manawatara and its monster friends, I should be able to buy my implant and audio module after I take down one. More. Kiwinuipāhue.

"Nate! Hurry up!" Ellie calls from farther up the track. "Let's get this done!"

"Don't rush him. If ya do, we might be out here all day," Jase screams back in a rush.

Slowing down a bit, I look at my little party and think back on the last few months. I think about where we were and what we've done to survive. I realize now that I don't want to die. I met with the dark and came back from it... and I don't feel like going back anytime soon.

Today, today will be my first real day of existence in the System. We have everything we need right here. Good friends, good hunting zones, and we're slowly getting the power we need to bring back our world. Right here, right now, *The Land of the Long White Cloud* is ours, and no monsters, aliens, or messed-up magic game System will take it from us again.

And I mean, c'mon! It's not like things could get any worse. Right?

Ah, fuck it all, I'm alive.

Nathaniel's Class, Skills, and Spell Information

Kaikiko Toa/ Vengeful Warrior (B)

Class Abilities

- Plus 1 per level in Agility, Constitution, and Perception
- Plus 2 per level in Strength and Willpower
- Plus 1 Attribute per level
- Plus 10% Elemental Resistance
- Plus 50% Mental Resistance
- Gain +25% combat bonuses when using Fighting Staffs, Bladed Fighting Staffs, Poleaxe, Short Spears, Long Spears, Clubs

Skill Tree

Tier 1	Haka/ War Thunder		Haumia's Trap	Tū's Gift
	1		1	2
Tier 2	Warriors Rage		Tāne's Sight	Trophy Hunter
	5		1	1
Tier 3	Heart of the Warrior	Rehua's Light	Meteoric Strike	Vindictive Fury
	1	1	1	
Tier 4	Warriors Resolve		Rangatira of the Pā/ King of the Hill	Shroud of the Fallen
	1			1

Tao Wong

Skill Descriptions

Warriors Rage (Level 5)

Increase Strength by 50% for 5 minutes

Cool down: 10 minutes

Cost: 50 Mana

Heart of the Warrior (Level 1)

Increase Constitution and Agility by 20% for 5 minutes

Cost: 100 Mana

Warriors Resolve (Level 1)

Increase Willpower, Perception, and Luck by 20% for 5 minutes

Cost: 150 Mana

(Base increase of 30% with 5% increase per level)

Te-koha-o-Tū/ Tū's Gift (Level 2)

Increase weapon attacks by 35% for 5 minutes

Cool down: 10 minutes

Cost: 50 Mana

(Base increase of 30% with 5% increase per level)

Rehua's Light (Level 1)

Heal 100 health per casting. User requires contact with target

Cool down: 60 seconds

Cost: 50 Mana

Haumia's Trap (Level 1)

Summon a covered 1.5m diameter and 2m deep hole with 1m long spikes that traps and stuns target for 10 seconds, causing 100 points of physical damage

Cost: 50 Mana

Trophy Hunter (Level 1)

Increased System Inventory by 10x10 slots and allows all quest items to be carried at no storage cost. For each equipped trophy, user gains 5% for every core attribute to the Vengeful Warrior class (Strength and Willpower), and 2% for each secondary attribute (Agility, Constitution, and Perception)

Cost: 5 mana regeneration per minute permanently

Rangatira of the Pā/ King of the Hill (Level 1)

The ground in a 30m radius from the spot you are standing transforms into a 30m tall multi-terraced landmass, with you top and center in a fighting circle with a radius of 5m.

Unusable when flying, floating in the vacuum of space, or floating in liquids. Restricted to outdoor use, or the inside of buildings, vessels, and caverns with ceilings exceeding 35m. Pā/ Hill lasts 30 minutes before reverting to original state

Cool down: 1 hour

Cost: 200 Mana

Haka/ War Thunder (Level 1)

Summons a squad of translucent Māori warriors who dance and chant a thunderous haka. Caster ignores all damage for length of spell-casting time. Instils fear upon enemy targets within a 200m range, stunning the targets for 5 seconds, and lowers their attributes by 20% for 5 minutes
Cost: 100 Mana

Tāne's Sight (Level 1)

Able to see a target's base information, titles, attributes, conditions, and effects
Cost: 5 Mana per second

Meteoric Strike (Level 1)

Summon and launch a flaming meteor from the void for 400 Physical + 100 Fire Damage, followed up by 6 smaller flaming meteors. On-hit the smaller meteors cause 50 Fire Damage, plus 20 damage/second of Fire Damage for 20 seconds to all enemies within a 5m radius
Cost: 50 Stamina + 200 Mana

Shroud of the Fallen (Level 1)

Caster is covered in a shield, with a strength equivalent to the health of all those he is seeking vengeance for. Shield lasts 30 minutes, or until its strength has been depleted. Limited to those wronged by a target or situation within one week, and fifty kilometers of caster at the time of casting. If not fighting for someone else, then shield equals the caster's health multiplied by 1.5
Cool down: 24 hours
Cost: 250 Mana

Vindictive Fury (Level 0)

Caster is engulfed in a storm of vindictive fury for 1 minute. They can only target those they are seeking vengeance against. Limited to those wronged by a target or situation within one day, and twenty kilometers from caster at the time of casting. All attacks are increased by 5% strength and speed for each victim the caster is seeking vengeance for. While active, caster ignores 30% of melee damage and 50% of ranged attacks. If not fighting for someone else, then vision is unimpaired, with strength and speed increases equal to the casters strength and agility multiplied by 1.5

Cool down: 12 hours

Cost: 200 Stamina + 100 Mana

Non-Class Skills and Spells

Instantaneous Inventory (Maxed)

Allows user to place or remove any System-recognized item from Inventory if space allows. Includes the automatic arrangement of space in inventory. User must be touching item

Cost: 5 Mana per item

Flight (Level 1)

Allows the user to hover and fly. Movement speeds based on agility

Cost: 20 Mana per minute

Tao Wong

The Not-Perfect-But-Good-Enough Simplistic English Speaker's Pronunciation Guide for Various Te Reo Words and Māori Names

Below, you will find a basic guide for how to say the various Te Reo words (the language of the Māori people) and Māori names that are used in the *Overture to Obliteration* short story.

You may notice that some words have multiple ways of saying them. This would be akin to an English speaker butchering the word Paris by saying Pa-ris, rather than the French way, Pa-ree, with the "R" rolled to make it almost sound as though there's an "L" hidden in there somehow.

The proper/ formal way will be listed first where applicable. This way is typically used by those who speak fluent Te Reo, those who teach or are actively learning Te Reo, many teachers, those who represent large bodies of people or organizations, and of course the odd person on the street. In terms of the short story, alien races like the Vaaharu would use this form by default, Ngaire would default to this manner, and Otiniara would use them depending on the situation and who he's talking to.

The other way of saying those words is used by a large number of average Kiwis. Nate, Jase, and O would primarily use these pronunciations. They may know the proper and formal way but tend to default to the colloquialized version.

It should also be noted that I have included some basic definitions, however, Te Reo words can hold multiple meanings. Those listed here are simple translations and are more for showing how they are used in the context of the story.

I hope you find the following information useful, and that it makes the reading of *Overture to Obliteration* a touch more immersive.

Te Reo Word or Māori Name	Simplistic English Speakers Pronunciation Guide
Te Reo *Basic Definition: Language of the <Māori> people*	T-eh Rai-Oh. *Rai* is said like the start of the word <u>Rai</u>n.
Māori *Describes: The Polynesian people native to New Zealand*	Mm-ou-ree. *Ou* said like <u>Ou</u>ch, and *Ree* is said like in the word T<u>ree</u>. Rs are rolled in this version of the pronunciation. Mou-ree *Mou* is said like the start of Mouse or Mountain.
Kiwinuipāhue *Basic Definition: Giant Plundering Kiwi*	Key-we-new-e-pah-who-e *Pah* sounds like the start of the word <u>Pa</u>th. *Note: This is a made-up creature*
Maraetōtara *Basic Definition: Gathering of Tōtara trees* *Describes: A Suburb of Whakatāne*	Ma-righ-a-toe-tra *Righ* like the word <u>Righ</u>t, and *Tra* like the word <u>Tra</u>in.
Nga Tapuwae O Toi *Basic Definition: The footsteps of Toi*	Nah Tah-poo-why Oh Toy Fun Fact: Few people use this name unless maybe they're listing it in documents, on signs and maps, or in some sort of official

	capacity. Locals tend to simply call this "The Bird Walk." Toi was the son of the founding Chief of Whakatāne
Whakatāne *Describes: A Town in New Zealand*	Fok-a-tar-knee. *Fok* is said like the word *Wok*, but with a "fff" sound at the start.
Rotorua *Describes: A City in New Zealand*	Raw-toh-roo-a *Toh* is said like the start of the word <u>To</u>fu. *Roo* is said like the start of the word <u>Roo</u>f. Rs are rolled. Row-ta-roo-a Fun Fact: Also known as Rotovegas
Kopeopeo *Describes: A Suburb of Whakatāne*	Cou-peh-awe-peh-awe *Cou* sounds like the start of the word <u>Cou</u>rt. *Peh* sounds like you're starting to say the word Pear. Co-pee-oh-pee-oh *Co* is said like the start of the word <u>Co</u>pe. Fun Fact: Also known as just Kope
Mokoroa *Describes: A hill in the Whakatāne area*	M-awe-ck-oh-row-a Rs are rolled. Mock-oh-row-a
Kaikiko Toa *Basic Definition: Vengeful Warrior*	Ki-key-co Toe-ah *Ki* sounds like the start of the word <u>Ki</u>te.
Kai Taua	Ki To-a

Basic Definition: Eater of War Parties	*To* like the start of the word <u>To</u>rn.
Haka Basic Definition: A traditional chanting dance of the Māori people of New Zealand	Ha-ca *Ca* sounds like the start of the word <u>Ca</u>r.
Haumia Basic Definition: Māori name for the god of all uncultivated food	Ho-me-ah *Ho* sounds like the start of the word <u>Ho</u>me.
Te-koha-o-Tū Basic Definition: Gift from the Māori god of war, hunting, fishing and agriculture	T-eh-co-ha-oh-too *Co* Sounds like the start of the word <u>Co</u>re.
Tāne Basic Definition: Human of masculine sex or gender. It is also the shortened name for the Māori god of forests and birds	Tah-knee Tar-knee
Rehua Basic Definition: Māori name for the star god with the power of healing	Rei-who-a *Rai* is said like the start of the word <u>Rai</u>n.
Kia ora Basic Definition: Hello/ Greetings/ Thanks, essentially an expressing goodwill or gratitude	Key-Ore-ah Roll the R for proper. Same pronunciation, just without the r-rolling for the other way.

Otiniara *Describes: A person's name*	Oh-tin-e-are-ah Roll the R for proper. Same pronunciation, just without the r-rolling for the other way.
Pio *Describes: A person's name*	Pee-or Soft r sound in *Or.*
Matetu *Describes: A person's name*	Mut-ah-too Mat-ah-too
Kai *Basic Definition: Food*	Ki *Ki* sounds like the start of the word <u>Ki</u>te.
Tumeke *Basic Definition: Too Much*	Too-meh-key
Pohutu *Describes: A street name in Whakatāne*	Poe-who-too
Mataatua *Basic Definition: Window to the gods* *Describes: The name of a famous waka/canoe*	Mah-tar-too-ah
Ngāti Awa *Basic Definition: River Tribe* *Describes: The local Māori clan*	Nah-tea Ah-wha *Wha* sounds like the start of the word <u>Wha</u>t.
Marae	Mar-eye

Basic Definition: Meeting House	*Mar* sounds like the start of the word <u>Mar</u>ch.
Iwi *Basic Definition: Clan*	E-wee
Ngāti Hokopū *Describes: A location/ organization in Whakatāne. They are a clan of the Ngāti Awa Iwi*	Nah-tea Ho-cou-poo *Ho* as in the way you would say <u>Ho</u>rse. *Cou* sounds like the start of the word <u>Cou</u>rt.
Ōpōtiki *Describes: A Town in New Zealand*	Oh-poe-tiki
Manawatara *Basic Definition: Mind/spirit Spines*	Mana-wah-tar-ah *Note: This is a made-up creature*
Tauranga *Describes: A City in New Zealand*	Tow-wrong-ah Rs are rolled. Tau-wrong-ah
Pāpāmoa *Describes: A Suburb of Tauranga*	Pah-pah-mau-ah *Pah* sounds like the start of the word <u>Pass</u>. *Mau* like the start of the word <u>Maul</u>. Pap-ah-mow-ah
Maunganui *Describes: Mount Maunganui is a Suburb of Tauranga. It's also the name of the mountain in the area*	Mong-ga-new-ee *Mong* like the word <u>Mong</u>olia. *Ga* like the word <u>Ga</u>rfield.

Te Puke *Describes: A Town in New Zealand*	T-eh P-ook-e *Ook* like the end of the word L<u>ook</u>.
Ruapehu *Basic Definition: A pit of noise or exploding pit* *Describes: A volcano by the name of Mount Ruapehu*	Ru-a-pay-who *Ru* like the start of the word <u>Ru</u>in.
Ngaire *Describes: A person's name*	Kni-ree *Kni* like the start of the word Knight or Knife. *Ree* like the end of the word T<u>ree</u>.
Moutohorā *Basic Definition: Island of the Whale* *Describes: An island off the coast of Whakatāne*	Mau-to-hor-ah *Mau* like the start of the word <u>Mau</u>l. *To* like the start of the word <u>To</u>rn. *Hor* is said like the start of the word <u>Hor</u>se. Mow-tor-hor-ah *Tor* is said with a soft r. *Hor* is said like the start of the word <u>Hor</u>se. Fun Fact: Few people use this name unless maybe they're listing it in documents, on signs and maps, or in some sort of official capacity. Locals tend to simply call the location "Whale Island."
Kora *Describes: A New Zealand band whose band members are part of the Kora family*	Co-rah *Co* is said like the start of the word <u>Co</u>re. *Fun Note: Kora (the band and family) are from Whakatāne*
Ka Mate	Ca Mah-ta

Basic Definition: Will/ 'tis Death	*Ca* sounds like the start of the word <u>Ca</u>r. *Ta* like the start of the word <u>T</u>ake.
Ka Ora *Basic Definition: Will/ 'tis Life*	Ca Ore-ah *Ca* sounds like the start of the word <u>Ca</u>r.
Whakaheke Tangata *Basic Definition: Slayer of Men*	Fok-ah-heck-eh Tounge-gah-ta
Tū *Basic Definition: Māori name for the god of war, hunting, fishing and agriculture. Full name is - Tūmatauenga*	Too
Rangatira *Basic Definition: Chief*	Rung-ah-tear-ah
Pā *Basic Definition: Fortified Village (typically atop a multi-terraced hill), or blockade*	Pah *Pah* sounds like the start of the word <u>Pa</u>ss.

Intermission Six

"M?" Vir called to his friend as he noticed her grow white. He'd seen it before, seen the flashbacks, the moments of disruption. No matter how much the System helped, provided increases in Willpower or flushed chemicals, the human mind was not meant to handle the loss and pain the survivors had suffered. Some, like Amelia, did better, functioning with little issues. But even then, a smell, a laugh, an image could trigger memories.

Even among his Truinnar guards, Vir had noticed some minor issues. For Truinnar, side-effects were more due to the constant stress of living in a Dungeon World, in a domain that was constantly challenged by other Galactic powers. That some actually found the entire process relaxing – due to their escape from the Barony – was ironic.

"I told you, don't call me that," Amelia sniped at Vir. She shook her head, discarding the document to the interesting, but not important, pile. That pile would be assigned to one of the guards to follow up on, using mundane and then Shop information networks. Any person with a unique Class or were cheaters like John needed a careful watch. And while not everyone in the world was as blatant about their presence as the Champions, they were all sill powers. Powers that could be used when the next crisis happened.

"Of course. M." The virtual world meant that when she threw the data slate at Vir's head, the slate just disappeared before hitting him. Together, in companionable silence, they worked. Until Vir shot up in his chair, his jaw dropping.

And then promptly disappeared.

"What the hell?" Amelia said, staring at the spot where her partner had been. A flick of her hands brought up the last document Vir had viewed.

Phoenix Rising

By R.K. Billiau

Chapter 1

The average person lives four to six years after an early onset Alzheimer's diagnosis. Dan's came eighteen months ago. He could feel his mind melting away. Some days were a haze of memories jumbled together as if lived all at once. Today he could remember the look on his wife's face the first time he forgot who she was. He took a deep breath to steady himself.

When he started having trouble remembering he chalked it up to his time with the Army in Iraq. 'Gulf War Illness', they called it. A strange cocktail of maladies that afflicted tens of thousands of servicemen. The litany of afflictions was as long as Dan's arm and memory problems topped the list.

Dan knew something else was going on when he started hallucinating. The lights would overwhelm him with brightness, his pupils shrinking to a speck as he squeezed his eyelids closed. Shadows would pop out at him making him jump. Sometimes sounds wouldn't process, coming into his mind as a garble. His wife broke down the day they got the diagnosis, while Dan sat rubbing his hands, stunned into silence.

He sat on his bed, eyes still heavy with sleep, not quite ready to start the day. His mother, Susan, broke his reverie, knocking on the door jamb to rouse him.

"Dan, we've got to get ready to go soon, do you need help? Monica followed Jason to the mechanic so she could give him a ride back. I swear breaking cars must be genetic as often as he has to get something repaired. He drives just like you! Anyway, I'm going to bring you to your appointment, we are going to leave a little early to avoid traffic." He smiled weakly, thankful for her selflessness.

"No… I'm… I'll be ok. I'll be right there," Dan said sleepily.

"Well honey, let me help you get dressed, the appointment isn't too long from now," his mother said, moving into the room to help him out of his bathrobe and into the sweats his wife had laid on the bed. She reached out to touch him.

"NO DAMNIT!" he screamed like a precocious two-year-old. "I can do it myself today!" He jumped away from her touch, the anger filling him with a seething hot fury. He knew the anger was unfounded, that it was the dementia, but he couldn't control it, couldn't stop it, as if it had a life of its own. He snatched the clothes off the bed and stomped to his bathroom, slamming the door.

"I'll just be in the kitchen then, dear," his ever-patient mother replied. "I have a cup of coffee waiting for you along with your pills."

Dan leaned his against the bathroom door and slid to the floor, the anger fading just as quickly as it had come. The rage beast was letting go of its control over his mind. His head fell and he cradled his knees, eyes wet with salty tears. Was he even himself anymore?

When the first blue box appeared in his vision, he read it, then dismissed it as just another hallucination from his broken mind. A box, like a window on his computer, saying something about a 'Dungeon World'. A countdown appeared, and he waved his hand to shoo away the box. Was his mind this broken already?

A loud crash from below drew his attention so he stood and slipped into his clothes. He noticed his reflection and made eye contact with the man in the bathroom mirror. He barely recognized himself. Dark, disheveled hair falling into dull eyes with heavy bags. Unattended facial scruff that was long past five o'clock shadow. He shook his head, disgusted, and left the room. When his feet hit the top of the stairs, more boxes appeared in his vision.

Congratulations! You have been spawned in the Shasta National Forest (Level 100+) zone. You have spawned in the level 80 section of the Forest.
You have received 5500 XP (Delayed)
As per Dungeon World Development Schedule 124.3.2.2, inhabitants assigned to a region with a recommended Level 25 or more above the inhabitants' current Level will receive one Small Perk.
As per Dungeon World Development Schedule 124.3.2.3, inhabitants assigned to a region with a recommended Level 50 or more above the inhabitants' current Level will receive one Medium Perk.
As per Dungeon World Development Schedule 124.3.2.4, inhabitants assigned to a region with a recommended Level 75 or more above the inhabitants' current Level will receive one Large Perk.

Dan shook his head violently to clear the box away and lost his balance. He crashed into the wall, his body sliding down the stairs to the bottom, arms flailing to grab onto anything that would stop him. At forty-eight his body was still healthy, and a firefighting career had made him strong, so he suffered no damage except another wound to his pride. He slammed his fist into the wall, the pain evicting the rage.

"Dan! Are you all right? It's time to make that switch, we can't have you living with stairs like these!" His mother, just shy of seventy, was still strong and healthy. She and some friends had started a walking group in town and on any day could be seen together talking and power walking in their 1980s sun-visors and hip packs. As strong as she was, she was still an older woman, all of 120 pounds soaking wet, and had to struggle to lift her adult son.

"What are you talking about?" Dan asked, not knowing if he didn't remember, or if he had never known. He used the wall as leverage to aid her in getting him up.

"Monica and I talked about moving you two into the mother-in-law unit so you wouldn't have to deal with the stairs," his mother replied as she gave him a once over to check for any injuries. "Are you okay? Does it hurt anywhere?"

The simple question sent Dan's mind spiraling. Flashes of memories ripped through his consciousness replacing his awareness of the present with brief moments of his past. The woman in the room was pressing her hands to his chest, probing him, the words coming out of her mouth mere noises that made no sense.

"Get AWAY!" Dan shouted and brushed the strange woman away. He dropped to the floor, put his head between his knees and rocked.

He looked up to see his mother, worry contorting her face as she stared at her son. "Dan? Honey? Can you get up?" She steadied him as he got to his feet.

"What's going on?" he asked. The boxes appeared again in his vision, and again he shook his head to make them go away. They made no sense. "Weren't we supposed to be going somewhere?"

His mom nodded, her concern melting to resolve. "We've got your doctor appointment in Shasta Lake. You have to eat first though, dear." She held her hand out to him and squeezed his when he placed it in hers. She guided him to his seat and the familiarity of his mom doting on him, feeding him and making sure he had enough to drink calmed him down.

As Susan helped Dan with his medication, she chattered on about the latest meal she was preparing for someone in town who had just had a baby. When she noticed Dan had cleaned his plate she stood up. "Do you want some more? It's no problem to make more," she asked.

Dan shook his head and rubbed his stomach. "I'm stuffed."

Susan smiled at him. "Good, I packed some snacks in the car anyway in case you get hungry. We should probably get going." Dan stood up and she led him out the door to the car then paused before opening the door to the passenger side and letting Dan in.

Chapter 2

Dan's mom drove them down I-5 from their small town on the outskirts of Shasta National Forest towards the city of Shasta Lake. The roads were quiet, with few travelers, only a couple cars in the distance ahead of them. Dan balled his fists, squeezing tight enough to make the knuckles go white. He couldn't remember where he was going, only that it was important. He would have asked his mom but these weird boxes, like windows on a computer screen, kept popping up in his field of vision.

The boxes were offering him choices of a class, things like Pyrokinetic, Mage and Ranger. It read like when he used to play Dungeons and Dragons. Dan tried to pay close attention to what they were saying, but the boxes kept flickering from one thing to another, as if there was a video glitch. He couldn't concentrate very well, anyway. He had something important to do. He looked out the window as the landscape passed by, trying to kick start his mind into remembering. Another box appeared describing a Blue Mage as a countdown in the corner ticked seconds indicating there was a little under fifty minutes left.

They had only driven a few miles before Dan blinked and waved away another screen. He had been jarred back to reality when the car slowed, and his mother cursed. "What is it? What's going on?" he asked. He couldn't remember hearing his mom curse before.

She didn't answer, her knuckles white on the steering wheel as she muscled it onto the shoulder. The power steering no longer working, she pushed the brake, stopping the car.

"The car just died... I don't get it..." She tried the ignition, turning the key over and over to no avail. Dan stared at her, face blank as he tried to force his mind to function. Another box appeared.

Incoming System message: An entity has determined you are a match for a symbiotic partnership. Would you like to accept? Entity: Phoenix. Warning: this is permanent.

Dan shook his head trying to get the box away. His mom needed his help. The box did the weird glitch thing and reappeared in his vision. He didn't know why this kept happening but he was becoming quite aggravated with the hallucinations from his broken mind. To make it go away he thought 'accept' at the box and it flashed yellow and disappeared only to reappear.

Symbiotic relationship formed.

Congratulations! World First. As the first individual to form a symbiotic relationship, your symbiosis has been upgraded from **Commensalism** *to* **Mutualism***.*

A voice spoke in Dan's mind, startling him.

< **"I see neither time nor space can provide a permanent escape from the System, once again I am caught within its clutches and bound to the life of a mortal."**>

"What is this?" Dan asked in a shaky voice.

"It's okay, dear, I'll just try to reach Monica or AAA and we can get towed," his mother said, as she once again tried the ignition. Dan jumped when his mom started smacking her phone against the dash. "What...is...wrong...with this thing?!" she gritted through her teeth and took a deep breath, her voice going back to normal. "Dan, do you have your phone?" She turned to look at him, but he didn't register it as the voice spoke again.

< **"Daniel Jay Burns, I am the Phoenix, you have accepted the contract of symbiosis with me and now our lives are entwined."**>

Dan shook his head violently again. The hallucinations were getting worse. He didn't remember the doctors ever telling him he would hear voices like this. "No, NO! Stop talking to me!" he shouted pressing his hands to the sides of his head. His mother frowned as she watched him.

"It's okay, dear, it's me, Mom. I'm just going to check your pockets for your phone." She reached to pat his leg where his pant pockets were. "I'm not going to hurt you, honey."

"Not you," Dan said. "The voice in my head... first the boxes, now a voice. I... I think it's getting worse."

< **"I assure you Daniel, your mind is not broken. In fact, it is only through one such as you, I may form this bond. In order for a Phoenix to bond with another sentient, that sentient must have a disjointed mind. It is the nature of our abilities to be in flux, embracing change and rising from chaos."**>

His mom froze, making eye contact with her son. "What did you say? Something about boxes?"

"Yeah... I saw... boxes. Like computer windows. I don't-"

"You saw them too?" His mom cut him off.

"Wait... you saw the boxes?" Dan asked. His breath quickened and his eyes bore into hers.

< **"It's always difficult on Dungeon Worlds for the natives. You have my sympathies. This communication takes much out of me, however, and I cannot keep it active very long. I can sense your thoughts and perceive some of what you perceive. I can tell you are in grave danger. You must get to a lower level zone soon or you will die."**>

"-y the car isn't working, or the phones?" His mother finished her question which Dan only half heard as he focused on the voice in his mind. "Dan? Please be okay, I need you to be able to help us." The worry in his mom's voice sent another cascade of memories through his mind. The day his father died, his mother's grief as she dealt with the loss, her voice when she learned of Dan's condition. Dan shook his head, and this time the memories cleared away, leaving him lucid.

"Mom. We have to go; we aren't safe here," he said with confidence and unbuckled his seatbelt.

< **"Your technology will no longer work now that the System is in place. You must go south, towards where there are more humans. You can be safer there, then you must get stronger, strong enough to free me from my prison."**>

Dan closed his eyes and visualized his thoughts going towards the voice in his mind.

"Can you hear me?"

< "Yes, Daniel, I can hear you. I tire though and must end this communication soon.">

"What is this 'System' you're talking about? What kind of danger are we in?"

The voice in his head made a sound like that of fire popping on hot sap and Dan recognized it as laughter.

< "That question is one I cannot answer any better than you I am afraid. The System is the System. It entraps worlds without care, civilizations rise or fall within its embrace and entire races have died seeking that answer. This is your new life, your new world. I urge you to find safety, you must level at least once for our bond to help you, but you must get to a lower level zone and soon. I must rest now, but I will leave you with this.">

With those last words came a blinking mail notification in Dan's field of vision as the presence left his mind. Dan smiled as the brain fog cleared, and he was suddenly clear headed. His mom placed her hand on his shoulder. "Dan?"

"Yeah, I'm here. Sorry, I'm not gone yet. I was just.... talking to the thing in my head. It told me we have to go south to get as far away from the forest as we can."

"What did those boxes mean? Do you know something?" his mother asked as she also unbuckled and got out of the car. "Why isn't the car or my phone working?"

Dan stretched, flexing his muscles as if preparing to exercise, reveling in this moment of lucidity, while worrying about how long it would last. He opened his mouth to respond but snapped it shut as an explosion to the northwest cut off what he was about to say. He watched as a pillar of dark smoke began rising into the sky.

Chapter 3

Dan's mom gasped and clenched his arm. "That's near town. What could have happened?" she asked. They stared at the rising cloud of grey smoke, twisting up into the blue sky.

"I don't know, but I don't think it's good." Dan spoke without looking away from the smoke. "The voice in my head told me our technology won't work anymore now that we're a part of this... System. Maybe it has something to do with that."

"You really saw the boxes too, then?" his mother confirmed. "And this...voice? That's part of it? I didn't know what to make of them before, and we were in such a rush to get you to your appointment I ignored them. What does this mean, is it aliens or something?"

Dan shrugged. "I'm not sure. But the voice in my head- it called itself the Phoenix- told me we have to get to a lower level zone, or we might die."

She looked at him and raised her eyebrow. "What in the world does that mean?"

"I think it's like in that video game Jason plays, World of Warfight or whatever. We have numbered levels that tell us how strong we are. Creatures and other stuff do as well. We must be in an area meant for higher levels."

"I don't understand any of that." Dan's mother gripped his arm tighter. "I remember seeing a screen that said I could pick a class or something, but then you fell down the stairs and I ignored it to help you. How do I get that to come up again? How do I know what level I am?"

Dan shook his head, his default motion for trying to separate reality from fiction. "I don't know. I don't even know what class I am. I think I saw a message about classes but don't think I ever got one." The blinking message icon in Dan's field of vision drew his attention. He attempted to look at it, his eyes going wild and swirling in every direction until he gave up and tried to send a thought at it like he had the voice. The screen opened to reveal a message from the Phoenix.

< "I cannot help until my energy recovers, but by becoming a symbiont with me I have been able to craft a class package utilizing your perks you have gained. This package should contain everything to ensure maximum survivability based upon your life experiences.">

Do you wish to accept the class package? Yes/No
Warning: Accepting this class package will consume all perks!

Dan didn't know what to do with this information. He didn't know if the Phoenix would make the best decisions for him or was offering things that would only help itself. He directed a thought towards the System to ask about available classes. A massive list popped up with most options grayed out as un-selectable. He thought 'perks' and an even larger list bloomed.

"I don't have a class yet. It looks like I can choose one, but there are so many choices," he said. "The voice, the er… Phoenix I guess, created a class package to help survivability, but I don't know if I can trust it."

"How do you know all of this?" his mom asked.

"I just thought 'class' into the System, and it gave me a list, the same for perks."

Susan's eyes went blank for a moment then she focused back on Dan. "Oh my, there's so many!"

"It's kind of intimidating," Dan said. "I know we should get going but we probably need to try to figure this out first. I want to at least figure out a class. I think we need every advantage if we are in a dangerous area."

"It's going to take us a while to walk back, can't we do it as we walk?" Susan asked.

"We could, but wouldn't you rather be prepared, just in case something happens on the walk?"

Susan gave that a seconds thought, then sighed and opened the door to the car to sit on the seat.

"That makes sense, I'm just worried," she said as she kicked her feet in the dirt. She reached through the car and grabbed her purse, pulling out a baggie of cookies. I'll just give this list a look then… what in the world is Magical Chef?" She took out a cookie and nibbled at it then handed the bag to Dan who rolled his eyes at the proffered treats. He was still full from breakfast, but took the bag anyway. He had learned it was easier to just take the food than be constantly asked if he was hungry.

Dan walked to the hood of the sedan and sat on it, opening the list of classes. He began to parse through it but as the information entered his mind, he felt his lucidity slipping. He placed his hands on the hood to steady himself and the words began to jumble, the letters swirling and making no sense. His vision narrowed, and he heard a scream come from somewhere nearby. Sweat beaded on his forehead. The car felt like it was swaying beneath him and he lost his grip, his clammy palms slipping out from under him. He slid down the hood and into the dirt. His tenuous grip on reality started to fade as his eyes fell on the source of the screaming; his mom dangling in the air by her ankle. His eyes slid down the length of the tendril hoisting her into the air, a massive plant pulling her to a gaping Venus-flytrap like maw.

NO! Dan thought. Not now! With no other options as his world started to fade to a cacophony of sounds, lights and memories, he latched onto the one thing he thought could help his mom. He opened the message from the Phoenix and accepted the class package it contained.

Congratulations!
You have gained an Advanced class:
Phoenix
5500 Delayed XP applied

The Phoenix is an extremely rare class. By utilizing the Ability – Rebirth, you gain access to Skills from another class (your Subclass) dictated by a segment of your memories. WARNING! Using Rebirth alters what memories you have access to and may cause physical appearance and personality changes. Experience gained is divided between your base Class and Subclass.

Phoenix Class Abilities:

+2 Per Level in Constitution, Strength and Agility. +3 Per level in Intelligence,
Willpower and Charisma. Additional 4 Free Attributes per Level.
+99% Fire Resistance, +50% Mental Resistance. Greater Elemental Affinity: Solar.
Class Skill:

Rebirth – Activating this Skill will cause the system to create a new personality based on your current memories and experiences. This new personality will have a Subclass that starts at level 1. New personalities drawn upon the matrix of your memories and are therefore always a version of you.
Phoenix Class Pack Perk Selection
Large Perk – Phoenix Advanced Class

Medium Perk - Gifted: You have a natural ability to learn quickly. All skills are gained +10% quicker. +10% Skill Level increase for all skills.

Small Perk - Paradise Plumage: Created by the master artisans of the planet Paradise, this living outfit is a second skin that uses the thoughts and feelings of its wearer to form its shape and design. Regenerative - will regenerate from even a single cell. Soulbound - Cannot be taken or given away. Though it may simulate the look of armor, it offers no protection. Shared Fate - This item shares its owners' resistances.

A scream ripped out of Dan's throat. A molten burning started in his veins and melted its way through his blood and muscle. His world was nothing but fire and light as it felt like his very essence was being burned away to make room for something new. He thrashed on the dirt ground, flailing wildly before going utterly still. Then the world went black.

Chapter 4

Danny opened his eyes to a scene he didn't recognize. He was lying on the ground next to a car. He sat up and looked around. His tent was gone, as were the tents of the rest of the troop. Was this a prank? He glanced down to make sure he hadn't been robbed of his clothes, but there it was, his scout uniform in red, gold and brown. Danny shook his head. Wasn't the uniform supposed to be green and tan?

He stood up and brushed himself off. Brow furrowed; his eyes darted around searching for clarity. He was at the edge of a forest, next to a highway, the straight multi-lane road disappearing into the horizon. He and his troop had hiked a good fifteen miles into the forest the day before. How had he gotten to a highway?

"Okay guys, this is really funny. You totally got me!" he shouted into the air, thinking at any moment the rest of the troop would pop out to surprise him. How he could have slept through all of this? Had they drugged him?

"Guys!?" he shouted again to no answer. He inspected his surroundings. The car in front of him was strange, not like any Buick he had seen before. The modern ones were boxy with sharp lines; this one was rounded and sleek. He shook his head again and blinked. As he did so, a blue box covered in text popped into his vision.

"AHHH! What the hell!?" he screamed and backed up, waving his hands, and landed on his butt, puffs of dust floating up around him.

Danny batted at the box unsuccessfully. It didn't seem to harm him, so he read it instead.

Congratulations! You are now: Level 1 Phoenix.

Congratulations, you have experienced your first Rebirth! (System Assigned) Based on a compartment of memory, you have been assigned the Subclass: Wilderness Scout, and will now have access to the Skills from that class. No attributes are gained from Subclasses.

After reading through the text, the box disappeared, and a floating icon of a blinking question mark replaced it in the top right of his field of vision. After studying it for a second, it disappeared, and another box appeared in the center of his eyesight.

Quests
Save Your Mother -
Save Monica and Jason -
Escape to Lower Level Zone –

"What in the world?" Danny's stomach dropped at the first quest and he eyeballed it to get more information.

Quest: Save your mother from certain death. Taken right in front of you, your mother was brought back to the lair of a carnivorous plant. Time is running out.

Danny jumped up out of the dirt. He didn't know what was happening, but he knew he wasn't on his Scout trip anymore. Something... different was going on. He didn't know where these boxes came from or what they meant, but if this one about his mother was true, he knew he couldn't waste time. He spun around, eyes darting about for any sign of whatever creature had his mom.

Danny's eyes popped open when he found what he was looking for. This thing wouldn't be too hard to track. There was an indent cleared in the dirt, about two feet in width, running past the bushes and through the trees. It seemed to move on a single, large foot, like a snail. What shocked him was the strange glowing yellow haze above the creature's trail. When Danny tried to touch the haze he realized it reacted the same way all the other elements of the System did. He guessed this must be the way this 'System' showed his tracking Skill working. With a smirk Danny set out to follow the obvious trail, when a voice in his head stopped him.

< "**Daniel, I see you have accepted my class selection. Things should be a little easier now. You must go quickly; the world becomes more dangerous with each passing moment.**">

"*Who are you? What is going on?*" Danny asked. He thought he should be more freaked out by all these strange occurrences, but he was calm as if he'd experienced this before.

< "**Ah, yes. I remember now how weak the mental stability is in a new Phoenix. In time that will change. Communicating like this is very taxing for me, and we do not have long. This too will change, as you grow stronger. You have Skills that will aid you in this, although the System will always anchor itself first in your memories, it is nothing if not self-preserving. Meanwhile, I must show you something, a way to protect yourself.**">

Danny stood at the edge of the road, while visions filled his mind. He watched as strange birdlike creatures flew through the endless skies of a world filled with heat and light. The creatures spread their wings, absorbing the energy from the brilliant suns in the sky. They used this energy to create updrafts of heat to glide on, they converted it into sustenance, and breathed great gouts of flame from their mouths. Danny could feel the connection the birds had and felt something within him stir. As the images faded, he lifted his hand and staring intently, beyond the skin of his palm, he willed a ball of flame into existence.

< **"Good, you have seen how your Affinity can be used. Practice with it, master it. Your Solar Affinity will be a great tool for your survival. Now, I must rest. Please, escape to a safer zone."**>

Danny beamed. He could feel his connection to the very heat and light of the sun itself. Like heartburn within his chest, but not painful and filling his whole body. If he had more time, he would explore this further, but he dismissed the ball of flame and set on the path to save his mother.

"Thank you for showing me this. I will use it well," he sent back. *"I have to save my mother before I can escape."*

Danny could feel a spike of worry and fear emanating from the dwindling presence within his mind. He started off then, following the path the creature had left for him, hoping that if this was a dream, it wasn't about to turn into a nightmare. Whatever the creature was it did not move with any kind of regard for covering its tracks, so Danny assumed it must be of low intelligence. Or perhaps it was so powerful it had no need for protection. He shivered and hoped for the former.

He recognized many of the typical trees and shrubs, but this didn't feel like the forests he had grown up around. Now and then a plant would catch his attention, unlike any he had ever seen. A plant made of interlocking vines that moved like it was blowing in the wind, shrubs with thorny branches and strange multicolored berries, even a sad looking tree with dimly glowing leaves. Several times plants would have a light aura of green or red or blue, when he looked closer at a plant with a green aura a box titled 'Wilderness Survival' popped up stating the plant was edible.

The fauna was no exception to change either. He passed a handful of squirrels and birds, a couple butterflies. But oddities still made their presence known. He gave a wide birth to a spider as big as his hand that was draining the fluids out of something dark in its web. None of these had any auras, and Danny wondered if it was because they were creatures or if maybe his Skill wasn't high enough to get any good information.

Danny hurried, realizing that the warnings the Phoenix had given him must be true. The hair on the back of his neck stuck up and his adrenaline perked, on even higher alert than he was before. After what seemed like ages, he stopped in his tracks. Ahead of him stood a massive green plant covered in a soft fuzz, much like a Venus flytrap. Surrounding the plant were half a dozen smaller versions of itself, each with a tendril wrapping around the larger plant, entering a slimy orifice. The huge plant's mouth-like structure was closed with a human sized lump within it.

Chapter 5

"What. The. Hell?" Danny whispered out loud. All the botany and plant-based merit badges he had earned had not prepared him for giant man-eating plants. He wished he had his machete with him so he could wade in there and hack away but he didn't have any tools. After a quick scan, he saw a long, broken branch from a nearby tree. It was about as straight as a dog's leg, but it was better than nothing.

He shrieked when a tendril wrapped around his ankle and yanked him to the ground. He dropped his makeshift weapon as he was dragged towards one of the smaller plants. Prying at the restraint around his ankle, he did his best to dig his heels in. Wildly grabbing at anything within reach, he found no help as the giant tendril continued to pull him, unaffected by his escape attempts. Danny eyed the plant in his path, its gaping mouth-leaves open. This one, like the others surrounding the huge plant, was about the size of a large dog, so he knew it wouldn't be able to eat him on its own. That wasn't very comforting, however, as the rest of the plants detached their tendrils from the huge plant and made their way over to him in a slow and silent death march.

The silence of the scene added a level of dread Danny had never experienced. Movies always had monsters making terrible noises as they attacked their prey. It made sense, plants didn't have vocal cords, but it was eerie in the extreme. Danny yanked on his leg to free himself, but the tendril was stronger than he was and didn't budge. He scrambled in the dirt as he neared his slow demise. He flung a handful of dirt and rocks at the open mouth-thing just as it pulled his leg up and closed around his foot.

The dirt and rocks had about as much effect as mean words and Danny's heart sank while the rest of the plants spat their tendrils at him, catching any part they could and pulling his body taut as if he was being drawn and quartered. Beyond having parts of him engulfed by plants, the tingling in his foot warned him that something bad was happening, then those areas started to go numb. At least if he was going to die it wouldn't be in agony.

Danny thrashed and kicked as much as his body would allow, when one of the smaller plants wrapped its tendril around his neck and started squeezing. With his head pulled back taught, Danny got to watch as the plant that was choking him made its way closer, its mouth open wide towards his face. He fought for all he was worth, wrenching on the tendrils wrapped around his body, but there were too many, and they were too strong. The mouth-petals closed over his face and he screamed in terror while the toxins entered his skin and began to do their numbing work.

"NO!" Danny screamed, his voice muffled against the slimy interior of the plant, as the fear threatened to make him lose his mind. He shut his eyes and concentrated, remembering the vision the Phoenix had shown him, of other Phoenix's harnessing the solar power of the sun. He pictured his vascular system, the winding maze of arteries and veins and focused intently on filling them with the energy of the sun. The numbness started to melt out of his body, and he could feel his temperature rise, leaving the pain of plant digestive enzymes behind it. Danny screamed and tensed his muscles as the numbness burned out of his body.

Toxins dripped into his mouth from the petals enveloping his head and he could feel the bile in his throat burning its way up as he gagged on his own mortality. With a heave he let the burning bile out, a sliver of hope that maybe if he threw-up in this plant's mouth it would dislodge him. Instead, burning hot flames shot out of his mouth like a flame thrower, searing a hole through the meat of the leaf and bringing fresh, sweet air into his lungs. The plant around his head shuddered, losing its ability to grip him and fell away, leaving only the tendril tightly wrapped around his throat, squeezing the life out of him.

Danny was not about to go down now though: not now that he knew he could breathe fire. He attempted to reproduce the flame shooting out of him, aiming his mouth at the next plant wrapped around his hand. The pain coursing through his body was tremendous as the numbing agent burned away. Danny fought through the pain, refusing to pass out though his head pounded, and eyes begged to close. He focused intently and finally shot another gout of flame from his mouth and burned away the plant attached to his hand.

Holding his hand and wiggling his fingers directly in front of his face, he marveled that it had come through the conflagration unscathed. He grasped the tendril around his neck, pulling on it to free himself as the black spots of suffocation began to seep into his vision. The heat in his body got more intense and what he had mistaken as burning from the acidic enzymes escaped through his pores and enveloped his whole self. A pleasant warmth suffused his entire body as heat waves emanated from him. Soon his skin started to glow as he called upon his Solar affinity and raised his temperature hotter and hotter. His veins danced and his skin tingled with the sensation, like the time he'd snuck into the liquor cabinet and took a swallow of his dad's dark golden whiskey.

He opened his eyes and light burst forth from them, his entire body now lit up like a lantern filament. The plants wrapped around him exploded into bursts of sap as their cuticles melted and ruptured. Danny fell to the ground panting, surrounded by the charred husks of the smaller carnivorous creatures.

Immature Mutated Caryophyllales (Level 3) Slain *5

+1500 XP

He lay on the forest floor catching his breath, dumfounded by everything that had just happened. He sat up, brushed himself off, and noticed a flashing notification in the corner of his vision. Beneath that, he saw three bars of varied colors, red, blue and yellow. The bars were all well below half full and judging by his current state of battered tiredness, he assumed they were a representation of his state of being. He stood up on shaky legs and warily looked around for any more of the smaller plants. Seeing none, he focused his attention on the largest of them. "Okay, you big bastard. It's your turn now."

A tendril from its base unfurled and cracked against him like a whip, tearing open the skin on his arm and sending him crashing back down to the ground. Danny learned that the red bar in his eyesight must represent health, as it dropped drastically low.

Nothing in him wanted to get up again, but he knew lying there was going to get him killed, and he rolled to the side as fast as his body would allow. Willing himself to ignore the pain, Danny attempted to summon the heat energy like before. Another whipping made him lose focus as his health bar dropped to 20%. Desperate, he lunged towards the base of a nearby tree to for cover. Rolling behind the trunk he sucked in ragged gasps of air and tried to calm himself. Slowing his breathing, Danny focused and tried summoning the burning energy again.

His skin began to heat up and an orange glow radiated from his body. Danny stepped from behind the tree, and true to form the plant whipped its tendril at him. This time, however, Danny leaned into it, raising his arm to block, and gasping as another 5% of his health disappeared. But now he had the upper hand. The tendril had wrapped around his arm, and Danny grabbed it with his free hand forcing contact and mentally pushed the burning sensation from his arms and hands onto the plant.

The plant yanked, pulling Danny off his feet and dragging him towards its base where a host of shorter tendrils covered in dripping thorns awaited. Danny had only seconds and shoved with all his mental might, his hand and arms erupting in brilliant white light. The tendril around his arm ignited as the blue bar in Danny's vision plummeted. He realized that must represent how much he could use his Solar power and that he didn't have much of that energy left. The plant's tendril waved in the air, trying to cool down.

With a roar, Danny summoned the energy again, forcing it out of his mouth in a torrent of heat and hate. The inferno of flame landed at the base of the plant igniting the writhing, thorny tendrils and causing the plant to stiffen in pain. He watched as his blue bar drained completely and the jet of flame sputtered out, leaving him breathing hard. The plant rocked a final time and its huge leafy mouth fell to the ground, opening up and spilling out a body.

Elder Mutated Caryophyllales (Level 5) Slain
+650 XP

Danny rushed over to the figure, thankful that his flames had not reached her. It was a woman, her skin melted in places and charred in others, patches of her clothes melted away. It was a woman, but it was not his mother. His mother was only in her late thirties and this woman, while familiar, looked much older. She lay there, unmoving. "What?" Danny asked, to no one but himself. "Who is this?"

Chapter 6

Danny rolled the older woman onto her back. He tilted her head and opened her mouth, peering inside to ensure there was no plant material blocking her airway. Satisfied, he moved two fingers to her neck. He blew out a breath he didn't even realize he was holding when he felt a strong, albeit slow, rhythmic beating. She showed little sign of the trauma, a decent abrasion on her right calf and hefty bruise around the left ankle along with some of the burned spots he had noticed earlier. Her white hair was speckled with bits of forest and her clothes had certainly seen better days. Large holes spotted the floral fabric, barely hanging onto her small frame. She laid there completely still, her chest rising and falling.

He needed to get her out of there. Who knew if there were more carnivorous plants lurking in the trees? With a puff of breath, he acknowledged the flashing exclamation mark in his field of vision.

Quest Complete: Rescue your mother.

Reward: 3,000 XP

Level Up!

You have reached Level 2 as a Phoenix. Stat points automatically distributed. Class point automatically distributed as designated by symbiont (Phoenix). You have 4 free Attribute points.

Level Up!

You have reached level 2 as a Wilderness Scout. No attribute points gained for Subclasses. You have 2 free Class points to distribute. These Class point may only be spent on Subclass Skills.

Danny inhaled as he felt the energy coursing through his body. He couldn't describe what was different, but he felt... better... than just a few moments before. The flashing exclamation point faded. A glowing '+' sign appeared, but he ignored it and focused on the completed quest- his mother?

"What is going on? Is this some kind of time warp?" He had saved the lady and the System checked off the quest as if it was his mom. Could it really be her? He shook his head to clear his thoughts and with a sigh squatted down to pick up the strangely familiar woman. He began the trek back to the highway carrying her in a fireman's lift. He paused about a third of the way back when the yellow bar in his vision depleted to nothing and he somehow knew he couldn't go on. Blowing his breath out he swung the woman off his shoulders and laid her down, then plopped onto the ground next to her.

Looking at the woman again, it was uncanny how familiar she seemed. Her features were his mom's, only older. His eyes widened and jaw dropped as he noticed her wounds. Most of the burned flesh had the soft pink hue of new skin, the cuts and bruises were simply gone. He marveled at this and wondered how much it had to do with the strange boxes and this 'System'.

The day was strange, but perhaps the strangest thing was his overwhelming feeling of déjà vu: like he had experienced this before. A glance at his yellow bar showed it was half full. With a sigh he looked at the glowing '+' sign and thought at it, opening it up. Another box bloomed in front of him, labeled 'Status Screen'. He thought watching a person's wounds close before his eyes was amazing enough, but the sheer amount of data on this screen made him forget to breathe for a moment.

Status Screen			
Name	Daniel Burns	Class	Phoenix
Race	Human (Symbiont) (Male)	Level	2
Titles			
None			
Health	100	Stamina	100
Mana	100		
Status			
Alzheimer's (a -10% Intelligence, Variable, Periodic)			
Dementia (-10% Charisma -10% Intelligence, Variable, Periodic)			
Attributes			
Strength	15	Agility	13
Constitution	15	Perception	12
Intelligence	15 (14)	Willpower	19
Charisma	13 (12)	Luck	10
Skills			
Wilderness Survival	3	Tracking	4

Athletics	3	First Aid	3
Observe	3		
Class Skills			
Echoes of Past Lives	1	Rebirth	1
Spells			
None			

Unspent Primary Class Attribute points: 4
Unspent Subclass Skill points: 2

Another '+' sign appeared next to the attributes, a way to increase them with the unspent points. He perused the status screen, remembering his time playing tabletop RPGs like Dungeons and Dragons. This reminded him very much of a character sheet, although more advanced. He stopped when he got to the 'status' section, reading the two conditions affecting him. Alzheimer's and Dementia. Somehow, he knew these conditions to be true, albeit alarming. He kicked at the dirt. All these Skills and he gets landed with mental demise? Was this System just a product of a broken brain? What was he forgetting that he didn't even remember he forgot? That would certainly explain the old lady version of his mom and everything else that was so strange today.

The Skill; 'Echoes of Past Lives', caught his attention, and he focused on it to reveal more text.

Though others may not believe in your power of rebirth, you will never doubt it. You have memories which may reveal themselves as skills from past lives. The higher this skill, the more you will remember from past lives. Knowledge of system operations will always be preserved.

That made sense why he didn't freak out about the boxes or the voice in his head. The woman stirred next to him, snapping him to attention, and pushing away all thoughts of character sheets. He cradled her head in his hands, astonished that all her wounds had healed completely. Without the threat of danger and with a chance to further study her, Danny really saw the familiarity. He brushed his hand along her cheek and patted her shoulder. "M…. Mom? Is that really you?"

She groaned as her eyes opened. They opened and closed a few times, either adjusting to the light or perhaps to her new surroundings. Her physical wounds may have healed but the memory of being eaten alive would last awhile. She turned her head toward Danny and her eyes stayed open, big as saucers.

"No, no… no! Am I dead? Did we die?!" Tears formed in her eyes and she reached up to touch Danny's face. "Dan… Danny? Why… what… how are you so young again?" She grabbed him and pulled him close squeezing hard, and he knew for sure it was his mom.

"What happened to you? What is going on?" Danny asked, face smooshed in his mother's embrace, his own eyes filling with tears. "I was on my Eagle hike and woke up here, and everything is different, and you're old, and -" he stopped when his mom started laughing.

"Old?! I'm old!?" She laughed, breaking the somber tone, and soon Danny smiled as well. "Danny, I don't know what's going on any more than you," his mother said. "Except that a few hours ago we both started seeing these boxes filled with text, offering us weird stuff like Classes and Skills. Before I was grabbed by that... thing... you were forty-eight. Now you don't look any older than eighteen, and I am just as confused about everything as you are!"

Danny stood up and offered his hand, which she took and got to her feet. "This is a really weird day. You can see these boxes too?"

She nodded. "Yes, though we haven't really had much time to talk about it. I guess aliens are taking over or something." She looked around. "I thought I was going crazy at first, but then those plant things... well, I don't know what to think any more." Susan frowned and rubbed her eyes, a gesture Danny recognized as frustration, having seen it enough growing up.

"Well, whatever is happening, we're in this together, and we need to find safety somehow. Where is your car?" Danny said.

"Should be right at the road, but the car doesn't work, Danny. Nothing works anymore," she said, looking at him. The sight of him amazed her, looking just as he had all those years ago. "I just wish I knew what was going on." She touched his hand. "Especially with you, how are you so young? Do you remember anything else? When did this happen?"

Danny shook his head violently and Susan recognized the sudden movement as one he had adopted as the dementia had gotten worse.

"No," Danny said. "I don't know...I... remember a voice... in my head... I somehow just know things that I feel like I remember. But I just don't..." He shook his head again. "I don't remember..."

Susan embraced him again, recognizing the signs of a breakdown. She rubbed his back, talking in a slow, sure, voice. "Shh it's okay, it's okay, you don't have to remember." She took a deep breath and squared her shoulders, ending them embrace. "Come on, let's get to the car and see if we can find help." She grasped her son's hand, set her jaw and started walking.

Chapter 7

They traveled much faster now that they were both able to walk. During their travel they talked: Susan filling him in on his current life, and Danny filling her with nostalgia. Danny experienced that feeling of déjà vu he recognized as the 'Echoes of Past Lives' Skill. He knew his mom's words to be accurate, although he had a hard time believing he had a wife and child. Despite not actually knowing them, he knew he would have to save them. He turned to his mom to ask her what their next step should be, only to stop as he caught her staring at him.

Susan blushed, averting her eyes. "I'm sorry. It's just so… uncanny… you really are so young. It's like I jumped back in time thirty years."

Danny shrugged. "I don't know what's going on. I think it's this Rebirth Skill I have. It says it changes me when I use it or something."

"How do you know that?" Susan asked.

"It came up on one of those boxes when I woke up on the ground. It also says it on my status screen."

"Your what?" She looked at him confused. "That's the second time you've mentioned that, what is it?"

"My status screen? It's like a character sheet from the RPGs I used to play."

"That game with the dice?"

Danny chuckled, his mom had never got 'that game with the dice' but had still been nice enough to provide snacks and a place to host it for those weekends when he and his friends played. "Yeah, Mom, that one. Think about looking at your info and say 'Status'.

Susan's mouth popped open in shock as she began to read her status information. "What!? How? How does it know all this?" Something she saw on her screen made her face screw up, and her eyes began to water again. "Danny... how accurate is this?"

Danny shrugged. "I don't know. I mean it told me about my Alzheimer's and dementia that I didn't even know myself... or well, I did but didn't know that I knew. You know what I mean?" He shook his head as if trying to make his words make sense. "Why? What does yours say?"

Susan's face turned lit up and her happy demeanor seemed to radiate out of her. The woman Danny saw before him looked broken and tired. But she had a resolution that was contagious. Susan took a deep breath, a tear rolling down her face, as a huge genuine smile erupted.

Danny stopped walking and reached out to touch her arm. "Mom? What did it say?" he asked again.

She looked at him, her smile wide as she met his eyes. "It's nothing... just..."

"Just what?"

She held her hand out to him, and he observed as she flexed her fingers, the knuckles that had been bulging and swollen with arthritis now smooth. "Nothing, my... arthritis is just gone now, I guess. You live with something for so long and it starts to become a piece of you, then when it's gone, even if you feel better, you kind of miss it..." She turned away, and he felt like there might have been something more but decided not to press the issue further. "We need to move faster," Susan said. "We have to find Monica and Jason."

They finally exited the thick line of trees and in another ten yards over sparse grass and random litter, the freeway stretched across the landscape.

"Which way do we go?" Dan asked.

Susan pointed north up I-5. "We only made it a few miles out of Lakehead, it's a bit of a walk but at least we know we won't get run over..." She gave a nervous chuckle at her dark joke.

"Should we get going then?" Danny planted his feet toward the sun and held his hand out toward the horizon. He moved his hand slowly towards the sun, stopping when his pointer finger met it. "Looks like we've got plenty of daylight, let's not waste any of it."

Susan smiled, "Okay, let's go!"

As they made their way north Danny asked; "What class did you pick, anyway? Is it anything that could help us get there faster?"

His mom smirked at him. "Oh, I don't think so. There were a few options that were so weird sounding, Anything-Goes Okonomiyaki Master or Magical Chef. I was looking at one called Gastromancer when I was grabbed, and I accidentally selected it. I think it's some kind of food wizard. But I have to tell you, Danny. I don't get all this weird computer stuff. You know me and technology- I can't even figure out the DVR box."

Danny stopped walking. "Your what? What's a DVR box?"

"I don't really even know," she said.

They laughed and started walking, following along the shoulder of the large road.

"Where did you get that outfit, anyway?" Susan asked. Danny told her about his perks, and they continued to share what little they knew about the System while they walked. At some point Danny opened his sheet and wondered where to assign his free Attribute points. After careful consideration he put half into Strength and half into Constitution. He could tell his class was designed to focus on Willpower and Intelligence, but his last experience attempting to carry his Mom showed him he needed to increase his physical stats to maximize how much help he could be. He left his Skill points alone, not wanting to make a rash decision, he just hoped he wasn't making a mistake.

Danny and his mom had figured out a walking pace that kept them moving quickly while keeping their Stamina at equilibrium. Susan seemed to have a never-ending supply of snacks, candies and treats in her bag which she kept offering to Danny. He smirked as he munched on the things she gently forced on him.

Their jovial mood soured eventually when they came across a car that had driven off the road and crashed headlong into a tree. They rushed over to check the driver but found him dead several yards in front of the car, having been propelled through the windshield. Susan cried at the sight of the poor broken man, and Danny put his arm around his mom in a comforting hug and pulled her away so they could continue their trek. He briefly considered the fact that gruesome death would probably be a much common event in this new world, but shook his head, not wanting to borrow worry. They passed other cars, abandoned on the side of the road like theirs, the occupants nowhere to be seen. With only about a mile to go, they came to the section of road that went over the waters of the Sacramento River arm of Lake Shasta.

Ahead of them was a pile-up of several cars, smashed hunks of metal and broken glass. A large fuel truck looked to have lost control and tipped over, blocking part of the southbound lanes and half the northbound. Thankfully the massive multi-thousand-gallon fuel tank had not ruptured. The southbound lanes had a couple vehicles that looked like they had played bumper cars and lost control, crashing into the guardrail. Behind the semi was another car, a sedan that had rear-ended the truck, crumpling like an aluminum can.

Without hesitation, they ran up to the vehicles to look for survivors. Danny pulled up short when he detected no movement, then noticed trails of blood leading toward the edge of the bridge. He followed a trail to find blood splatters over the guardrail. With a tremor in his voice he shouted out to his mom. "It looks like there might have been survivors here, but something dragged them into the water!"

"Stay away from the water then!" she shouted back. He jumped back from the edge taking her advice. "Let's get around this, the southern edge of town is close, hopefully it'll be safer there."

They moved toward the wreckage and threaded their way through the vehicles. A Subaru laying on its side caught Danny's attention. "Mom, come give me a hand here, I found a couple bikes on the rack of this car!"

"It's been years since I've ridden a bike," Susan said, helping unfasten them.

"No worries Mom, I hear it's just like riding a bike!"

She paused at his lame attempt at humor and gave him a raised eyebrow. She opened her mouth to retort but her words changed into a scream as her eyes widened at something behind Danny.

Chapter 8

Danny whirled to see what his mom was screaming at. A shiver went down his spine at what he saw. Climbing over the guardrail was a humanoid with giant, unblinking eyes. Its skin was a tough looking scaly, black, its mouth full of needle-sharp teeth and its hands and feet ended in webbed claws. A strap wrapped around its chest held a spear.

Fear spurred Danny's actions, and he worked faster to detach the bikes. He considered running but knew the bikes would be much faster. Susan was frozen, unable to tear her eyes away from the creature.

"It's real… there really are aliens…" she whispered as her face paled.

"Mom! Snap out of it! We've got to go!" Danny pushed on her shoulder while he untangled one bike and set it to the side. The creature, now on the bridge, yelled something at them and leveled its spear. Danny ignored it, ripping the other bike free from the rack. The creature made another terrifying noise and stalked toward them.

Danny grabbed his mom and shoved the handlebar of a bike in her hand. "Go, Mom! Get to the town! I'll distract it!"

She grabbed the handlebar more out of reflex than a desire to obey. "Danny, no-" she gasped as the creature raised its spear to throw.

"Don't argue with me, dammit!" he shouted at her. He could use his new powers, and she was way more likely to get hurt than he was. Why wouldn't she just listen? Danny grimaced, his features contorting in an angry look. His mother's face snapped around to look at his. In that instant he saw something within her, something that said she understood or at least had experienced that anger before. She got on the bike and shoved off, wobbly at first, but picking up speed.

The creature shouted more words in its garbled language and pointed at Susan as she pedaled away.

"Hey, fish face! Ignore her!" Danny shouted. He had no idea if the thing could understand him. He searched, grabbing and throwing the first thing he could find, a bike pump, hitting the thing in its chest. The creature turned to him; its spear still raised. Why hadn't the thing hadn't thrown it? Was it just an intimidation tactic?

He must have guessed right as the creature put the spear back into its strap and pulled something out of a belt pouch around its waist. A tangle of braided rope attached to a few spheres. A weighted net. It had put away it's weapon and brought out something to capture with. Danny didn't know what was worse, knowing that this thing was what had taken the people from the car crash, or that it wanted them, and him, alive. He looked down the road to see his mother riding into the distance and prayed that she would make it.

Danny wished he had run. The creature wound up and threw the net with unerring accuracy: he tried to dodge but was too slow. His stomach sank as the net wrapped around him, the weights wrapping tightly like bolas, and he was dragged to the ground. The smell of dead fish assaulted his nose as he struggled to free himself. As the creature approached, it was obvious it wasn't made to walk on land. Its webbed feet were long and floppy like scuba fins, causing it to move with a strange, slow gait.

Danny waited, biding his time for the creature to come closer. He sought the solar energy contained within him and pulled it close to the surface of his skin. It felt easier this time, like a natural reflex to his spiked adrenaline. As the creature reached him, it warbled in its strange language, and grabbed an end of the net, dragging it and Danny along the pavement towards the guardrail of the bridge. He dug his fingers into the ground, grasping at anything to stop him, his breath coming in shortened gasps. With bloodied nails, panic was setting in. He couldn't focus, and he felt the solar heat retreating from his skin. He had to do something. This couldn't end now; it wasn't his time. He refocused, channeling his fear into his Solar Affinity.

With its back turned to him, Danny forced the solar energy up towards his mouth again and spat at his captor's back in a blazing inferno. He couldn't tell if it would hurt the thing or not, and was pleasantly surprised when it hit, burning through the creature's clothes and the harness holding its spear. The scream it made when the flames touched its skin was unearthly and Danny watched as its flesh burned and flaked off as if it was sandblasted away.

The creature fell to the ground, rolling and screaming in agony. Danny used the remainder of his blue energy bar to blast the solar power out of his skin through his pores, incinerating the net holding him. As the ashes blew away in the wind, he got up to run when the creature's hand closed on his foot. Danny could do nothing to get free from its vise-like grip. His blue energy bar had not recovered enough to use his solar power again, and he desperately searched for anything to help him.

The creature was still howling in pain, its flesh flaking off in huge chunks, like unsecured newspaper in a campfire. Danny noticed its spear then, laying on the ground next to him where it had fallen when the harness burned off. He snatched it up and with as much skill as someone who had never held a spear before and stabbed it down on the creature's wrist. It screamed again and reflexively released Danny and fumbled at its belt. Danny wasted no time and with the spear in hand, ran and mounted the bike he had freed. He pedaled for all he was worth, holding the spear across the handlebars.

As he put distance between himself and the sea monster, he heard a loud bleating noise and the waters all around the bridge started to churn. He turned his head to find the source, and saw it blowing a large conch horn. He pushed his bike faster, his calves burning with the effort. He sped down the road only just avoiding the massive sucker-covered tentacle that leaped out of the water toward him.

"Holy crap! What is that thing!?" he shouted out loud, riding as hard as he could to get away and off the bridge.

He glanced back to see two more of the fish creatures climbing the guardrails. He was thankful they were slow on land and was just starting to feel relieved at the distance he was putting between them when the huge tentacle picked up one of the smashed cars on the road and threw it at him.

He wouldn't have believed his eyes if he didn't have to avoid the car flying towards him. He wasn't sure his heart had ever beat so fast. He screamed as the car slammed into the asphalt a good ten feet to his side, the cacophony as it scraped across the ground making his whole body flinch. A last glance back showed the creatures across the bridge hollering in his direction, raising their spears. He put on speed and hoped he could find his mother.

Chapter 9

Danny pedaled hard, sweat breaking out on his forehead, eyes peeled for any sight of his mom. A movement to his side caught his attention, sending his elevated heart rate up even higher. He breathed a sigh of relief when he saw it was his mother, who had hidden behind a dead car on the side of the road. He slowed down then but motioned for her to hurry up.

"Why did you stop? We need to keep moving!" he yell-whispered, no idea what other monsters might be lingering nearby.

She jumped on her bike and rode up to him. "I was just watching to see what was happening. I couldn't leave you behind. Danny, you can't scare me like that! You could have died! What were those things?"

"I don't know what they were, but I think they wanted me alive, which scares me more than if they had tried to kill me."

Her eyes filled with tears, but then a look of anger crossed her face. "Don't you ever tell me to leave you like that again! You can't do that to a mother, tell her to leave her son to die!"

Danny wanted to console her somehow but only had words to offer. "I'm sorry, I just, I have powers now that can help me, and I knew I might stand a chance to get away. I needed you to go try to save Monica and Jason."

"I know. I'm just so sick of this damned world. The things I… we… have had to go through since your diagnosis. Then this alien invasion or whatever it is. It's just so much."

"I know Mom. I'm sorry. I don't know what it's been like since the diagnosis, but this world with its strange monsters attacking us, it's a lot. I love you though, and I will do everything I can to protect you."

They rode in silence for a bit after that. "Powers, what do you mean you've got powers?" she asked.

He smiled, thinking of the energy he could summon. "It's like, fire powers. It's from something called an elemental affinity. I guess I have a connection to Solar energy. I don't know exactly what that means, but I've been able to create a lot of fire out of my mouth and body. It's pretty neat, actually."

She looked at him askance. "You breathe fire and it's 'pretty neat'?" she asked.

He barked a short laugh. "Hah, yeah, I guess that's a bit of an understatement."

"We're getting close now." Susan pointed towards a green sign that read 'Welcome to Lakehead,' and 'Population 430'.

"Wow, this is a real small town," Danny said.

"It's where you retired from firefighting. You loved the small town and river here," Susan said.

Danny shook his head, trying to remember the things she was talking about. He had that weird déjà vu feeling again as they rode. He felt like he knew everywhere they passed. He was pretty sure if he closed his eyes his body would take him back home. They rode through the small town taking a few side streets.

"Where are all the people?" he asked.

"I don't know, with the cars not working maybe they are just in their houses?" Susan responded.

They rode until they got to a large red two-story house with a detached garage that had been converted into a mother-in-law apartment. Susan pulled into the empty spot of the driveway with Danny right behind her. They dismounted and his mom waved her hand towards the house.

"This is it," Susan said and pointed at the Tahoe in the driveway. "Monica's car is still here. I don't see Jason's though."

"Jason has a car? How old is he?" Danny asked.

Susan blinked at him, her smile melting into a frown. "You really don't remember?"

Danny felt the heat rise in his face as he lashed out. "How the hell am I supposed to remember!? As far as I know it's still 1987!" he screamed.

Susan only stared at Danny as he panted, his face red. She turned her whole body towards him, keeping her hands behind her back. She spoke in a calm tempered voice. "I'm sorry, Danny. I know this is hard for you." She slowly approached him from his right side and placed an arm on his bicep. "Would you like to go in?"

Danny shook his head, not in response to the question but to clear the anger away as he absorbed his mom's soft demeanor. "Yeah, let's go inside," he said.

Susan turned, walking towards the door on the side of the house. She took her keys from her pocket, fumbled with them a bit, and pushed one into the lock of the door. As it was opening, a weight slammed against it, shoving it closed again. Susan jumped back, startled, and tried turning the knob again only to find it was locked.

"Who is it? What do you want?" came a female voice from inside.

"Monica? Monica, it's me, Susan! Open the door!" Danny's mom yelled.

"Susan? Who's that with you?" the voice, presumably Monica, said.

"It's... well... it's a long story, but this is Danny," Susan said, her hand pressed against the door. It was quiet for a long moment. "Monica, it's really me, what's going on?"

"Prove it," Monica said.

"What? Prove what? Monica, what is going on, why won't you let me in?"

"Prove that you are who you say you are. Prove that you're Susan. I don't know that guy with you, and Susan left town hours ago. How do I know you're who you say you are?" Monica's voice sounded strained, like she was trying to shove all the emotion out of it but failing.

Susan stared at the door, then looked at Danny who simply shrugged.

"Alright" she said. "I was at your wedding and tried to calm your ass of a father down. When I called him a drunken idiot, he threw his drink at me and stomped off. I thought you would never forgive me."

Susan was just about to say something else to break the long silence that followed, when the lock clicked, and the door opened. A petite brunette in her 40s stood behind the door and Danny felt a wave of unexplainable emotion looking at her. He couldn't recognize her, but something within him felt he should.

"Susan?" the woman said and rushed out to embrace the older woman, dropping a large knife. "Susan! It IS you! Where's Dan? So much is going on." Monica stopped and looked warily up and down the street, biting her lower lip. "Come in, you have to come in. We need to lock the doors."

Monica ushered the two of them in the house, her movements frantic as she scooped the knife back up and dead bolted the door behind them. She pressed her back against the door, breathing hard.

"Quickly, come this way, we have to help him," she pointed at Danny, "if you want him to live," Monica said and walked through the kitchen toward what looked like the living room.

"Monica, you need to slow down and tell me what's going on!" Susan called behind her as she followed. Danny scanned the kitchen; the sense of déjà vu overwhelming him, and went after the two women. He picked up his pace when he heard his mother gasp.

"My God, Monica!" Susan exclaimed, her hand over her mouth. Danny rounded the corner to see a boy, no, a young man, tied to a chair with earmuffs over his ears, and a gag of cloth tied around his mouth. "What have you done to Jason!?"

Chapter 10

Susan moved to help the young man, Jason, out of his bindings when Monica grabbed her arm.

"DON'T!" she yelled, then her eyes darted toward the door they had just entered from. In a lowered voice she said "This is for his own good, it's protecting him. Something weird is going on, something that has all the men in town freaking out. If you don't want your friend here," she pointed to Danny, "to suffer the same fate, we need to do the same to him."

"Does it have to do with the boxes and this new 'System' that seems to have taken over?" Danny asked. He felt strange looking at her and the young man in the chair. He felt... protective... over them but didn't know why. It must have had to do with his 'Memories of Past Lives' Skill.

Monica looked at him, an eyebrow cocked. Her face screwed up as she did a double take between the man in the chair and Danny.

"Susan... who is this? What happened to Dan?"

Susan put her hand on Danny's shoulder. "We've had a strange day as well. This is Dan. This... System... changed him."

Monica took Danny in, her eyes going from top to bottom and back to his face. "What are you talking about?"

Danny nodded towards her. "It's true, I am Dan. Or well, I go by Danny. I... don't remember you... I'm sorry..."

Monica tensed up, a war of conflicting emotions making their way across her face. "You don't remember me?"

"He can't remember anything past his teenager years," Susan said. "The System took over and our car died on the way to the doctor. Dan was still Dan then. But then I was almost eaten by some plant monster and he saved me, looking like this. I've spent a lot of time with him, and I can assure you it is Dan."

Monica looked right at Danny, her stare piercing into his eyes. She squinted, cocking her head in different directions. "I don't... how is this even possible?" she asked.

"It's the System. I became something called a Phoenix, like the one from the story, I guess. Although the stories never mentioned voices in your head," Danny said. "I guess I have a Skill called 'Rebirth' that changes me based on whatever memories are dominant. When I accepted the class, the System assigned me a rebirth, and I woke up like this." He shrugged, waving his hands over his body.

Tears filled Monica's eyes, and she embraced Danny, her head on his shoulder leaving wet stains. Danny wrapped his arms around her, his hands falling comfortably at her waist. His body knew hers. Just as he was about to say something, a strange sound caught his attention. "What is that noise?" he asked.

Monica pushed away, her face going white. She looked to Susan. "Get him in a chair! I'll try to find more rope!"

"Is that... singing?" Danny said looking around for the source of the noise.

"What are you talking about, Monica?" Susan said at the same time. "I know it's hard to believe this is Dan, but-"

Monica cut her off. "It's not that! The sound! We have to block out the sound!" She grabbed two throw pillows and pressed them to the sides of Danny's head, covering his ears.

"It IS singing!" Danny said, pulling at the pillows.

"What are you talking about? I don't hear anything?" Susan said.

"I don't hear it either, but all the men seem to. Now help me!" Monica shouted, but it was too late. Danny wrestled the pillows away, enraptured by the sounds he was hearing. The women attempted to re-cover his ears, to hold him back as he started walking towards the door.

"NO!" Monica screamed and moved in front of him, both hands on his chest, pushing him back.

Danny felt the heat of anger well up within him and he slapped Monica's hands away. She yelled in pain as his suddenly hot skin burned her. Danny kept walking towards the door, each step slow but determined. "That music is so beautiful…" he whispered as his anger dissipated along with the rising heat of his body.

Tears flowed down Monica's face and she turned to Susan. "We have to get Jason out of here! If he hears it, he'll be lost too!"

Danny shouted, making the women jump… "Hello! Who's singing!?" He ran to the door and flung it open. Outside was a creature, with the legs of a bird, a feather covered torso and the head of a woman. It opened its mouth as if it were singing…

"So beautiful," Danny said as his jaw went slack, and he stood by the open door, fascinated as the creature made its way into the house, followed by three of the strange humanoid fish-people they had seen on the bridge. The three figures plodded in, clearly uncomfortable as they walked on their long, webbed feet.

"We have to save Jason," Monica whispered under her breath, eyes red and cheeks wet with tears.

"What do we do?" Susan asked. "What is that-" She jumped to move when one of the fish-man leapt at her, knocking her to the ground. Monica screamed and raced to the room where Jason was, only to be slammed to the ground as a weighted net wrapped around her. Danny stood there, half aware of everything going on, but so enraptured by the singing, he was unable pull himself away to act.

Monica continued to scream, fighting and kicking with all she had as the fish-man hoisted and carried her on its shoulder outside, the net dragging behind them, its gills flared. Another fish creature pulled out a spear like the one Danny had taken, and leveled it at Susan, motioning towards the door, while the final one moved past everyone toward Jason while he was struggling to get free of his restraints. Jason fought until the fish-man removed his headphones. Instantly he froze, turning his head towards the door and the birdlike woman beside it.

The fish-man next to Jason cut his bonds and the young man walked up to the birdwoman, who led both men out of the house. On the road before them was a strange conveyance; a floating cube of water, held together by fields of energy. The water moved and splashed but did not fall from its invisible walls. Several more fish-men were swimming within it, with one at the front wrapped in seaweed like vines. As Susan and Monica were brought closer to the cube, a metal platform extended from the bottom. The women cried out as they were thrown onto it. One fish-man tied Susan's wrists and arms together and signaled to the other in the water. The creature wrapped in seaweed pulled a few strands, the cube levitated and started to glide down the street. The fish-men climbed their way back into the tank, seeming relieved to no longer rely on their ineffective feet.

Behind the women, Danny watched in mute fascination, mentally fighting against the bonds of the song as they made their way down the streets, toward the marina. His mom and supposed wife screamed as electricity suddenly raked across their skin. One of the fish-men swam close to their station on the platform, its head bobbing in what could only be laughter as it pulled one of the seaweed strands and another shock burned across them.

They rode like this until they reached the marina. Every time one of the women would move or speak, they were shocked. The alien parade came to a halt when they reached the marina. What must have been at least half the town's inhabitants were there, the women strewn together in nets. The men were standing at rapt attention, willing prisoners of two other birdlike women, mouths opened wide in song. Water sloshed as the tank set down, and the bird-woman brought Jason and Danny to the rest of the men.

Two of the fish-people in the conveyance propelled themselves through the water like dolphins and leaped onto the ground, while the pilot of the strange contraption pulled a vine. The floating fish tank began hovering again and turned towards the boat launch where the energy dissipated, and the tank water assimilated into the lake.

One of the fish-men brought his mouth to the ear of the bird-woman who had led Danny and gestured toward him. She then pulled him from the group, toward the fish-man. Danny saw that its clothes were burned through, the flesh underneath new and healed. This had been the one he had burned on the bridge. His shock at seeing it completely undamaged turned to dismay as it picked up the spear Danny had stolen and cracked him in the face, knocking him to the ground, blood spraying out of his mouth. Danny gasped in pain and felt the hold on his mind lessen a bit from the act of violence, only to have the singing take control a heartbeat later.

"Stop it! Leave him alone!" Susan shouted while she flailed in her net and Monica covered her face in her hands and screamed next to her. The creature looked at them and chuckled in pleasure. Two other fish-men grabbed hold of their nets and dragged them to the center of the parking lot leading toward the boat launch, where a large, round stone dais sat. The parking lot had always been there, but the dais was a new addition. In the center of the platform was a table, or altar, engraved with sharks. Their captors roughly threw them down and using stakes, drove the nets into the ground, digging into the flesh of the helpless women.

The lead fish-man picked Danny up by the throat and carried him to the altar. The rest of the fish-men stood to either side of him and began chanting. They held Danny's arms and legs as the leader pulled out a vicious, wavy dagger, and held it in the air shouting out what must have been a prayer in a strange language. The singing subsided, and Danny's eyes darted around wildly, as the power controlling his body suddenly dropped away and he shook his head violently as if to dispel what he saw.

Monica, unable to take her eyes off the scene, recognized that head shake as the one her husband picked up when he started to lose his mind to dementia.

"It really is him," she whispered, her voice rising in pitch to a scream as the leader of the fish-men leveled its dagger and plunged it toward Danny's heart.

As the blade descended a message box appeared in Danny's vision.

Mortal Danger imminent! Would you like to activate Rebirth?
Yes/No

Without hesitation, Danny selected YES.

Chapter 11

That scream. Burns recognized that scream. Memories poured into his mind like smoke, images burning their way into his retinas. He knew that scream. It was the same scream he had heard that night in the Jones fire. He had saved a woman... Monica... he remembered, following the screams to a home and pulling out a woman trapped by a fallen bookshelf. It was later he learned her name was Monica. He struggled to remember more and felt like he was trying to grab the smoke in his mind. With a shout, he woke, jerking up.

Burns looked around, his eyebrows scrunched down. He appeared to be at the marina in Lakehead. He had been there many times to go fishing, but something was off this time. It might have been the embossed stone slab he was lying on, or maybe it was the corpses surrounding it. Three bodies around the slab, blackened and charred. Looking closer he noticed that all three of them only had a vaguely human shape. A couple seemed to have fins and the other had singed feathers strewn about. He shook his head, trying to piece together what was going on. He wasn't concerned, even though charred freaky alien bodies were all around him.

A System message popped into his vision.

Congratulations! You have completed your first True Rebirth!

Warning: You must gain a level in your base Phoenix class before you may use this Skill again.

Congratulations! You have learned the Skill: Rebirth Fluctuation

Your stats fluctuate between rebirths to accommodate your current Rebirth Subclass.

Burns brought up his status screen.

Status Screen			
Name	Daniel Burns	Class	Phoenix (2)
Race	Human (Symbiont) (Male)	Subclass	Pyromancer (1)
Titles			
None			
Health	170	Stamina	170
Mana	160		
Status			
Alzheimer's (a -10% Intelligence, Variable, Periodic)			
Dementia (-10% Charisma -10% Intelligence, Variable, Periodic)			
Attributes			
Strength	17	Agility	15
Constitution	17	Perception	12
Intelligence	16 (15)	Willpower	22
Charisma	16 (15)	Luck	10
Skills			
Wilderness Survival	3	Tracking	4

Athletics	3	First Aid	3
Observe	3	Flame Burst	3
Class Skills			
Echoes of Past Lives	1	Rebirth	1
Spells			
None			

A Pyromancer… was that a wizard or something? He felt like all of this should be alien to him, but accessing the System was… natural… somehow.

< "**A rebirth already?**" > the Phoenix asked him.

Burns looked down at himself. "*I must have had to for some reason. What happens to me when I go through 'rebirth' anyway?*"

< "**What happens to you is different than what happens to a true Phoenix. The System can only copy our abilities. You become 'phase-shifted' for a period of time while the System scans your last mental state to determine your next state of being.**">

"*Phase-shifted? What's that?*"

< "**You become invisible, and undetectable to normal and magical means, and may pass through solid objects.**" >

Burns cocked an eyebrow. "*I become a ghost?*" Burns got to experience the unique feeling of an inhabitant in his mind rolling its eyes.

< "**Have you at least made it to a safe zone yet?**" >

With those words his quest log opened and the Quest 'Get Somewhere Safe' highlighted. Burns shrugged, not knowing how to answer the Phoenix.

"I'm in Lakehead, at the marina. I'm on a..." He looked down to get a better inspection of the stone slab. *"... an altar of some kind?"*

< **"An Altar? New Dungeon Worlds always get the worst crowd. Lakehead.... is in the opposite direction of where you need to go. You are headed into more dangerous territory; you must turn back!"** >

"Yeah... well... I don't really know why I'm even here..." Burns shook his head, trying to jog his memory. *"There has to be a reason. I've always liked it here, it's where I thought I would retire."*

< **"That may be, however it is no longer a zone that is safe. You must make it out! If you die, I will be trapped here forever, or worse."** >

"Then help me! Help me remember why I came here!"

< **"I cannot. I cannot see into your mind, or at least not into the mind of your past self. You will never be the same any longer, such is the plight of those of the Phoenix. To be reborn over and over, but never fully remembering who you were from one life to the next."** >

Burns grunted, looking at his status screen again. There had to be a reason he was here in Lakehead. With a sigh he sat down and gave serious thought to what he was trying to remember. He closed his eyes and memories of that scream came to him.

Burns shook his head violently trying to force the memories to make sense. After a moment he caught his breath and his mind started to clear. *"I think... I think I'm here to save my girlfriend.... and someone else... an older woman?"*

< **"If such is the case, you must act with speed. It is imperative you escape the zone into a safer area and quickly. The longer you wait the more dangerous it becomes. Tell me, does the altar have any markings?"** >

Burns scrubbed the soot off the stone. "*Yeah, it looks like embossed reliefs of, a huge shark or something. My memories showed me weird fish things, and there are some bodies around me that look like them. Wait, why are there burned bodies around me, anyway?*"

< "If you select a rebirth while you are in danger, you experience a fiery rebirth, exploding out in flames that deal Fire and Holy damage. You become incorporeal during the time of your memory reconstruction. The creatures you burned are most likely Nagashiu, water people that live only to sacrifice sentients to their warped Shark god." >

"*Shark god? That's a thing?*"

< "It is a being like any other, though with a powerful class that is tied to its people's religion." >

Burns shook his head. Shark gods were almost too much to handle. "*How powerful is the explosion I cause?*"

< "I assure you it is quite powerful, though that is not the only reason for the death you caused. The Nagashiu are water based and thus many of them are very weak to Fire, as well as Holy damage." >

"*What about this feathered-human thing?*"

< "Most likely those are Sirens, they often work with the Nagashiu. Be cautious, if there are Sirens about, you are in much danger for being male. Their song can enthrall you." >

Those words sparked another memory in Burns' mind, of a song so beautiful he wanted nothing more than to listen to it forever.

"*Yeah, I think I may have experienced that already,*" he said.

< "The Sirens are also weak to Fire and Holy attacks. Though many of them have gear to mitigate that. If you have killed several with your

rebirth, it is likely that they are lower level. They are never alone though, and I would hazard to say that the Nagashiu have most likely bought some territory on this world. I must leave now, I get stronger as you do, but am still so very weak. I will leave you with this; Your memories may be lost, but your soul recognizes your past. Trust your instincts. Now go, get to safety!" >

Burns felt the presence leave his mind and took a deep breath, checking himself over. He wore his standard firefighters' uniform, navy slacks, and a shirt with a crimson collar, embroidered with SLFD on the pocket.

"Trust my instincts," he mumbled to himself. He stood up and stretched, wondering what he was going to do now. He closed his eyes and thought about it, memories of that scream coming back to him. "Monica, I have to save Monica. But where is she? Why is she here in Lakehead?" He clenched his eyes shut, remembering.

They had spent plenty of time together in the area, out on his boat, fishing, and enjoying the river. A smile fluttered across his lips and he felt a slight tugging in his mind. Opening his eyes, he looked towards the small town and stepped off the dais in the direction he felt pulled to go.

Chapter 12

Burns walked through town. He saw cars in designs he didn't recognize, but with just a small shake of his head he chalked it up to his memory and rebirth. What surprised him was how empty the town was. Lakehead was not big, capping out at around 400ish population, but normally he would see some people out doing normal things, mowing their lawns, walking dogs, or driving around.

He supposed today wasn't a normal day, with Nagashiu and Sirens in the town, but still, it bothered him how empty it was. He came up to the house he was feeling pulled to, the front door striking a chord of deep déjà vu. He walked up to the door to find it locked. Hesitating a moment, he closed his eyes and shook his head, trying to remember. A wide grin spread across his face and he reached for the potted plant on the ground next to the door, lifted the plastic pot within the ceramic to find a house key underneath it.

He unlocked the door and went in, and it felt like coming home. As soon as he entered the kitchen, his mouth dropped. Drawers and cabinet doors were left open, food left on the counter, even the refrigerator door was open. He looked inside the fridge, moving things around in the darkness of its unlit bulb. The lukewarm beer called to Burns, he popped the top on one and sipped the beverage as he continued his tour through the house.

On the otherwise empty dining room table was a framed picture with a note beside it. He set his beer down to look at the picture, and a sob tore out of him. In the picture was a man he knew to be himself though older, with Monica. The years had been kind to her and though he had roughened with age, her loveliness had only increased.

Tao Wong

There was a young man in the picture with them, in his late teens. Burns' heart accelerated as he examined the young man. He didn't know his name, but he knew it was his son. He popped the picture out of the frame and folded it into his breast pocket. They were the reason he was here in Lakehead instead of finding safety in a lower level zone.

He picked up the note next, recognizing the cursive handwriting as his mothers.

Danny,

I don't know if you will find this note or not, but felt I had to leave it just in case. I've explained to Monica (your wife) and Jason (your son) about your rebirth thing, as best I can anyway. She thinks I'm crazy, but it was the only thing that gave Monica enough hope to snap out of the shock of watching you "die" right in front of us. When that blade came, she thought you were dead for good, but when your body turned white hot and exploded out with heat and light, burning those horrible creatures, I knew you would be back. I hope you will be back.

Several of the creatures died in the explosion and the rest ran off. We've gathered together, the whole town, and are going to Shasta Lake. You would be so proud of Jason. He seems to understand this 'System' much better than the rest of us. He kept referencing video games and ended up getting us organized and even figured out who could be effective in battle. I hope it doesn't come to that. I told him what happened to us on the bridge, but he says we'll be able to figure something out.

I told the town that these creatures would return and everything you told me the Phoenix said about getting somewhere safe. I think everyone is in shock over how easily we were all captured and want to get to the city as fast as possible. Many people have loved ones there anyway and wanted to get back to them. If you find this note, please, come south and meet up with us. We left a bike in the garage for you. I love you; WE love you.

Mom

Burns folded the note up, putting it in the same pocket as the picture. He took a deep breath, shook his head and walked to the garage. A quick glance outside showed him that the sun was nearing the western horizon. He had once known a trick to telling time just by looking at the sun's position but couldn't quite remember how to do it. Regardless, he knew by the length of the shadows it was getting late in the day and he didn't have too many hours of daylight left.

He hopped on the bike and took off towards the highway. He rode in the center of the lane, pedaling as fast as he could. Burns didn't how long ago they had left on their trek, but hoped he'd catch up with them. He kept an eye on his stamina and noticed riding the bike seemed very efficient in terms of stamina use vs. speed and found a rhythm that kept him pedaling consistently while not expanding more stamina than he regenerated.

He hadn't been riding long when he saw the bridge ahead of him with a swath of people, maybe half the town, looking like a ragged group of gypsies. They had bikes with bike carts interspersed throughout, but most of the people were on foot, pulling wagons and wearing backpacks. Burns road through the crowd, making his way to the front where he recognized the young man, Jason, directing people.

"Look," Jason said to a group of older men and women as he pointed to a car laying on its side. "These circles? They look like sucker-prints to me. I think this is pretty good evidence of what my Grandma was talking about!"

"Hey kid, I get that you might think so, but why the hell are aliens going to bring giant squids or whatever to live in our lake? I'm not saying she's lying, but it's been a crazy day, maybe she's just mistaken," said an older man in checked flannel and blue jeans with a rifle strapped to his back.

"I'm right here you know; I can hear you," Susan said, her eyes steely. "What I saw was not a hallucination. Don't confuse my kindness for stupidity." She cut off as she noticed Burns riding up. "Danny!" she shouted and ran towards him. Jason looked at the man on the bike, recognition dawning on him.

"No way. It's actually real." Jason ran to Burns and grabbed onto him. "Dad? Is that you?"

Burns let the young man hold him for a moment, then gently pried them both off. "Mom, you haven't called me Danny in years." He looked at the young man, recognizing him from the picture in his pocket. "You must be Jason, I'm sorry...I... I don't remember..." Jason pulled back, the delight on his face fading.

"Ah yeah. Grandma told me you might not. I'm sure it would hurt a lot more if it hadn't happened before." He tapped on the side of Burns' head. "I'm just glad to see you. And alive! I gotta go get Mom!" He hugged Burns again then took off into the crowd of people.

"What's going on here?" Burns asked.

Susan gestured to the people near the flipped over car. "We're trying to figure out the best way across the bridge. Nobody seems to believe me about the giant tentacle we saw that threw a car at you." The man with the rifle turned from his examination of the bridge.

"Is this the fella that was with you Susan?" the man asked, squinting at Burns. "I swear I know you from somewhere. I'm Roy." He stuck his hand to shake Burns'.

"Dan," Burns said and completed the handshake, then looked back at his mother. She looked older than he remembered, but he had no doubts who she was. "I'm sorry, Mom, I don't remember what happened."

Roy crumpled his face and turned red. "You don't remember a car being thrown at you?! By a monster octopus?!" He threw a sideways glance at Susan. "Well that settles that. You really are full of crap." He turned and walked towards the bridge.

"Wait!" Susan shouted after him. Roy threw his hand up in a non-response and kept walking. Another voice called out, a voice Burns recognized, and he felt his heart twitch.

"Dan!" Warm arms embraced him from behind and he closed his eyes, inhaling the scent of his girlfriend. "Susan was right, you did make it back!" He could feel the wetness of tears on his back and turned to embrace her.

"Monica, I'm so sorry you had to see that. I am back, though. But you should know… my memory is still a mess."

"We've been dealing with that; we can deal with it still," she said as she kissed him.

Dan pulled back to look at her, her face cradled in his hands. "It may actually get better, that's what my symbiont, the Phoenix, says anyway."

Jason, next to Monica, looked at him. "What's a symbiont?" he asked.

Burns opened his mouth to respond when screams erupted through the crowd. He turned to see a huge tentacle reaching out from the water over the side of the bridge. He barely had time to register it before the tentacle grabbed onto Roy, who had turned to run back towards them, and yanked him over the edge into the water.

Chapter 13

If 'chaos erupted' could describe anything, this was it. The small group of people surrounding Burns and his family scrambled back, some falling on their butts in their mad dash to escape. Onlookers from the larger group who had seen what happened screamed and ran like wild. Mothers shielded their children's eyes.

Burns was used to chaos, having been a firefighter, and he knew how to handle a crowd of panicking people. He jumped onto the car and started shouting. "Everyone calm down! Back up! Stay away from the water and move back further down the road!" He waved both hands in the air, as if he were directing traffic.

Jason began directing the group back, while Monica helped calm the most panicky and Susan offered everyone snacks. Soon everyone had moved a few dozen yards down the road. Burns made his way over, taking Monica's hand and standing in front of the crowd. The fear emanating off them was palpable, and he tried his best to speak in a calm but loud voice.

"Everyone, I know what you've seen is terrible and we will need time to process. But we need to calm down and work together to figure out a way over this bridge," he said.

"Why do we even have to leave!? Why can't we stay in our homes?" A female voice shouted from the crowd.

Susan spoke up. "We went over this! Those things will just keep coming back, it's not safe here!"

A woman came out of the crowd holding a young child on her hip, trying to calm the girl. "Why do you think that? We saw them burn when that boy exploded, we can fight back!"

"No. We can't." Burns said. "This... System we are all in now, it's dangerous and where we are is deadly to us. We need to get to a safer area, or we could all die."

"How do you know this?" asked an older man near the front of the crowd.

Burns gave it a moment's thought. He didn't know how much he should share about his new status without sounding crazy. "You all have been seeing system messages pop up into your field of vision, right?" A few heads nodded, so he continued. "Well part of what I got from the System was a bit of knowledge about the System. Everything is assigned a level, a measurement of its strength and ability to survive. We-" he gestured towards the crowd and himself- "are all level 1. But Shasta Forest, the area we are in, is much higher- level 60 or 80 or something."

Jason's face paled at this information. "It really works like that? Like a game?" he asked.

Another man spoke up. "What does that mean? I don't get it."

"Well if this System is like the way a video game works, then basically we are so insignificant to the things that live in this area, that we could be killed by accident," Jason responded.

The crowd rumbled at this, the younger generations nodding their heads in understanding. Burns witnessed little pockets of conversations going on. "We can worry about all that later, though!" he shouted. "What I know is that we must get to a safe zone now, and the city of Shasta Lake should be that zone! We need a plan to get across this bridge, then we need to move as fast as we can to the city."

An older woman complained, "That's almost 20 miles! We'll never make it! Some of us are too old or weak to walk that far."

Burns smiled at her. "That's where the System helps us," he said. "Somehow, we have all become a part of it, so we have a set amount of energy that replenishes pretty quickly when you rest for just a little bit. I think you'll see that we are all hardier than before."

Burns turned to look at the vehicle strewn bridge, sighing in frustration. There were about 6 cars in the pileup, with a Pacific Fuel truck jackknifed across both lanes. This gave him an idea. "Does anyone have any… wind magic or anything? Something that can move stuff?"

Most of the people looked at him like he was crazy. "Oh, right. Everyone concentrate and say 'status'." Jason and some younger members of the group did so right away, and Burns watched as they were reading things he could not see. Once again chaos erupted in the group, though this time it wasn't the chaos of panic and fear, but surprise and maybe even a little excitement at what everyone saw.

He gave them all a small amount of time to look at their status screen before addressing them again. "I know there is a lot to process there, but I urge you to not do anything to your status until we can get to a safe area and spend some time learning about this System. I need to know if anyone has any kind of wind or air manipulation abilities, something that can help me spread a liquid? Also, did anyone bring a gun?"

After some jostling, several people came forward with guns, and two, who did not. One of them, an older woman covered in turquoise jewelry, spoke, "My status thing says I have a spell called 'Wind Blast' but I'm not sure how it works."

Burns smiled at her and took her hand, setting her up in the location he wanted while directing the others with guns to their stations. "I'm not sure how it works either, maybe try pointing your finger and shouting the name of the spell or something?" The older woman looked at him dubiously, then pointed her finger towards some bushes on the side of the road and shouted.

"Wind Blast!" Nothing happened and her face reddened.

"Um, maybe try concentrating on making a blast of wind, I guess?" Burns suggested.

This time the woman pointed towards the side of the road but said nothing, a look of hard concentration clear on her face. A massive gust of wind rocketed from her hand and blew the bushes fiercely. The woman fell over out of surprise and Burns moved to help her up, but she lay back on the ground laughing. "Oh, that was wonderful!" she shouted. "It was so easy, so amazing!" She pointed her hand in a different direction and blasted another gust of wind, laughing with pleasure once again.

Burns grinned and let her have her fun, looking to the other person, a woman who looked barely out of her teens, who had also come up front. "Do you have some kind of wind magic also?" he asked her.

In response, the young woman held up a stick she was carrying and pointed it towards some rocks on the side of the road. "Wingardium Leviosaaah!" she shouted, and a handful of rocks began to float into the air. Her face took on a look of concentration as she flicked her hand in a circular movement, the rocks to follow her motions.

Burns gave her a strange look. "Was that from those kid wizard books?"

The woman rolled her eyes at him. "It's Harry Potter!" She flicked her wrist, and the rocks went flying across the road. Her features softened then. "It's not really the spell from the books, I have 'Telekinesis' I just wanted to flavor it up a bit." Her smile lit up her whole face, obviously smitten with her new wizard-esque ability. "This is amazing!"

The crowd seemed to agree, and Burns witnessed many grins and excited cheers coming from them as pockets of conversations broke out while people tested their abilities.

"Yeah, well, it's nice to see the silver lining in all this. Here's what I want you to do," Burns explained his idea to his helpers. "I need you guys to shoot holes in that fuel truck, then you girls- I want you to use your abilities to cover as much of the bridge as you can in the fuel that leaks out. Spread it on as much surface area as you can. These sea creatures are weak to fire and I'm thinking if we make it an inferno up here, we can do some hefty damage and hopefully send them running."

"Won't shooting the truck make it explode, though?" one of the gun wielders asked.

"Haven't you seen that episode of MythBusters?" the Harry Potter fan responded. "They showed that it's pretty much impossible."

"How will we get through the fire though?" he asked, acknowledging what the girl said.

"I can take care of that, I think," Burns responded. They seemed satisfied enough with the plan, and everyone got into place. On Burns' mark they fired, their guns destroying the quiet of the day. The crowd practically flinched in unison, and they all held their breath. Just as the girl and MythBusters had said, the fuel truck did not explode, even as holes were punched through it. At his direction, the two women began their magic and spread the fuel all over the bridge, the harsh fumes wafting over to the waiting crowd. With a moment of concentration, Burns tried out his Class Spell 'Flame Burst' and sent a jet of fire streaking low across the pavement, causing most to shield their faces as the fuel ignited the bridge into a burning conflagration. A handful of people broke from the crowd, running back to a safer distance, unsure of what would happen next.

The flames followed the fuel up the lines of gushing liquid from the tanker truck, and soon it was spouting fire from everywhere, black smoke pouring out into the air. "Okay," Jason said. "The bridge is on fire… now what?"

Chapter 14

"Now," Burns said, "we draw out the squid thing." He hopped into an abandoned vehicle and popped it into neutral. "Everyone give me a hand pushing this thing down the road, let's get it to roll across the bridge!"

He muscled the steering wheel aiming the car straight down the empty lane, and hopped out so he could keep one hand on the wheel while pushing. Several others from the group came and helped push, while most remained at a much safer distance from the flames. With a final heave, the car rolled down the road and onto the burning bridge.

As hoped, the tentacle snaked its way out of the water and lashed at the thing moving across its bridge.

"Look! Upriver!" someone shouted and Burns' eyes turned that way. What he saw startled him and he shivered at the sheer size of the creature. A chorus of screams erupted from the crowd. The tentacle was attached to a large squid-like body, its giant head and a single eyeball poking out of the water, as it latched another tentacle onto the bridge support and began hoisting itself up. The massive squid body was easily the size of the fuel truck near them, with four tentacles, and a multi-faceted eye like an insect's.

Burns turned his attention back to the rolling car, hoping the flames would be enough to hurt or scare off the otherworldly beast. A hope that was dashed as the tentacle seemed to ignore the fire altogether. It grabbed the car, lifted it up, and dragged it into the water. Everyone watched silently, their eyes darting with fear.

"Great, now what? We are literally burning our bridge here," Harry Potter girl said, a little too nonchalantly for their current situation. Burns turned to the group to field other ideas when he saw several members' faces turn ashen, their mouths dropping. Spinning back around, he witnessed another tentacle on the other side of the bridge rise out of the water along with the first. Both tentacles began slamming onto the top of the bridge, fuel and flames spraying in all directions. Its strength was such that cracks started forming in the pavement, and stifled sobs could be heard from the group behind him.

Burns cast his fire bolt spell at a tentacle. As it hit, there was finally some kind of reaction from the creature. A blister formed where the spell had hit. This seemed to anger the creature as it began flailing the burned tentacle. In its angry lashing the beast slammed a tentacle dead center on the fuel truck, crushing it and spraying hundreds of gallons of fuel out like a shaken soda can.

The spray of liquid caught fire as it flew in every direction, leaving burning spots on the water where the gasoline floated, and causing a wave of flame heading towards the group. Everyone screamed. Burns could feel the flames, as if he was connected to them, and before he even registered what he was doing he pushed at the flaming spray of burning fluid and ripped the flames off. The flameless fuel sprayed against him and the first row of people. Behind him members of the group ducked or raised their arms in protection. Before them, floating in the air, was a roaring, crackling ball of burning energy.

Burns marveled at it. The crowd was silent, awing at physically impossible stunt they had just witnessed. Burns ignored the chatter that broke out among the group behind him, concentrating on the ball of flame and compressing it smaller and smaller. He could feel the intensity of the temperature rising as the ball shrank. Burns noticed his mana bar draining as he toyed with the flame, and not wishing to waste any more mana, he flicked the ball of burning hot energy, now just the size of a golf ball, towards a tentacle. The flaming sphere hit dead on, then continued through the tentacle, cauterizing the wound as it burned.

The bellow of rage and pain that ripped out of the mouth of the massive undersea creature was unearthly. Many of the people covered their ears, some dropping to their knees from the sheer volume of it. Burns closed his eyes, concentrating on his elemental affinity. In his mind's eye he could see the flame, like a living entity dancing across the bridge. He could feel the connection to it through the conduit of the sun's light.

"Everyone get ready to run across the bridge on my mark!" he shouted; his eyes still closed.

"It's still burning! Are you crazy!?" a voice shouted back. Without a response he raised his hands in the air, imagining what he wanted to do, he spread his hands wide apart, and like some twisted scene from the Bible the flames parted to either side of the bridge, forming massive, burning walls of fire. He concentrated on the walls, and began pouring his own energy into them, somehow knowing this was the catalyst that would cause the creature to avoid the flames.

As if his thoughts brought the idea to life, the tentacles caught in the flame started smoking and burning. They retreated into the water as the creature screamed again.

"GO, GO NOW!" No one moved. Jason stood at the front of the crowd and spoke loudly. "I get it seems like a crazy idea, but this whole world is crazy now. We don't have another choice!" With that he spun on his heel and dashed across the bridge, unscathed.

Burns screamed as sweat from concentrating began to break out on his brow. "You. Have. To. Go. Now!" he shouted through clenched teeth. After another small group of people made it through the flames, the rest of the group charged through.

Burns could sense the fire being drawn to the fumes of the fuel-splashed people and he fell to his knees as he concentrated harder on holding the flames off. He heard screams as a few people were singed but he managed to keep the fire away.

The squid thing slammed the bridge from underneath, shaking it and causing some of the group to falter. Several others helped them up, and they quickened their pace as the creature took its fury out on the bottom of the bridge over and over. Cracks formed in the concrete and members of the group shrieked.

Burn's mana bottomed out, and he felt the flames roar back to the center of the bridge, where the remainder of people were still crossing. With sheer willpower and drawing on the sense of his affinity, he separated the flames again, this time his stamina bar draining completely. At long last, the group made it over the bridge, and he groaned at the stress of his power as he took his first few faltering steps through. The creature continued to pummel the bridge, and a particularly hard hit knocked Burns to the ground, his concentration failing.

He closed his eyes as natural physics took over, the flames rolling back to engulf the entire bridge. Burns screamed in anticipation of his painful, burning end, squeezing his eyes closed as if it would be less painful if he didn't watch. When no pain came, he opened his eyes and gazed in wonder as the fire flickered across his body. He smiled. This would have been very helpful as a firefighter.

He strolled through the flames, marveling at the absurdity of flames dancing on his skin to no effect. In his contemplation, Burns had forgotten one thing: without his energy fueling it, the fire had become mundane once again. He paid the price of his cockiness as he registered that the creature had stopped bashing the bridge and once again a tentacle snaked out of the water and wrapped itself around him, squeezing.

Burns gasped as his ribs cracked, his health dropping by 40% in an instant. He knew he wouldn't last long like this and shook his head violently, trying to rack his brain for a solution. An image popped into his mind, a memory perhaps, he couldn't tell, of his body covered in flames. He was wearing his old scout uniform, the memory melting away in his confusion. The image remained, however, of himself wrapped in fire, and he called out to his affinity, attracting the flames from the bridge to himself. Just as before, the fire ripped free from the fuel, leaving a large patch of it on the roadway. Burns willed the fire to wrap itself around him, feeding it the small amount of mana he had left.

Flame surrounded him like a shield. Willing the flames to stay, he concentrated again on his affinity. The tentacled creature bellowed as its fleshy protuberance started cooking. The smell of barbecued calamari came to his mind, but he had no time to revel in the scent as the creature flung him away, sending him in a fastball special towards the group of people that had made it across the bridge. He cried out, covering his face and trying to douse his flames, hoping to do so before he crashed into them, a human Molotov Cocktail.

When no impact came, he opened his eyes to find the Harry Potter girl, her makeshift wand pointed straight at him, holding him aloft with her power. A thin trickle of blood dripped from her nose as she sat him down.

"At least I made it across," Burns said, then passed out, falling face first to the ground.

Chapter 15

Burns woke to the periodic squeak of a wheel that needed oiling. "Ugh," he moaned.

"Dan!" Monica's voice exclaimed from the bike pulling the trailer he rode in. "You're awake! I thought I'd lost you again. Are you okay? I would stop, but it's starting to get dark and we want to get to the city. The zone we're in is only level 30 now, so we are a little safer."

"How long was I out?" Burns asked.

"A couple hours, we stopped a few times to check on you, but you seemed to be healing fine. It's weird though, I can literally watch your body repair itself."

Burns checked his health and saw that it was at about 90%. He still had a few aches and pains but felt good overall. "I think this System will take some getting used to," he said.

Monica barked out a laugh. "Coming from my husband who is 20 years younger than a day ago, but still has memory issues."

Burns smiled, laying his head back down on the bike trailer. They rode like this until the next time they stopped for a stamina recharge break. Burns had been right. Traveling, even for the older folks, worked much better in this System as they could stop to let their stamina recharge and be on the move again. Eventually they crossed over the large bridge on I-5 that spanned the rise of Lake Shasta.

They watched as down below the houseboats used for recreation across the massive lake were taken over by more things in the water. Huge tentacled beasts, more fish-people. Some were just driven into the rocks.

"This world will need some serious help," Burns said. As the day began to close, they made it across the bridge, the zone dropping even further in level. They entered the suburbs of Shasta Lake, and several messages bloomed into Burn's view.

Quest Completed - Get Somewhere Safe!

Quest Completed - Save Your Wife and Son!

Hidden Quest Completed - Save the Residents of Lakehead!

Congratulations! You have gained a level x2 in Phoenix. Stats automatically assigned - you have 2 free points to spend.

Congratulations! You have gained a level x3 in Pyromancer. No attribute points gained for Subclasses.

Burns breathed a sigh of relief. He had made it, his family and even most of Lakehead were safe. For now, anyway.

***

At the bottom of the deepest point of Lake Shasta, several Nagashiu stood around a scrying bowl watching the humans as they entered the town. One of them, a large female with an ornately decorated crest on her head looked to the male, a muscular creature wearing a badge of authority. "My chief," she said, "why do you let the humans go? They would have provided an enormous sacrifice to Shethlglth. He would have blessed us greatly!" The female did not hide the anger in her voice, a challenge to his authority.

"Silence, witch," the male said, and backhanded her, slamming her into the wall. With a wave of his hand the scrying pool went blank, and he picked the witch up by her throat. "You would spend all our resources on a single benefit. This is why you will never supplant me; you seek only what aids you now while I think for our future." He casually tossed her to the ground. "That tribe of humans will bring us sacrifices for months to come. We will raid them and sacrifice them over time, making sure our altar is never empty."

The witch coughed, blood from her mouth dissipating into the water. "But what about the Phoenix? Your father will not forgive you for allowing it to kill our scouts."

The male Nagashiu chuckled, an evil grin coming to rest on his toothy face. "I have already taken care of that particular nuisance," he said.

***

Deep space, the Forbidden Zone. Aboard the starship Forsworn a light flashes, followed by a beep. A stasis tube begins its opening cycle, releasing the occupant within. Before it can process its surroundings, a message appears on the large, main screen of the ship.

Automated message: A Phoenix has been found. Funds have been withdrawn from your account and placed within escrow awaiting verification.

Time since last awakening: 997 years.

\#\#\#

One Last Conversation

"Seven Advanced Classers we didn't know of. One crippled Master Classer. And four interesting Basic Classes," Rob Markey, the elected leader of Earth stared at the summary provided to him. He had no time to read the full details of the reports, not yet. Not until his people had worked up more information of the groups. Among other things – if they were alive or still on Earth.

"That's about it. Those are the ones we should look out for," Amelia confirmed.

"I'm glad our tip went to good use," Rob tapped the data slate. "But, you didn't need to talk to me for that. My people would have handled it. So, what do you want?"

"A bit blunt, aren't we?" Amelia said.

"Peter was the diplomat. I was just a politician. And my promotion was a political compromise," Rob shook his head. "There were. Are, better people for the job."

"Well, we were lucky you survived anyway," Amelia said. "Enough about the past. I wanted to know why you're collecting all these people. Where so many of our people have been going?"

"Going?" Rob said, his face carefully neutral.

"Yes. Going. They're not on Earth. And, I note, a lot of those who have disappeared are friends of Ingrid's. So…"

"It's classified."

"Even to allies?"

Rob nodded. "Let's just say that we need them to help an old friend."

Amelia paused, staring at Rob and then she rolled her eyes as realisation struck her. "Again?"

"Just a continuance." Ro shook his head. "I've said more than I should. And don't pass this on. Not to your employer."

"I'm sure he knows already," Amelia smirked. "They still talk, much to my partner's chagrin."

"I bet," Rob said, chuckling. He sobered up as a light chime notified him of another call. "Anything else?"

In answer, Amelia cancelled the call, her holographic form disappearing, leaving Rob alone in his office. He sighed, looking at the call notification and could not help but wince.

Really, sometimes, he missed John. As brash, unthinking and violent as he was, the Master Classer had a way of managing the Fist that he lacked. They just did not respect a non-Combat Classer in the same way.

Then again, he wouldn't exactly want to be in John's place right now. At least he was safe.

The End

Enjoying the System Apocalypse?
Rebel Star, the next book in the series is available now!
https://readerlinks.com/l/960891

Biographies

Craig Hamilton is gainfully employed as a technical sales engineer who dabbles at writing in his free time. Most of his work days are spent translating tech speak and specifications for a non-technical crowd. When not working, Craig appreciates playing tabletop RPGs or board games with friends. When his inner-introvert demands a break from polite company, Craig can be found sprawled on his couch with a good book or playing a video game with spaceships and entirely too many spreadsheets.

Alexis Keane - Hey there! Alexis here, welcome to my author bio! So, a little about me. I live in England (you know, that place where it never stops raining and the inhabitants never stop complaining about the weather) with a dog and far too many books (if such a thing exists).

I could launch into a laundry list of places I've been and things I've done, but this isn't a CV, and I doubt you really want to read it all (neither do I, tbh). So, let's talk about us, have a chat, just you and me. So, about us! We both love video games and hate Season 8 of Game of Thrones (seriously, wtf, bro).

Oh! And reading. That's okay, I guess. Either way, we're here for one of two reasons, because we love LitRPG or we're trying to singlehandedly deforest the Amazon (those trees deserve it). We've read (or listened to) everything there is to read and we're constantly on the lookout for something new and exciting. Because that's what we're here for. Having fun; not listening to some bore who doesn't know when to shut up about themselves. If we wanted to do that, we'd visit LinkedIn, right ☺?

Anyway, I loved every minute of writing this story, and I hope you'll have a blast reading it. Or *had* a blast reading it, I have no idea where this bio is going to be placed… waaaaay up here at the top of the story, or down here at the end. Or somewhere else entirely (I heard R'lyeh is great for author bios this time of year). But I'm waffling on here and all those annoying professional marketers are screaming at me to push my platform… so, uhhh… here, I guess… https://alexiskeane.com/platform … you know… that's an awful way to make an

exit… *Thestarwarsprequelsarethegreatestmoviesevermadeandjarjaristhebestcharacter*… fight me.

L.A. Batt is a New Zealander who has made a hobby out of backpacking his homelands and beyond in-between bouts of working in hospitality, retail, radio, deep-sea fishing, gaming news and reviews, I.T., and more. Now Luke (that's what the L stands for) is throwing his wits and wiles into the wonderful world of crafting stories to spellbind fans of fantasy, adventure and science fiction.

RK Billiau is the best selling author in his household. He feels strange writing about himself in third person, so just know that he has a wife, a ridiculous amount of kids, a few pets, is a geeky used-to-be-gamer who now games by living vicariously through reading and writing LitRPG. When he isn't drowning in children, he works for a nonprofit medical outreach bringing free healthcare to people in his local community. Follow him here:
http://Rkbilliau.com
https://www.facebook.com/rkbilliau

Ix Phoen writes in order to read the stories they can't find elsewhere. They have a hidden archive of unpublished ideas, books, and more, guarded by fierce monsters including Uncertainty and Perfectionism. "Rebel Within" is the first of Ix's novellas to battle its way to freedom in search of an audience. Now that the Impossible Boss has been defeated, a trilogy is planning to fight for the right to be self published over the coming months. Watch @IxPhoen on Facebook and Instagram for progress updates.

Tao Wong lives in the Yukon, writing away the long winter months. He's a long-time martial artist, scifi and fantasy reader and lover of food. Tao wrote the System Apocalypse one long winter as he decided to set the end of the world in the cold north. To his surprise, the post-apocalyptic book found a fan base and he's been writing since.

For more information on the System Apocalypse and his books, visit his website: http://www.mylifemytao.com

Subscribers to Tao's mailing list will receive exclusive access to short stories in the Thousand Li and System Apocalypse universes: https://www.subscribepage.com/taowong

Or his Facebook Page: https://www.facebook.com/taowongauthor/

Or support him on Patreon direct at: https://www.patreon.com/taowong

More Great Reading

For more great information about LitRPG series, check out the Facebook groups:

- GameLit Society
  https://www.facebook.com/groups/LitRPGsociety/
- LitRPG Books
  https://www.facebook.com/groups/LitRPG.books/

For more information on the System Apocalypse and his books, visit:
http://www.mylifemytao.com

Books in The System Apocalypse series

Main Storyline

Life in the North

Redeemer of the Dead

The Cost of Survival

Cities in Chains

Coast on Fire

World Unbound

Stars Awoken

Rebel Star

Stars Asunder

Anthologies

System Apocalypse Short Story Anthology Volume 1

Comic Series

The System Apocalypse (On-going)

Made in the USA
Monee, IL
12 January 2022